'To that end, Lady Colin Campbell is publishing her first novel in 2005. *Empress Bianca* is about "a woman who murders two husbands and makes off with billions of dollars". She pooh-poohs any domestic homicide Freudian score settling connection. "Darling, I don't have murderous instincts," she grins. "I am not a vengeful person."' - *Jeremy Hilder, Independent on Sunday*

Praise for *The Real Diana:*

'You've really caused a stir with this book!' - *Richard & Judy*

'Explosive ... The most sensational book of the year' – *Mail on Sunday*

'Startling new revelations from the woman who has written the headline-making biographies about Princess Diana-astonishing' – *Hello! Magazine*

'Britain is buzzing about The Real Diana' – *Victoria Mather, The Early Show, CBS News*

'Some Palace watchers note that she has an impressive roster of well-placed contacts and credit her with writing the most believable Diana biography' – *People Magazine*

'Lays bare the facts about Diana's affair with James Hewitt and the reasons for Diana's death in 1997' – *Evening Standard*

'Bombshell revelations by Lady Colin Campbell, the former wife of a cousin of the Queen of England' – *Ireland on Sunday*

'A tribute to a truly remarkable and outstanding woman' – *Later Living*

'Lady Colin Campbell is a highly successful and prolific author, most famous for her two biographies of Diana, Princess of Wales' – *Sarah Wicker, chatshow.com*

'If you are maintaining a Diana library, Lady Colin Campbell's books are now must haves' – *Royal Book News*

Empress Bianca

Also by Lady Colin Campbell:

Lady Colin Campbell's Guide to being a Modern Lady
Diana in Private
The Royal Marriages
A Life Worth Living
The Real Diana

Empress Bianca

A Novel by

Lady Colin Campbell

Dynasty
Books

Dynasty Press Ltd
36 Ravensdon Street
London SE11 4AR

www.dynastypress.co.uk

First published in this version by Dynasty Press Ltd, 2008
copyright MDP Group of Companies 2006

ISBN-13: 978-0-9553507-0-2

Edited by Ken Hollings
Typeset by Charlotte Lee Pike & Modern Graphic Media

Cover Artwork by Stuart Grunsell, Broadworks
Photography by David Chambers
Styled by Jenny Iggleden
Jewels from the private collection of Lady Colin Campbell

Printed and Bound in Canada

This book is dedicated to my sons
Dima and Misha.

Prologue: September 21, 2000

When your mother is reputed to be one of the richest widows on earth, and you know that she ranks alongside Catherine the Great when it comes to getting away with murder, you tread carefully. Very carefully. Even when you are telephoning to offer her your congratulations.

In Mexico, it is four o'clock in the morning. Pedro Calman Barnett has been to a party given by his sister-in-law, Dolores, and this being Mexico City, he has had a fair amount to drink. He isn't even tipsy, however. Just relaxed. Should he call his mother or shouldn't he? He toys with the idea. There are pros and cons either way, and he turns them over in his mind while getting undressed.

Meanwhile, in the eight-bedroom house she has rented on Carlisle Square in London, his mother Bianca Mahfud is just awaking on the day for which, in some ways, she has spent her whole life preparing. Today is the day that will mark the culmination of her dreams and ambitions, when her status will finally be recognized beyond dispute by the only people who truly matter to her.

This evening, in the piazza at Brunswick House, one of the former royal palaces situated near Richmond by the Thames, Her Majesty Queen Elizabeth The Queen Mother is scheduled to unveil the brass plaque dedicating the massive Henry Moore sculpture, which Bianca Mahfud has bought for a reputed £4,000,000 - although actually costing less than quarter of that amount, the price having been inflated by Bianca's public relations people - and donated to the British nation in memory of her late husband, the billionaire banker Philippe Mahfud.

As the soft morning light eases its way into the room, Bianca unhurriedly savours the anticipation of her moment of glory, with patience born of the knowledge that satisfaction is assured and cannot be denied. The wait, Bianca knows, will only heighten the pleasure.

The telephone rings, but Bianca does not answer. It is many years since she has answered her own telephone. The ultimate practitioner of the luxurious arts, a quintessential devotee of gracious living, Bianca would never dream of answering her own telephone. To do so would be to defeat the purpose of her carefully constructed lifestyle, one so lulling, so captivating, so seductive, that those who have fallen under its spell include kings, presidents, first ladies, princes, princesses, servants, lovers, family, lawyers and of course, billionaires. Especially billionaires.

The telephone gives one discreet buzz: her signal to pick up the receiver.

'Hello,' Bianca says. Her voice is deep, lush and soothing, like molasses flowing over rocks. Her accent, clear even after one word, is that elegant combination of British, American and the indefinably foreign that is so characteristic of the upper reaches of the International Set.

'Hi Mama, how are you?'

Pedro. The dreaded Pedro. Pedro who was always trouble, even as a little boy, who would always take the side of the servants and level judging eyes at his mother when she was only trying, in her own mind at any rate, to run an organized household and provide a certain standard of comfort for her family.

'Oh, hello Pedro,' Bianca says in that sugary tone which, Pedro knows, is reserved for those she feels threatened by. 'How kind of you to call. It must be the middle of the night where you are.'

Pedro knows that she does not like him. That he discomfits her. That even the sound of his voice makes her retreat into the burnished shell with which she covers herself at will. A polished shell of charm. Of such superficial and empty correctness that it feels as if she is consulting some guide to etiquette and enacting its recommendations with feeling but no heart. Pedro cannot remember a day when he ever thought that his mother felt anything but uncomfortable in his presence.

'I rang to wish you luck on your big day,' Pedro says, torn as always between the pleasure of witnessing his mother squirm and the natural tendency of a son who wants the one thing he has always been deprived of: his mother's love.

'Thank you, Pedro,' Bianca says, her tone losing some of its reserve.

'You must be very excited.'

'I am. I am. This really is the most wonderful day of my life. Imagine, the Queen Mother no less unveiling Uncle Philippe's statue then coming to dinner afterwards. What a coup. *Toute Londres* will be here.'

Bianca has such spontaneous charm and energy when she lets her guard down that Pedro finds himself responding to the thrilling quality which is a natural feature of his mother's magnetic personality. Caught as he is by an attraction towards someone he is fully aware he must guard against, Pedro understands that Bianca also suffers her share of conflict because of him. She is a Jewish mamma, a Mediterranean mamma; she cannot quite bring herself to be indifferent to her own flesh and blood.

'What a pity Uncle Philippe can't be here this evening,' she says, sending Pedro hurtling down another byway. 'He'd be so proud.'

Pedro can hardly believe that his mother has just uttered those words. Philippe Mahfud would be proud indeed to witness the wife who arranged his murder glorifying herself with his money by presenting a statue in his memory to a nation where he never lived and about which he cared nothing. Just so she can enter the portals of royalty and snag herself a prince or duke in her ever-upward quest. Even though Pedro has his mother's measure as few others do, he is nevertheless so taken aback by her comments about Uncle Philippe that he is lost for words.

Pedro can almost hear Bianca, ever sensitive to the thoughts and feelings of others, listening to the silence.

'Well, don't you think Uncle Philippe would be proud of your mother?' she asks, the sugar in her voice returning as her guard rises again.

'Anything you say, Mama.'

'Anything I say? What is this? Did you call just to bait me?'

'No. I called to wish you well.'

'Then why are you making yourself so disagreeable?'

'I'm not making myself disagreeable. I haven't said anything.'

'You can't play dumb with me, Pedro. I'm your mother. I gave you life and I love you, but I'm also onto you. I know what's in your mind, and I have to tell you I didn't think it was funny the first time you came up with your crackpot theory nor do I think it's funny now.'

'Listen, I really didn't call to upset you. I only wanted to let you know

3

I'm thinking of you.'

'You know, Pedro, you could've been here with us this evening. Don't ever stop to think how much it breaks your poor mother's heart to know that she can't ever have all her children with her at one time...because I can't rely on you? It's bad enough what you've done to yourself, but what about what you've done to me and to your brother and sister? I want you to think about that. Think about how much happier our family would be, if we could all share things together.'

'There's no winning with you, Mama, is there?'

'This isn't a race, Pedro. This is life. Take my advice and try to loosen up a little. Now get some sleep. We'll all be thinking of you tonight when Queen Elizabeth unveils the Henry Moore. Bye-bye and thanks for calling,' Bianca says, and rings off.

The Connaught is Antonia Najdeh's favourite hotel. Ever since she first stepped off the pavement at Carlos Place in Mayfair and into the foyer, smelling the beeswax with which the wood is polished, she has loved the place and used it as a benchmark for measuring tone. To her, the Connaught is also a repository of treasured memories. Her first stepfather, Ferdie Piedraplata taking her to Sunday lunch for some of the roast beef and Yorkshire pudding that is a renowned specialty of the house. Princess Grace of Monaco, at the pinnacle of her glamour and beauty, gliding out of the lift into the foyer in a rose-pink ball gown, the silk rustling as she and Prince Rainier make their way to their waiting car for the short ride to Buckingham Palace, where The Queen is hosting a prenuptial ball for Princess Anne. The pride as Princess Grace stops and says to the young girl who always, but always, comes a poor second within the family circle to her adored older brother Julio: 'Aren't you Caroline's little friend from St. Mary's?'

Bianca Mahfud's only daughter, Antonia can still feel how she glowed and grew within herself as she saw the head porter look at her kindly, noting the Princess of Monaco's acknowledgement that she is someone of consequence and not just the also-ran who is always in Julio's shadow in the family circle. That moment of recognition might have been a small and insignificant incident of kindness to Princess Grace, but to Antonia it was the boulder upon which the river of her life changed course.

Antonia gazes at her five children and Leila Barnett, her aged grandmother, and smiles. Her expression reflects her contentment as they breakfast together, having flown in from their respective homes in Cuernevaca and Beirut for the big night. Unlike many of her peers, Antonia appreciates how lucky she is. She does not have troubles like her brother Pedro. She is happily married to Moussey Najdeh, the scion of one of Lebanon's richest Jewish families, with whom she lives in a palatial villa beside the Bay of Jounieh where St George slew the Dragon. She has four children of her own as well as raising her brother Julio's child, Biancita, as if she were her own. Uniquely, she gets along with everybody within the family circle and is still alive: a state she does not take for granted, having seen two stepfathers die tragically and a brother be as good as dead before her.

Antonia's grandmother notices her smile. 'Happiness is a wonderful thing, eh, Antonia?' Bianca Mahfud's mother speaks in that heavy Arabic-Spanish accent which conflicts completely with the remnants of her Slavic-like beauty, still visible even at the great age of ninety-seven.

'One never needs to explain anything to you, Granny. You can always read what's on people's minds.'

'My greatest joy is to look through your eyes and see what I hoped for when I was your age. Sadly, with me it was not to be. At least, not after we came to Mexico, and Bianca moved up in the world when she married your father. I think it's a terrible thing when a child is ashamed of her parents because they're middle-class, and she pretends to her friends that they're aristocrats. At least your father always made us feel welcome. He's a good man, your father.'

'But things were all right between you and Granny before she met Daddy, weren't they?'

'Oh yes. That was during the war.' Leila never referred to it as the Second World War. 'Mexico wasn't the country it now is. It was sleepy. Really colonial. Grandpapa and I were making our way in the world.' Leila breaks off to laugh with Antonia, who understands the underlying message: you can never acknowledge around Bianca Mahfud that the Barnett family ever had to make their way in the world.

'In those days, it was easier than it is now for Europeans to arrive and get established. Grandpapa was always an ambitious man. He worked hard, and he encouraged me to get out and meet people. He understood in a way I didn't how good for business it was for us to get into the right circles. With his English accent and what he used to call my "exotic" background, he got us accepted in solid, middle-class circles. We weren't high society, but we had a very nice life. A villa in a good area. Three servants. And while he worked as a surveyor, I solidified our position socially. We worked as a team, you see. He insisted that I go to every coffee morning, lunch and tea party I was asked to, provided, of course, that the invitations were from the sort of people he wanted us to mix with. I can't pretend I didn't enjoy myself. It was a lovely life. All those canasta afternoons. Those meetings of the Women's Club, with all the smart ladies dressed to kill in hats, gloves and furs. Yes, fox furs were all the rage then, and we used to wear our fair share.

'Your Mamma was the first baby to survive. I'd had three miscarriages and two stillbirths before her, so you can imagine how much she was loved.

'Of course, in those days, ladies from the middle and upper classes didn't spend as much time with their babies as you girls do nowadays. Maids were two a penny, to use one of Grandpapa's favourite expressions, and the values of the age meant that we turned our children over to nannies and nursemaids and got on with our lives, establishing the family so that we had a good position among our peers. Your mother was ultimately able to benefit from that when it came time for her to marry. In those days, you must remember, the only career open to girls was to marry, and to marry as well as their parents could manage.'

'Were you always so clear-sighted about your ambitions?'

'Oh yes. There was nothing shameful about being refugees and about making your way in the world from scratch. At least, not in 1939 when we moved to Panama, and later, when we moved from there to Mexico. The world was in turmoil. Everyone except Neville Chamberlain, the English Prime Minister, expected war. We were among the lucky ones who were able to get out. We brought your mother up to be aware of how fortunate she was to have a comfortable life in a safe part of the world, and she certainly behaved as if she recognized that fact while she was growing up.'

'I remember as a little girl thinking how happy you and Grandpapa were together,' Antonia says.

'We were. Like you and Moussey. Two lovebirds,' she giggles, clutching herself in fond, almost embarrassed, memory of the fulfilling marriage she had.

'Granny was hot stuff in the old days,' Ramsi, her younger grandson, interjects, chewing toast and marmalade. The other grandchildren laugh.

'I suppose I was,' Leila says as Antonia raises a finger and scolds, fondly but firmly: 'No talking with your mouth full.'

'This is not the beach at Acapulco. This is a dinner table,' Yasmine, the youngest child, mimics her mother. 'Or a breakfast table, at any rate.'

'Don't interrupt your great-grandmother,' Antonia says as she joins in the laughter.

'The one thing we've been lucky to have in our family,' Leila says, 'is an example of happy marriages. I am a firm believer that the only people who ever have happy marriages are those who have experienced happy marriages in their own family life. I know that sounds ironic, taking into account the things people say about your mother, but you have to hand it to her: she knows how to keep a man happy as long as she wants to keep him.'

'I love Granny,' declares Yasmine's elder sister, Little Leila, standing up for Bianca. 'She takes me to Gucci and Ferragamo and buys me anything I want.'

'It's OK for grannies to spoil their grandchildren, darling,' Leila Barnett says. 'That's what grannies are for. But good mummies do not spoil their children. If they did, how would the children learn right from wrong?'

'You don't spoil us,' Yasmine says, looking at Antonia.

'That's because she's a good mummy, and she loves you.'

'Do you love Granny?' Yasmine asks Leila of her daughter Bianca.

'Yes, I do, darling. Just because a mother sees her daughter's faults doesn't mean she loves her any the less. It simply makes loving her that much more painful. But you're too young to understand these things. Now, since you've finished your breakfast, why don't you run next door and get yourselves ready for a day of serious shopping?' Leila says.

The five children, although none of them is strictly speaking a child any longer, sidle off into their bedrooms to get ready.

Antonia sips from a glass of freshly squeezed orange juice that is only marginally inferior to that served at the Hotel Nacional in Havana. 'You know I've always loved Mama and would never do anything to harm her,' she says, stepping into forbidden territory. 'But I'm worried about her. You know... all those stories going the rounds suggesting that she killed Uncle

Philippe.'

Leila nods sagely, her expression unreadable, at least to her grand-daughter Antonia.

'What do you make of them?'

Leila shrugs in a way that conveys everything and nothing at the same time.

'I need to know, Granny. You have answers that I need to know.'

'Let me put it this way,' Leila replies affectionately. 'I hope you never have to live with the knowledge that any child of yours has the blood of not one, but two, people on her hands. Now, do be a dear and pass me the toast. And never let on to your mother that you believe she's anything but the most wonderful person on earth. She's not like other people. It's not so much that she doesn't have feelings as that she can turn hers on and off in a way ordinary people cannot. She is, I have to say, an extraordinary woman in every sense of the word. That's both her blessing and her curse... and ours too.'

'So you think she really had a hand in...'

Leila cuts off her granddaughter in mid-sentence. 'There are some truths that are best left unsaid. All that matters is that you know in own your mind what the truth is.'

Part One: Bernardo

Chapter One

The infant who would grow up to become Bianca Mahfud was born Bianca Hilda Barnett in Jaffa, Palestine, in 1930. Her background was as incongruous and exotic as she herself would turn out to be. Her father Harold Barnett was a Welsh surveyor who arrived in Palestine with the British Army after the Great War, when the British Mandate came into effect. Her mother was Leila Milade, a Palestinian whose paternal family owned orange groves in Jaffa and whose mother was from a Jewish mercantile background.

But for the Great War, Leila would never have met, much less married, an Englishman. There were already enough suitable families in Palestine from which to select a husband; and, in the ordinary course of events, her father Joseph Milade would have spoken to one or two fathers with sons of a suitable age and arranged for them to call upon the Milade family with a view to arranging a marriage when Leila had turned seventeen.

That was how things were done in those days. The fact that Leila was Jewish by religion would have made no difference whatsoever to her desirability, for Jews, Christians and Muslims lived in harmony, having done so for over a thousand years and to such a degree that intermarriage between the religions was an accepted feature of national life.

Bianca Mahfud's parents met one afternoon in 1920. Leila Milade was being driven home from school in the family buggy when the sound of a motorized vehicle backfiring frightened the horse, causing it to bolt. But for the quick reaction of Harold Barnett, then an army sergeant stationed in Allenby Square, Leila might have been killed as the horse tore towards the main thoroughfare. Harold, however, grabbed the horse's stirrup and brought it to a halt without even considering the danger to himself. Only afterwards, when Leila was thanking him in French, a language he knew slightly from his time in France during the Great War, did he notice how extraordinarily beautiful was this blonde-haired, green-eyed creature with the high cheekbones and lush lips. Taking her to be French, Harold's commanding officer ordered him to see her home.

So began the friendship, then courtship, of Leila and Harold, which ended four years later in their marriage. This was a period when the unthinkable was becoming acceptable. Like many other parts of the world, the old order in Palestine was giving way to a new one, and in Joseph Milade's household, a Britisher - any Britisher - was desirable by virtue of his nationality alone. Moreover, Harold Barnett behaved towards the Milades with respect, and once Bianca's father established that his 'intentions were honourable', he was happy to give his blessing for the marriage between Leila and the handsome Welshman who had now left the British Army and gone to work as an apprentice surveyor with the Palestinian Railway in Jaffa.

Harold Barnett was an ambitious man - a trait his daughter would inherit from him. He had no intention of spending his whole life as a railway surveyor, and within two years of his marriage to Leila Milade, while she was producing first one, then another stillborn baby, he studied at night to become a qualified surveyor. By the time Bianca came on the scene, eight years later, her father was a qualified surveyor with his own practice, employing an assistant, a clerk and an office boy.

It was into this prosperous but solidly middle-class and respectable world that Bianca Hilda Barnett was born in 1930. Because her mother was Jewish, she too was Jewish, and while she, and indeed her mother, shared Harold's British nationality; from the moment she could remember she considered herself to be more Middle Eastern than English.

Harold and Leila would never have left their home in Jaffa had it not been for the political situation in Europe after Adolf Hitler was appointed Chancellor of Germany in 1933. Harold was worried because Palestine, as a former part of the Ottoman Empire, had been allied to Germany in the Great War, and he was only too aware that the Palestinian people resented the presence of the British who were occupying that country, having reneged upon their promise to the Arabs that they would be given their freedom in return for helping get rid of the Germans. Having watched the Pathé newsreels and seen Germany invading the Sudetenland, dismantling Czechoslovakia and, in March 1938, occupying Austria, he said to his wife Leila and his father-in-law Joseph Milade: ' No Jew or Britisher is safe in Palestine. We must emigrate.'

To Leila and Joseph, emigration was not an alien concept. The Milades had cousins who had done well in Jamaica and Tanganyika.

However, Harold opted for Panama, a country where they knew no one, and no one knew them; but it had at least the merit of being totally independent of either Britain or Germany. Moreover, it had the Atlantic Ocean between it and Europe, where Harold was convinced a conflagration was imminent.

Harold, Leila and eight-year-old Bianca boarded the SS *Sao Paulo* in Lisbon, Portugal just after England and France declared war on Germany, following its invasion of Poland. They landed in Panama on Saturday, September 23 1939.

Within two weeks, Harold had rented a comfortable three-bedroom apartment in the South District with a view of the Caribbean Sea in the distance.

While Harold went from surveyor to surveyor, looking for work, Leila hired a housekeeper who had once worked as a lady's maid with the Honorary Syrian Consul and so spoke kitchen Arabic. Harold found a job four weeks after his arrival, and they were on their way to duplicating the solidly respectable life they had enjoyed in Palestine. Harold's energy and initiative were such that it was not long before he was cultivating clients with a view to setting himself up in business on his own: something he did within twenty-one months of landing in Panama.

Like most eight-year-olds, Bianca was blithely unaware of the pressures governing adult life. Being Palestinian, Leila was inclined to follow the Middle Eastern tradition of letting her daughter know the realities of their lives, of allowing the child to see behind the worries of having to change country. Of having to find an apartment. A car. A school for Bianca. Harold, however, being English and the man of the house, held sway in the British manner. 'Not in front of Bianca,' was his guiding motto. As he scurried around town from their room at the Don Pedro Hotel to find the apartment which he did with that treasured glimpse of the Caribbean Sea; as he looked for a job; as he went down to the docks to arrange for the delivery of the furnishings they had shipped with them; as he and Leila discussed Bianca's schooling, Bianca remained oblivious of everything but the final result. To her child's eye, it all seemed so seamless, so effortless. She would, as a consequence, spend the rest of her life moving home and country without a glimmer of anxiety.

Although Harold and Leila had radically different views on how much information to provide a child, on the issue of Bianca's education, they were in perfect accord. 'It's crucial that she mixes with nice girls,' Harold said. 'The friends she makes in childhood might stand her in good stead for the remainder of her life.' Ever practical, Harold solved the problem of finding out where to educate his daughter in an unfamiliar country by resorting to the simple expedient of getting the British Consulate to inform him where the diplomats sent their daughters. And so it was that Bianca Barnett was enrolled at the Catholic Mercy Academy in Panama City as Bianca Barnett Milade. She was seated, in Latin alphabetic fashion, in front of Begonia Cantero Gonzalez: something that seemed to be without any importance whatsoever at the time, although it was the first step along Bianca's route to success and murder.

At the very moment Harold, Leila and Bianca were walking down the gangplank of the SS *Sao Paulo* in Panama's harbour, halfway across the world, in Bucharest, a motor vehicle was pulling into the courtyard of Palatul Cotroceni, the official residence of the King of Romania.

Emanuel Silverstein had been one of King Carol II's jewellers since that monarch had returned from exile in 1930. Before that, he had enjoyed the patronage of his father, the late King Ferdinand, after whom Emanuel named his only son, and Queen Marie, who was then one of the most famous women in the world. Emmanuel Silverstein was used to coming to Palatul Cotroceni. At least three or four times a year, His Majesty's Equerry would telephone his shop on the Boulevard Regina Maria with the suggestion that 'Mr Silverstein might care to call at the palace.' The Equerry always indicated what to bring with a comment such as: 'His Majesty would appreciate it if you could provide him with some examples of your more important earrings in coloured stones.' Courtiers, Emanuel Silverstein had learned, are so cultivated, so well mannered, so used to having their own way that their every command was couched as a request, their every direction as a suggestion. Their world, the royal world, was truly one where velvet and satin reigned, where the occupants were not merely rich but were bred to a mode of behaviour, a standard of cultivation and pedigree that separated them from other beings.

This time, however, when the Equerry telephoned, his direction, while delivered as smoothly as ever, took Emanuel Silverstein's breath away. 'His Majesty wants to cast a wide net this time and would like you to bring whatever stock you have available for purchase.'

This could mean only one thing, Emanuel Silverstein realized. The King was preparing to flee. 'Remember every detail of this visit,' he had cautioned his son as they rode together to the Palatul Cotroceni. 'It may well be your only one.'

As Emanuel's motor vehicle came to a stop, four sentries who were obviously watching out for their arrival stepped forward. 'Mr Silverstein,' the most senior officer, a major, said, 'May we assist you with your boxes?'

'Thank you, Major,' Emanuel Silverstein replied, indicating the back seat and the boot, which were packed to capacity with black velvet boxes in various shapes and sizes.

Emanuel Silverstein barely had time to adjust to the glare of the sun before an elderly gentleman stepped forward from beneath the portals leading into the palace's trade entrance. 'Mr Silverstein,' said this tall, elegant, silver-haired gentleman with military bearing as he extended a hand, 'it is indeed a pleasure to see you again. In times like these, one does treasure one's old friends.'

'Hospodar Malinescu, this is a surprise. May I have the honour of presenting my son, Ferdinand? Ferdie, this is Hospodar Major Malinescu, His Majesty's Equerry.'

'How do you do, young man?' replied Hospodar Ion Malinescu, one of the King's oldest equerries. 'Welcome to Palatul Cotroceni. We hope we will have the pleasure of seeing you over the years, the way we have seen your father and your grandfather before him.'

'Thank you, sir,' replied Ferdie, intent on remembering every detail, as the old gentleman extended his hand in greeting.

'Times really are as bad as I fear,' Emanuel decided, utilizing one tiny but significant scrap of information to intuit the reality of his - and Romania's - predicament. In the sixty years that he and his father before him had been 'attending at' Palatul Cotroceni, not once had any member of the Royal Household ever shaken their hand. According to the rules of the day, 'gentlemen' - that is, courtiers, landowners, the gentry and nobility - shook hands with other 'gentlemen'. It was no more thinkable for a Court official to shake the hand of a tradesman than for Mr Emanuel Silverstein, to shake the hand of a shop assistant or a waiter or the man who delivered his coal. Yet here was Hospodar Ion Malinescu, late of Her Majesty Queen Marie's Dragoons, shaking his hand, and, as if that were not enough, young Ferdie's as well.

'Yes, young man, we expect to see a great deal of you in the future,' Malinescu said as he led father and son down a series of magnificently furnished corridors, his tone of voice convincing neither Emanuel nor Ferdie. 'He's trying to be brave,' thought Ferdie. 'But he's frightened and in despair.'

'Everyone I have spoken to supports His Majesty's decisive actions in these difficult times,' Emanuel Silverstein said, picking up the political thread of Malinescu's comments in the hope of gleaning some useful information.

'As well they might. It's either the King or the Iron Guard, and we all know they want Corporal Hitler,' Malinescu said, as he led them into an antechamber whose splendour defied anything young Ferdie had ever seen - even in the motion pictures.

'Do have a seat,' Malinescu continued, indicating a pair of Louis XVI sofas with newspapers spread on a table between them. 'His Majesty will only be a moment.'

Malinescu withdrew while Emanuel and Ferdie settled themselves on the sofa facing the French window. The newspapers, father and son could see, were full of the assassination two days before of Prime Minister Armand Calinescu and of the attempt ten minutes later by seven members of the Iron Guard, the Romanian fascist organization, to seize the radio station. They had interrupted a broadcast of waltz music to announce that the death sentence passed upon the prime minister had been executed, but not before the radio announcer had cried out: 'They are killing us - a band of Guardists!'

The newspapers all recounted how the conspirators were arrested before they could escape, and their accounts differed little from the account King Carol wrote later that day in his diary, 'The eight assassins were executed at the scene of the crime, the two or three Iron Guard leaders first.' Before Ferdie had a chance to finish reading, Hospodar Ion

Malinescu ushered him and his father Emanuel into the King's presence. Surrounding Carol, who was standing in front of his desk, were several piles of Emanuel Silverstein's velvet boxes, containing his shop's entire stock.

'Mr Silverstein,' Carol said as soon as the formalities of receiving Emanuel Silvestein and Ferdie had been dispensed with, and Hospodar Malinescu had withdrawn from the room. 'You have an interesting selection of jewels here. One might almost say something for every taste, certainly something for every occasion.'

'Your Majesty knows that my family has a tradition of trying to satisfy our clients.'

'That's true enough, Mr Silverstein,' King Carol said, opening one of the larger boxes and removing a diamond and ruby tiara, which he held up towards the open window. 'Half Bucharest can attest to that. Even my late mother swore by your workmanship and the quality of your stones.'

Both father and son could see the remainder of the parure that the King had left in the box.

'It is ironic that you look at that particular piece, Sire. Her late Majesty, your mother, admired that particular parure only four years ago. She said it reminded her of one that belonged to her aunt. She lamented the fact that she was no longer of an age to justify acquiring it.'

The parure consisted of the finest Burmese rubies and diamonds, the smallest stones being of three carats, the largest extending, especially with the rubies, to sixty carats; a ring of one large, square-cut ruby surrounded by diamonds; matching bracelets to be worn on the left and right arms; and the *pièce de resistance*, a necklace in the Tsarist style, the back dripping almost as many square cut rubies and diamonds as the front. Whoever wore this necklace would have to possess the dual aspects of a fine cleavage and a slender back, a feat well known in Europe to be within the reach of Elena Lupescu, the King's mistress.

'That would be Aunt Menchen she was speaking about: The Grand Duchess Vladimir of Russia. She had the finest collection of jewels in the world. Queen Mary has many of them now.'

Emanuel Silverstein shifted his weight from one foot to the other. He remained silent, an expression of attentiveness and pleasantry suffusing his countenance. Years of experience with high-ranking clients had taught him the golden rule: after the initial pleasantries, remain silent. Allow the client to do all the talking. Let him drive the conversation in the direction he wants it to go.

Ferdie looked at his father, who smiled almost imperceptibly. King Carol turned around, still holding up the tiara, and said to Emanuel: 'You guarantee all these items as being of the highest quality?'

'Absolutely, Sire.'

'In that case, Mr Silverstein, I will have them all.'

'All?' Emanuel Silverstein said, not quite sure whether all meant all of the parure or all of the jewels.

'I think so,' King Carol said. 'Everything.'

'Everything,' Emanuel Silverstein repeated.

Ferdie had never seen his urbane and self-possessed father at a loss for words before.

'I think so, Mr Silverstein, but I must ask you to be discreet. Presumably you won't have too much difficulty restocking from Antwerp.'

'No, Sire.'

'Take your whole family. Visit while you can. But do so quickly. The world we live in has become terribly unpredictable, and while I have done my level best to ensure the liberty of my people by toeing a neutral line, the fact remains that Chancellor Hitler cannot be relied upon. We live in very uncertain times, Mr Silverstein.'

'The situation is a worry, there's no denying that, Sire,' Emanuel Silverstein said.

'Have a word with Major Malinescu. He will help you with your travel permits.'

Hospodar Ion Malinescu glided into view, as if from nowhere, and King Carol thanked Emanuel Silverstein and Ferdie for 'attending upon' him before retiring to the adjoining room while Hospodar Malinescu escorted them out.

Emanuel Silverstein's thoughts reeled as he walked down the familiar corridors to the tradesman's entrance. So much of what King Carol had said could be taken in two ways. Was Carol suggesting that the time might have come for him to leave Romania? Was the King hinting that he could not protect his Jewish subjects against Hitler, or was Carol merely being pragmatic? Was his main concern that Emanuel Silverstein should restock the shop so that no word would leak out as to where its contents had gone? By the time he reached the shop on Boulevard Regina Maria,

Emanuel Silverstein had decided to take advantage of this opportunity to emigrate.

That night, Emanuel waited until Ferdie and his younger sister Clara were in bed before speaking to his wife. 'We have to face facts. Romania is not safe. The King's declaration of neutrality might buy the country time, but if either Hitler or Stalin wants Romania, this country's done for.'

'You're right,' Hannah Silverstein said. 'Last month's pact of friendship between Nazis and the Soviets makes it almost inevitable that Hitler or Stalin, or even both of them, are eyeing us up for occupation. There's not much to choose between them. The Nazis despise the Jews, while the Soviets hate capitalists.'

'Where to go, that's the question? The King has offered to help with our travel permits, but I'm not inclined to head towards Belgium. He proposed I take you and the children to Antwerp - to restock, he suggested. But I'm nervous in case the Germans overrun Belgium the way they did in the last war. Look at what they've just done to Poland.'

'You have to decide where you want us to live and what you intend to do once we get there. It seems to me, once you've made up your mind, a lot will fall into place.'

'I'm not sure if any country in Europe is safe for Jews anymore, and, whatever our official religion, we are classified as Jews in the eyes of the Axis Powers. Can England and France really check the might of the Germans? I wonder.'

'Manny, as long as we are together as a family I don't care where we live. It's important that you know that.'

'You are the most precious woman, Hannah,' Emanuel Silverstein said, bending to kiss his wife.

'You remember my cousin Rachel Finkelstein, from Lake Constanza, don't you, Manny? She married a rabbi's son, and they moved to Mexico City in Mexico. She's the one who died in childbirth. He had a dry goods shop and did very well.'

'I didn't know you still kept in touch with him.'

'I don't, but her sister does. We write each other twice a year. I even have a snapshot she sent me last year of Rachel just before she died. Would you like to see it?'

'Sure,' said Manny.

Hannah walked to her dressing table, opened a drawer and pulled out a large bundle of letters neatly tied with blue satin ribbon. She untied the ribbon carefully, looked through the last few letters then pulled out an exotically stamped one. From it, she withdrew a grainy black and white photograph of her cousin Rachel standing beside a bearded man and a little girl. There was a pyramid behind them. Hannah turned the photograph over, looked at the inscription on the back and said to her husband as she handed it to him: 'That's the Mayan Pyramid in the background. Rachel thought it the most beautiful city. Very bustling. Very nice people. And no anti-Jewish feeling whatsoever.'

'Mexico,' Emanuel Silverstein said, taking the picture and studying it. 'I'm trying to remember what I've read about it. Is it still a Spanish colony?'

'No. It's been independent for over a hundred years.'

'Is it prosperous?'

'Very. It has oil like us and silver. But it has a much smaller population than ours, though it's vast in size.'

'You think maybe we could make a go of a jewellery shop in Mexico City?'

'I don't see why not. At least we'd be safe until the war is over. Then we can always return here if we want to.'

'That's decided, then. Mexico it is. But we'll go to Antwerp first to buy new stock. Hopefully the German Army will be too busy occupying Poland to bother about invading Belgium for the next few weeks. I'll speak to Hospodar Malinescu first thing in the morning about our travel permits and settling the account.'

Hannah took her husband's hand and kissed it gently. 'You're a good man, Manny, and a wise one too. With God's help, we're doing the right thing.'

'We are, Hannah. We are,' Manny said sombrely. 'It might be the only chance we have for freedom. We have to take it.'

Chapter Two

Five years had elapsed since Manny and Hannah Silverstein arrived in Mexico City with their children Ferdie and Clara. In that time, much had changed for the family, and Manny was convinced that the ease with which he and his family had settled in that Latin American haven was largely due to three things. First, but not necessarily the most important, was the fact that he had landed with total financial liquidity and was therefore in a position to purchase, outright and for cash, a beautiful villa in San Angel, the most gracious part of the city, near the famous San Angel Inn, while at the same time procuring premises on the chic Calle Reforma for what was now one of Mexico's leading jewellery establishments. Second, Manny and his family made a point of wearing their prosperity lightly. Where others resorted to arrogance or authority, his family convinced with charm, good manners and quiet statements of wealth. Third - and in Manny's view, of crucial importance - was his decision to show respect for the society he had moved to by changing the family name from the European-sounding 'Silverstein' to the Spanish equivalent: Piedraplata.

Too many émigrés, Manny felt, were so intent on preserving their old ways that they insulted their new hosts by being pointedly foreign. Well, he had no axe to grind against the Mexicans. On the contrary, he considered himself to be in the debt of such a welcoming inclusive nation.

Mexico had spared him and his family the suffering that many of his European friends and relations had been forced to endure in the Old World since Hitler's rise to power. This had been especially true for

Romanians. Their country entered the war on Germany's side in 1941, when the resettlement to the East of everyone the Silversteins had known from the Jewish community had begun. Ominously, none of these friends and relations wrote anymore, and, while Manny had heard the rumours circulating in the Jewish community about concentration camps in Germany and Poland, he remained hopeful, marking the silence of his loved ones down to the inevitable breakdown in communications that came in wartime, especially when the tide turned, as it now had against the Axis Powers.

Manny had done well since arriving in Mexico, and as he walked out of his office into the showroom of the Piedraplata jewellery shop on the famous Reforma, past display cases showing fine jewels, many of whose stones he had bought in Antwerp before setting sail for Central America, he reflected upon how fortunate he was to have had King Carol II as a client.

As Manny made his way towards the entrance of the shop, he stopped, in the courtly fashion that he had learned in Bucharest from his royalist clients, to greet the mistress of one of his major clients. She explained that she was looking for a birthday present. This particular lady, Manny observed, careful to eradicate all trace of the thought from his expression, either had an unheard-of quantity of female friends, all of whom had several birthdays a year, or she was feathering her nest against the day of despatch. 'One's friends do so appreciate it when one remembers anniversaries,' Manny said as respectfully as if he were speaking to his former King and then instructed the attendant to show the Señora the new range of emerald brooches, inspired by the Duchess of Windsor and designed by Fulco, Duca de Verdura. The lady in question could not help noticing the kindliness that emanated from Manny's eyes as he spoke to her, for, despite his best endeavours to conceal his thought processes, Manny was a compassionate man and did not condemn a beautiful woman who guarded against an uncertain future by gathering her rosebuds while she could.

Mario, Manny's driver, was standing directly outside the shop, the motor of the Rolls Royce purring. Before Manny could even cross the pavement, Mario had the back door open, and Manny sank into the well upholstered comfort of the car's interior. Today was a special day, especially for someone like Manny, who valued education above all else. It was his daughter Clara's graduation, and he did not want to be late for so important a ceremony. He tapped the dividing glass and instructed Mario, who was just pulling out into the traffic, to drive faster than usual.

As the Rolls Royce glided through traffic, people stopped to look at it, peering inside to see whose it was. It was at times like these that Manny realized how wise he had been not to leave this car behind when he was departing from Romania. Rolls Royces had been difficult enough to obtain in 1937, when Manny had imported this one from London, and they were a rarity by 1939, when he had fled Romania in it. Now they were almost like talismans: comfortable, reliable, prestigious, providing visible and unspoken proof of their owners' elite provenance, and impossible to procure in wartime. In Mexico City as much as in Bucharest, London or even Berlin, they were the best calling card for anyone who needed to establish his credentials without words or to assess another's worth. Doormen, head waiters, *maîtres d'hôtel* and bank presidents all took notice when Manny pulled up in his Rolls Royce, and they gave the vehicle's owner the respect such a possession commanded.

Harold Barnett noticed the Rolls Royce as it pulled into the school. Ever on the lookout for anyone or anything that would advance him, he turned to Rabbi Julius Finkelstein, brother-in-law of his employer in Panama and his host in Mexico City while he, along with his wife Leila and daughter Bianca, explored the possibilities of moving to Mexico to take advantage of the country's wartime boom.

'Do you know who owns that beauty?' Harold asked.

'That's my late wife's cousin by marriage,' Julius replied, laughing out loud, 'Emanuel Silverstein, or Manuel Piedraplata as he's now known. He's become the biggest jeweller in Mexico in the space of five years. Would you like to meet him?'

'I'm sure I would,' Harold said.

For all Harold Barnett's hopefulness, the meeting that took place between him and Manny was as flat as the Maracaibo Lowlands, Manny's attention being focussed solely in the direction of his daughter Clara, who was graduating with honours. In any case, Manny disliked opportunists, and from the moment Julius introduced them, he had Harold Barnett pegged as one.

From Harold's point of view, however, the encounter was not entirely unsuccessful. For days afterwards, little realizing what the future held for his daughter Bianca and Ferdie Piedraplata, he kept on joking half-seriously with her that, when they moved from Panama to Mexico, she should 'set her cap' at Ferdie. 'He's tall, dark and handsome,' Harold observed. 'With his wavy, dark-brown hair, tanned complexion and green eyes, he could be mistaken for a South American. Julius says he's also an unusual young man, in that he loves to work as hard as he likes to play. So you'd be both rich and in compatible company, for we all know how much you like having a good time too.'

To an extent, Harold's assessment of Ferdie's prospects as a husband was accurate. In the five years since the young man's arrival in Mexico, he had changed from a gangly seventeen-year-old boy into a young man who appeared to be everyone's dream. Aside from his good looks, he had made the transition from calm and studious teenager to an exceptionally energetic and imaginative young man with an aptitude for business. In this and all other respects, he had turned out even better than his father and mother had hoped. Indeed, in the last year, Manny had noticed that Ferdie's enthusiasm for business was so pronounced that it had a vocational aspect to it. The very word 'business', when used by Ferdie, was filled with an unusual power and passion. It was almost as if he were in love with the whole concept of business, which was, of course, the answer to his rich father's prayers, for he had produced a son and heir who needed no encouragement to fill the shoes that fate had allotted to him.

But Harold's assessment of Ferdie wasn't based solely on what Julius had told him about the young Piedraplata. He was also using the information he had gleaned from a conversation he went to some lengths to overhear. He was sitting behind the family for the graduation ceremony, and he craned his neck to get within earshot of father and son while they were killing time waiting for the ceremony to begin. Their conversation had begun simply enough. 'So how are things going, Ferdie?' Manny had said in a tone that conveyed all the ease and closeness that existed between him and his heir.

'Great, Papa, the walls are up, and the roof will soon be on. The budget's coming in on target. It's going to be an attractive premises.'

'Our son's going to be a great businessman one day,' Manny's wife Hannah, now known as Anna, had interjected. 'Or we're all going to go bust. Who else but Ferdie could come up with the notion that the shantytowns which have sprung up on the outskirts of this city need an electrical shop?'

'And who else but his Papa has the wisdom to appreciate that our son has an aptitude for spotting gaps in the market that will, if his hunches are right, enlarge our fortune significantly?' Manny had said to Anna in a manner reminiscent to Harold of the intimacy that he and Leila shared.

'I hope your judgement doesn't turn out to be misguided faith. This is Ferdie's third project in the last ten months, and none of them has yet come to fruition.'

'The investment for all of them adds up to less than a three-bedroom apartment in a crummy part of town,' Manny had said. 'If they all fail, that - plus Ferdie's time - will be our total loss. On the other hand, if they succeed, the rewards will be incalculably greater. The risks involved are all reasonable ones, wouldn't you say so, Ferdie?'

While Harold Barnett was listening in on this conversation, Bianca was sitting beside Sarita Finkelstein looking over the assembled group that she would soon be joining as a student, unaware that her life was about to change in ways she would never have dreamed possible. It all began innocently enough, with Sarita saying: 'My best friend's over there. She's really nice. I'll introduce you after the ceremony so you can have another friend before you join our class in September. She's the one with the long brown hair in the pink bandeau and the pink dress, standing beside that boy in the blue blazer with the black hair. You'll really, really like her, I promise. Her absolute all-time favourite movie star is Clark Gable, followed by Lana Turner.'

'That girl in the pink dress beside the boy in the blue blazer with the rust-and-aubergine striped tie is your best friend?' Bianca enquired sweetly, caring not a jot about the girl but smitten by the stunning-looking boy beside her. Even though she was only sixteen, she was already very aware of boys, of her appeal to them and of their attraction for her.

'Yes. That's Alicia and the dreaded Bernardo. Yuck. All he can ever think about is cars and tennis. But Alicia's great. Do you think she's pretty? Mama does, though I can't say I'm sure. But she really is very, very nice.'

'She looks pretty from here,' Bianca said, eager to find a way to meet the brother, 'but I'll be able to give you a better opinion when I meet her after the prize-giving.'

'I'll introduce you. I've told her all about your coming to live in

Caracas, and she's just dying to meet you.'

'I'm looking forward to meeting her too.'

As soon as the prize-giving and graduation ceremony came to an end, Bianca jumped up. 'Come on,' she announced to Sarita. 'Let's go meet Alicia.'

With that, Bianca linked arms with Sarita and propelled them through the throng of parents and children until they reached the spot where Alicia was standing with her parents and brother. Relief and excitement washed over Bianca in equal measure as she stood in front of Mr and Mrs Calman, with their daughter Alicia on one side and their son Bernardo on the other. 'Alicia, this is Bianca. You remember me telling you all about her?'

' Hi, Sarita,' Alicia said. 'Hi, Bianca.'

'And this is the dreaded Bernardo,' Sarita added, only half in jest.

'Hello,' Bernardo said in a deep voice that made Bianca go weak at the knees.

Never one to miss a trick, even at that tender age, Bianca smiled first at Alicia, said 'Hi,' quickly then flashed Bernardo her most dazzling smile.

'Why are you the dreaded Bernardo?' she asked as she leaned into him with a self-possession and confidence in excess of her years, subtly rocking her hips.

Bernardo laughed. He had never met a girl quite like Bianca before. Not only was she beautiful but she was also being straightforward, in the way that boys usually were, and girls generally weren't. 'Alicia and Sarita say I'm obsessed with cars.'

'All men like cars,' Bianca said, knowing very well that by calling Bernado a man she was putting him into a category that no one else would have done in the Mexico of that time. But Bianca was already accomplished in the art of making people feel good, of flattering them so openly that they melted. This was something she had learned from - and practised upon - her father ever since she was a little girl, and she now put it into effect with an urgency she had never felt before. Already, she was in love with Bernardo Calman, and she was going to make sure he fell in love with her too. 'My father loves his Packard as if it were his second daughter,' she continued. 'It's natural for men to like cars. If I were Alicia and Sarita, I'd be worried if I had a brother or a friend who didn't like cars.'

Bernardo could hardly believe his luck. Here was this beautiful and delightful girl actually talking to him in a way that removed all the awkwardness from the encounter. Already he was under her spell, even if he did not yet know it. 'So what's your favourite car, then?' Bernardo asked. 'Mine's the Bugatti.'

'So is mine. Isn't that a coincidence?'

'Or an indication that both of us have good taste,' Bernardo retorted playfully but sexily.

'A lover of the Bugatti and with a sense of humour,' Bianca said, laughing cheekily. 'Next you'll be telling me that you play tennis and I'll know that I'm in the presence of a perfect specimen of masculinity.'

'I don't believe this. Sarita didn't tell you, did she? Sarita, you surely didn't tell Bianca that I'm my school's tennis champion.'

'Of course not,' Sarita snapped, sure that she must deny the revelation if Bernardo was asking about it. 'Why would I bother telling my friends anything about you?'

'Thank you, Sarita, I love you too,' Bernardo said, rather more good-naturedly, Bianca decided, than her friend deserved.

Bianca pulled back and thrusting out her pelvis slightly, placed an arm on her hip in a pose reminiscent of a Schiaparelli mannequin.

'My God,' Bernardo thought, his loins stirring at the sight of Bianca's subtle display of sexuality, 'this girl is provocative.'

'Bianca' he said, hoping his penis would not become embarrassingly engorged with blood, 'how about a game of tennis tomorrow at the Town and Country Club?'

'I'd love that, but I must warn you, I'm a very average player.'

'Somehow I suspect we'll enjoy the game, nevertheless. Shall I pick you up at eleven in the morning?'

Tennis the following day led to more games of tennis, which led to the holding of hands and much staring into one another's eyes for the remaining five days of Bianca's stay in Mexico City. On her last evening Alicia and Bernardo came round to Sarita's house, and Bernardo drove the four of them to the American Ice Cream Parlour for sundaes. When he dropped them back home, Sarita and Alicia left them in the car and went to sit under the poinciana tree at the front of the house.

As soon as they were alone, Bernardo moved towards Bianca. She responded in full measure, and the next thing they knew, his lips were on hers, his tongue parting her mouth as their limbs intertwined, and he urgently pressed his erect manhood against her thigh.

'I love you,' he said.

'I love you too,' Bianca replied.

'Will you be my girl?'

'I already am,' Bianca said, never at a loss, even at that tender age, for an unexpected and endearing riposte.

The following morning the Barnett family went back to Panama to wind up their life there and organize their move to Mexico. For the six weeks that they were due to be apart, Bernardo and Bianca pledged to write each other every single day. For the first two weeks, their letters, though not particularly long, were filled with passion and desire, then Bernardo's stopped. At first Bianca was perplexed but hopeful. By the end of the third day, however, hope was turning to humiliation and perplexity to rage. When, at the end of that week, she had still not received another letter, she accepted an invitation from Begonia Cantero Gonzalez to make up a foursome at the pictures. This proved to be a particularly fateful event, for that was how she met Hugo del Rio, the twenty year old son of a prosperous merchant who resided with his parents in some splendour a short drive but a world away from where the Barnetts lived in decidedly middle class style in Panama City.

No sooner did Hugo clap eyes upon Bianca than he fell utterly in love with her. By the end of the evening he was hinting that he would one day want to marry her and by the end of the week – a week in which the postman remained stubbornly emptyhanded as regarded letters from Bernardo - he was suggesting eloping with her. Never slow on the uptake, Bianca realized that Hugo's attitude meant that his family would never approve of a girl of such unillustrious lineage as her. Intermingled with a feeling of resentment that anyone would have the gall to disapprove of her daddy's little princess, was the realisation that here was an opportunity to salve the wound of Bernardo's rejection while meeting her father's target of moving up in the world, so when Hugo, patently caught up in the convulsions of a great passion, suggested that they marry in secret that Saturday, she hesitated only momentarily before agreeing to do so with the proviso that she continue living at home until she could she break the news to her parents – her father in particular – in her own time. It says a lot about Bianca that, even at that early age, she had no hesitation in reversing her decision as soon as she appreciated what a mistake she had made. This came about as suddenly as Hugo's presence in her life, for, upon returning from her midday marriage, she walked past the silver-plated tray in the vestibule where the maid customarily left the letters after clearing out the letter box, to see not one, but eight, letters from Bernardo. So there had been a problem with the postal services. Shaking with relief and anticipation, Bianca grabbed them off the tray and fled into the privacy of her bedroom, where she read them and discovered that Bernardo, her real love, was going out of his mind wondering why she had not replied to his letters. Not for a moment did Bianca hesitate about how best to get out of the fix she now found herelf in. She went straight to her father when he got back home later that evening and confessed tearfully that she did not love Hugo or want to live in Panama when her adored father would be in Mexico, and sat back confidently as he uttered the words she knew he would : 'Don't cry, Princess. Your Daddy will make it all good. Everyone makes mistakes from time to time. We can get the marrriage annulled.' At that point, Harold's ambition got the better of his reason and he allowed himself to hope momentarily. 'Although the del Rios are a very classy lot and you can do a lot worse than being married to one of them. Maybe they'll want to open up a branch of their shop in Mexico City. Is he a nice boy?'

Knowing what her father was angling for, and intent on averting him immediately, Bianca started to wail as if death would be preferrable to marriage to Hugo del Rio.

Feeling dreadful, Harold hugged his daughter protectively and said, 'There, there. Don't worry. Your old Daddy will take care of everything. I'll go to the lawyers on Monday and have them begin proceedings to annul the marriage. I'm sure the del Rios will be willing to co-operate. One thing, though. You mustn't see or speak to that young man again. Ever! Is that understood ?'

'Yes, Daddy,' Bianca said, inwardly relieved that her father, and not she, would have to break the devastating news of her change of heart to the lovesick Hugo. 'And one more thing, Bianca,' Harold said. 'Make sure you never breathe a word of this to anyone. No one – and when I say no one I mean no one – must ever know about any of this. Don't even breathe a word of this to your mother. As far as you or I or the rest of the world is concerned, this marriage never took place. Understand ?'

'I understand,' Bianca said meekly, glad that her father could so painlessly – to her at any rate – erase this most inconvenient of marriages. When she returned to Mexico, Bianca and Bernardo took up where they had left off. This being Mexico in 1944, however, nice girls simply did not stray beyond certain boundaries, even though nice boys did everything in their power to entice those nice girls into allowing acts which would ruin their reputations and preclude them from taking their assigned places in middle-class circles as wives and mothers. The result was that there was a tremendous build-up of sexual energy which could only be relieved through necking, protestations of love and the phenomenon known in that circle as 'scrubbing', an act which involved the boy rubbing himself fully-clothed against the girl's equally fully-clothed body, until she brought it to a halt with cries to desist or, as frequently happened with Bernardo and Bianca, the heat of the moment became so intense that the flames of passion expended themselves beneath the worsted of his trousers and his cotton underpants.

Harold and Leila Barnett were lenient parents, although Harold frankly had higher expectations for Bianca than a middle-class boy like Bernardo Calman. It is possible that the young couple's relationship might not have flourished the way it did – he called to see her every afternoon after school for an hour, and they spent every waking moment of their weekends together – but the news from Europe was so momentous and alarming that it put the harmless antics of the youngsters into perspective; and even stricter parents than the Barnetts found themselves tolerating conduct in their children that would have been unthinkable even a year before.

Although the war news was welcome to those who supported the Allies, it came at a price for the Barnetts, as it did for many people in the New World with relations stuck behind the Axis lines or serving with the Allies. Harold's only sibling was killed in action in France in September 1944. Palestine provided hope for Leila until the concentration camps gave up their secrets, and the influx of Jewish refugees from Europe turned that peaceful Middle Eastern haven into a powder keg, which would explode during the next three years, annihilating two of Leila's brothers, along with many other Palestinians of all religious faiths. For the Piedraplata family, living a few miles across town from the Barnetts, but a eon away in terms of lifestyle, the news was equally bleak. Every Silverstein in Romania was annihilated. All of Hannah's relatives were also exterminated. None of Julius Finkelstein's relations was ever heard from again. Manny and Anna Piedraplata, like her cousin by marriage Julius Finkelstein, now found themselves the rump of an extended family that no longer existed. It was a chilling and debilitating time for them all.

The first time Ferdie and Clara fully understood the enormity of what their parents were facing was over dinner one night in late 1945. That very afternoon, Julius had telephoned his late wife's cousin to tell her that he had just opened a letter from Poland confirming that his sister-in-law and Anna's cousin Bella, her husband and six children had all been gassed in Majdanek Concentration Camp in November 1943. The family were trying to absorb this latest tragedy when the normally urbane Manny burst out, his face contorted with pain: 'It's beyond comprehension that any human being can behave like that towards another human being.'

Clara stretched her hands across the dinner table and stroked her father's compassionately. It was at moments like these that she was glad she had foregone her second year at Vassar College, the American university it had always been her dream to attend, where she was studying for a degree in philosophy. As the news from Europe had started coming in that April of 1945, when the British had liberated Belsen, and as her parents reeled under the shock of losing all their extended family, she had opted to transfer to Mexico City University so that she could be on hand should her parents need her. It was a decision she would never regret making. Her presence at home in Mexico became even more vital when, within a matter of months, Ferdie started to fall to pieces.

Ferdie, always so vital, so active, so full of ideas and enthusiasm, had become the mainstay of the business since their father had withdrawn into himself following the dreadful news from Europe. By August 1945, he was running the jewellery shop on the Reforma instead of Manny. While his father spent most of his time at home, Ferdie had stepped into the breach with all the capability the elder Piedraplata had ascribed to him. Where Ferdie found the time to run the other three projects he had developed on his own during the previous two years, no one knew or even questioned, for those were days when people were grateful to be alive and making money at a time when so many million others had either died or been rendered penniless. But Ferdie not only ran those businesses but also did so with outstanding success; he was even trying to dig his father out of his deep depression with ideas for other business projects that he wanted to start up. It was therefore with a profound sense of shock that Clara witnessed the events of February 24 1947 as they unfurled.

She had got up, as was her habit, at seven o'clock in the morning. She bathed before going into the family dining room, where a full English breakfast of bacon, eggs, fried mushrooms and tomatoes, plus poached kippers, awaited her. As she ate, she noticed that Ferdie was not up before her. This was unusual for him, but she thought nothing of it, for Ferdie had not managed to rest much of late. Indeed, he was so frequently up late into the night and always awoke so early in the mornings that she used to tease him about his ability to go without sleep. This had proven to be especially true after he found himself a girlfriend in the shape of Fernanda Veira Fernandez, with whom he spent most evenings, paying her court in the Mexican manner at either his house or hers or occasionally, out on the town with friends. There had been talk in the family, albeit muted, that Ferdie might even propose to Fernanda, who was a nice girl from a nice family, even if she was neither outstandingly beautiful nor highly intelligent nor even particularly amusing. Had she been older, the Piedraplatas might even have been inclined to describe her as 'somewhat dour', but because of her youth they simply said that she didn't have much personality, although they readily conceded that she had a lovely character and a pleasing disposition. As Clara left the breakfast table to dress for university, she supposed that Ferdie, who had returned home last night long after she had gone to bed, was merely sleeping in for once.

Early that evening, however, when Clara returned from university, she was met by her parents who were standing by the front door, awaiting her arrival. 'We need to talk,' Manny said, leading the way into the drawing room. Immediately, Clara knew that something was very wrong. The drawing room was only ever used for guests or emergencies, the less formal sitting room being the family room of choice.

'What's happened?' Clara asked, by now so well used to earthshattering announcements that she thought there had been news of yet more terrible deaths of yet more relations.

'It's Ferdie,' Manny said.

'Ferdie?' Clara repeated disbelievingly.

'There's something very wrong with him.'

'What do you mean, Papa? What could be wrong with Ferdie?'

'He's been in his bedroom all day. He refuses to get up. He won't talk to us. He refuses to let us call the doctor. He's still in the clothes he had on last night. He doesn't even want your mother to pick up his jacket and tie, which he's thrown down on the floor...'

'Oh, Papa,' Clara said, a wave of relief washing over her. 'He's most likely just tired. He's been burning the candle at both ends, working very hard and then being up half the night with Fernanda and her friends. You mustn't lose all sense of proportion. Maybe you ought to think about going to the office a bit more. It might do you good.'

'Don't patronize your father,' Anna said. 'Go. Take a look for yourself. You'll see what he means.'

Clara, sympathizing with her parents as she did and appreciating the strain they had been living under since the end of the war, got up, confident that she would walk into her brother's bedroom and see Ferdie resting. After all, what could have happened in the thirty-six hours since she had last seen him to bring about the reaction - indeed, the drama - which her parents seemed intent on creating out of a simple lie-in? Clara was therefore utterly unprepared for the sight greeting her when she opened the bedroom door, saying, 'Ferdie, it's Clara. May I come in?'

Ferdie's response was a soft groan. She pushed open the bedroom door and entered the room. There, lying on the bed, was her brother: still in the trousers of his Prussian-blue pinstriped suit, the jacket and tie now neatly hanging in the armoire, thanks to his mother, but with the starched white shirt unbuttoned to reveal his hairy chest and his socks still on. Worse, however, than the state of the normally fastidious Ferdie's clothing was his expression. He looked wretched, haunted even: his eyes sunken in a way that was wholly unnatural and betokened real illness. Yet he did not look sad. Rather, he looked as if the life had been wrung out of him, as if he had been crushed beneath a boulder. As soon as she saw her brother's expression, Clara understood why her parents were so worried.

'Ferdie,' Clara said, making her way over to sit by the side of the bed. 'What in God's name has happened?'

Ferdie shook his head on the pillow.

Clara took his hand. 'Ferdie, something must have happened. Is it Fernanda? Did she break up with you?'

Once more Ferdie responded by shaking his head.

'Is one of the businesses in trouble?'

Again, only the shake of the head.

'Are any of the businesses in trouble?'

That elicited the beginnings of a smile before he shook his head again. 'What is it, then? Are you just tired?'

'I must be. I've never felt like this before,' he said.

'Don't you think you should let Papa and Mama call the doctor?'

Ferdie shook his head again, this time vigorously.

'You've been driving yourself too hard. You're suffering from exhaustion. The doctor can give you something to make you feel better.'

'Rest, that's all I need. Rest. And peace and quiet. Sorry, Clara,' Ferdie said, allowing his sister to hold his hand, 'but I don't have the energy to talk. Maybe tomorrow, OK?'

Clara kissed him on the forehead. 'Have you eaten anything at all?'

'Soup. That's all I want. But not now...later.'

'I'll get Cook to bring some.'

With that, Clara kissed her brother again and left his bedroom.

Standing in the passage to greet her were their parents. 'Well?' Anna said. 'See what I mean?'

'I do see what you mean, Mama,' Clara said as they walked back into the drawing room. 'I've never seen anyone look like that before. It's hard to put it into words, but he just looks so odd. Still, I don't think there can be anything very wrong. I mean he was lucid. If his thought processes had been disturbed, I'd say we do have something to be worried about. But they aren't. He's just wrung out.'

'It's more than that,' Manny said. 'I can tell. A father's instinct, if you prefer. I do wish he'd let us call the doctor.'

'Your father's right. I've seen many people exhausted in my life, and none of them has been quite like Ferdie is.'

'Maybe you should call the doctor if you're so worried, even though Ferdie doesn't want you to,' said Clara, who actually agreed with her parents.

'That's not a good idea,' Manny said. 'He'd take it as a mark of disrespect if we went over his head. He's a man now. He's not a little boy. We have to respect his wishes, even if we don't agree with them.'

'Then maybe you ought to go into his bedroom right now, Papa, and tell Ferdie that, while you will respect his wishes not to call the doctor, you insist, as his father and employer, that he take a break for a few days.'

'That's a good idea,' Anna said.

For the next five days, Ferdie stayed in his bedroom. In that time, he left his bed only to relieve himself. He did not change his clothes for the first two days. Only on the third morning, when Anna insisted that he change into pyjamas, did he finally strip off the trousers, his socks and his white shirt. Not once, however, did he brush his hair, wash his face, brush his teeth or take a bath. Exhaustion was on thing, both his parents and sister agreed, but this was something else. What none of them realized, because none of them had ever seen it before, was that they were witnessing the first severe manifestation of the downside of hypermania. The manic phase, which they had also failed to recognize, they had been observing for some considerable length of time prior to his collapse. His tremendous energy, his plethora of ideas (all good, but nevertheless, an extraordinary amount of them), his boundless enthusiasm – all the things the family believed were what made the adult Ferdie Piedraplata so extraordinary – were also the indications of a hypermanic personality at work. It would take several more cycles of exuberance and collapse before any of them, Ferdie included, realized what the problem was. Thereafter, hypermania, with its peaks and troughs, would cast a pall over the rest of Ferdie's life.

Chapter Three

That first manifestation of the down phase in Ferdie's illness lasted only a few weeks, after which he gradually bounced back with all the energy, and flair that were characteristics of his personality. Never one for idleness, as soon as he was fit, he once again applied himself to his true vocation: the creation and expansion of a great fortune. Meanwhile, across town on the outskirts of Chapultapec, in a far more ordinary part of the Federal District, as Mexico City was sometimes known, than San Angel, where the Piedraplatas lived, Bianca Barnett was preparing to marry the man of her dreams - or, at any rate, the man of her dreams of the moment.

It was in mid-October 1948 that Bianca's wedding day dawned warm, bright and sunny. The weather was neither too humid nor too hot. A perfect day for a wedding, in fact. The marriage ceremony was due to take place that afternoon at the Chapultapec Synagogue, followed by a reception at the Barnett house, which was two streets away from Julius Finkelstein's, in that modest but good area. In the four years since his arrival in Mexico, Harold Barnett had enjoyed a measure of success that allowed him to live well. The one-storey house he had built the year before was spacious, with three bedrooms and two bathrooms, as well as a living room, dining room, a family room and servants' quarters with laundry room, bedroom, lavatory and shower. It sat on half an acre of land, which Leila had had their full-time garden-boy landscape with attractive flowerbeds and bushes. To the poor, the Barnetts seemed rich, even though to the rich, they were poor.

To the beggar woman from the shantytown a mile and a half down the road who pushed her face between the closed wrought-iron gates of the Barnett residence, as Harold rather grandly referred to his house, the scene unfurling before her eyes was one of unimaginable wealth. She stood outside that October afternoon and watched the wedding preparations as the houseboy, the gardener, three waiters on secondment from the Jewish Club and three housemaids beavered away, opening up trestle tables which they then draped with white damask table cloths before setting them with what looked, to the beggar woman, like fabulous silver tableware but was actually only nickel-plate. She feasted her eyes as small but beautiful floral arrangements were set down at regular intervals upon the five longer trestle tables or put in the centre of the eleven smaller tables seating four apiece. She was entranced when chairs which looked as if they were made of gold were placed before each place setting, little realizing that they were merely ordinary metal chairs coated with goldcoloured paint: a solecism which would have been regarded as the ultimate in vulgarity by the very people Harold Barnett was trying to ape, had he known any well enough to invite them.

When the rows of electric lights were draped from pole to pole, and the nickel-plated candelabra brought out and placed upon each table, the beggar woman closed her eyes and imagined the glow they would provide later that evening, when the reception was in full swing, with the band playing and the guests being wined and dined. She hoped that no one would shoo her away, and indeed, no one did until a beautiful blonde lady, followed by two men carrying buckets of flowers, came outside. As the lady was walking towards a wooden arch, a tall man in pinstriped trousers, a crisp white shirt and a black bowtie came up to the woman and said, in a harsh tone of voice: 'What do you want? Go on! Off with you!'

The woman stepped back and would have run off had she not noticed the beautiful blonde lady turning around and gesticulating towards the starched and pinstriped man. 'Come and see me,' the vision of loveliness appeared to be saying. 'Let her stay.' The beggar woman edged towards the roadside and waited until he had walked across to his mistress. Sure enough, within moments he confirmed by gesture that her interpretation of the beautiful blonde lady's actions had been accurate, so the beggar woman stepped back towards the gate and once more pushed her face between the black iron bars. Having done so, she watched, again entranced, as the beautiful blonde lady directed the dressing of the arch with a quantity of pentas, lilies and other flowers whose names she did not know but which, she had no doubt, cost more than she and her whole family had to live upon for a year. The rich, she decided, really do live in another world, one free of the cares and concerns which daily oppress those who are less fortunate. How she would love to make the leap, if only for an hour, from her life to the one unfolding before her eyes, but she knew the futility of such hopes.

After the arch had been dressed to the beautiful blonde lady's satisfaction, she retreated back into the house. By the time she reemerged, dressed in a long, pale-green chiffon tea gown and a matching hat, the beggar woman had gone.

The beggar woman therefore did not see Leila take up her position in the backseat of the new green Mercury coupe with which Harold had replaced the Packard for the ride to the synagogue, nor did she see Bianca step out of the house a few minutes later and wait, patiently, while her bridesmaids - all in long apricot dresses - unravelled her long tulle train before helping help her into the Austin Princess limousine which the British Consul had lent Harold for the journey from the house to the synagogue and back.

'You've made your Daddy very proud, Bianca,' Harold said as the Consul's chauffeur started up the engine. 'I don't think I've ever seen a more beautiful bride than you.'

'Not even Mummy?' Bianca said teasingly.

To Harold, the height of feminine beauty had always been his wife, followed by his daughter, who closely resembled her mother; he knew that Bianca was mischievously prodding him to find out which one of his two loves was the more beautiful in his eyes.

'Oh, your mother made a magnificent bride, but if I have to judge, I'd say you've aced her.'

Satisfied, Bianca leaned over and kissed her father on his cheek.

Harold suddenly looked as if he was about to cry. 'It's unbelievable to think that my little Bianca is getting married,' he said as the tears slid down his cheeks. 'I don't know what your mother and I are going to do without you.'

'Daddy, it's not as if I'm going far. We'll be living only five minutes away in Lomas, and Bernardo is already working with his father twenty minutes from home. Nothing's going to change except where I lay my head at night. Promise.'

'Promise?' Harold said, a plaintive expression in his eyes.

Bianca thrilled at the look. She basked, as she had always done, in her father's adoration. Although she would never admit it to Bernardo, she needed her father's love almost as much as she needed Bernardo's, for Harold Barnett had been the mainspring of her self-esteem: the person in whose eyes she had always been perfect and for whom she had never been able to do any wrong. 'Don't be an old silly, Daddy. Of course nothing's going to change. You surely don't think I'd ever let a little thing like a husband come between us, do you? Now, come on, don't blubber. You did enough of that last night, and I can't have you setting me off again. I have to walk up the aisle a well groomed bride, and I fear a tear-stained face will be incompatible with that.'

'Quite right,' Harold said, putting on a brave smile and trying to banish his tears.

Ever since Bianca had become engaged to Bernardo Calman three months beforehand, Harold had been dreading the day when his baby would leave home. Try as he might to reason with himself that he was lucky to have such a nice and obliging young man as a prospective son-in-law, he had never been able to shake the feeling of doom, loss and horror at what would happen once Bianca adjusted to married life and found that she did not need her father the way she once had. In an attempt to let go, Harold had been telling himself these last three months that it was inevitable that Bianca would grow up and marry, and he must count himself lucky that she was marrying someone of Bernardo Calman's calibre.

Bernardo Calman, although not rich, was unusually easygoing. He was good-natured almost to a fault. He was simple and direct. He made no pretence of the fact that he worshipped Bianca. From the very outset of their relationship, he had met the Barnett family on their terms and had fitted in so well that Harold would have thought he was obliging to the point of weakness, had it not been for the fact that Harold himself was obliging of his daughter to that same ineffable point. Moreover, while Bernardo had no money of his own, and did not appear to have a glittering future in front of him the way Ferdie Piedraplata did, he was from a prosperous family of builders and had joined the family firm, not as an employee, but as a junior partner. He was therefore a man with prospects, as Harold would put it, and while he would never provide Bianca with the life Ferdie Piedraplata could, he would nevertheless provide her with a good and comfortable lifestyle, and ultimately, Harold comforted himself, it was the fact of comfort, more than its degree, that really mattered.

Leila Barnett also approved of Bernardo Calman, not only for the same reasons that Harold did but also for one very private reason of her own. Bernardo Calman was Jewish. Leila and Bianca were Jewish. Although Leila loved Harold and had never regretted marrying him, the world had changed in a way that would now make it impossible for her to marry a Christian, or for her father to approve of her doing such a thing. After all that had happened to her people since the days of her own marriage, Leila was delighted that Bianca was reaffirming her Jewish identity instead of stripping her descendants of it. Moreover, this marriage precluded her from having to tell her Christian husband that she didn't want her Jewish daughter to marry out of the faith, out of her own people. Of one thing Leila was sure. After all the suffering her people had endured in Europe throughout the last decade, the last thing she would have wanted was a Christian son-in-law, inevitably bringing yet more Christian blood into her family and diluting for all posterity the strength and heritage of the Seed of Abraham.

Although Leila had helped her daughter to get dressed, even she was startled by the radiance of the bride when Bianca took up her position at the entrance of the synagogue. She was absolutely ravishing in a longsleeved, jewel-necked white organdie and lace bodice with a heavily gathered floor-length skirt and a long train over which flowed, like the fizz upon a glass of champagne, an even longer tulle veil. This was attached to her hair by a tiara of faux pearls, partially obscured by a heavily gathered layer of tulle that had been pulled down over her face for the walk down the aisle. Even that single layer of tulle covering her face, however, did not did not detract from her beauty or her radiance. Rather, it enhanced it, giving Bianca a mysterious air that was at once romantic and glamorous.

To the wedding guests, none of whom had known the Barnetts before their arrival in Mexico, this was one of the weddings of the year. The Barnetts were already accepted as members of bourgeois society, in part because Harold had never disabused anyone of the notion that he was a wellborn British gentleman. In fact, Harold Barnett fostered that notion, despite the fact that he had been born anything but a gentleman. His father was a railway worker from Llangoglen who moved to Gwent before he was born, his mother being a domestic servant with a local solicitor's family.

What saved Harold from a life of unfulfilled potential was saving Leila Milade's life. But for that fortunate occurrence, he might well have been condemned to a life of class limitations, of unredeemed and unremitting boredom. Of knowing his place and taking it for granted for the remainder of his life. It was ironic, as Harold knew only too well, that the Milades had accurately judged his measure because he was a foreigner in a foreign land.

Had they been English, they would have dismissed him as soon as he opened his mouth and betrayed the remnants of his humble Welsh origins. Instead they heard what they thought was the sound of a middleclass British gentleman: someone who might not be rich or grand but who, judging by his manners and his deportment, must be well bred.

As a foreigner, Harold had made the leap from the working to the middle class. Thereafter, there was never any question of his ever returning to Britain to live. He liked being a British gentleman, and he could only be taken for one so long as he lived outside of Britain and the English-speaking world. And as long as he spoke a foreign language. The result was that Harold seldom spoke English, except to Bianca, Leila and the staff at the British consulate, who invariably made allowances for the British abroad. Harold was easily able to adhere to the habit of a lifetime when he stood up to make his speech as father of the bride, if only because none of the guests spoke English. Flanked by the flowered arch, a microphone in his hand, he welcomed his guests in Spanish and proceeded to sing the praises of his daughter in the tongue of the land.

Bernardo, whose only language was Spanish, did the same in his speech, while Bianca sat back and enjoyed the high point of her life.

To Bianca, it seemed unlikely that life would ever get better than this. Here she was, marrying the man she craved and embarking on a life that would doubtless provide her with a Latin version of the American dream: handsome husband, three or four children, an active social life, increasing prosperity. Ultimately, there would also be a big house with four bedrooms and en suite bathrooms designed by Mexico's leading architect - whoever that happened to be by the time she and Bernardo could afford that realization of the dream. She was going to have a perfect life, with love, money, kids, happiness, servants and a place in bourgeois society so that she could keep herself gainfully amused while Bernardo did a man's work and brought home a man's wages.

At the end of Bernardo's speech, Bianca rose to cut the cake with him. This was the end of the speeches, she knew, and she felt a sense of rising expectation as soon as she and Bernardo cut the cake and he fed her a slice, which she sexily took from his fingers, her teeth brushing provocatively against the skin of his fingers as she did so. Then the cake was whisked away by the houseboy to be cut up in the kitchen before being distributed amongst the guests who rose and toasted the health and happiness of the bride and groom in champagne.

As was typical with brides and grooms of that time, Bianca and Bernardo were in an inordinate haste to down their champagne. No sooner did they drain their glasses than they flew into the house to change into their going-away outfits. This caused an amused ripple of laughter from the guests, all of whom understood the new bride and groom's sense of urgency. These, after all, were still the days when newlyweds literally could not wait to get into bed, to unleash all the pent-up ardour that the rules of bridal virginity had confined them with until this moment. The result was that most brides and bridegrooms in those days behaved exactly as Bianca and Bernardo did, the bridal couple being invariably the only people at their own wedding reception who left just as the fun was starting.

Once Bianca and Bernardo were in the house, however, they were restricted by the prevailing customs of the day, aimed at discouraging the bride and groom from temptation until they were safely alone in their honeymoon suite. The bridesmaids helped Bianca out of her wedding dress and into her pale-blue silk suit with matching hat and gloves in her bedroom, while Bernardo's best man performed the honours of removing his studs in the guest bedroom.

Only after Bianca and Bernardo were fully clothed were they allowed out of their respective dressing rooms. Bianca, looking like the young matron she had now become upon matrimony, walked arm in arm down the stairs with Bernardo, dashing in a new bespoke pinstriped suit. Word spread that the bride and groom were ready to take their leave, so all the single girls assembled at the foot of the steps leading up to the front door.

With much jollity and feeling very grown-up because she was the first bride in her group of friends, Bianca threw her bouquet into the assemblage of single girls. It was caught by Sarita Finkelstein. That task done, Bernardo scooped Bianca up into his arms and carried her to the second-hand Plymouth coupe that his father had bought the young couple as a wedding present.

It was less than a fifteen-minute drive from the Barnett house to the Imperial Hotel downtown, where Bernardo's father had reserved the Bridal Suite for the night as an additional present to his son and daughter-in-law. The following afternoon they would board the SS *Duque de Medinacelli* for a cruise, stopping in Trinidad, Cartagena, Panama and Miami.

Bianca eagerly surrendered her virginity to Bernardo before the bottle of champagne they had ordered could be delivered to their suite. In retrospect, it seemed to her that one second they were entering the suite fully dressed, and the next they were urgently stripping amidst a flurry of sensual kisses. Thereafter, events were almost staccato in their pace.

Bernardo's naked body, pulsating with desire. Her hand moving down to touch the instrument of desire which she had never dared touch before, even though she had often sensed it through her clothing and been sorely tempted to have just one little feel. Bernardo groaning with pleasure and moving her towards the bedroom. The imperial-sized bed and the feel of the silk counterpane as Bernardo eased her down upon the mattress. The heat between her legs and the yearning to be occupied by this man whom she loved and desired. The pain as Bernardo edged his way in - gently, lovingly - all the while telling her how much he loved her and how much he wanted her. After he entered fully, the sensation of pain intermingled with desire: the harbinger of pleasures to come once her body had become used to having a man inside her. The embarrassment afterwards, when they were finished and she saw the blood upon the counterpane. Bernardo manfully taking control: 'They'll be used to this. Honeymooners use this suite all the time. You go and have a relaxing bath while I ring for room service and have them send it to the laundry.'

Up until their wedding, Bianca and Bernardo had been so compatible that it seemed as if they could not possibly improve upon that state of affairs. This, however, turned out to be untrue. They quickly became obsessed with each other sexually, which only enhanced the pleasure they derived from one another's company when out of bed. By the time they returned from honeymoon, ready to implement their plans for a happy home life by trying for the first of the four children they wanted, their unity of purpose was evident for all to see.

As Bianca and Bernardo settled down to married life, this unity did not diminish. It was almost as if they were the living embodiment of a complementary couple. Both of them liked socializing with their friends and their families, dining out most evenings or having friends or family in to dinner. Both of them went every Saturday and Sunday to the Jewish Club to swim and to play tennis.

Ten months to the day after their marriage, Bianca, who had learnt three months beforehand that she was expecting twins, gave birth to identical sons. The delivery was relatively easy at first, and she had opted, like most of her peers, to be anaesthetized. When she came around, she also behaved in keeping with the mores of her time and waited until she had freshened up – which included combing her hair and putting on lipstick and powder – before seeing anyone but the nursing staff, whose conduct she found decidedly odd. The explanation was not long in coming. Bernardo, his parents and hers had all seen the babies and knew of the tragedy, which was that the firstborn Emilio had been strangled on the umbilical cord and only the younger son Julio had survived.

Bianca experienced a strange, almost panicky feeling as she held out her arms to receive her son. Anticipation mingled with fear. 'Suppose I don't like him?' The thought flashed across her mind: one she had never had before. She took the sleeping baby and cradled him in her arms. He had the dark hair and eyes of his father but the features of his mother. 'He's so beautiful,' the new mother said, unwrapping the muslin in which he was swaddled and looking with awe at the being she had helped to create. Somewhere between the moment when she started to unwrap his swaddling and when she had to return him to the nurse, Bianca fell irrevocably in love with him. Thereafter, her heart and soul belonged to three men: her father, her husband and her son, although in a matter of weeks Julio supplanted Bernardo and Harold as the love of her life.

Two years after Julio's birth, Bianca produced another son, followed by a daughter, Antonia, in 1953. These were halcyon days for the young Calmans as well as for Mexico, which was experiencing an era of unprecedented economic expansion that made it the fastest growing Latin

American economy. Everyone in Bianca and Bernardo's peer group was prosperous. Everyone was young. Everyone was healthy. The future seemed to be as unclouded as the Mexican skies, with one bright sunny day following another in the Federal District of Mexico City.

At first, Bianca was happy and fulfilled both personally and socially. Life was everything she had ever hoped for or imagined. She had a handsome husband whom she loved and who adored her. They made love at least twice a day and sometimes, at weekends, three and four times. Although she did not always climax, she was a born sensualist and found the whole process of lovemaking gratifying as long as Bernardo made her feel desired - which he had never failed to do. She had three lovely children, all of whom she loved, although she was also the first to admit that she regarded Pedro as rather awkward and thought Antonia dull. Bianca had an active social life, one which emulated her own mother's and followed the established pattern of her class: coffee mornings, lunches, tea parties, dinners *en famille* or with friends, dinner parties, cocktail parties, dances, tennis parties, swimming parties and the occasional – very occasional - cultural evening at the opera, the ballet or a concert. Life, in fact, was one constant round of pleasure and gratification, and by the time Antonia was four years old, Bianca was growing dissatisfied with so much contentment. It was as if she needed a challenge, something to stretch her, some grit in her life to provide a bulwark against boredom. Could this, she sometimes asked herself, really be all there was to life? Was her existence always to be one long round of pleasurable events, unrelieved by anything unexpected? So much pleasure had become a chore.

However, to find work with which to occupy herself would have been unthinkable for Bianca. A working wife would have dishonoured her husband, declaring to the world that he could not support his family. It was an expression of failure. Instead, Bianca's discontent festered. By 1957 it was only a matter of time before it burst apart the apparently blissful existence she was leading.

Ferdie was by now well on his way to being one of the richest men in Mexico, although he still did not own the family business outright. His father remained his partner, something that might have bothered many fathers and sons but did not perturb either Manny or Ferdie. There had never been any doubt that Manny would leave his share of the family business equally to Ferdie, Clara and their mother; and for his part, Ferdie saw nothing amiss about his mother and his sister deriving benefits from his talents and hard work. To him, as to most other people in their world, the family was what counted first and foremost, and the idea that Ferdie would ever hive off, having used his family business as the springboard, and increase his own fortune without increasing theirs was unthinkable.

The family name and the name of the company, Calorblanco, with its emblem of a white flame, were by now known in every household in Mexico, Ferdie having diversified into everything from food shops and electrical stores to clothing stores and garages which sold both new and used motor cars.

Aside from Ferdie's tremendous energy, Calorblanco owed its extraordinary rate of growth to another of those chance encounters that would shape all of Ferdie's life. On a visit to Antwerp in 1949 to buy jewelry for the shows that the company now owned in Mexico City, Cuernevaca, Acapulco and five other Mexican cities, Ferdie had stopped off in London. He had never been to England before and, although the capital was in the grips of the British Labour Government's austerity programme and the overall impression was one of greyness, a chance encounter in an electrical shop changed the way he looked at funding, thereby paving the way for the massive expansion of the family business which followed.

Ferdie had arrived in London with an American electrical razor. He disliked shaving with razor blades. To him, there was something morbid about a man shaving himself with a sharp implement. It was difficult to say whether this distaste was his unconscious seeking to preserve him against temptation or whether it was simply his innate fastidiousness and sensitivity: Ferdie disliked pain and mess in equal measure and would go to great lengths to avoid both. Whatever the reason, his predilection for Remington razors was the reason why he walked into McCarthy's electrical shop on Piccadilly and made a great discovery when the shop assistant asked: 'Cash, cheque, account or hire purchase, sir?'

'What's hire purchase?' Ferdie asked, aware that his English was hardly fluent but also curious, as always, about what he did not know.

'That's when you buy something and pay for it in instalments, sir.'

'That's not the same as "on account", is it?'

'No, sir, "on account" means you take the item, and we invoice you for it. "Hire purchase" means you pay a portion of the selling price upon purchase and the remainder in instalments, say, over six, twelve or eighteen months.'

'Interesting,' Ferdie said, immediately spotting the possibilities of applying the same principle to purchases made in Mexico.

Ferdie walked out of McCarthy's realizing that he had been handed the means to expand the family business. No longer would he have to exercise patience, the way he had been doing, opening one electrical shop here, another there, a jewellery shop elsewhere, all the while making sure their financial base was covered so that any losses could be absorbed without affecting the overall performance of the business. The percentage the purchasers paid upfront in a hire purchase arrangement meant that there was an increased cash flow, which could be used to provide other goods for other purchasers. The sky was the limit if the system worked, as it seemed to be doing in England.

By applying the principle of hire purchase, no longer would a businessman have to aim his market at the moneyed classes. The poor also had needs and were a vast untapped market, if only the limits of their purchasing power could be enlarged. Hire purchase seemed to be the way to do it. With hire purchase, he could sell a labourer an item he might want - or, indeed, need - without either the labourer or the business having to fully finance the purchase at the time it took place. In effect, expansion could be financed in part by the customers instead of the banks, thereby keeping bank loans to a minimum.

Ferdie returned to Mexico City eager to try out this new idea. 'It seems sound,' Manny said. 'Like all good ideas, it is simplicity itself. I wonder why we didn't think of it before.'

On the principle that everyone needs to eat, and that food degenerates in a warm climate, Ferdie, who had already successfully opened electrical shops near two of the poor districts in Mexico City, decided to open twenty small refrigerator shops all over Mexico. For all his adventurous-ness, Ferdie was an innately cautious person who never took an unnecessary risk and always sought to create safety nets in case of unforeseen eventualities. This quality was one that he brought to bear not only in his business life but in his personal life too. It was also what propelled him to open up the refrigerator shops in working-class districts, shrewdly realizing that the poor needed credit and would not want to shop in affluent areas, where they would be led to feel that their presence was at best tolerated and at worst an intrusion.

It was this careful quality that had also led Ferdie to call off his engagement with Fernanda. With hindsight, he could see that he had treated her unfairly, but breaking up with her had seemed the only sensible thing to do at the time. This was at the time of his third bout of depression, eighteen months after the first and nine after the second. After the first one, he had ascribed his condition to overtiredness and had actually been so touched by the way Fernanda reacted that he had proposed marriage, even though he did not feel ready to settle down; but after the second bout, he began to question whether his personal life might not be having a hidden effect on his frame of mind. He therefore resolved to sever relations with Fernanda if he had a third bout, which he did two months before their wedding. This cancellation caused a furore in the smart Mexican social circles in which they moved. Fernanda was perceived as being blameless. Fiancés did not break off engagements with nice girls from nice families on a whim, after all. They only did so if the girl was found to be lacking, which Fernanda was patently not. The reaction of both his friends and his parents' friends so jolted Ferdie that he shied away from forming an attachment with another girl from a good family. In truth, it was just as well that he did, because most parents of such girls would not have allowed their daughters out with Ferdie Piedraplata after what he did to Fernanda.

In the nine years between ending his engagement to Fernanda, Ferdie developed a reputation in Mexico for being a playboy, even though he felt himself to be merely a man whom circumstances had cast into the twilight world where the living was fast and the women faster.

He travelled extensively on business. Always, he went first class, crossing the Atlantic on such liners as the SS *United States*, the *Queen Elizabeth* and the *Andrea Doria*. It was on one of those crossings that he met the Duke and Duchess of Windsor. Thereafter, whenever he was in Paris, he called in upon them at their Bois de Boulogne residence, unless, of course, they were all in New York, in which case he merely went up a floor to their apartment at the Waldorf Towers, where Ferdie customarily stayed. He was well on his way to earning a reputation as a sybarite when he first encountered Gloria Gilberto, Mexico's leading soprano, a tall, slender, statuesque brunette who resembled the movie star Delores del Rio and had been rated as a potential challenger to Maria Callas, although, it has to be said, more in the Mexican than the Greek or American press.

The whole course of Ferdie's life altered when he went backstage at La Scala in Milan to congratulate her on the fine performance she had given in the title role in Bellini's *Norma*. Upon meeting her, Ferdie felt something he had not experienced since first dating Fernanda. There was an immediate sympathy. A desire. A feeling of possibilities above and beyond the ordinary. Gloria, moreover, was no girl. She was a woman. An experienced woman of the world. A woman who promised excitement, satisfaction. An interesting, indeed fascinating, woman. Two years older than Ferdie, she had lived for ten years with the multimillionaire Prince Vittorio dell'Oro, a man two and a half decades her senior. There was no chance of her becoming the Principessa dell'Oro, however. That role was already filled, by a hawk-nosed Papal *contessina* who had provided the prince with eight children, the last of whom was only four years old, despite the fact that he and his wife were never together, save for family holidays.

Although Gloria's prince and his *contessina* were effectively separated, divorce was not a possibility in Italy in the fifties, and the nature of the relationship between Gloria and her prince was therefore not exceptional. Indeed, Italy at that time had many couples who were not married (at least, not to each other) but who, like the prince and the soprano, were accepted as established couples. In some ways, Gloria was even happy about the situation. She was only too aware that, but for Italy's archaic ban on divorce, she might never have been the declared consort of a prince because the Italian aristocracy seldom married outside of their own caste; and Gloria was only one of many women who secretly hoped that the state did not reform its divorce laws and force public humiliation upon them when their men refused to marry them.

Within days of their meeting, Ferdie asked Gloria to join him in Capri for a long weekend. 'Why not?' Gloria told herself, aware that a single multimillionaire with his future before him was a better prospect than a married multimillionaire with a past.

That first night in Capri, Ferdie and Gloria consummated their romance. From his point of view, it was interesting, exciting and fun. From hers, it was also interesting, exciting and fun; but neither of them had been profoundly moved by the other, even though they both wanted to meet someone with whom they could fall in love and ultimately marry.

By the end of their time together, they had enjoyed themselves enough to be prepared for more, despite the fact that what they had experienced was far from the real thing, merely a pleasant diversion.

However, they both wanted it to be more than it was, and in their anxiety to mistake it for something more profound, neither of them listened to the inner voices as they whispered their doubts.

For Gloria, the moment to listen ought to have been when Ferdie told her he loved her after they had made love on the morning of their departure. Pleasant as they were to hear, those three magical words seemed slightly out of place. Slightly optimistic. Slightly anticipatory. They were words she wanted to hear, words she might even want to hear from him one day, but if she had been honest with herself, she would have acknowledged that she did not want to hear them from him at that time and in that place.

As for Ferdie, he ought to have listened to his doubts that first time he said 'I love you,' to Gloria, for, as he was doing so, a small voice within him said: 'No, you don't. Not yet. You might one day, but you don't now.' But Ferdie ignored his inner voice, rationalizing that if those three words might one day be true, it was all right to use them now. After all, he lived in Mexico City, Gloria in Rome; and they could hardly conduct a long distance romance without some declaration of intent.

'I'm so glad you do,' Gloria responded, as the gap between the words she was uttering and her true feelings started to hit her.

Tactics. Tactics. A girl had no other option but to use tactics unless she was prepared to ruin her chances. And Gloria was not about to do that. Not with someone who was as attractive, as interesting, dynamic, interesting and rich as Ferdie Piedraplata.

'I don't want to lose you,' Ferdie said.

'Nor I you.'

'You're not coming to Mexico for a while, are you?'

'I wasn't planning to.'

'I've got a hell of a week of appointments ahead of me. All unbreakable. In Madrid, Barcelona and Paris.'

'I'm singing in London next week and New York the week after.'

'Would you ever give up your career for the right man?'

'I suppose I would, though he would really have to be the right man, because my career is more to me than making money. It gives me so much else besides.'

'I can see that.'

'The difficulty with being a soprano is that your voice reaches its peak, just as mine is doing, just when you're at your most marriageable. Life really presents opera singers with cruel choices. Do you marry and give up your career, or do you have your career and give up marriage? Needless to say, the voice begins to decline just as you're losing your attractiveness as a woman. It's as if a sadist created the choices for a female singer.'

'Surely there are men who won't make a woman choose between him and her career?'

'I don't know of any, except Giovanni Battista Meneghini, who isn't a man at all,' Gloria said, referring to her rival Maria Callas' ancient husband, who was more manager than lover.

'I wouldn't force you to choose if we were married.'

'You're an exceptional man in that case.'

'So I've been told,' Ferdie laughed.

'No, I mean it,' Gloria said, raising her head from his chest and looking at him directly. 'You are an exceptional man. Most wouldn't allow their wives the liberty of having their own career.'

'I have to return to Mexico next week, but why don't we meet in New York week after next?'

'Sounds like a good idea, as long as you realize that I'm working and have rehearsals as well as the performance, and I'll have to cosset my voice. Being around a soprano isn't all fun and games, I can assure you.'

Ferdie laughed. 'You're a woman after my own heart. I like professionalism and dedication.'

Two weeks and five days later, after another intensive period of being together, Ferdie proposed over a late dinner at Le Pavillon, the legendary French restaurant on East 57th Street. 'I'd love to say yes,' said Gloria. 'We get along so well and have so much in common. But we know each other so slightly.'

'That's true. But I feel we have something special. Either we can see each other occasionally and hope it amounts to something - thereby reducing the chances of things working out between us - or we can have a leap of faith and commit to making it work. But I'm a reasonable man.

At least, I hope I am.' Ferdie laughed. 'And you're right...we don't know each other as well as we could. So why don't we go into this with our eyes open? If it works, great. If it doesn't, we have a friendly divorce after a year, and I give you a settlement and alimony for, say, ten years, and we remain friends. That way, we have everything to gain from things working out and nothing to lose if they don't.'

'You'll be losing the settlement and alimony.'

'I'd be happy to give them to you. You'd have taken a leap of faith. That courageousness alone warrants its own reward. We'd have had an interesting – shall we say? – experiment...not that I mean to trivialize what we would have had between us. Two people who get married will always have a unique bond, and I would hope we'd always want what's best for each other.'

'Ferdie, it will be an honour and my privilege to be married to someone as big-hearted as you,' Gloria said, seeing for the first time that Ferdie was not only exceptionally desirable but also that rarity, a true life-enhancer.

Chapter Four

It all began innocently enough at a recital of *lieder* at the Wigmore Hall, which also happened to be Gloria's second appearance at that prestigious London venue since becoming Señora de Piedraplata. The audience was more of a mixture than usual: some ladies in long dresses and some gentlemen in black tie, although the majority were in lounge suits or short dresses. A good sign, Ferdie knew from Gloria. Society audiences were notorious in classical music circles for being the worst, with the result that the more ladies and gentlemen there were in formal attire, the more a performer dreaded appearing before them. 'They mask their lack of knowledge either with excessive appreciation or a pronounced lack of it, believing, erroneously, that too overt a display of enthusiasm might unmask them,' Gloria had explained to Ferdie shortly after their marriage, the first time she released a palpable breath of relief at the sight of the poorer-dressed members of the audience. 'It is therefore a relief for a performer to know that the larger percentage of the audience is in street clothes and has not come for social motives but because they love music and want to hear the performer perform.'

When Gloria Gilberto de Piedraplata came out onto the stage, she was pleased to see that there was indeed a healthy percentage of genuine music lovers among the tuxedoed crowd. As she sang, she was encouraged by their response. Pauses were honoured, instead of being filled with inappropriate clapping, and at the end of the song, she received applause which was just measured enough to inform her that this audience knew its music. By her own accurate estimation, she had been good, but she had not warmed up fully, so she was not as she ought to be, and both she and the audience knew it. Only a few of the smart crowd clapped too exuberantly, but she was able to discount them good-naturedly because the weight of their numbers did not unbalance the scales of proper musical appreciation.

By the end of her second song, 'Melancholie', from Robert Schumann's *Spanisches Liederspiel No 74*, Gloria had warmed up enough to be almost excellent. This time the applause of the knowledgeable was less measured, but it was only at the end of the first half, when she was in full flow, that the informally attired section of the audience really erupted into vociferous appreciation, shouting *'Brava!'* to Gloria, who was now performing at the absolute limit of her talent.

Great recitals are a marriage of performer and audience, and by the time the second half of the programme was under way, this September evening in 1959 was becoming one of the most memorable recitals in *lieder* history. Neither Gloria nor the music-lovers in the audience wanted the occasion to end. Finally, after her fourth encore, the audience, many of whom knew that the Wigmore Hall allocated only so many minutes to each recital, after which it had to be cleared or the staff would have to be paid at overtime rates, marked the occasion by refusing to stop their applause. Even after she had departed from the stage, they clapped for a further four minutes until Gloria had to come out one last time, take another bow and, blowing kisses to them, say: 'Thank you. Thank you so much. But it really has to be "goodnight" this time.'

An audible but affectionate groan of disappointment rippled through the audience as one or two diehards screamed, 'More, Gloria, more!'

Resorting to humour, Gloria waved at them as if she were about to depart on one of the ocean liners upon which she had been photographed so frequently over the years. Appreciating the joke, the audience erupted into laughter, and within seconds most of them began drifting out through the exit doors.

About forty of them, however, formed a queue on the left-hand side of the hall, in front of the door leading to the reception room backstage.

These were the die-hard aficionados, the musical cognoscenti. Some were musicians themselves, others members of the London musical scene, music-lovers who mixed in music circles and whose sole claim to fame was their love and knowledge of music. Standing out from this crowd were three people in black tie: two men and a tall, willowy, blonde woman. She was attractive rather than beautiful, obviously well bred, aquiline features, a Norman Hartnell dress, and a Georgian *tremblant* diamond brooch some six inches in length, with a central diamond of at least eight carats, and another thirty or so carats dispersed throughout the roses, leaves and stem.

'Her phrasing's exquisite,' the younger and better-looking man said.

'Très Elisabeth Schwarzkopf,' the older and decidedly unattractive man added.

'She's even better looking than Elisabeth Sckwarzkopf,' the girl said.

'And the style of the woman. The way she moves. That dress. The jewels.

'Balenciaga and Van Cleef, I'd say.'

'Amanda can always be relied upon to know precisely where a lady's costumes and jewels come from,' the younger man laughed.

'That's what comes from having gone to school at Roedean,' Amanda replied, joining in the laughter. 'Those South American millionaires' daughters were an education in themselves. Not to mention their mothers, none of whom would be seen dead, even at ten in the morning, without complete maquillage, couture dresses and jewels to die for. They turned grooming and its accoutrements into an art form, I can tell you.'

'And you learned their lessons well,' the older one teased.

'Thank you, Hugo,' Amanda said, as they approached Gloria Gilberto, who stood, flanked by Lillian Hochauser and her impresario husband, Victor. Victor Hochauser stepped towards the older man, who was a music critic for *The Times*. As they started to talk, a tall, good-looking Latino brought Gloria a glass of champagne. By way of thanks, she pecked him on the cheek.

Amanda recognized the man from his photographs in the gossip columns and glossy magazines as Gloria Gilberto's husband. She was surprised at how sexy he was in the flesh. In his pictures, he always looked stiffer, more cardboard, like a Scott Fitzgerald character rather than a living, breathing, *fuckable* man. She felt her loins stir just as Hugo was introducing her to Gloria Gilberto. After a few pleasantries, Amanda moved on, only to be introduced to Ferdie Piedraplata by Lillian Hochauser.

'Your wife is such a fine artist,' Amanda said, aware that good manners required her to limit her conversation to the purpose of her visit.

'Yes, she is, if I do say so myself. I don't think it's immodest to agree.' Ferdie laughed heartily. 'After all, I have nothing whatever to do with her talent, and, in the absence of being able to take the credit, I feel that anything less than recognition on my part would be laying claim to what isn't mine.'

'What an adorable man,' Amanda thought and laughingly riposted: 'I've never heard modesty described in quite those terms before. Of course, you're absolutely right. A wife's talent is not her husband's, and to treat it with false modesty is not only unacceptable possessiveness but also trespassing on her territory.'

Just then, Lillian Hochauser came up and spoke to Ferdie so softly that Amanda could not hear what the other woman had said. She did, however, hear Ferdie's response: 'Absolutely. It will be my pleasure. Our pleasure, I mean.'

Lillian Hochauser returned to the group consisting of her husband, Gloria and the two tuxedoed men. 'Mrs Piedraplata would like to extend her invitation to all of you to join us for dinner at the Mirabelle.'

While the others were accepting the invitation, Ferdie said to Amanda: 'You will join us too, won't you?'

'I'd be delighted,' she replied, wondering if she was imagining things, or did Ferdie find her as attractive as she found him?

A possible answer to that question came towards the end of dinner, after the forty or so other guests had departed. It was clear that this was the end of the evening. All their glasses were empty, and so was the restaurant, the waiters standing by politely. As he pushed back his chair to indicate that dinner was at an end, Ferdie said: 'This evening has been such fun. I've never before enjoyed myself so much in your lovely country. My wife leaves for New York the day after tomorrow, and I shall be a grass widower for two days. Shall we repeat this at the Ritz the evening of her departure? As long, of course, as you have no objections?'

'Of course not,' Gloria said. 'Enjoy yourselves.'

'We won't be able to come, I'm afraid,' Lillian Hochauser said. 'We have a Festival Hall recital being given by another artist.'

'We're game,' Hugo said. 'As long as you want us without the esteemed Mr and Mrs Hochauser.'

'I take it that means Gloria is getting a good review?' Ferdie laughed.

'More than good,' Hugo replied. '*Glowing*, my dear Señor Piedraplata.'

'In that case, we must celebrate.'

'You do that,' Gloria said good-naturedly.

Two days later, both of Amanda's concert escorts telephoned to cry off.

She toyed with the question of whether she should go on her own or cancel as well. Two things made her decide not to back out. The first was that Ferdie had not called off the evening, and because she liked him, she did not want to leave him in the lurch in a strange country. The second was that she liked him so much she wanted the opportunity to get to know him better. Being the lady she was, however, Amanda was not about to involve him or herself in anything compromising or disagreeably surprising, so she telephoned the Ritz Hotel and left a message explaining that the numbers had shrunk, and he was to let her know if the evening was still on.

Ferdie received the news after returning from an appointment with his Savile Row tailor. 'How elegant of her to give me an out,' he thought as he picked up the receiver and asked the operator to connect him to the telephone number she had left with her message.

'Amanda? Ferdie Piedraplata here. As long as you're up and running for this evening, I can think of nothing I'd like more than seeing you.'

'Shall I join you at eight-thirty, as planned?'

'I wouldn't dream of letting a beautiful young lady fight her way across London on her own. I'll send a car and driver for you. What's your address?'

'One hundred and twenty-one, Eaton Square,' Amanda said.

'I know Eaton Square well. It's so elegant. Your family home, I take it?'

'Oh no,' Amanda said. 'Mummy and Daddy could never afford anything so grand. The estate eats up all their money. They have a maisonette on Queen's Gate Terrace. I share with my cousin, Duckie. Her father is Lord Paulington, of the Starboard Shipping Company,' she added by way of explanation, assuming, rightly as it turned out, that Ferdie would know precisely of whom she was speaking.

'Not Piers Paulington, surely?' Ferdie said, having learned when dealing with the English that one had to speak in their disclaiming manner, otherwise one jarred. 'I do business with him. In fact, we had lunch only yesterday. What a small world it is. I'll have my driver with you by eight-fifteen.'

At six o'clock, Amanda was in the library, idly flipping through the latest issue of *Tatler & Bystander*, in which both she and Duckie were featured, when her Uncle Piers arrived home from the office.

'You'll never believe whom I'm having dinner with this evening,' Amanda said. 'A business associate of yours.'

'Are you going to keep me dangling, or are you going to tell me who it is?' Piers asked.

'Ferdie Piedraplata.'

'The richest man in Mexico, they say...though one always has to take what *they* say with a pinch of salt.'

'Is he seriously rich?'

'Without a doubt. Whether he is actually the richest man in Mexico may be a moot point, but what is indisputable is that the man is a veritable Midas. Everything he touches turns to gold. He's recently branched out into shipping, which is how we met, and I have to tell you, watching him in action has been an education in itself. Nice chap as well.'

'I thought so too. We had dinner the other evening after his wife's Wigmore Hall recital...that is, James and I trailed along with Hugo, who was writing it up for *The Times*.'

'Charming woman. Beautiful too. We've been to dinner with them once or twice and had them to dinner last year when they were here for Royal Ascot. Apparently, she's on the way to being a huge opera star. The next Callas, they say. Not that I can abide all that screeching. I understand that they married very quickly, but that it's worked out well and they're happy together.'

'I liked her. Him too.'

'Give them my regards.'

'I'm only seeing him. She left today. She's doing Lucia at the Met in New York.'

'Well, have a good time, my dear.'

During dinner, the attraction Amanda felt for Ferdie became so overpowering that she had to excuse herself and go to the ladies' room to calm herself down, lest she succumb to the temptation to lean across the table and kiss him. 'This is ridiculous,' she scolded herself in the mirror.

'He's a happily married man. He's years older than me. He most likely hasn't even noticed that I'm a woman. Hit terra firma, girl, and don't let your feelings run away with you.'

Having managed to get some kind of grip on her emotions, she returned to the table. Ferdie, ever well mannered, stood up. She took her seat. He resumed his. They reached for their napkins and, inadvertently, their hands touched. Amanda felt as if she had been electrified. Powerless to mask her feelings, she looked in Ferdie's direction and saw him experiencing the same thing. They were both caught up in the moment, in emotions that were too strong to conceal. He slid his hand over hers, while she blushed as never before. For a moment their gazes locked. He smiled slightly. So did she, wanly - afraid and hopeful at the same time. He took her hand in his. He stroked it. Almost imperceptibly, she leaned towards him. 'I'd like to kiss you right now,' he said, slipping their hands under the table so that they could continue to hold hands without being observed.

'I wish you would,' Amanda said, overcome with desire. 'I love this man,' she thought to herself as she looked into his eyes.

Ferdie's expression changed. It was a combination of desire, pleasure and seriousness. 'This is so unexpected,' he said. 'I did find you very attractive over dinner at Mirabelle...truth be told, even at the Wigmore Hall...but this is something else. You're a very bewitching girl, you know.'

'And you're a very bewitching man,' Amanda said.

'I have to tell you I don't like emotional mess. Affairs are very messy things. They're not my style. And you don't strike me as the sort of girl who would just hop into bed with a married man.'

'I'm not. But I suspect that I would with you, if that were the only thing on offer.'

Ferdie raised Amanda's hand to his lips and kissed it.

They looked at one another in silence. The moment gave way to silence. Before it became awkward, Ferdie slipped Amanda's hand under the table, placing it on his leg. 'Let's look at this sensibly,' he said. 'One must always be sensible when confronted by anything of importance. What's happening here has never happened to me before. I take it I'm not wrong in hoping that you feel the same way?'

Amanda shook her head.

'I've heard about it,' he continued. 'Some of my friends have even had it happen to them. A *coup de foudre*, I believe it's commonly called.

Doubtless you've read about such things in those romantic novels that you ladies are all so enthralled by. Am I right?'

Amanda, not trusting herself to have a voice, shook her head again.

'The question is,' he went on, 'where do we go from here? I'm a married man. My wife and I have a good marriage. However, if I'm frank, and I'm going to be only because you deserve the truth, our marriage has never reached the heights that I suspect a relationship with you would. That's no criticism of my wife. She's a good woman. But marriage is like any other relationship. Its boundaries are defined by the personalities involved. For better or for worse, the relationship between Gloria and myself has never been as electrifying as the one between you and me already is. To my way of thinking, what's happened between us is a gift, whether from God or nature or Cupid, doesn't matter. We have the beginnings of something wonderful here. I just don't see how we're going to realize it. I'm married. Even if you wanted to become my mistress, I would not allow it, not only because I respect you too much but also because we'd gradually kill what we have between us. If marriage has taught me one thing, it's that relationships need commitment to flourish. We would need to be married, to share our lives together, to wake up and go to sleep together, to have common goals, to strive and to worry together...even at times, to fight together. Is this making sense to you?'

Amanda nodded, almost dejectedly. Ferdie raised her hand and kissed it again. This time he replaced it on the table, cupping it with his.

'Since I'm in a confessional mood,' he said, smiling, 'I have to tell you that my personal life matters a very great deal to me. Aside from my wife, whom we'll keep out of this for the moment, I have only my parents, my sister and my niece. All of our family was exterminated during the war. You don't have anything against Jews, do you?'

'No. Why? Are you Jewish?'

'Yes and no. My parents converted. I was christened a Romanian Orthodox and have been received into the Catholic Church. By blood, however, I'm totally Jewish. Now where was I? Oh yes. I have a suggestion to make. How would you feel if we were to keep away from one another for three months...no communication whatever... and meet up again and see if we still have what we have between us now? And, if we do, then we explore the possibility of getting married. What do you think?'

'You mean we begin an affair after three months, and if it turns out that we're really in love, you get a divorce and we get married?'

'You've put it much better than I ever could.'

'Three months is a long time when you feel the way I do,' Amanda said.

'I know,' Ferdie said. 'It is for me too. But we must test ourselves. It's not only our own happiness that's at stake. There's also my wife to consider.'

'Three months it is, then,' Amanda said resolutely, shaking his hand and showing him the courage that he already sensed she possessed.

Ferdie laughed. 'Only an English girl,' he said, the tears streaming down his face, 'would shake the hand of the man in a situation like this.' He took his hand, brushed it against her cheek, and, as she started to laugh too, said: 'Amanda, I love you.'

Amanda heard nothing from Ferdie for the following six weeks. This was a period of exquisite torture for her, wondering if Ferdie would, at the end of this sentence, feel the same way as she still did. For Ferdie, it was also a period of intense conflict, and more complicated because he did not have only himself to consider the way Amanda did. Although his feelings for Amanda did not diminish, nor did his feelings towards Gloria alter. He was still enormously fond of her. He still valued her and enjoyed her company. The one thing that had changed was their lovemaking. And this was a profound change.

Gloria noticed it too. Almost immediately, in fact. 'Ferdie, is something bothering you?' she asked the third time they made love after their return to Mexico.

'No,' Ferdie said gently, knowing that Gloria had sensed the change and wanted the reason for it.

'Are you sure?'

'Of course I'm sure,' he said less sharply than he would ordinarily have done.

Gloria looked at him quizzically, shrugged her shoulders. 'If you say so,' she replied then walked into the bathroom.

As far as Gloria was concerned, something had come between them, whether Ferdie would acknowledge it or not. He was more distant than he had ever been. Even during his periodic attacks of depression, there had always been an emotionally available dimension to their relationship.

Yet she now sensed that this was no longer the case. That he was holding something back. That she was not as important to him as she had been.

Proof came to Gloria in an unexpected way. For three days following that verbal exchange, Ferdie did not approach her to make love. This in itself was unusual, for they had always made love at least twice a day except during his periods of depression. At first, Gloria wondered if she was not witnessing a new manifestation of depression. By the end of the second day, however, she had to admit to herself that his behaviour in every other way was so patently different from depression that the problem had to be something else. When they made love on the third day he put so much vigour into it that she had to ask herself what he was compensating for. Once the suspicion of infidelity crossed her mind, Gloria became as vigilant as a lioness stalking her prey. She waited until he was almost asleep one night. 'Ferdie, is anything wrong?' she asked, trying to keep her tone light.

'No,' he said soporifically.

'You wouldn't, by any chance, be having an affair with anyone, would you?'

'I don't have affairs, Gloria.'

Having hit another brick wall, Gloria decided that watching and waiting was the only mature way to deal with whatever it was that was happening. She had to wait a week before a further opportunity to catch another glimpse into Ferdie's soul offered itself for, unusually for him, Ferdie did not try to make love to her for another seven full days. When, at the end of that period, he initiated relations, she embarked upon the encounter with an eye for any microscopic detail that might provide a clue as to the real nature of the subject. In so doing, Gloria became a partial observer to the scene she and Ferdie were enacting.

'Maybe he's just settling down to married life,' she concluded afterwards, 'and is starting to take me for granted, like most other married men do with their wives.' Although she had not been officially married to Vittorio dell'Oro, the prince had never taken her for granted. He had never made her feel, as Ferdie now did, as if she didn't quite exist as a real person. This sensation, of somehow being dampened down, was new and discomfiting and ultimately demeaning, she decided. It was almost as if Ferdie were using her physically. As if he had reduced her to a receptacle for his carnal pleasures.

Gloria was profoundly shocked at the thought. 'Secondary masturbation,' she reflected. 'That's what our lovemaking feels like now. I don't like it one bit.'

Quite what the solution to the problem was, Gloria did not yet know. Men, especially Latin men, disliked anyone probing into their sex lives. 'A woman has to be so careful what she says or does,' she decided, perplexed about how she could resurrect the feeling of intimacy which had previously existed in their lovemaking.

Towards the end of the fifth week, Ferdie turned to Gloria one morning and mounted her without preamble. Without even the most basic foreplay, he inserted himself into her and pumped away until he climaxed. Not once throughout this encounter - for that is what it was, at least to Gloria - did he kiss her or touch her with any sensuality or affection. When he had relieved himself, he got up, went into the bathroom and took a shower before returning to dress for work. As he went about preparing for the coming day, Gloria resolved to say something. 'You don't have anything on your mind, do you, Ferdie?' she asked, sitting up in bed and ringing the buzzer twice for her maid to bring her breakfast.

'No,' Ferdie said matter-of-factly.

'You're sure?' Gloria asked, a wave of anger and frustration welling up within her.

'Sure I'm sure,' Ferdie said, as if he were speaking to one of his buddies.

'And you're not having an affair.'

'No.'

'You know I'm leaving for Rome next Tuesday, don't you?'

'Sure,' Ferdie said.

'It's fine for me to go, I take it.'

'Of course it is. Why wouldn't it be?'

'You're not having second thoughts about me pursuing my career, are you?'

'Of course not. A deal's a deal. I don't go back on my word.'

'Ferdie,' Gloria said intently, changing her tone. Ferdie stood, looking, waiting. Gloria looked at him, opened her mouth as if to say something, closed her mouth and, obviously thinking better of it, instead said: 'I hope you'll miss me.'

'I always miss you when you're away,' Ferdie said as he tucked his shirt into his trousers, slung his jacket over his shoulder and came over to the bed to kiss her on the cheek. 'Enjoy your day, darling.'

Ferdie did not touch Gloria again until the morning of her departure when he once more mounted her for yet more perfunctory sex before kissing her goodbye with the chasteness that young nephews reserve for aged great-aunts.

'If this is what's in store for me for the rest of my life, I don't want it,' Gloria decided while inspecting the cases her maid had packed for the journey. Although the marriage had never quite taken off with the bang she had hoped for, there had been compensations in the form of Ferdie's commitment; the luxury of their everyday life; the lavishness with which they lived and travelled; the type of person she met as Ferdie's wife. After all, Mr and Mrs Ferdie Piedraplata functioned on a wholly different level from the way either Gloria Gilberto the opera diva or Prince Vittorio dell'Oro ever did. Not for Ferdie and Gloria the limits of music and aristocracy. Thanks to Ferdie's extraordinary business acumen, and to the wealth it generated, they moved among the leading lights of the world, whether political, business, social or musical. If an associate of Ferdie's was a lord, he was not just any lord, but one who was tremendously rich and vastly influential. If he was a socialite, he was not part of the flock but a leader of the field. If he was a businessman, he was not merely rich, but very rich and well connected. This world that Ferdie had introduced her to was a revelation, not only because of the wealth but also the influence that such wealth created. There was a feeling that anything was possible.

No, strike that: easy. Anything you wanted was yours for the asking.

Ferdie's world was the elite of the elite, and there was no doubt that such wealth had its advantages, although such compensations were not enough to tempt Gloria to stay in a marriage where she felt she was being taken for granted.

Gloria, of course, was not stupid. She was not about to make so hasty a leap into the unknown. She intended to watch and wait and see. But, for the first time since her marriage, she started to think in terms of it ending rather than continuing. The upshot was that Gloria telephoned Vittorio dell'Oro as soon as she was shown into her suite at the Excelsior Hotel in Rome.

'Vittorio, it's Gloria.'

'Gloria,' he said excitedly, the pleasure evident in his voice. 'What a surprise! I've waited two years for this call. Why didn't you ring before?'

'It wouldn't have been fair to any of us, Vittorio.'

'Things have changed?'

'Things may be changing.'

'I can't say that I'm sorry. I've missed you.'

'There have been times when I missed you too.'

'Shall we have dinner tonight? At our old favourite? Say, nine?'

'I'm staying at the Excelsior.'

'*Bella*, it will be wonderful to see my little treasure again.'

Although Gloria did not intend to sleep with Vittorio that night, she did. All their old passion returned in force. Afterwards, as she lay in Vittorio's arms, she could not help but contrast the way she was now feeling with the way she had felt after Ferdie, even at the best of times. With Vittorio, she was bathed in desire. In fulfilment. In oneness with her man.

'Vittorio,' she said, 'how would you feel if I told you that I think I made a mistake in marrying Ferdie?'

'*Bella*, I'd say that's wonderful. We can go back to the way we were.'

'On one condition. If your wife dies or if Italy changes the law, you marry me.'

'But naturally, *Bella*,' replied Vittorio, a true gentleman whose word was his bond.

At that moment Gloria understood that, no matter what the reason for Ferdie's recent change of heart, marrying him had been the right thing to do, if only because it had made her marriageable in Vittorio's eyes. As the ex-wife of one of the richest men in the world, she had been elevated socially and was now on a par with Vittorio's set in a way she could never have been before, when she was merely Signorina Gloria Gilberto, successful soprano from Mexico. Finally, the one stumbling block, which had always perturbed her in her relationship with Vittorio, had been removed. Marriage was no longer an impossibility. That was all Gloria needed to hear for her to make up her mind.

'I'm going to ask Ferdie for a divorce,' she said.

Vittorio held her tightly. He kissed the back of her neck, stroking her back sensually. 'I've been praying to the Virgin for this day for the last two years,' he said intensely.

'Vittorio,' Gloria laughed. 'That is outrageous. Who else but you would think it acceptable to pray to the Virgin for another man's wife - and when you're another woman's husband too?'

'No, *Bella*. You have been my true wife for ten of these past twelve years, and I have been your true husband. Your husband and my wife have been social arrangements. The Virgin knows where my heart lies.'

With that, Gloria turned over to face Vittorio and kissed him. 'Thanks for taking me back, Vittorio,' she said, silently thanking Ferdie for removing the one impediment from her relationship with the man she had always truly loved.

Chapter Five

As she dressed for her old school friend Sara Finkelstein de Cohen's party, Bianca had no more idea that she would one day marry Ferdie Piedraplata than she did that all her social ambitions would be realized beyond her wildest dreams. As far as she was concerned, this May evening in 1963 was nothing more than an opportunity to climb another rung up the ladder of Mexico City Society.

For Bianca, all that was important in life remained focussed upon the social circles in which she moved in the Federal District and to which she aspired. Society was the platform upon which she could assert herself. Upon which she could strive and attain, allowing her to earn an achievement that would add grit to her life and make getting out of bed more of a challenge than the seamlessly pleasurable - and pointless existence - of the Mexican matron ever could.

As Bianca looked into the mirror and peered at the image reflected back at her, she saw a woman already approaching middle age, with blonde hair blunt-cut to the shoulders and backcombed to within an inch of its life. It was a very young look. Very trendy. With her large green eyes outlined in heavy black eyeliner - top and bottom - and further accentuated with long, thick, black false eyelashes; green and white eye shadow highlighting the distance between the eyes and eyebrows; a hint of blusher and a pale pink lipstick, Bianca projected an image of perfect but youthful grooming.

'I don't look a day over twenty-eight,' she said to herself, consoling herself with the thought. 'Not bad for a woman approaching her mid-thirties.'

In Bianca's circle, half her contemporaries looked at least ten years older than she did; the other half, fifteen years older. To Bianca, her looks were of overriding importance, because she functioned in a world where a woman's achievements were made possible by beauty and charm while at the same being circumscribed by the wealth, position and accomplishments of her husband. Although Bernardo Calman was a successful man, and she had been moving inexorably up the social ladder with him, Bianca's ambition was now to become one of the leaders of Mexico City society. To that extent, therefore, her ambition was outstripping Bernardo's position, but she was intelligent enough to see that it was realizable, as long as she poured the unique gifts of beauty, charm and energy, with which she had been endowed by nature, into her quest.

Bianca got up from her dressing table and peered at herself in the full-length mirror. She was as slender as if she dieted and exercised constantly, her ample bosom sexily filling out the line of her low-cut dress. She nodded approvingly at what she saw, for reflected back at her was an undeniably beautiful woman radiating sex appeal, who, unlike many another beautiful woman, had no anxieties about her looks. Indeed, one of her rarer characteristics was how completely for granted she took her beauty while at the same time relishing all the attention it brought her.

Bianca delighted in a compliment the way few other women did; and the look of lust that so frequently overcame men when they were talking to her never failed to generate a genuine thrill within her. Nor did she mask that delight. She gave expression to it in a way that thrilled men right back. Whether it was with a low chuckle, the batting of her long eyelashes or a finger fleetingly placed on the arm of the man with whom she was flirting, Bianca always, but always, conveyed her appreciation of the man who appreciated her, for she had learned one of the secrets of being a successful woman, which was that few men could resist being appreciated and in as obvious and direct a manner as social mores allowed.

Unusually for a woman who was so attractive to men, Bianca also got along well with other women. They never found her a threat, not even when she had their husbands drooling over her. Partly, this was because Bianca was careful to reserve her most pungently sexual conduct for the moments when no woman could overhear her, but partly it was also because she courted women as much as she courted men. Flattery - or, as she would put it, 'displaying appreciation' – laid on with a trowel was the secret of her success and always had been. She had learned the art as a little girl sitting on her father's lap and had used it lavishly thereafter, safe in the knowledge that the one thing no one wants to rectify is another's splendid opinion of oneself.

Lavishness had actually become an increasingly pronounced feature of Bianca's personality in recent years. In the social world as in so many other areas of her life, once she hit upon a mode of behaviour that elicited the responses she required of it, she repeated and refined it. In the case of her lavish demeanour, this worked so well socially that she had already begun to acquire quite a reputation in Mexico City for being a hostess. This, she knew, was her passport, visa and residency papers for the upper reaches of Mexican society, where nothing, save money and lineage, counted more than entertaining. In the absence of a great fortune, the Calmans were providing the only other means for acquiring an enviable social position: superb hospitality. Twice a year, therefore, at the end of April and the beginning of September, the Calmans hosted a large cocktail party for two hundred, during which they served every drink known to humanity and food that was always a combination of Lebanese and Mexican. The mix was both exotic and unusual, and the hospitality truly Middle Eastern in its splendour.

To establish herself further, Bianca had started two years previously to throw a dinner dance that she hoped would become one of the fixtures of the Mexico City social calendar. She had already originated the format she intended to perpetuate – the latest 'in' band until six o'clock in the morning, at which time Kedgeree, scrambled eggs and bacon, fried sliced mushrooms, fried sausages and kippers – a full English breakfast – were served. Bianca had started to play up her Britishness in a way her father never did, wisely using it to provide her with a distinction and a distinctiveness that she would otherwise have difficulty laying claim to.

She therefore made it known to all her friends that she invariably sent out engraved invitations that she had printed in London by Smythson of Bond Street, who, she claimed, were the English Royal Family's stationers. Lest anyone miss where their invitations came from, each envelope had that firm's name embossed on the flap, and Bianca was assiduous in letting everyone know that her family had always used the Queen's stationers, thereby reinforcing the Barnett family's reputation for aristocratic connections - a reputation she was cultivating - while at the same time standing out from the crowd of Mexico City socialites by sending out invitations unlike anyone else's.

For all her efforts, Bianca was only too aware that she had not yet reached the pinnacle of society to which she aspired. For all her achievements, she was not yet even properly on the periphery of the upper reaches of Mexican society, dominated as it was by no other female than Amanda Piedraplata, for Mr and Ferdie Piedraplata were the couple to know. Theirs was indisputably the most eminent social position in Mexico, before even the President and his family, who were viewed as transients while the Piedraplatas were regarded as holders of positions whose permanence transcended the changes in political climate.

Ferdie and Amanda lived like a latter-day imperial couple in a recently completed Frank Lloyd Wright palace in Lomas not far from the Chapultapec Palace where the Mexican Emperor Maximilien and his Belgian Empress Carlotta had briefly lived while he reigned in the nineteenth century.

For sheer, up to the minute splendour, their maze of concrete, glass and flat roofs was unsurpassable. *Architectural Digest* said so. *House and Garden* said so. *Harper's Bazaar* said so. Everyone said so. Their country house, situated on a man-made island in Cuernavaca, a two-hour drive from Casa Piedraplata in Mexico City, was a nineteenth-century palace built by Emperor Maximilien during his reign. Rumour had it in Federal District drawing rooms that Ferdie Piedraplata had instructed I.M. Pei, the celebrated architect who practised in the United States, to design another modern palace on the site and to tear down the ill-fated Emperor's palace to make room for it.

Whenever Bianca thought of Ferdie and Amanda Piedraplata, life's injustices bore down upon her slender shoulders. Why did they have to clutter up their circle with presidents, government ministers and foreigners? Why couldn't Ferdie be more patriotic? More Mexican? Why couldn't he and Amanda choose their friends from the same circles that she and her friends did? Nice, well-off, social Mexicans. Every time the Piedraplata parties were covered in the society pages of the newspapers, the only Mexicans present were the boring old president, his boring old wife, his boring old ministers and their boring old wives as well as a sprinkling of Oligarchs who featured in the red-velvet bound Families of

Mexico. Or the wretched International Set. Super-rich and super-beautiful people like the Fiat king Gianni Agnelli, the Queen of England's cousin David, Marquess of Milford Haven, Chase Manhattan Bank's David Rockefeller, or Aristotle Onassis with Maria Callas.

One of the more charming features of Bianca's personality was the complete lack of envy she possessed. She was not upset because they had what she wanted. She merely wanted an invitation to the party. She was therefore perfectly sincere when she asked herself why they couldn't give fellow Mexicans like herself and her peer group a chance to meet them, when all she wanted to do was bask in the glorious light that their luminous presence cast. Life was just too unfair: Bianca was convinced of it, still puzzling over how best to engineer a meeting with Ferdie Piedraplata and his wife Amanda.

'You would think,' Bianca said to herself for what must have been the thousandth time, 'that it would be easy enough to meet people who live in the same city. It's not as if I want to become friends with them. I don't. I merely want them to attend one of my parties each year, and for Bernardo and myself to be asked to one of theirs in return. That's hardly a lot to ask.'

With the gift of clarity that would hold her in good stead throughout her life, Bianca knew precisely what she wanted from the Piedraplatas. She was equally clear about what she did not want. She did not want a close friendship, for Bianca knew from the newspapers and gossip on the social scene, that Amanda was the niece of an English lord, and while Bianca never let on to anyone – not even to Bernardo or her children – that she was fully aware of her father's humble antecedents, over the years she had come to realize that there was a good reason why her father avoided speaking English or being with the British. She was not about to blow his cover – and incidentally her own – by befriending an Englishwoman who would be ideally placed to unmask her father for being the commoner he was. No, her ambition, so far as the Piedraplatas were concerned, had nothing to do with friendship. She simply wanted the kudos of being recognized by her peers as a member of the Piedraplata social set. Nothing more, nothing less.

Since Sara had told her that Ferdie and Amanda were attending the party, Bianca had resolved that, even if she had to move heaven or earth to create the opportunity, tonight was the night she was going to set her foot on the first rung of the Piedraplata ladder. Intent on looking her best as well as her richest, Bianca put on the emerald and diamond parure that Bernardo had given her for her thirtieth birthday. 'Proper grown-up jewels,' her father had called them. They were dazzling. And they had dazzled her friends. But, she had no doubt, they would be very secondrate compared to Amanda Piedraplata's fabled jewels. 'Still,' she consoled herself, 'at least they show I'm not penniless.'

Sure enough, when Bianca walked onto the Cohen veranda in Lomas, there was Amanda Piedraplata 'holding court' with two other women dressed in midnight-blue taffeta, in what looked suspiciously like a Balenciaga cocktail dress. On her bodice she was wearing the most obscene amount of sapphires Bianca had ever seen in her life. Rather than being envious, however, she was bedazzled. One of those stones alone was worth twice the whole of her parure, and she knew it. Amanda Pedraprata would also know it. 'What a display,' Bianca said to Bernardo. 'If you owned jewellery shops like the Piedraplatas, I would also drape myself in every jewel I could. Have you ever seen a more fantastic sight in your life?'

No sooner were the words out of her mouth than she heard someone behind her call her name. 'Bianca? Long time no see. How are you, you fabulous thing, you?'

'Begonia?' Bianca asked, almost disbelievingly. 'Can it really be you? After all these years?' Begonia was the Panamanian girl who had sat behind her at the Academy in Panama City and who was responsible for introducing her to her unrecognised first husband Hugo del Rio, whom not even Bernardo knew about. Although they had never been close friends, they had been friendly enough: on the periphery of one another's circles. Bianca hoped that Begonia was equally ignorant of that secret from her youth.

'Can you believe it?' Begonia replied. 'Nineteen years! The last time I saw you, you were barely a teenager. Now you're a knockout.'

'It's sweet of you to say so. You're looking great yourself. So soignée. As if you had just stepped off a plane from Paris.'

'In a manner of speaking, I did. I married someone called Raymond Mahfud. Although his family are originally from Baghdad we've been living in Beirut, which is called the Paris of the Middle East, and in its own way it's very Parisian. I don't mind telling you, though, it's great to be back in Latin America.'

'Will you be staying, or are you just visiting?'

'No. We're here to stay. Raymond is opening a branch of the Banque Mahfud here.'

'So you married a banker?'

'I sure did,' Begonia said with the merest hint of resignation.

'But how exciting! It is exciting, isn't it?'

'Not if you don't like parties eight nights a week and dinners with all sorts of people about whom you really couldn't care less but have to be nice to. I believe they call it being a Corporate Wife.'

'But you must meet the most fascinating people.'

'It depends what you mean by "fascinating". Even people who are genuinely fascinating, because of what they do, are pretty mundane around a dinner table. Unless you're actually working with them, they're really very ordinary.'

'People like who?'

'People, I suppose, like King Hussein of Jordan and Nubar Gulbenkian.'

'Well, I'm sure I'd find King Hussein or Nubar Gulbenkian interesting, even if it were only over a dinner table.'

Begonia laughed. 'Oh, Bianca, it's so good to see you. You haven't changed a bit. Not really. You're the same wonderful, funny, enthusiastic Bianca we all knew and loved.'

'Life was made to be relished, no?' Bianca said, laughing.

'Come,' Begonia said, taking her former classmate by the hand. 'I want to introduce you to my husband and his brother Philippe. They're going to be working together in partnership with Ferdie Piedraplata.'

Light at the end of the tunnel. Finally. Begonia was offering on a plate what Bianca had expected to have to acquire through her own resources. Clearly Begonia was someone she should add to her circle of friends and not only because she liked her, although she did. If she developed a friendship with Begonia, Bianca was aware that she would in the ordinary course of events meet Ferdie and Amanda Piedraplata at the house of Begonia and her husband on a regular enough basis to develop a solid social acquaintanceship. Mexico City social life followed an established pattern whereby people who were in business together fraternized outside business hours at each other's houses and clubs. 'It's wonderful to see you, Begonia,' Bianca said, light-headed with anticipation, as Begonia walked her across the veranda onto the lawn. 'We must swear not to lose touch again. There are so few kindred spirits in Mexico.'

'We'll have a lot of fun.'

'Yes.'

'Ah, here's my guy,' Begonia said, stopping in front of a short, squat, podgy, balding man in his late thirties. 'Isn't he the sweetest, most loveable man you've ever seen? Darling, I want you to meet an old school friend: Bianca Barnett. Bianca, my beloved Raymond Mahfud.'

'It's actually Bianca Calman now,' she said, stretching out her right hand for him to kiss. He took it and shook it.

'Did the Academy churn out only beauties, or am I mistaken?' Raymond said with a glint, more of humour than anything else, in his eye. 'You're almost as beautiful as my wife.'

'Almost,' Bianca laughed good-naturedly, knowing very well that she was much better looking than Begonia. 'And she was named after a flower, while I have to make do with merely being the colour of one.'

'I can see that my husband likes you,' Begonia said, wagging her finger playfully at Raymond, who started flirting mildly with Bianca.

'"Like" is not the word. If I were not married, I would throw down my cloak for you to walk upon. Fortunately, Begonia knows she can trust me. My eye is the only thing that roves.'

'You're funny,' Bianca said, laughing appreciatively.

'Your country is beautiful and exciting,' Raymond continued, changing tack. 'It reminds me of home. Have you ever been to Baghdad?'

'No,' Bianca replied, 'but I want to one day. My mother's from that part of the world. She's Palestinian.'

'Ah, then we share a common bond,' Raymond laughed. 'We both shook off the yoke of the Ottoman oppressor.'

'But we're Jewish.'

'So are we.'

'I didn't know you were Jewish,' Bianca said to Begonia.

'I wasn't. But I am now.'

Another short, squat, podgy, balding man walked up to them at that point. Before Begonia even introduced them, Bianca knew it was Raymond's brother. 'Philippe, I want you to meet my old school friend, Bianca Calman. But you're not allowed to flirt. She's safely married.'

'But I'm not,' Philippe Mahfud replied. 'Though it's not for the want of Begonia trying. You're the first friend of hers I've met in ages who isn't marriage material. And what a pleasure it is to meet you.'

Tempted though she was to riposte, Bianca limited herself to a throaty laugh, sexy and appreciative. It wouldn't do to flirt too outrageously with a strange man in front of his sister-in-law. Not when she hoped the sister-in-law would assist her in reaching the pinnacle of her ambition: admission into the social circle of Ferdie and Amanda Piedraplata.

'There's my husband,' Bianca said, catching sight of Bernardo in the distance and signalling him over. 'You must meet him. He's the most darling man in the world if I say so myself, present company excepted, of course. Do you remember him? Bernardo Calman?'

'I didn't know him, Begonia said. 'You must remember that our time together was spent in Panama, not here.'

'Of course, silly me. I met Bernardo when we moved here from Panama.'

Just as Bernardo was approaching from the left, Amanda and Ferdie Piedraplata came into view on the right. Torn, Bianca could not decide whether she was glad that she would have the distraction of introducing her husband at the same time as Begonia was introducing her to the Piedraplatas - thereby distracting her and reducing the rush of adrenaline which might overcome her - or whether she was rattled because one of the decisive moments of her life was being adulterated. Fortunately for Bianca, Ferdie and Amanda came up to their group just before Bernardo reached them. The alternative, that Ferdie and Amanda might shy away rather than break up an introduction, was a distinct possibility, although Bianca could see the likelihood of Bernardo arriving after introductions were underway. This, indeed, was what he did, slipping in beside his wife and taking her hand in his.

Bianca was careful to say 'How do you do?' as demurely as possible, while Begonia made the introduction to Ferdie. She purposely saved the full force of her charm and her warmth for Amanda. This was a wise move on her part. In the eyes of a good many people, the wife of a rich man comes a very poor second to her partner. Bianca was wily and she understood the power of womanhood.

Moreover, she was no rebel. On the contrary. She had respect, almost reverence, for the code governing feminine conduct. She functioned by the rule that no sane sensible woman ever undermined another woman who was not a direct competitor for the hand of a man. No sane sensible woman ever trampled on the toes of another woman – unless, of course, she was after her man. That objective aside, a woman always respected the feminine code and functioned through other women, not through their men. To function through a man when he had a wife was to call the whole principle of feminine solidarity into question. It was to declare yourself a traitor to the feminine cause – and the feminine cause was a woman's cause – every woman's cause. Bianca's cause.

Bianca's one ambition in life, after being happy, was to climb to the rung on the social ladder where she would be acknowledged as one of Mexico's elite socialites. Bianca therefore grasped the initiative of this special moment and stepped back just enough so that she, Begonia and Amanda formed a triangle. The men, they all knew, usually preferred speaking among themselves, and now that Bianca had subtly broken up the group into two segments, she set about working the magic of her charm upon Begonia and Amanda in varying but deliberate degrees.

'I always thought you must photograph well because it's impossible to find a bad picture of you,' Bianca said to Amanda, hoping that her charm would work its old magic. 'But you look so much younger in the flesh that I now see I was wrong. Don't you think so, Begonia?' she added, taking care to include her schoolmate, her bright and smiling eyes flicking from one to the other.

'It's true. Trust Bianca to notice it and say so. She was always so outspoken and generous, even as a young girl. One of the few pretty girls in the school you never felt threatened by.'

'Why, Begonia, that's one of the sweetest compliments I've ever received. Two compliments in one, in fact. You'd better be careful, or you're going to give your old school friend a swollen head,' Bianca said, tongue in cheek, for it was obvious to both Begonia and Amanda, who were also pretty women, that Bianca was as used to compliments as they were.

Amanda smiled. 'That's very kind of you, but I confess I seldom like myself in photographs. I look as if I'm the same generation as my mother or the Duchess of Argyll. Quite what the answer is, I don't know.'

'I wouldn't concern myself with it if I were you. How could a newspaper picture capture your eyes? They sparkle more than the most fabulous jewels ever could. And what a colour! If you were an actress, they'd be comparing your eyes to Elizabeth Taylor's. Wouldn't they, Begonia, my beautiful friend?' Bianca said, taking care to keep Begonia suffused with the glow that she was spreading elsewhere.

'Do you have children, Bianca?' Begonia asked.

'Yes, three. Two boys and a girl. And you?'

'One,' Begonia said. 'A boy. But we're going to get a daughter soon.'

The way Begonia phrased her reply caught Bianca's attention. She wondered whether she should ask if Begonia's son were adopted or not but decided against doing so in such a public place. Instead, she thoughtfully acted as if she had not noticed the implication and said: 'Boys are great, aren't they? One of my boys is the absolute love of my life, though that doesn't mean I love my other son or my daughter any less.

'Do you have children, Amanda?'

Bianca could have sworn that Amanda blushed at the question, but she could not be sure, as the half-light might have been playing a trick with her eyes. 'Not yet. We've only been married for three years so there's still plenty of time. But I do want at least two: a son and a daughter. My husband teases me and says I display all the qualities of a typical Jewish mamma, even though I'm not actually Jewish.'

'Then your children will be very lucky. Raymond tells me I'm a typical Jewish mamma too. He says I'm the best mother in the world after his own, of course, with whom no earthly presence can compete,' Begonia said pithily. 'As far as he's concerned, not even the Virgin Mary was a patch on her.'

Amanda and Bianca erupted into laughter.

'What is it about Jewish men and their mammas?' Bianca asked as their laughter subsided. 'I'm sure the reason they make good husbands is that they are such adoring sons. I really pity a woman who doesn't marry a Jew. That's where you're lucky, Begonia. You didn't marry one of those Panamanians or Mexicans who give their wives so much trouble. That's why you're glowing with fulfilment.'

'As are you,' Begonia replied.

'Yes, I'm a lucky girl, and I know it. I have the most wonderful husband in the world - after the two of you, of course,' Bianca said then added as an aside: 'plus three gorgeous children and a father that I frankly worship. My mother isn't too bad either, though it must be said that she and I don't always drink the same brand of tea.'

The women then rejoined the men, and the conversation shifted to beach houses. Begonia, who was always on the lookout for signs of the state of a marriage, observed Bernardo slipping his hand into Bianca's. It was Begonia's inflexible maxim that she would never become friendly with unhappily married couples, believing that marital unhappiness was as contagious as whooping cough. She watched as they remained holding hands long after they needed to and, when they stopped doing so, touched each other fleetingly but lovingly while they spoke to everyone else in the group. Bianca, she decided, could become her friend.

Begonia had also noticed in the past that the Piedraplatas enjoyed a good marriage as well. They too touched more than the average married couple and, when they were separated and talking to other people, Begonia had observed the way Ferdie and Amanda kept on looking across the room at one another, as if each were checking to see that the other was all right. It was, Begonia concluded, lucky for her that two such young and attractive couples could be so happy. Perfect additions to the group of friends she hoped to acquire against the loneliness she would otherwise feel in a country where, she had reason to believe from Raymond, they would stay for a very, very long time, possibly even for the rest of their lives.

Without realizing it, in her desire for friendship, Begonia Mahfud had just become the catalyst for changing all their lives forever.

Chapter Six

New York: 1965. The last thing on the mind of either Ferdie or Amanda Piedraplata was Bianca Calman, her charm or her ambitions, as the first snow of the winter fell at lunchtime that November afternoon. By five o'clock, there was a fluffy white blanket covering the Columbia-Presbyterian Hospital in uptown Manhattan, and Ferdie was nervously pacing up and down by the window of his father's room, looking out at a view that was both beautiful and bleak at the same time.

'Where's the damned oncologist?' he said, looking at his watch. 'He was due here fifteen minutes ago.'

'He's most likely running late, darling,' Anna Piedraplata said quietly. 'Why don't you and Amanda find a Coke machine and get a drink?'

Amanda looked at her mother-in-law. Her expression conveyed that whatever Ferdie wanted would be fine with her. Ferdie, his mother knew only too well, was a handful. Impatient. Volatile. Nervy. Edgy. Self-willed. But always fascinating. And kind. Decent too.

For Amanda, dealing with Ferdie, whether he was well or ill, had been made immeasurably easier by the support of his parents. Early on in the marriage, Anna had given tangible evidence of her and Manny's support for their son's aristocratic and loving wife by pressing a velvet pouch containing a perfectly matched, twenty-two millimetre double length of South Sea pearls - worth the price of a brownstone on the Upper East Side in New York - into Amanda's hand one afternoon with the words: 'These are for you. For you to remember that Ferdie's father and I appreciate the way you treat our son more than words can express.' Anna

Piedraplata recognized that Ferdie, the most compassionate and generous of men, was lucky in having married a woman with a commensurate degree of compassion and generosity of spirit.

Anna, however, was Ferdie's mother: not his wife. As they waited for the oncologist to see Manny, Ferdie was getting on her nerves. 'Go on,' she encouraged. 'Go get a Coke. No point remaining here, working yourself into a frenzy. I'll send the nurse for you when the doctor arrives.'

Just then the door opened, and Dr Abraham Mankowitz stepped into the room. He was dressed in hospital whites and had a stethoscope dangling from his neck. 'Good afternoon,' he said pleasantly and generally, but without a jot of levity in his voice. 'Sorry I'm late.'

'That's OK, doctor,' Manny said, shifting his weight from one side of the bed to the other.

'How are you feeling today?'

'Tired. Very tired. I don't think I've ever felt as tired as I do right now.'

'Would you prefer that we speak alone?'

'No, doctor. You've met my wife, son and daughter-in-law,' Manny said, looking around at Anna, Ferdie and Amanda. 'You can talk freely in front of them.'

Ferdie shifted his gaze from the beautiful, snow-clad grounds of the hospital to Dr Mankowitz. Before the oncologist had a chance to say anything more, he had already assessed the situation. 'The news is bad,' Ferdie told himself.

'Mr Piedraplata, the results show that you have late stage-three Hodgkin's Disease. There's quite a lot we can do to make you comfortable. For instance, we can give you steroids, which will give you a lot more energy than you have at present and will counteract a lot of the tiredness you've been suffering.'

'Is fatigue a symptom of the disease?' Manny asked.

'It is. We can also put you on Cytoxan and Vincristine. We've been having encouraging results from them for some time now. There's a lot we can do...'

'To make my father comfortable,' Ferdie said, crossing from the window to the side of the bed.

'Yes, sir,' Dr Mankowitz said. He was at least fifteen years Ferdie's senior, and as soon as he uttered that one word 'sir', he confirmed to the four Piedraplatas that he must have read about Ferdie's tremendous wealth. The fortune, however, was not Ferdie's alone. His sister and parents were equal partners, so Ferdie was only a quarter-owner of the fabled Piedraplata fortune.

'Why not an operation? Can't you operate? What about a cure?' Ferdie asked, his voice tinged with desperation.

'Mr Piedraplata, Hodgkin's Disease is a cancer of the lymphatic system. There's much we can do, but when it has spread to the liver, as it has in your case, Mr Piedraplata,' Dr Mankowitz said, shifting his focus of attention from son to father, 'surgery is not a valid option.'

'What are we speaking about in terms of time, Doctor?' Manny said. 'You can tell me. I'm a tough old warhorse. Give it to me right on the chin.'

'Four to six months, if nothing else goes wrong.'

'What could go wrong?' Ferdie asked.

'You must take extra special care not to catch so much as a cold. Don't go near anyone with flu,' Dr Mankowitz said, looking directly at Manny. 'Hodgkin's Disease is indicative of the fact that you have a flawed immune system. If that weren't the case, you wouldn't have Hodgkin's Disease. The drugs we give you will also affect your immune system. You'll have very little resistance. Many patients with your condition are not carried off by the disease but by a bug they thought was harmless. I can't emphasize that enough.'

'So it's only a matter of time?' Anna said to the doctor, as the tears poured down her cheeks.

'I'm sorry, Mrs Piedraplata.'

'You wouldn't feel slighted if we asked for a second opinion, would you?' Ferdie asked. 'Maybe Sloan-Kettering will offer us some hope.'

'I wouldn't discourage you from trying there,' Dr Mankowitz said, looking directly at Ferdie. 'If I were in your shoes, I'd also get a second opinion. Maybe even a third. However, I'm sorry to tell you this but oncology is a narrow enough field, and you'll find that the experts at Sloan-Kettering are interchangeable with the doctors at Columbia-Presbyterian in terms of knowledge and treatment. Truth be told, we all know each other and exchange information.'

'Thank you for your honesty, Dr Mankowitz,' Manny said. 'It's much appreciated. Really.'

'We'll begin a course of treatment tomorrow,' Dr Mankowitz said. 'I'd like you to stay in New York for at least another three or four weeks. Once we establish how you're responding to treatment, we can look at things again. Maybe then you can return home to Mexico, and our regimen can be implemented by the doctors there.'

'Will I have to stay in hospital the whole time?'

'I see no reason why you can't leave here after a week or ten days and check into a hotel.'

'You can use my rooms at the Towers,' Ferdie said, referring to his suite at the Waldorf Towers with the modesty that Amanda had taught him was the mark and true sense of good breeding.

'I'm sorry I can't be more encouraging,' Dr Mankowitz said. 'I truly am.'

'It's all right, Doctor,' Manny said. 'I'm an old man. I've lived a full life. I've been more richly blessed than most. My only regret is that I die without having a grandson.'

Dr Mankowitz left the room. Anna immediately got up from the chair where she was sitting, and sat on the bed with him, holding his face in her hands and kissing it as their tears co-mingled. 'We'll do all we can, Manny,' Anna said. 'Anything you want, we'll do. I just can't believe it's come to this.'

'Papa, I'm sorry we haven't given you a grandchild,' Ferdie offered. 'Amanda can tell you it hasn't been for the want of trying. That's true, isn't it, darling?'

'Yes. We've been to doctors here and in England, Papa. We've even been to the Queen's gynaecologist. They all think we might never have children of our own, but they can't be sure.'

'So why don't you adopt?' Manny said.

'Papa, we're still young. Every day there are medical breakthroughs. I figured if we exercise a little patience, everything might turn out all right,' Ferdie said.

'And if it doesn't? Do you have anything against adoption?'

'It's an option we've been considering,' Ferdie replied. 'But only as a last resort.'

'And what if there is no medical miracle? What if no breakthrough comes? Or it comes when you're sixty? Ferdie, a couple don't make a family. They make a couple. Family is God's greatest gift. Is all the knowledge and wealth - spiritual wealth, I mean, not money - that our family has amassed over the centuries to die out when you and I die? What about what my father taught me, and his father taught him, and I taught you? Aren't you going to hand that on to a son? You do realize that if you don't, you will be the end of the line, and it will all die with you.'

'But Papa, an adopted child won't have your father's blood, or yours or mine.'

'All this rubbish that people talk about blood...don't they realize that this was the basis of Nazism? Blood without heritage is nothing. Heritage without blood is still heritage. I am speaking about heart. About culture. About knowledge. About spirit. That's what I want to keep alive.'

'So you think I should adopt a son?'

'Do you want a son?'

'Of course I do, Papa. It's the only thing I don't have in life that I truly want. Amanda too.'

'And a daughter,' Amanda interjected with a smile as she wiped away her tears.

'You're a lucky man to have this girl,' Manny said to Ferdie. 'We couldn't have wished for a better daughter-in-law. Remember that and always take care of her. You'll never go wrong with her by your side, of that I am sure...eh, Anna?'

'My sentiments exactly,' she said, nodding her head and wiping away the tears.

'I will die a happy man if I can hold my grandson in my arms, if only once,' Manny said. 'Now you ladies leave us men to talk business for half an hour, if you please.'

Anna got up and kissed her husband on the cheek, then she and Amanda left the room together, Amanda stepping aside to let the elder woman exit first through the door that Ferdie now held open for them.

'You'll soon be on your own, son,' Manny said as soon as the door was shut. 'Your old Papa won't be here to act as a sounding board. I remember how lonely I felt when I no longer had my Papa to talk things over with. Money creates such isolation. You have to be careful whom you trust. My advice to you is: never put a hundred percent of your trust in anyone who isn't a member of our immediate family. Don't completely trust any friend or partner. Never forget, the world is full of people who seem kind and decent and trustworthy until you discover that they aren't. Your mother is no businesswoman, so she won't be of any use to you when you discuss the mechanics of business, but she's a good judge of character...she understands what motivates people. Your best ally, however, will be your sister Clara. With her mind and knowledge of the world, she combines a lot of your mother's virtues with a businessman's perspective.'

'But Papa, Clara lives in Italy.'

'She does, it's true, but she nevertheless has a gift for business. Take my word for it. She runs Calorblanco Europa far more efficiently than either you or your mother has ever given her credit for. Even putting aside her business acumen, her general knowledge alone is worth five consultants. And she's much sharper about people's baser motives than you are.'

'I suppose I do sometimes find it difficult to accept that people I like can be as self-interested as they sometimes are.'

'Ferdie, this is not a criticism. My only concern is to protect the family from the vultures that will encircle you all once I'm gone. They will, believe me. You have a reputation - a just reputation - for kindliness. Is there another businessman in Mexico, or indeed the world, who has done more for his workers than you have done for ours? Every time I think of the Calorblanco Foundation, my heart bursts with pride at having a son like you. Who else but you would have had the idea to build schools throughout the length and breath of Mexico for Calorblanco workers' children? Who else but you would have subsidized those schools, paid the teachers, given the children uniforms and schoolbooks at below cost? Set up adult education classes? Is there another businessman in Central America who has built housing developments for his workers? Who rents those apartments and bungalows out to the workers at a cost to ourselves? Do you remember when you had the idea to build that first medical clinic for the workers in Taxco? How many clinics and hospitals do we now have? Twelve? Fifteen? All fully staffed. At no cost to our workers. No, Ferdie, you are a good man with a big heart, and I love you all the more for it. Hopefully, one day your son will give you the opportunity to be as proud of him as I am of you. You have exceeded every hope and dream I had for you, but your Achilles' heel is your big heart, which you must guard against, otherwise you will let in people who will take advantage of you. When I'm gone you'll have no one to turn to except your mother and Clara.'

'I'm sure I'll manage, Papa.'

'I'm not sure you will, Ferdie. That's the point I'm making.'

'Clara lives in Italy, Papa. I can't very well call her every time I need to work something through.'

'Why not? You can afford the cost of the telephone call.'

'It just doesn't seem particularly practical. And I do have some good men around me. Look at Raymond and Philippe. They're great guys. They're on the ball. Our interests coincide on many levels. They're even Jewish.'

'I would especially warn you against Raymond and Philippe. Yes, they're charming. Yes, they're capable. Yes, they've done well with the Banco Mahfud Mexico and even better with the Banco Imperiale, but I want you to remember that they owe most of their success to our funding. But for our backing, the Banco Imperiale would not exist. While their interests coincide with ours in a limited way, in other respects their interests clash with ours.'

'Let me remind you that you're the one who encouraged us to start up Banco Imperiale.'

'I know. I know. Undeniably the Mahfud boys are brilliant and energetic, and they've served our purpose well in giving us footholds in other countries. We were uncomfortably focused on Mexico for awhile, and though I have nothing but thanks for the welcome Mexico has given us, we as a family must never forget that one day in the future Mexico might also turn against us, as Romania would have done had we stayed there – and as it did with all our relations who did stay there. We're lucky that Calorblanco is a family concern and all our interests coincide, but with the banks, that is not the case. You must never forget that today's partner can become tomorrow's adversary. Our money is what is propping up the Mahfud brothers, Ferdie. Without us, Banco Imperiale would not exist and Banco Mahfud Mexico would fold, or at the very least, struggle to survive. Either way, don't rely too much on the Mahfuds. See them for what they are. Lean only on your sister. I know you're selfwilled and don't like to be curbed, but in this, I am begging you, listen to me. If you do not, the potential for disaster is too horrific to contemplate.'

'Papa, I appreciate what you're saying and why you're saying it, but you mustn't worry. The business will be in good hands, I promise. I'll take care of it for you and for Mama and for Clara.'

Later, a tearful Ferdie and Amanda left Anna with Manny and headed back to downtown Manhattan. Between 168th Street and 59th Street, they discussed adopting a son, and by the time they reached 48th Street, they had agreed that Amanda would telephone Begonia Mahfud, the only person they knew who had adopted children, to see how she and Raymond had obtained their children.

'Raoul Goldman in New York,' Begonia said. 'He's one of the top "baby" lawyers. He finds Jewish babies for Jews; Arab babies for Arabs. Chicano? Japanese? A mixture of Serbo-Croat and Thai? No problem. Raoul Goldman always finds your baby.'

'I don't mean to sound crass, but what are his charges like?' asked Amanda, who hated speaking about money.

'He bills according to the time he spends on your case, and - be warned - according to what he perceives the depth of the prospective parents' pockets to be. His fees range from $5,000 to $15,000, which is frankly exorbitant, and there's also no way of checking to see whether he has really spent the time he says he does on any particular case. To people like Raymond and me, however, the price is well worth paying. Raoul Goldman's babies are always healthy, intelligent and good-looking. Truth be told Amanda, if I'd had my children myself, I couldn't have done better.'

Armed with that information, Amanda and Ferdie deliberated over who should make the call to Raoul Goldman. 'Better an English accent on the end of the line than a South American one,' Ferdie said, shrewdly factoring in the advantage his wife would have over him.

First thing the following morning, Amanda made the call. The receptionist put her through to someone with a slight Bronx accent who answered in a way Amanda found both amusing and unusual.

'Raoul Goldman.'

'Hello, Mr Goldman,' she started, sucking in her breath. 'I am a friend of Begonia Mahfud, and she has recommended you, as my husband and I are interested in adopting a baby. Is it possible to have an early appointment with you?'

'I can see you a week on Thursday at five-thirty,' Raoul Goldman said. 'Will that be you on your own or you and your husband?'

'Don't you have an earlier appointment?' Amanda said, plainly disappointed.

'Afraid not. But if something comes up and I have a vacancy, I'll give you a call.'

'It's just that my father-in-law is dying and we want him to see his grandson before he goes,' Amanda said, thinking that she sounded like a nutcase or a liar.

'I'll see what I can do,' Raoul Goldman said, making a note of Amanda's telephone number.

As soon as she rang off, Ferdie said, 'He'll ring back later today or on Monday with a cancellation. Mark my words. It's the oldest trick in the book. Keep 'em hungry and anxious, and they'll be keener. It's the guiding motto of all hucksters and hookers. The guy sounds like a real operator.'

'What do we care, so long as he provides us with a healthy baby boy?'

'True,' Ferdie said.

Raoul Goldman did not call later that day or the next, or even the day after that. He did not ring on the following Monday or on the Tuesday thereafter. On the Wednesday his secretary telephoned at eight-thirty in the morning to say that a vacancy had arisen for five-forty five that afternoon.

Amanda jumped at the opportunity, but Ferdie, still distrustful, remarked: 'What sort of operation does this man run, that he has his secretary working at such an early hour of the morning?'

Ferdie had the opportunity to find out just what sort of operation Raoul Goldman ran later that afternoon when he stepped out from beneath the canopied awning of the Waldorf Towers into the black Lincoln Continental limousine that he invariably hired whenever he was in New York. Within ten minutes, the driver had pulled up at Raoul Goldman's office on nearby 44th and Broadway and leaped out, opening the door to a tight-lipped Amanda and a less visibly nervous - indeed, almost pugnaciously curious - Ferdie.

The lobby of the building was functional rather than elegant, as was the waiting room in Goldman's office on the twelfth floor. Whatever the lawyer did with the money he made, Ferdie decided, he certainly wasn't spending it on lavish offices: that was for sure. Even the receptionist seemed drab and mousy in a world where the beauty and charm of receptionists were often yardsticks by which companies and men of the world indicated the measure of their success to the incoming visitor.

No sooner did Ferdie and Amanda announce themselves to the mouse than she pointed to two plastic chairs against the wall facing her and said in a graceless voice that could have come straight out of a Jimmy Cagney gangster movie: 'Have a seat. Mr Goldman will see you in a few minutes, but first you need to fill out these forms.' With that, she shoved two eightpage documents towards them.

While the mouse was running furious fingers over the typewriter and fielding telephone calls in a hive of simultaneous activity, Ferdie and Amanda filled out the forms, which covered everything about them from their ethnic origin, through their religion and the state of their marriage, to their annual income.

'I must say, these questions are pretty intrusive, aren't they?' Ferdie whispered to Amanda.'Don't answer anything about money.'

The forms completed, the mouse rose from her swivel seat and, walking round the desk, stuck out her hand for Ferdie and Amanda to hand them over.Without a word, she spun on her heel and took them into her boss's office. Within seconds, she returned to find Ferdie rummaging through the pile of magazines for something to read. The most tempting seemed to be the new issue of *Time* magazine, which he began flipping through, impatience crackling in the air with every flick of the page. Amanda, meanwhile, was serenely working her way through a battered August copy of *Vogue* while smiling at her husband, the mouse noted, every few minutes.

Eighteen minutes to the second after they had taken their seats, a stylishly dressed woman, whom Amanda recognized as Amaryllis Goudanaris, the third wife of the Greek shipping tycoon Stavros Goudanaris, stepped out of Raoul Goldman's office. Swathed though she was in sable, the brightest thing about her was her smile as she bade goodbye to first Mr Goldman and then the mouse.'Thank you so much, Miss O'Brien. Have a nice weekend. And God bless you.'

'You too,' Miss O'Brien said, sounding as if they were old friends.

Just then the buzzer rang twice, and Miss O'Brien leaned forward and said to Ferdie and Amanda: 'Mr Goldman will see you now, if you please.'

With that, Amanda and Ferdie stood up and headed into Raoul Goldman's office. If such a thing were possible, it was even more dingy and depressing than the reception room, but the baby-man Goldman seemed oblivious to that as he waved them in the direction of two chairs in front of his desk, while he continued the telephone conversation he was having.

Although Ferdie tried to glean something of what the conversation was about, it was difficult to discern what he was discussing, for his comments were uniformly monosyllabic. After about ninety seconds he rang off then turned his gaze to Ferdie and Amanda and said, in a manner that was so straightforward as to be brusque: 'So what can I do for you?'

Amanda blushed. Ferdie, taking an instant liking to the lawyer, said equally to the point: 'We want a baby boy.'

'I see that you've been to Harvey Mickleman and Sir Godfrey Pennington,' Raoul Goldman said, holding up the forms. 'Fine doctors, both of them. Decent men too.'

'You know Sir Godfrey?' Amanda said, unable to erase the trace of surprise from her voice.

'I sure do. He was adopted, you know. Does all he can to assist in placing babies. But you're not here to talk about that sort of thing. If we can cut to the chase, I take it you want a baby that reflects your own ethnic backgrounds?'

'That's right,' Ferdie said, his words overlapping with Amanda's. 'If that's at all possible.'

'When?'

'As soon as possible,' Ferdie said.

'You mean, like tomorrow, if a baby is available?' Raoul Goldman said.

'Well, maybe not quite tomorrow, but in a few weeks or months.'

'You'll need to have a Home Study. A Home Study is a social worker's report that delves into all your circumstances. Your home life. The state of your marriage. The reasons why you want to adopt. A description of the home the child will be placed in. It's really a social worker's picture of your life. It's a way of seeing that you're suitable. Without it, you can't adopt.'

'We live in Mexico, though we do have rooms here,' Ferdie said.

'Rooms?' Raoul Goldman said with some surprise.

'My husband means, we have an apartment here.'

'Oh. I thought for a second you were renting rooms in a boarding house.'

Amanda and Ferdie laughed. 'Our apartment is in the Waldorf Towers,' Ferdie replied, 'one floor down from the Duke and Duchess of Windsor's.'

Raoul Goldman laughed too. 'Those must be some rooms.'

Looking through the completed forms some more, he said, 'If you have an apartment in the city, we can process the adoption as if you're American residents. That will make things easier. Quicker too.'

'You don't have a baby for us already, do you?' Amanda said.

'No. But we have the possibility of two at the moment that might be suitable as long as they're boys. You're lucky. One of the commonest ethnic combinations is Jewish and British. All those horny teenagers in Westchester and Connecticut... They never seem to learn. We still don't have abortion on demand in New York, and – judging by the way things are heading – I don't think we ever will. It's a tragedy for those teenagers and their parents, but the answer to an adoptive parent's prayers.'

'You mean two girls are pregnant with babies that might suit us?' Amanda said hopefully.

'The two babies are a combination of English and Irish and Jewish,' Raoul Goldman continued. Both sets of parents are teenagers from nice professional families upstate. All nice looking kids. One of the girls is a raving beauty. A dead ringer for the teenage Elizabeth Taylor. The other girl is more the Grace Kelly type. Elizabeth Taylor is due in January, Grace Kelly in February. Interested?'

Ferdie looked at Amanda, who nodded almost imperceptibly. 'Sure,' he said, locking eyes with Amanda.

'Will you still want the baby if it's a girl?'

'No,' Ferdie said without referring to Amanda.

'Ferdie,' Amanda said, her tone an unreadable mixture of several different emotions.

'Just a boy. That's all we want,' Ferdie said. 'A boy.'

'At least for now,' Amanda said. 'My husband's father is dying, you see, and he wants to hold his grandson in his arms before he dies.'

'My father lost all his relations during the Holocaust,' Ferdie said apologetically, 'and his one unfulfilled ambition is to have a grandson. He says he doesn't care about blood. All he wants is someone who can carry the banner of our heritage into another generation.'

'That's as noble a sentiment as I've ever heard,' Raoul Goldman said.

'You know, Mr and Mrs Piedraplata, we hear many different reasons for why people want to have children. Most of them are good. Many are touching. But I've never heard anyone describe the desire for a child in quite those terms. Your father must be quite a man.'

'He is,' Ferdie said quietly.

'I'll do what I can, but you must have your Home Study ready, and you must be approved by one of the adoption agencies on our approved list before we can turn a baby over to you. I don't mean to sound discourteous, but we have to protect the babies as much as the prospective parents, so we have to satisfy ourselves that those little mites are going to people who will take good care of them.'

Raoul Goldman rose from his desk for the first time since Ferdie and Amanda had entered his office. 'Marie will give you the details of the social worker and the agency on your way out.'

'Is that all there is?' Amanda said, rising to her feet.

'It's simple, but it's also difficult,' Raoul Goldman said. 'I always warn my parents: birth is arduous. It doesn't come without pain. Adoption is another form of birth. Prepare yourself for the unexpected, for the unexpected is what will happen.'

Raoul Goldman was wrong. The entry into the world of the baby who would become Manuel Piedraplata Junior was smooth for both his birth mother and his adoptive parents. He was born at the Windlesham, a private hospital on East 54th Street between Third and Lexington Avenues, on the Friday January 14 1966 at nine forty-six in the morning. As soon as the baby, who weighed eight pounds four ounces, was born, he was whisked to an adjoining room, where he was cleaned up and put in the nursery. His birth mother was not even given the opportunity to hold him.

Raoul Goldman was having breakfast at his apartment on Ocean Parkway in Brooklyn with his wife and their two daughters when he received the telephone call to say that the baby had arrived and that he was healthy. He thanked the obstetrician for the call, went back to the table to finish his breakfast then called Ferdie and Amanda at the Waldorf Towers. Ferdie answered.

'You have a son. Eight pounds four ounces. Black hair. Possibly light eyes, though they're all born with light eyes, so he might end up with brown eyes. He's a little beauty, the doctor tells me.'

'When can we see him?'

'You can pick him up tomorrow, if you want,' Raoul Goldman said, telling him where the baby was. 'At about two-thirty.'

The following afternoon, a nervous Ferdie and Amanda showed up on the Nursery Floor of the Windlesham Hospital to be handed a tiny sleeping bundle swaddled in white and swamped by a shock of long black hair. 'He looks like you,' Amanda said to Ferdie as the nursing sister handed the baby to her. 'I don't believe it. He has your hair, your mouth and your chin.' Amanda felt her heart leap.

'Here, let me,' Ferdie said, extending his arms for the baby. The sister looked vaguely disapproving but nevertheless placed the baby in his arms.

'Hiya, son,' he said, his face awash with delight. 'How's my little champ? What a cute little guy you are. Come on, give your Papa a smile.'

'He's a bit young for that, Ferdie,' Amanda laughed. 'Babies don't smile for the first few months.'

The sister's response was to hand Amanda two sheets of paper, densely typewritten. 'This is his recommended feeding schedule. Please follow it carefully.'

'Thank you,' Amanda said, refraining from mentioning that she and Ferdie had already hired a maternity nurse. She took the papers and put them away in her handbag, while Ferdie paced up and down with the baby, talking to him as if this were his closest companion.

From that moment onwards, Manolito - as the baby would thereafter be called within the family - became more Ferdie's son than Amanda's. It was Ferdie, already totally besotted with his son, who took little Manolito in his arms to the car, and it was Ferdie who cooed over him all the way uptown to the Columbia-Presbyterian Hospital, where Manny had been taken the Wednesday before when he started passing blood. When they reached the hospital it was Ferdie who stepped out of the car with the baby in his arms, and when they reached his father's room it was Ferdie who handed him the baby with the words: 'We brought you your grandson, Papa.'

Manny, his last wish granted, cradled the baby in his arms, wiping away a tear with the back of his hand. 'You've made my life complete,' he said, looking from father to son. Six weeks later Manuel Piedraplata, formerly Emanuel Silverstein, was dead.

Chapter Seven

Bianca had not intended the affair to take the course it had, nor had she intended it to last as long as it did. Her aim had been pure and simple: to bind herself more closely to the Piedraplatas. With that objective in mind, she had pursued every avenue open to her. First, she had tried befriending Begonia. That had worked for about three weeks, but by the fourth week, Begonia began making excuses for why she could not come for coffee or for a swim or for tennis. By the eighth week, Begonia would take and return only one in five of her telephone calls, and by the tenth week, when she dropped in unexpectedly to see Begonia, Bianca suspected that the other woman was lurking in her bedroom and was not out, as the maid had claimed.

'I don't see why you're so upset if Begonia Mahfud is too busy to be your latest best friend,' Bernardo said of Bianca's increasing frustration. 'You have plenty of friends already. Lay off her for a while then ask her and Raymond to a dinner party with Philippe and that Polish woman who's new in town. That will keep the friendship on the boil but in a more manageable way from her point of view, since she's so busy. What you don't seem to understand, Bianca, is not everyone has as much time on their hands as you do.'

Bernardo was right, of course. Bianca saw that instantly. Distance would preserve the relationship and keep it on a social level. It would also spare her the pain of being rebuffed again, for the one thing Bianca, a naturally affectionate person, had difficulty coping with was being spurned.

Since the original plan of befriending Begonia to get to Amanda Piedraplata was not working out the way she had expected it to, Bianca did as Bernardo suggested and put the relationship with Begonia on a more impersonal footing. That not only worked well but surprisingly so.

Every invitation Bianca issued for dinner was reciprocated within a month by Begonia. Every invitation from Bianca to a cocktail party was followed by an invitation from Begonia to one of the fashionable Mexico City restaurants. And always, Philippe, Raymond's unattached brother, was seated beside Bianca.

That was how it all began. In the age-old Latin tradition of friends dropping in without invitation, Philippe started to call by uninvited to see Bianca and Bernardo. He would stay for supper and chat to husband and wife after the children had gone to bed until Bernardo started to yawn. That was his cue for departure, and within months a ritual had been established with Philippe coming by once or twice a week without being invited.

This new addition to the Calman family circle was less unusual than it might have seemed to people who were unfamiliar with the way life was conducted in Mexican social circles of the day. The Calmans were known to be extremely hospitable, and Philippe was only one of about twenty friends who believed they had the licence to visit whenever the urge took them. What made Philippe's visiting exceptional was the frequency and regularity with which he did it, but even that did not arouse suspicion, at least not in their circle of friends.

Bernardo was of the firm opinion that Philippe was merely lonely and that he was killing time until he found himself a girlfriend or wife. It did not strike him as odd that Philippe would prefer being with the Calmans to being with his own family. The truth was that life never appeared dull in the Calman household with its constant stream of guests buoyed up by Bianca's vibrant personality. Meanwhile, life with Begonia and Philippe's brother Raymond might have been worthy, but it was also excruciatingly dull. Even their dinner parties were like squibs dunked in water. To Bernardo, it was therefore easily explicable why Philippe - and indeed, everyone else - would prefer an evening with his vivacious wife and himself to an evening with Raymond and Begonia, although Bernardo was not a foolish or careless man, and he was on the lookout for signs that Philippe might be 'sweet on Bianca'.

Many men had been 'sweet on Bianca', but Bernardo had always been vigilant in seeing off the competition before temptation had reared it's ugly head. So far as any threat from Philippe was concerned, his conduct was so patently correct and above-board and so devoid of anything sexual that Bernardo gradually relaxed his guard and even began to encourage his friend to escort her to functions that he preferred to avoid. The term 'walker' had not yet been invented to describe Philippe's function within the Calman family group, but within two years of meeting Bernardo and Bianca, he was indeed her 'walker' with the full approval of her husband.

The children, of course, had their own take on this new development. 'Philippe's in love with you,' they used to tease their mother. Bianca silently agreed. However, she was not interested in an affair with this man, whom she did not find in the least sexually appealing. Indeed, she was not interested in having an affair with anyone at all. She was happy with her husband, whom she still loved passionately and with whom the physical side of marriage was as satisfying as it had ever been. Their lovemaking had, in fact, become ever more rewarding with the passage of time. 'One of the best things in life,' Bianca used to say, 'is to make love with a man you're in love with and who's in love with you.'

The lacunae for Bianca were outside her personal life. They were centred round her need for interest and challenge in a world where women of her milieu had to restrict their activities to their social circles.

To outsiders, her ambitions, being centred round society, could be discounted as trivial, but to insiders, they would have been entirely understandable, had she been of a mind to confide her ambitions to anyone. She was not, however. Denial of social ambition was as crucial to success as the energy and resourcefulness that the Biancas of this world brought to bear on achieving their ambitions.

As for Bianca, there was nothing to be ashamed of in the way she felt. She needed something to strive for: something to give grit and purpose to her life. She needed the reward of accomplishment, although she was not consciously aware of it. She also needed the frustration of failure and the excitement of uncertainty, for success would have been meaningless without them. In the presence of a life with too much unearned fulfilment, she was seeking arenas where she could strive and stretch herself.

Over the two years in which her friendship with Philippe was ripening into something else, Bianca preoccupied herself fruitlessly with how she could achieve her ambition of entertaining, and being entertained by, Amanda Piedraplata. Of course, her ultimate ambition was not to become an acolyte of Amanda's. She wanted to befriend the queen of Mexican society so that some of the Piedraplata glory would rub off on her, along with some of their influence and clout. She was not deluding herself. She knew that her current rank in the social pecking order equated in aristocratic terms to somewhere between a countess and a marchioness. This might have been good enough for some but not for Harold Barnett's little princess, who had been raised from birth to believe that she could, by dint of her natural talents and her efforts, be at the very centre of things. No. Such a paltry rank was not where she saw herself. She wanted to be a princess in social terms, and until she had achieved that objective, she would not feel that she had realized her potential.

The route to royal status in Mexican society, as Bianca knew only too well, was through the Piedraplatas. Unless she was a member of their circle – even a peripheral member – she could have all the pretensions she wanted to being a top-flight socialite, but she would not be one, nor would she be acknowledged as one by the people who mattered socially.

As things stood, she occasionally saw Ferdie and Amanda at Begonia and Raymond's larger parties. This was not enough for the realization of her ambitions, but it was enough for her to discern that Ferdie was attracted to her. Pleasant though that fact was, it was not something upon which either of them was inclined to act. Indeed, had Ferdie been in the market for an affair (which he was not), Bianca would have been the last woman in Mexico who would have slept with him. To do so would have been to put herself for all time outside the magic social circle, which, Bianca was only too aware, had Amanda as its pivot. Bianca used her considerable resources whenever she was with Ferdie out of Amanda's earshot, to befriend him in the hope that he might be instrumental in having his wife accept one of the invitations she periodically sent them.

The Mahfud family still provided her with access to Amanda. For that reason, she welcomed Philippe into the bosom of her family, even though she found him dull, if amiable and obliging.

Philippe, on the other hand, seemed to find Bianca endlessly fascinating, which in a way she was. She had energy and charm and warmth. She was hospitable. She had a great sense of humour. She was strong and apparently invulnerable. She seemed unstintingly generous. And you knew, just knew, that there was a part of her hidden away from view and to which you could never gain access. She might, however, allow you glimpses of it, if and when you pleased her sufficiently. This hint of inaccessibility lent her an aura of mystery, which only heightened her appeal.

For two frustrating years, Bianca hovered around the Mahfuds, watching and waiting for the opportunity to advance her cause. Then, on New Year's Eve 1965, at her own party, Bianca took a gigantic step forwards – although it was only later that she recognized it as such.

The garden was glistening with thousands of tiny electric lights. The tables were groaning with food. The band was playing all the latest songs, and Bianca was keeping an eye out for Astrud Gilberto, who had accepted an invitation – supplied by Smythson, of course – but was running fashionably late. She was thrilled that Brazil's biggest singing star was attending, but even her attendance, together with a prince and princess of the Orleans-Braganza family from Brazil, could not completely eradicate the disappointment Bianca had to endure. Amanda and Ferdie had declined. Yet again. Amanda had replied – in her script with its upright looping characters so characteristic of upper-class British women – that she and Ferdie 'much regret not being able to attend owing to absence abroad'. Life was too, too unfair. Every time Bianca had thrown a party in the two years since she had first met Amanda at Sara Finkelstein de Cohen's party, her elusive quarry had not been able to accept her 'kind invitation' because she and Ferdie were out of Mexico. In the hope of nabbing the Golden Couple at a time when they would be sure to be in Mexico, Bianca had even changed the timing of her summer party.

Absence abroad had been the excuse again – or, to be more fair, the reason, for they were genuinely out of the country – this time in the South of France. 'Why can't those blasted Piedraplatas ever stay at home like everyone else?' Bianca had asked Bernardo when she received their latest expression of regret. And, to add insult to injury, the Piedraplatas had never once asked the Calmans to any of their functions, although Bianca could at least take comfort from the fact that they had a good reason for being out of Mexico on this particular occasion: old Manny Piedraplata was dying in New York.

All of this, and the myriad distractions which occupy a hostess, were on Bianca's mind during her New Year's Eve party as she cast an eye around the dance floor and received a shock that made her hands start to tremble. Philippe was dancing erotically with an American woman whom he had brought along as his date, a woman Bianca had pressed him to bring, because she needed Philippe to produce a possible love interest from time to time so that Bernardo's suspicions about his feelings for her could be kept at bay.

'What a tramp,' Bianca hissed to herself under her breath, alert to the danger of losing her adoring swain as she watched Philippe and the over-peroxided Bonnie Lee Haldane grinding their hips together. Although Bianca had no doubt that he must be aware, as she was, that Bonnie Lee Haldane was a two-bit floozy on the make, she could not take the chance of sexual attraction distorting his perception and transforming this tart into something more substantial. After all, if Philippe should fall for - or, indeed, make off with - any other woman, it would significantly reduce Bianca's chances of getting close to Ferdie and Amanda Piedraplata; and she was not prepared to take that chance.

Without missing a beat, she slapped her sweetest expression on her face and sailed onto the dance floor to speak to the couple beside Philippe and his bombshell. Having whispered the generalities to them that were the cover for her real purpose, she turned to Philippe and Bonnie Lee, whose elegant finger tips were positioned on his back and shoulder in a manner reminiscent of a praying mantis about to devour its victim, and said: 'Philippe, what a cruel man you are! You can't treat our guest so cavalierly. Look at the poor thing. You must be aware that foreigners are not used to the heat the way we are. If you keep on at this rate, you'll have her sweating from every pore, and we ladies don't like our maquillage ruined, do we, my dear?' she finished, smiling broadly at the astonished woman. With that, Bianca grabbed her American guest by one wrist, Philippe by the other, and led them away towards the bar.

Once there, Bianca indicated to one of the footmen that she wanted three glasses of champagne. They were drinking Louis Roederer NV and chatting amiably when the band struck up 'Blame It On The Bossa Nova', a hit by Eydie Gorme of which Bianca was particularly fond. 'My favourite song,' she declared. 'I can't possibly not dance this. Would you mind awfully if I stole your date for a few minutes?'

'Not at all,' Bonnie Lee replied graciously, her eyes as hard as steel.

'She's on to me,' Bianca thought, giving her one of her broadest and warmest smiles. 'Darling,' she said to the man nearest her, an old school friend of Bernardo's as it turned out. 'Do take care of our American guest and show her what Latin American hospitality is all about, while Philippe twirls me around the floor, will you?'

With that, she seized her prey by the wrist again. 'Come on, my old dancing partner,' she said, dragging him onto the dance floor with the first overtly flirtatious comment she had ever made to him. 'I can't think of anyone I'd rather dance this with.'

The bossa nova, of course, was hardly the sort of dance one would choose to set a romantic mood, but Bianca smiled and laughed her way through it as if she were having the time of her life. In reality, she couldn't wait for the song to end. She hated exerting herself on the dance floor, not because she minded the effort (lethargy was not one of her faults), but because she loathed ruining her clothes and makeup with perspiration.

Moreover, she would have wanted romantic music to set a romantic mood, but violent threats called for violent remedies. As soon as the song ended, she took control of the situation. Once more dragging Philippe by the hand, she said, 'Come with me. I must get them to vary the tempo. They're not playing enough cheek-to-cheek music. At the rate they're going, everyone will look like a thoroughbred after a race. It's time they gave everyone a break from all of this vigorous dance music.' She walked straight to the bandstand, excusing herself graciously on the way, and whispered her instructions to the bandleader. She then turned, smiled triumphantly at Philippe, slipped her arm through his and said, 'Let's really dance now.'

The band struck up *'Spanish Eyes'*. Bianca swung her body into Philippe's, and they closed in on each other with the naturalness of people who are used to dancing together. Philippe adopted the attitude they had always formerly had: correct, friendly and comfortable. Bianca, however, subtly edged in a degree closer than she had ever done before and applied the slightest amount of pressure to Philippe's hand and back. He responded by mirroring her actions.

'So far, so good,' Bianca thought, taking care not to dance so suggestively that the suspicions of any onlooker - Bernardo especially - would be aroused.

Four slow dances later the band changed tempo again, and Bianca indicated – by the slightest facial gesture – that the time had come to stop dancing. While she and Philippe were making their way off the floor, she said lightly and flirtatiously: 'Philippe, I do believe you've been trying to seduce me.' He blushed, giggled slightly as if he were a sixteen-year-old girl whose older and much more experienced boyfriend was making a welcome pass at her and squeezed her hand.

The evening after her New Year's Eve dinner dance, Philippe tried to kiss her, grabbing her clumsily in the drawing-room while Bernardo and the children were on the veranda having ice cream after dinner. He pressed his lips on hers and tried to stick his tongue down her throat.

Bianca pulled back. 'Not here, not now,' she said, relieved that he had shown his hand so completely. Although the incident might not have counted for Philippe – or for most women – as a success, to Bianca it did.

It showed her that he really did desire her but that he was also inept, at least in terms of seduction and kissing. This, however, was no bad thing. A woman always has more power over a man who isn't exactly a lady-killer than over one who is an accomplished lover. She was also intrigued to discover that she had not disliked the sensation of his lips on hers, nor had she been repelled, as she had feared she might be, by the taste of his saliva.

Although Bianca had not actually intended to begin an affair with Philippe, once the genie of his desire was out of the bottle, it proved impossible to stuff it back in. She was now confronted by a stark choice: either she gave him the license he sought or she refused and ran the risk of sullying the friendship. Reluctantly she allowed him to court her into bed.

It was with relief that Bianca discovered, three weeks into the new year, that her fear that she might find Philippe physically repugnant and thereby ruin their relationship was unfounded. True, he had a body that would have challenged the sexual desire of any woman with convention-al appetites. At five foot four and one hundred and seventy pounds, he was no Adonis, but he had a masculine build: muscles in all the right places.

Good broad chest. Good solid arms. Substantial, indeed protruding, stomach, but at least it was firm. His legs, while short, were muscular. And he was covered in hair, front and back; and to Bianca, a hirsute man was more appealing. Indeed, his back was as hairy as his chest, which was a mat of long, silky black hair. She already knew this, of course, from the countless times she had seen him swimming. What surprised her that afternoon when he dropped in unexpectedly at three o'clock, knowing that the children would be at school and Bernardo at work, and pulled her into the men's changing room of the swimming pool - built for her by Bernardo to celebrate their fifteenth wedding anniversary - was the frisson of attraction she felt when he was naked and his manhood fully exposed, his short but thick penis throbbing and his large, well-rounded testicles tight with desire. This, of course, should not have surprised her the way it did, for Philippe possessed the three essentials for attractiveness in Bianca's eyes. One, he desired her. Two, he was hairy. And three, he had a thick penis. 'Length is at best a luxury, at worst uncomfortable,' she used to say whenever the subject of Porfirio Rubirosa and Baby Pignatari, Latin America's two most famous lovers, was discussed around Mexico City dinner tables. 'But width is absolutely fundamental to satisfaction.'

'Oh, Bianca, I love you,' Philippe declared, pressing himself against her fully clothed body. 'I've loved you and wanted you since I first met you.'

'Not here, not now,' she replied between his fumbling kisses.

'Marry me. Marry me. You won't regret it. I'll give you an even better life than Bernardo does.'

Bianca raised her index finger and gently put it against his mouth, pleasure coursing throughout her body and soul. Philippe was hers, to do with as she pleased, and even though she did not really want him, she nevertheless thrilled at the idea of having someone so ardent and so useful in her power. If only she could keep him dangling forever, that would be ideal. 'We'll speak about this outside. I can't stay here any longer. If one of the servants discovers us, it will be a disaster.'

'I'll marry you, Bianca,' he said, trying to reassure her.

'I know, and I love you for it, but I have the children to consider.' With that, she pecked him on the lips and let herself out onto the veranda of the pool house.

Within minutes, he came back outside, a large bath towel covering the erection that had not quite disappeared. Bianca, noticing his state of arousal, felt another frisson, this time of satisfaction. It was so gratifying to be desired.

Before Philippe could say anything, she said: 'Darling, I want you to know how very happy you've made me this afternoon.'

'We need to be together properly,' he replied.

'In marriage or in bed?' she asked, sharp as a whip: a trait that never failed to quicken the pulse of this most astute of men.

'Both,' he said, reaching for her hand. She let him take it and allowed him to caress it, although she was not responsive the way she would have been with Bernardo. 'What about coming to the apartment tomorrow afternoon at siesta time?'

'Philippe, I can't slink into a man's apartment at siesta time, as if I were some common prostitute.'

'No one will know.'

'Your porter will, for one. It leaves us open to blackmail. No. I can't behave like that. I have a husband and children and a reputation to consider.'

'You can always divorce Bernardo and marry me. I'd love to be a stepfather to your children. You know Bianca, I'm a rich man, relatively speaking. I can take care of you. I may not be as rich as Ferdie, but I am worth a few million dollars.'

'You're going too fast for me. We haven't even slept together...'

'I know we'll be fantastic together...'

'That may be so, but I can't just leap from one marriage to another, Philippe.'

'We need to be together.'

'Not here. Not in Mexico. We would have to meet abroad,' she said, stalling for time.

'That's very clever, Bianca. No wonder I want you so much. You're so much more than a pretty face. I've always said that brains are the ultimate turn-on to a man with a mind. The problem, of course, is that so few women with brains look the way you do,' Philippe said, taking her hand and resting it near his penis. 'And let's face facts: a man doesn't go to bed with a woman's brains. You're the perfect package.'

She smiled, pulled her hand away and said: 'Maybe we should meet in New York in March. I'll tell Bernardo I'm going shopping for the new season's clothes. But you must tell him that you're going to Paris or some such place.'

Although Bianca did not enter into the affair with any enthusiasm, the March trip was an unexpected success. Although the sex was perfunctory and could not compare with what she had with Bernardo, she nevertheless did not mind sleeping with Philippe. He was so sweet and so ardent that she almost desired him and would have done so, had he been more proficient in bed. However, he was like many highly successful men: highly effective out of bed, totally deficient in it. Still, his acumen as a businessman made dealing with him easy, if only because he was used to making compromises as a part of deals. Therefore, when she insisted that they occupy suites on separate floors ('Just in case Bernardo is having me followed. I don't think it's likely, but you never know for sure') he booked a suite for her and, three floors beneath, a double room for himself which he never once slept in, although he was careful to stash his clothes there ('In case one of the staff is a private detective,' Bianca suggested.)

Bianca's nervousness and the precautions it forced upon them only added to the excitement of the occasion. 'If Bernardo finds out you were here, we can say that we ran into each other and linked up for companionship,' she said. 'And if he doesn't discover that you were here, we'll keep our mouths shut.'

Having lived in Lebanon and travelled extensively on business throughout Europe and the Americas as well as the Far East, Philippe was actually considerably more sophisticated than his new mistress. This sophistication now came to his aid, helping to seduce her and lure her more deeply into the relationship. He made sure he served up all the treats a great metropolis such as New York has to offer to those in the know. For the four days of the trip, he laid on the latest Broadway shows, lunched and dined at *Le Pavillon, La Côte Basque, La Grenouille* and the other fashionable watering holes. They danced at *Le Club*, the chicest discotheque in Manhattan, and Bianca was supremely impressed to discover that he had been one of its founding members. Clearly, she noted with surprised delight, this funny-looking and superficially dull little man had hidden depths.

By the time Bianca flew back to Mexico while Philippe made his way to Paris, their relationship had undergone a fundamental change, even though it was not enough to make her contemplate leaving Bernardo for him. It was on their second foreign assignation, however, that her respect for him surged, bringing her closer to the precipice she did not yet know existed.

Once more, Bianca and Philippe stayed at the Pierre, that most sumptuous of hotels on Fifth Avenue diagonally opposite the Plaza, where

Ferdie Piedraplata's good friend, Aristotle Onassis, kept a permanent suite.

Once more, they did all the things chic New Yorkers did, but it was when he introduced her to the magic of Mainbocher that she entertained for the first time the idea that one day she might...some time in the very, very far future...replace the solidly parochial Latin American Bernardo with the more cosmopolitan Philippe.

On the morning after their arrival in New York, he'd simply said to her: 'This afternoon, you're going to receive an invitation to visit the salon of Mainbocher. I've arranged things through the King of Morocco's sister-in-law, who's a friend of mine from Lebanon. If you'd like me to come with you, make the appointment for eleven o'clock tomorrow morning. Otherwise, go and choose whatever you want.'

Mainbocher was America's premier couturier. You couldn't just walk into his salon on the eighth floor of the KLM Building on Fifth Avenue without first being invited, because this man, who had made his name between the wars in Paris, did not have clients. He had house 'friends'.

These included the Duchess of Windsor, whose dress for her wedding to King Edward VIII had been his creation; Babe Paley, CZ Guest; Gloria Vanderbilt and every other luminary on the American social scene. Never in her wildest dreams had Bianca ever hoped to become a house 'friend'. Never had she imagined that she would reach the stage in life where she, Bianca Barnett de Calman, would have her own dummy made, the way all Mainbocher's other 'friends' did, and that it would repose alongside all the Ford, Rockefeller, Vanderbilt, Van Rensslaer, and Windsor ones, ready and waiting to be draped, pinned, pricked and fitted with a creation that would be hers, and hers alone. The idea that she, Bianca Barnett de Calman, would ever be able to spend $2,000 on a suit, the way Mainbocher 'friends' customarily did, had never occurred to her. Sure, she was well off and had a reputation in Mexico City for being a lavish hostess, but this was something else again.

Bianca at first was too stunned to reply to Philippe's invitation.

However, she was not so taken aback that she did not notice that Philippe had been too elegant to add that the bill would be sent to him, which she knew would be the case. He was also, she knew, too proud to say that he'd like to come with her, but she had no doubt that this was what he wanted.

'I wouldn't dream of going without you, darling,' she said. 'You must come and give me the benefit of your guidance.'

The following morning, the lovers were received on the dot of eleven by the *premiere vendeuse*, who introduced them to Main himself. He was so charming, confidential even, that Bianca could see why he had 'friends' instead of clients.

On that first occasion, Bianca chose – but only after consultation with Philippe – a magnificent emerald-green silk jacket with contrasting skirt and a burgundy boucle woollen suit with a plunging neckline. Those garments would perfectly complement the emerald parure Bernardo had given her as a present and would give her the opportunity to wear the necklace to cocktails instead of only with a long dress, as she had been obliged to do until then.

Philippe could not have planned his campaign of matrimonial seduction better. By now he recognized that capturing a prize like Bianca was going to be a long and exacting enterprise. He would have to bring to bear all the artistry that he used to ensnare clients into believing that only he, Philippe Mahfud, could provide the key that would unlock the door to their desires. The world of Mainbocher was only one of the many enticements he proposed to set before Bianca, until she realized that he, Philippe Mahfud, could give her a richer, broader, fuller, more interesting and fascinating life than Bernardo Calman.

In furtherance of his long-term objective, on their third trip to New York, Philippe said to Bianca on the day of their arrival, 'After lunch at The Colony, I have somewhere I'd like to take you.'

'Where?' she asked eagerly.

For Philippe, part of the pleasure of giving was the undisguised relish with which Bianca received. Like many other genuinely generous people, she understood the need not to spoil a giver's pleasure by receiving with anything less than wholehearted appreciation.

'Indulge me in my little mystery. Suffice it to say, it's an oyster awaiting its pearl.'

After lunch, the chauffeur drove them to the Frick Museum. The car pulled up, the driver leaped to open the kerbside door, and Bianca stepped out, wondering what was up. Philippe took her arm and escorted her inside. 'This is the setting you should have,' he said. 'This house contains one of the finest collections of furniture and art in the world. I want you to take it all in. This is the sort of thing you deserve. We could have the most fantastic life together, if only you'd leave Bernardo and marry me. We could have a house like this in Switzerland. Filled with museum pieces. A palace in the South of France. One of those pre-war co-ops on Fifth Avenue, again filled with furniture and paintings like these, for our trips to New York. The banks in Geneva and New York are doing fantastic business and are just crying out for me to spend more time in those cities. I shouldn't be spending as much time as I do in Mexico City. You're the only reason I do. I don't want to rush you into a precipitate decision, but I do want you to see, with your own two eyes, the sort of life I'm offering you.'

Not since childhood, when her father taught her that she was his little princess, had anyone so baldly indicated to Bianca that she was worth the absolute best of what life had to offer and that anything less was cheating her of her true worth.

Bianca melted. 'Philippe, I do love you,' she said, 'and what you're offering is tempting. Very tempting. But I can't just leave Bernardo as simply as that. He's been a good and loving husband. My parents adore him. His parents adore me... and his father has ultimate control over the purse strings. The kids love him and have a happy family life. I'll destroy my standing within the family unless I leave Bernardo very, very carefully.'

'But will you leave him?'

'Yes. But I need to lay the ground first.'

'How?'

'Well, if I could catch him out in some infidelity, that would be a good reason for seeking a divorce.'

'How can you do that when, by your own account, he never cheats?'

'That's my problem, not yours. He's my husband and the father of my children, and I must wrap up the marriage in such a way that I don't get the blame. Otherwise my life won't be worth living.'

Despite her reassuring words, Bianca was not about to make a precipitate or irrevocable move without first checking that she would be getting precisely what Philippe promised. When she returned to Mexico she therefore made discreet inquiries among their friends to ascertain whether Philippe Mahfud was worth as much money as he had indicated he was. She discovered he was worth even more.

With that discovery, Bianca became torn between staying with a man she loved passionately and whose world was limited and leaving him for a man she did not love passionately but whose world seemed limitless.

Sleeping with Bernardo was always such a joy. It was like being swept up in the arms of a god. 'What a difficult choice,' she said to herself. 'A man who has everything or a man who is everything.'

Unsure of what to do, Bianca was pulled in two separate directions.

One day she would avidly make love with Bernardo and ask herself how she could possibly give up such fulfilment. The next day, she would try to pull away, to loosen the bonds that tied her so firmly to him, only to bounce back when her desire for Bernardo, and his for her, proved too powerful an attraction.

'What's got into you?' Bernardo asked one afternoon after yet another day of Bianca being withdrawn for no reason. 'Since you returned from New York, you've been blowing hot and cold. Is something the matter with you?'

'No,' she said, seizing the opportunity he had unwittingly presented her with. 'But something's the matter with you.'

'With me?' he said incredulously. 'What have I done?'

'I've been told you're having an affair.'

'Me? An affair? You've got to be joking. Who told you that?'

'One doesn't reveal one's sources. You know that only too well,' Bianca said, assuming a haughty English manner.

'Come off it, Bianca. It's me you're talking to: Bernardo. Who told you that lie? I want to know. I demand to know.'

Bianca, surprised at how relieved and happy she was by his reaction, walked off, saying placidly: 'OK, Bernardo. You're not having an affair. I believe you. Shall we forget it?'

For the next month, they fell back into their established pattern of marital satisfaction. It is, of course, difficult to leave a man you love, so Bianca simply shelved the idea of withdrawing for the foreseeable future while enjoying the attentions of both her husband and Philippe, who still danced constant attendance upon the Calman family in general and upon his beloved Bianca in particular. She would have loved to keep her husband while availing herself of everything her lover had to offer, but she knew that life is not like that, and sooner or later she would have to make a choice which would terminate her relationship with one or the other of them.

The next stage came when Bernardo was out of the country on a business trip to Boston. 'Amanda and Ferdie are having a cocktail party the day after tomorrow for Prince Johannes von Thurn und Taxis. He's a German banker and does business with us. Would you like to come as my guest, and we can go out and have a quiet dinner afterwards at the Jewish Club?' he asked.

'What a good idea,' Bianca said, concealing her delight at finally receiving an invitation to the Piedraplatas, even if it was only a second-hand invitation. The tussle between love and personal ambition was now beginning in earnest.

The invitation not only caused Bianca to see Philippe in a favourable light but also made her ask herself whether she would ever achieve her ambitions as Bernardo Calman's wife. Obviously, Mr and Mrs Bernardo Calman were not big enough for the Piedraplatas. But since Bianca on her own was acceptable, maybe Bernardo was the deadweight that was preventing her from reaching her natural heights.

Bianca had never been so torn. So out of control with her own destiny, her own desires. Philippe was proving, for all his protestations of love, to be a tougher nut to crack than Bernardo had ever been. On the one hand, he offered more than she had ever wanted, with the result that even her ambitions and objectives had perceptibly altered since their affair began. On the other hand, he was the cause of her torment because she could not occupy his world without relinquishing the most intense pleasures that life with Bernardo afforded her. The real issue, she could see, was that she was being forced to choose between two sides of her own self. No matter which one she chose, she would have to give up something of great value.

Choice would mean pain. And she couldn't choose.

Realizing that an orderly withdrawal from her present way of life would never happen, if only because she really didn't want to leave a happy marriage - although she didn't want to give up the prospect of a richer life either - Bianca resolved to trust her instincts to make the choice for her, rationalizing that they would take her where she truly wanted to go.

She then unthinkingly followed them to the extent of greeting Bernardo, upon his return from Boston, with ardour. For the first two days, they spent as much of their time in bed as they could, making love as if they were newlyweds. On the third day, however, after Bernardo had gone to work, on an impulse Bianca pulled one of his shirts from the laundry basket and smeared the back of it with lipstick.

When Bernardo came home that evening he was confronted by a wife who was so convincingly furious that she took even her own breath away.

'What's this?' Bianca bellowed, waving the shirt back and forth. 'What is this? You tell me what this is!'

'I don't know what you're talking about,' was all that Bernardo, nonplussed, could lamely reply. 'What's wrong?'

'This is what's wrong,' she said as she continued to wave the shirt around and then slapped him on the shoulder with it.

'What's got into you? Stop that. You're hurting me.'

'Not as much as you've hurt me,' Bianca retorted, rolling the shirt into a ball and presenting her husband with the visible evidence of lipstick traces. 'Don't play the innocent with me. How could you, Bernardo? Who is she?'

'What in God's name is that?' Bernardo said, genuine panic in his voice.

'Lipstick. That's what that is. Lipstick, Bernardo. You know, the thing women wear. Women and whores. Who is she? That's what I want to know.'

'Bianca, I swear I don't know how that lipstick got onto that shirt. Are you sure it's my shirt?'

'Of course it's your shirt. Unless you now have a friend who his shirts made at the same place as yours and has the same initials as yours embroidered on them too.'

'As God is my witness, Bianca, I don't know how it got there.'

'God is always the last resort of the guilty, Bernardo,' she retorted chillingly. 'Who is she?'

'There is no one else. There's never been. You know that.'

'I'm going to New York either next week or the week after at the latest. I need some time to think. And don't you dare touch me in the meantime. I want you out of the bedroom and sleeping in the guest bedroom. I can see the way things are headed. The next thing you'll be bringing home is a dose of the clap. And, after you've infected me, you'll swear that you've never been unfaithful, and that I must have picked it up off a toilet seat,' she said witheringly, sweeping out of the room and slamming their bedroom door with such force that it reverberated through the rest of the house.

Three weeks later Bianca flew to New York. She checked into the Pierre and waited for Philippe's call. His plane had been due in from Paris earlier that afternoon, but it was delayed. She toyed with the orchids he always ordered for her room and idly ate one of the Lebanese dates in pastry which were his favourite sweet while looking at the television. On an impulse, she grabbed the sable coat he had bought her from Maximilien and headed downstairs to buy a packet of chestnuts from the vendor who was customarily positioned on the corner of the Plaza Hotel and Central Park. As she was taking the packet, she turned and there was Amanda Piedraplata at the top of the steps, having just left the Palm Court where she was having tea.

'I don't believe it,' Amanda said in her clipped, almost unfriendly tones. 'What a small world! How are you?'

'I'm well thank you. And you?' Bianca replied, careful to meet reserve with charming reserve.

'Never better,' Amanda said, her cheeks flushing. 'I've just been to see my baby daughter in the hospital. Tomorrow I bring her home.'

'That's wonderful. Congratulations. What's the baby's name going to be?'

'Anna, after my mother-in-law, and Clara, after my sister-in-law.'

'I'm delighted for you. I'm here for another five days. If I can be of any assistance to you, please don't hesitate to ring me. I'm staying across the road, at the Pierre.'

'You have sons and a daughter, if I remember correctly. They say the relationship between girls and their mothers is different from that between boys and their mothers. Has it been like that for you?'

'If you have the time,' said Bianca, seeing that Amanda was more accessible than she had ever been, 'why don't you join me at my hotel for a glass of champagne to celebrate? Then I can tell you all I know about sons and daughters.'

'Why, Bianca, that's very kind of you,' Amanda said in that slightly stiff, formal and surprisingly modest way of hers. 'I think I'd like that very much.'

'Would you prefer the bar or my suite?' Bianca asked as they entered the lobby.

'Whichever is the easiest.'

'At least, in my suite we won't have to shout over other people's conversations, and no one will be able to overhear us,' Bianca said.

With that the two women headed upstairs.

As soon as Bianca opened the door to her suite, she could tell that the other woman was surprised she was staying in such a lavish suite. 'How splendid,' Amanda said without side, sucking in her breath. 'And those orchids are to die for.'

'You know what we Latin American girls are like,' Bianca responded conspiratorially. 'We can't live without our orchids.'

She crossed to the telephone and asked room service to bring up a bottle of Louis Roederer Crystal Brut. 'Or would you prefer Dom Perignon?' she mouthed to her guest, cupping the mouthpiece with her hand.

'Whichever you prefer.'

'This is such exciting news,' Bianca said when she had hung up. 'Your own little girl. What does she look like?'

'She's gorgeous. Cute little nose. Pretty little mouth. A chin rather like mine, funnily enough, and I wouldn't be surprised if her colouring is also like mine. Her ancestors all have blue eyes and blonde hair.'

Bianca shrewdly and correctly marked down the extent to which Amanda was uncharacteristically forthcoming as excitement at the impending arrival. Hopeful though she was that this exchange might be the harbinger of a closer friendship, she did not delude herself that it would necessarily be anything but an isolated instance, and one, moreover, that Amanda might come to regret, if only because she was giving away more of herself than she might be comfortable with in more normal circumstances. And life in Mexico City for both Amanda and herself was an amalgam of normal circumstances, no matter how abnormal or extraordinary those circumstances might be to outsiders. Alert to the danger, Bianca nevertheless could not resist the pleasure of empathizing with someone so overflowing with joy and recklessly decided that, irrespective of the consequences, she would go along with the flow.

The champagne arrived. The waiter poured glasses for both ladies before placing the bottle in a silver ice bucket on the table and then withdrawing.

Amanda knocked back her glass so quickly that Bianca had to gulp some of hers in a gracious effort to keep a vague pace with her guest's consumption.

'Here, let me replenish you,' Bianca said, grateful that Amanda would at least afterwards have the excuse – if only to herself – of alcohol.

'Thank you. I do hope you don't mind me taking up your time like this.'

'Amanda, it's a pleasure. It's always good to see you. You're not taking up my time at all.'

Just then the telephone rang. Bianca turned to answer it. Amanda could hear a male voice on the other end. She noticed her hostess listening intently. Then Bianca said, 'I cannot believe how you tracked me down. This is my day for coincidences. You'll never believe who I ran into on the street and who's sitting here with me having a glass of champagne. Amanda Piedraplata! And you saw me leaving the hotel from a taxicab earlier today, and now you're calling to tell me you too are in town. This is providential. You must come over and join us for a glass of champagne. Yes. Right now. I'll leave word at the front desk. They'll show you up.'

Amanda started looking perplexed, albeit pleasantly so. 'Philippe Mahfud,' Bianca said as soon as she hung up, her cover story already in place. 'Can you believe it? He saw me leaving the hotel as he went by in a taxi and rang up to see if I was staying here. Isn't the world the smallest place?'

Of course, Philippe was downstairs in his room, so he actually had to kill some time in order to make his arrival seem convincing to Amanda.

However, he was soon sitting with the two women, sipping a glass of champagne, listening to Amanda recount her delight in adopting such a beautiful little girl, unaware that his life was about to take the most unexpected of turns.

'I hope Ferdie isn't going to be cross with me for adopting the baby without his knowledge,' Amanda remarked. 'You know how difficult he can be, Philippe.'

With that, she turned, looked at Bianca and said: 'My husband has periods every six months or so when he's almost impossible. There's nothing one can do but accept it. Unfortunately, he's coming out of one at the moment...it's already lasted about four weeks, hasn't it, Philippe?

That's partly why I came here in the first place. I've learned to keep away at a certain point. It's best for our marriage, otherwise the good bits will become sullied by something which is beyond everyone's control.'

Some innate sense of wisdom told Bianca not to utter a word. She therefore nodded sympathetically, fixing her gaze on Amanda, who was revealing an intense side of herself that she had never suspected existed beneath that cool and rather prim exterior.

Returning to Philippe, Amanda continued: 'This whole business of the baby has been so unexpected. I telephoned Raoul Goldman, just to keep in touch really...he's the lawyer who found our son... and Begonia and Raymond's children,' Amanda said as an aside to Bianca before turning her attention back to her husband's business partner, 'and he said he had this day-old baby girl. The couple earmarked for her didn't want her when they discovered her father is half-Jewish...can you believe it? He knew I wanted a daughter eventually and asked me if I was interested. And this, Bianca, is where things get a bit tricky. I telephoned my husband...I was hoping he's have turned the corner and been open to reason...but we didn't even touch upon the purpose of the call, because it was so obvious that he has not yet returned to his normal self. You know what I mean about Ferdie when he's in that frame of mind, don't you, Philippe?'

'You did the right thing in not broaching the subject until he's in better shape,' he said reassuringly. 'It really isn't possible to get through to him when he's in this condition.'

'I thought I'd go and see the baby. Well, it was love at first sight. She was mine from the moment I saw her. No doubt about it. She was already my daughter. I loved her as much as if I'd just given birth to her myself. The bonding was instantaneous. I could not imagine, having seen her, how I could live my life without her. Raoul was with me, and I agreed there and then to adopt her. He's processing the papers, and I'll take her back to Mexico next week. I only hope Ferdie doesn't throw a fit. He's the most easygoing man normally, Bianca, but he does get bees in his bonnet, and once he does, there's no changing his mind. He has a thing about control and respect. I know he's not going to be pleased that I've gone ahead and got the baby without his knowledge or consent. I only hope he'll understand how the situation developed and not hold it against the baby. He's such a good father to Manolito. He absolutely worships him. And to think I was worried before we adopted him that his feelings would be affected by the way we came to have the baby.'

'He also loves you totally,' Philippe said. 'Even if his nose is out of joint for a while, I'm sure any damage done will be superficial, not fundamental. You might have a rough two weeks, but I predict things will blow over.'

'That's what I'm banking on,' said Amanda.

Chapter Eight

'You what?' Ferdie exploded, moving menacingly towards Amanda. 'You what? What did you say you did?'

Amanda trembled. She had never felt such overwhelming fear in all her life. 'Ferdie, if you'd just look at her, I know you'll love her.'

'Look at her? Are you crazy, woman? Why would I look at her? She's not my child. She's never going to be my child. Why would I want to look at her?'

'She's as much our child as Manolito...'

'Oh no, she's not. Manolito is my son, our son. She's not my daughter. She's your daughter. You want her: you keep her. But let me make one thing clear...I am not having a daughter foisted upon me.'

'Ferdie, please...be reasonable...'

'Be reasonable? That's rich coming from you. You go shopping in New York and come back with a baby your husband knows nothing about, and you tell me to be reasonable. Your problem, Amanda, is that you've got too big for your boots. I've made you too secure. You've grown so overconfident that you think you can go behind my back and adopt a baby just because you want it. What about me? What about what I want? You didn't even consult me.'

'Ferdie, if only we could take things more calmly...'

'Calmly? How many men would take having a child foisted upon them calmly? You tell me that, Amanda.'

'I had to make up my mind there and then. Raoul couldn't wait for me to come back home and speak to you about it...'

'And you couldn't phone me, I suppose...'

'I did, Ferdie, but you were in such a vicious mood...'

'Vicious mood? That's what you think of me when you're simpering and whimpering and beating around the bush...? Woman, I knew you were trying to work your way around me...I'm not your husband for nothing...I can tell when you're dancing around trying to get your own way, instead of giving me a clean clear choice...'

'Please, Ferdie. Please. Let's not argue. I love you and would never do anything I thought would really upset you...'

'I notice your use of the word "really". So it's fine for you to upset me slightly? To take advantage of me slightly? To use me slightly? What we're talking about is the degree of liberty you've given yourself. That's what we're talking about here.'

'You're twisting what I said. I didn't mean it like that...'

'You meant it like that, all right, Amanda. What you didn't mean was for me to find you out. You've overstepped the mark. You'd taken advantage of me. You've disrespected my rights as a husband and as a human being. This isn't something that we can paper over. There's a larger issue at stake here. Superficially, it's about the baby, but beneath that, it's about whether I'm to suck salt and pander to a woman who's now so puffed up with her own importance that she thinks she can impose her desires and her will upon me.'

'I can't believe you really mean any of what you're saying. You have to know that I'm not like that.'

'All I know is that you've begun to believe your own publicity. You remind me of some B-grade movie actress from Hollywood who thinks she's so popular that she can rub the studio chief's nose in the mire.'

'Ferdie, please... Please...I'm begging you... Please try to understand that I didn't intend to disrespect your wishes or desires. Why would I? I love you. We have a happy marriage. We have a wonderful family life... I honestly thought I was adding to our happiness. I concede that I haven't handled things well...'

'You must have realized that your actions would cause a problem...'

'Well, I was nervous about how you'd take the news...'

'Now you know. I'm outraged that you could have taken my life and my destiny into your hands without so much as a word to me.'

'What can I do to make things better?'

'Send the baby back.'

Amanda felt her blood run cold. Instantaneously, she started to shiver.

'You don't mean that,' she said.

'I do.'

'You can't mean that.'

'I can, and I do.'

Amanda started to sob. 'No, Ferdie, no, you can't... That's the cruellest thing you could do... Please...please... Say you don't mean it...'

'I mean it, Amanda,' Ferdie said coldly. 'If you value our marriage, you'll send that baby back.'

For three days Amanda looked for a sign that Ferdie was softening. She tried affection to no avail. Sex to no avail. Showing the baby to Raymond and Begonia, who came for dinner at the end of the third day she was back in Mexico City, to no avail. Ferdie simply walked out of the drawing-room as soon as she appeared with little Anna Clara. He didn't make a point of departing, so the Mahfuds did not realize that anything was amiss, but he nevertheless did not return until the baby had been taken back to the nursery.

By this time Ferdie was no longer occupying the marital bed. He had moved out without warning or discussion and taken up occupancy of one of the guest bedrooms the night of the baby's arrival. Amanda had no choice but to confront the fact that Ferdie's obstinacy and pride might well prevent him from ever relenting. As she turned things over in her mind, she believed that the only hopeful sign was that he had not mentioned anything about separation or divorce. It was a straw to clutch at, but only a straw, for he had withdrawn emotionally and sexually, and Amanda saw the evidence of it everywhere.

Although she was hopeful that Ferdie would return to her bed once he had calmed down, as she looked back on the last few days, she found his reactions dispiriting. 'I'm not going to let my pride get in the way,' she told herself on the second night of their separation and had gone into the bedroom where he was sleeping and tried to snuggle up to him, hoping that one thing would lead to another and that they would effect a complete reconciliation through the reestablishment of conjugal relations.

Ferdie, however, had pulled himself away from her in such a manner that she was made to feel unclean.

Amanda knew Ferdie better than anyone else, so she gave him time to calm down and start to miss her during the next seventy-two hours. On the evening of the fourth day after her return she decided she must try again, but when she attempted to open the door to the bedroom Ferdie was using she found it was locked. This alarmed her, for he had raised the drawbridge and had made himself inaccessible in a way he had never done before. These were oppressive days for Amanda, but they were not without their consolations. Anna Clara was a truly adorable baby: beautiful, goodnatured and everything a mother could ask for. Manolito was also captivated by her, which was a relief, for coping with a jealous toddler would have been too much.

Amanda received her first glimmer of hope when Manolito dragged Ferdie into the nursery and showed him Anna Clara. Amanda stood by silently, her heart in her mouth, as Manolito encouraged his father to touch the baby. Anna Clara, who only cried if she was hungry or dirty, kicked her little legs sweetly and grabbed onto Ferdie's finger. Manolito, touched, kissed the baby, then his father, babbling away happily, utilizing the few sounds he could make as if they were a language everyone, especially his father and mother, could understand.

'Surely Ferdie will relent now,' Amanda thought as she witnessed this scene.

That night, Amanda's hopes soared when Ferdie knocked on the marital bedroom door just as she was about to turn off the light. 'Yes?' she said, knowing only too well who it was, while her heart skipped a beat.

The doorknob turned, and Ferdie entered. He was in his pyjamas and dressing gown.

'Come in, my love,' she said, sitting up in bed and patting it, hope suffusing her.

'I want a divorce,' said the man whom she thought had finally returned to the marital bed.

In shock, Amanda stuffed her fist in her mouth and started to sob uncontrollably. When she was finally able to speak, she babbled rather than talked. 'Oh, my God... No...Ferdie...no...'

Ferdie remained standing. He looked at her silently, impassively, as if she were a stranger about whom he felt nothing. Unable to believe that a man who had loved her so completely only a few weeks before could now be indifferent to her, Amanda jumped out of the bed and threw her arms around his neck, resting her head on his shoulder and smelling the sweet scent of his body. This act of intimacy brought on a fresh wave of anguish for her, without altering his inflexible stance one jot, and she could feel him stiffen. She wondered if she would survive the pain of it. Amanda was in such agony that she half expected her heart to give out, but to her surprise it continued beating as she clutched the husband she loved utterly.

After the longest moment of Amanda's life Ferdie reached behind him, took her hands in his and removed them from around him. He impassively handed them back to her, as if he were a butler presenting a houseguest with a drink on a tray.

'It's no use,' Ferdie said. 'You've destroyed what we had. Love is like a delicate vase. Once it's broken...'

Immediately comprehending the enormity of what he was saying, Amanda fell to the ground and clutched her husband's ankles, wave after wave of grief engulfing her.

In what she would later view as the worst response Ferdie could possibly have had - because he removed her ability to be angry with him - he gently reached down, picked her up, placed her on the bed, kissed her cheek and said: 'I'm sorry, Amanda. I wish it could be otherwise, but it can't. It gives me no pleasure to cause you pain. You've been a good wife, and we've had a marvellous marriage. But it's over.' He paused, and she started to sob once more.

'I'll take care of you,' Ferdie continued in the caring tone of voice she knew only too well. 'So don't worry about the practical side of things. Get yourself a good lawyer from England to negotiate with mine. Take my advice and don't use a Mexican. He'll only cheat you. Get your uncle to recommend someone suitable. I'll settle a million US dollars on you, outright. No strings attached. With that, you'll be able to buy a brownstone in New York or a house in London and still have enough left over to give you a good income, if it's properly invested. I'll even help you with your investments, if you want. Now try to get some sleep, and we can talk some more in the morning.'

For the rest of her life, Amanda would be amazed that she actually got through the rest of that night without expiring from a broken heart. She could hardly believe that her marriage was ending because of her urge to love the baby daughter she now had. Had she committed adultery or made Ferdie's life unhappy or even been a flagrant bitch, she could have more easily accepted why this was happening. But for it to end because of love - especially the love of a child - was too acute an irony.

The following morning, it was a dispirited and broken Amanda who dragged herself out of bed. However, she did not deviate from her routine, for she understood the importance of keeping the fabric of normality intact as the stitches of her life unravelled. She therefore splashed cold water on her face, brushed her teeth, fixed her hair. Then she put on a silk dressing gown and went straight to the nursery, as she would normally have done, where she looked in on the sleeping Anna Clara and Manolito, who was already awake and playing with his nurse.

Amanda played with her son for a few minutes before returning to the cot to look at the cause of all her trouble. Anna Clara was still sleeping peacefully, a tiny, angelic, defenceless bundle of goodness, completely unaware of the turmoil her presence had caused. Amanda felt her heart tug and knew that she would not change anything she had done, even though the price had been higher than she could ever have imagined.

Fortified by this knowledge, which lightened the load of anguish slightly - but only slightly - she headed downstairs to join Ferdie for breakfast on the terrace underneath the lignum vitae tree. She had no hope that he would have changed his mind during the night, for something in his behaviour told her that the end had come. But still, it would be comforting to adhere to old habits. Once she joined him, Ferdie was kind and gentle, but Amanda could tell her previous assessment of the hopelessness of her situation was accurate. He was closed to persuasion.

'How do you want us to do things?' she asked, meaning, as he knew only too well, who was going to live where.

'I'll continue living here. I'll keep the country place, naturally. If you want to live in Mexico, you can buy yourself something here. A million US dollars is a lot of money, Amanda. It will go a long way here, though I question whether you've put down sufficiently deep roots to justify remaining here. I suspect, ultimately, you'll be happier in New York or London.'

'If I have to be on my own, I suppose the most sensible thing for me to do is return to London. New York is fine to visit, but I can't imagine living there.'

'A wise choice,' Ferdie said, reaching across the table and cupping his wife's hand. At that moment, Amanda felt as if she were caught up in a surreal comedy of errors that was anything but funny. She could hardly believe that she was sitting where she was, having this conversation with this man about this subject: and that he was cupping her hand affection-ately and protectively, with all the affection a loving father or brother would have for his daughter or sister.

'Of course,' she said, tears beginning to stream down her cheeks despite her desire to present a tearless façade, 'you can see Manolito whenever you want. I'll tell my lawyer to give you all the access you want. I can see that it will be difficult for you, with me living in London and you in Mexico, but with a bit of goodwill on both sides, I'm sure we'll come to an arrangement that will make the best of a bad situation.'

Ferdie removed his hand. He looked levelly at Amanda.

'Manolito stays here with me.'

'What do you mean?' she said, her voice icy with panic. 'I can't leave Manolito here with you.'

'You'll have to. It's non-negotiable.'

Amanda stiffened. 'Then I'm not leaving Mexico,' she said firmly.

'Even if you stay in this country,' Ferdie responded with all the calm of a practised negotiator, 'Manolito lives with me. Permanently. You can visit him, but he cannot live with you.'

Amanda felt her blood run cold again. Could this be the same man who had made love to her countless times over the years? Who had looked across many a room to see that she was all right and for her to reassure him that she still loved him, still noticed him, still paid attention to him? Was this the humanitarian who had built assisted housing for his staff as well as hospitals and schools?

'Ferdie, how can you do this?' she asked gently but pointedly, her tears drying with the cold blast that had emanated from him.

'If I don't do it to you, you'll do it to me,' he said, again with the calm of the experienced negotiator.

'But Ferdie, I'm his mother. I love him totally. How can you expect me to live without him?'

'I'm his father. I love him totally too. And I'm not going to live without him. He's my son. He's the carrier of my family's heritage into the future. I'm bringing him up so that he'll be a Piedraplata. If you bring him up, he'll be your son. He won't be a true Piedraplata. He'll carry your heritage into the future, and if you remarry, he'll carry another man's. No,

Amanda. It's only fair. You have Anna Clara,' Ferdie said, using the baby's name for the first time since her arrival in Mexico, 'and I have Manolito.'

Speechless, she sat rooted to the chair, frozen with shock.

Ferdie stood, placed his napkin on the table and said: 'Don't fight me on this, unless you want to lose everything, including the settlement and Anna Clara. This is the way it has to be, and this is the way it's going to be. Accept it, and I'll always be here for you. Fight me, and I'll win.'

He then walked away, turned back just before entering the house and said: 'You can stay here till you get used to things the way they're going to be. I'm not pushing you out onto the street. I know it's going to be difficult for you to leave Manolito and me and make a new life for yourself with a little baby. There's no rush. But maybe you could start to make plans to leave. Shall we say, by Easter?'

The sensation of being trapped in the wrong life welling up within her, Amanda simply nodded her head.

'I leave it up to you what you tell your friends. For my part, I intend to say nothing to anyone except Raymond and Philippe, and my mother and Clara of course. But I will be going out on my own from now on. No point playing happy families, if we're going to part company.' With that, Ferdie walked into the house to leave for work.

Confronted by a situation she could never have imagined in her worst nightmares, Amanda resolved to keep things as amiable as possible.

It was Ferdie's habit, when home from work, to play with Manolito downstairs until his son's bedtime. In the past, she had sometimes taken part in this activity, depending on her schedule. She decided that, from now on, she would keep out of Ferdie's way during his playtime with Manolito and would instead stay either in her bedroom or in Anna Clara's room, until Ferdie had finished playing with Manolito. Then, and only then, would she go into his room to say goodnight to the son she was going to lose.

That first night, already aware that she would soon have to relinquish custody of Manolito to Ferdie, Amanda experienced an overwhelming sense of unreality as she tucked the boy into bed. 'Soon,' a voice told her, 'the day will come when you can no longer undertake this simple but important maternal activity.' As she looked down on him, and he looked back at her, puckering his lips for a kiss, she asked herself how she would ever find the strength to leave him behind.

Feeling like a character in the wrong film, Amanda kissed Manolito, said, 'Goodnight, darling, sleep tight,' and walked back to her bedroom, the tears streaming down her face. Just then Ferdie came out of his room, and their paths inadvertently crossed.

'I'm off for dinner,' he said blandly but courteously. 'See you tomorrow.'

'Good night, Ferdie,' Amanda replied, trying to keep her voice as level as possible.

He was on his way to dine at Bianca Calman's house.

How Ferdie came to dine at Bianca's said a lot about the woman who would soon take Amanda's place. Ferdie had been true to his word, telling no one but his mother, sister and partners about the impending separation. Within minutes of informing Philippe and Raymond, however, the brothers had been on the telephone to give their respective women the news. Begonia and Bianca were both surprised, as everyone else who knew the Golden Couple would be, but it was the latter who seized the moment. 'Darling,' she said sweetly to Philippe when he gave her the news, 'you must bring poor Ferdie when you come for supper this evening. My heart goes out to him. He must be beside himself, especially as he hasn't been well of late. The last thing you want is Ferdie having a breakdown. I promise you, I'll do all I can to help tide you over this period with him. You know I'll always do anything I can to keep my Philippe happy, don't you, darling?'

'I'm the luckiest man alive to have a woman like you. I can't wait for the day when we're married,' he replied. 'I'll just buzz Ferdie and see if he wants to come.'

When Philippe gave Bianca the answer she yearned for, she resolved to do everything in her power to make the most of this chance, even though she did not yet know what advantage she could obtain from it.

She and Bernardo, who had not yet come to a final decision regarding their future together, struck just the right note that first evening with Ferdie, as Philippe had known they would. They welcomed him unreservedly, taking care not to allude to Amanda or his problems even once, and treated him as if he had always a close member of their inner circle. Bernardo was particularly careful not to fawn over him, which might have made Ferdie uncomfortable, and although Bianca's fabled charm was very much in evidence, she spread it evenly between the men and her children.

Ferdie was enchanted with the warmth of his hosts and the vibrancy of their conversation. Dinner at the Calmans, he had been told by Philippe, was always a time for intelligent discourse about current affairs, although this was frequently relieved with gossip, for they were also much taken with the current affairs of their social circle and could be relied upon, as on this occasion with Ferdie, to provide a sparkling array of ideas and affairs for the delectation of everyone around the table. By the end of the evening, Ferdie was so relaxed and stimulated by the company that he was loathe to leave when Philippe rose to go, saying, 'It's time for me to get to bed. Thanks for yet another marvellous evening, Bernardo and Bianca.'

Reluctantly, Ferdie got to his feet as well. 'Thanks for having me, Bernardo... Bianca. I've enjoyed myself thoroughly. I've often heard about evenings with the Calmans from Philippe. Now I understand why he's such a fixture here.'

'Drop in whenever you want,' Bernardo said, showing traditional Latin American hospitality. 'Our home is your home.'

'Yes, you must,' Bianca said, noticing that Ferdie was almost puckering his lips when looking at her. 'He does fancy me,' she said to herself, not for the first time.

Although Bianca was right, the last thing on Ferdie's mind at that time was starting another relationship with any other woman. He was still emotionally frozen by the events leading up to his estrangement from Amanda and, in this period of transition, really only wanted to mark time with congenial and undemanding company. From such small acorns are mighty oaks produced.

The following afternoon, Ferdie was conducting a meeting concerning Banco Imperiale business in Geneva. At the end of it, he turned to Philippe and said: 'I'm at a loose end this evening, and I'd prefer not to stay at home. Better to keep out of Amanda's way. If you're not going out, why don't we do something together?'

'I mentioned to Bianca that I'd drop in for supper.'

Ferdie looked at Philippe hopefully.

'If you won't find it too boring,' said Philippe, aware that it was in his interests to keep the senior partner happy, 'why don't I ring her and ask if I can bring you along as well?'

'That sounds like fun.'

'There's never a dull moment around them, that's for sure,' said Philippe, pleased that Ferdie seemed to be so taken with the charms of what he now considered to be his future wife and family.

This set a pattern for the next six weeks. At first, Philippe was pleased to take his business partner along to the Calmans, but with the passage of time, his tolerance waned. The other man's perpetual presence was evolving into an intrusion and, although he never manifested personal interest in Bianca, both Philippe and Bernardo began to watch him closely lest an attachment was forming.

For her own part, Bianca found herself having virtually identical conversations with both her husband and her lover. 'No, Ferdie has never telephoned me. No, he has never tried to kiss me. No, he has never even held my hand. Or brushed past me closely. I've never met him for lunch. I've never had tea with him. I've never had an assignation with him. He's never once indicated by word or deed that he has any interest whatsoever in me as a woman. He's just lonely. At a loose end. Using our friendship to tide him over until Amanda leaves. Doubtless, he'll spread his wings once she does, and then life will return to normal, with Ferdie making himself as scarce as he did before his separation.'

Although a part of her told Bianca that what she was saying was true, another and less rational part told her that it wasn't. 'Suppose, as Bernardo puts it, Ferdie is sweet on me?' she asked herself. 'Suppose he is more than sweet on me? Suppose he is falling in love with me? Or has fallen? Does he know about my relationship with Philippe?'

That, Bianca realized, was something she would have to find out, because the answer could have a crucial bearing on her options. The opportunity came one afternoon when Philippe was complaining to her over the telephone about Ferdie. Taking a deep inaudible breath, she said in her sweetest tone of voice: 'You've always said that no one knows anything about us, not even Raymond and Begonia. I take it that applies to Ferdie as well.'

'Of course it does,' her lover replied, knowing how terrified his mistress was of discovery until she was safely divorced from Bernardo.

'You'd think he'd have the perspicacity to at least query the nature of our relationship.'

'Oh, he did,' Philippe said airily. 'On the way home the second time I

125

brought him over to you. I said that of course there wasn't anything between us. I said I liked the whole Calman family. I said how stimulating and welcoming I found you all, and he accepted that. In fact, he said he also found your family exceptionally stimulating and welcoming. I asked him if he was drawn to you, and he said, "Which man wouldn't be?" before going on to say that you were another man's wife and he'd never touch a woman in those circumstances. Since then, he's said from time to time that yours is his ideal of what family life should be. I think he's hoping to meet someone like you, Bianca, and marry her as soon as Amanda's out of the picture. Do you know anyone who would fit the bill?'

'Let me put my thinking cap on,' she said sweetly, a warm glow coming over her. 'Maybe I can ask one or two spare girls around. Casually. So that he doesn't suspect anything. Would you like me to do that?'

'Yes,' Philippe said, hoping to be rid of the unwelcome competition.

One of the outstanding features of Bianca's personality was the speed and sureness of foot with which she moved whenever she was presented with an opportunity. While the average person would still be thinking about what to do, she would have already done it and progressed the scenario to new heights.

This was never truer than on this occasion. Already Bianca had been formulating the makings of a plan in case it turned out that Ferdie knew nothing about her affair. So, no sooner did Philippe hang up than she put the first stage of it into operation, telephoning Oriente del Valle, a refugee from Cuba, the scion of a once wealthy family that had fled from Castro at the time of the revolution. She now worked as a receptionist to the most fashionable gynaecologist in Mexico City. Tall, red-haired and green-eyed, she was attractive rather than beautiful. She would doubtless have married well had her world not collapsed but, shorn of her position, she had reached the age of thirty-four without having once received the matrimonial stamp of approval. However, what made her the perfect single woman, from a married woman's point of view, was her personality.

Loyal and sweet, she tried to be good fun and was a good sport, but ultimately, she was also somewhat dull because her personality lacked the spice of anything negative. Oriente never thought ill of anyone, never had a negative opinion on anyone, and, whenever others did, she always spoiled their fun by injecting a deflating dose of worthiness into her comments. Although men were initially drawn to her, a little of Oriente went a long way, and by the fourth meeting, you could see their eyes glaze over beneath the weight of her virtues.

'Oriente? Bianca here. I hope this isn't a bad time to call. You only have a minute? That's fine. I won't keep you. Are you doing anything for dinner tonight? No. Good. It's only us, *en famille*, but with Mexico's most eligible bachelor being served up for the main course. I do so want to find him a suitable wife, and I can't think of anyone who'd be better for him than you. Now, you mustn't breathe a word of this to anyone, especially to him. He's paranoid about girls wanting him for his money, and I'm not going to let on that this has been arranged. You must promise me, on your mother's life, that you'll never tell him that I've done this, not even if you marry him. Swear it. Good. Just remember, he's very shy, so you must do your best to draw him out. He can be hard going at times, but you've got a heart of gold, and I would so love to see two of my favourite people in the world happy together. This is our little secret, right? Good. See you at eight-thirty.'

Having orchestrated the distraction that would divert Philippe, if only for half an hour, Bianca advanced her stratagem by telephoning Ferdie. 'I wanted to be sure you're coming for dinner tonight. You are? Fabulous. I need you to help me. I'm hoping to match Philippe up with Oriente del Valle. Yes, I know you know her. She was at that party you had at your house last year for that German prince whose name I can't remember. Yes, she does lack sparkle, but she has everything else, and Philippe does so deserve a good woman. 'Then, as airily as a robin's feather sailing through a breeze, Bianca delivered the *coup de grâce*. 'Just because you and I haven't had ideal marriages doesn't mean that I've lost my faith in the institution. One of my main ambitions in life is to see Philippe happily married. But you know how uneasy he is around women he doesn't know well. I need you to help nudge him in the right direction. If we all help Oriente and him along, I'm hoping they'll click.'

Ferdie laughed. 'You are an incorrigible romantic, as your husband is always saying. I'll help. Of course I'll help. It would be great if Philippe could find himself a wife, and I somehow don't see him doing that without a little push from his friends.' Then he paused, became sombre, and said, 'I had no idea you and Bernardo were having problems.'

'No one knows,' Bianca said, her voice breaking as if she were about to cry. 'He has another woman.'

'I'm sorry to hear that.'

'One tries to put a brave face on these things,' she said, assuming a manner she took to be stiff upper-lip English.

'You are truly an exceptional woman,' Ferdie said, his voice filled with admiration. 'Bernardo must be insane. He's a lucky man to have a wife like you. Any man would be.'

'That's the best compliment I've received in ages. Maybe ever,' replied Bianca, always lavish with her praise. 'I'd better let you get off the phone before you turn my head anymore. See you later. At the usual time.'

Encouraged by the way that bit of preparation had gone, Bianca now needed to neutralize Bernardo. This she did when they were dressing for the evening. 'I'm trying to make a match between Oriente and Philippe,' she said to him. 'At dinner, I'm going to seat everyone in a very eccentric manner on purpose. I'll dot the children around the table. Julio on my left, Pedro and Antonia on yours. Ferdie on my right. If you ignore Oriente, Philippe will have no one to speak to but her. With a bit of luck, he'll realize what a lovely girl she is, and we'll have a lovely wedding to look forward to.'

'You're such a romantic,' replied Bernardo, who only ever saw what his wife wanted him to. With that, he leaned over, kissed her on the back of her neck, cupped her breasts and said: 'I'm so glad you've stopped accusing me of seeing another woman since your return from New York. I could eat you right now.'

'I wish you would,' she replied, feeling herself respond, 'but not now. I don't want to have to put on my makeup again.' Despite the fluctuations in their relations since she had first accused him of infidelity, the sexual attraction between them still remained strong. They were still in love with one another, and she still found him irresistible with the result that Bianca had not kept to her plan to push for a divorce but had embarked instead upon a torrid kiss-and-make-up phase with him. This, as things turned out, served her purposes even better than if she had planned them.

Having finished dressing before Bernardo, Bianca left him standing in front of the mirror brushing his hair while she went to the drawing-room to put on some background music. She chose Frank Sinatra and Stan Getz, hoping to set the mood with something cool and romantic.

She then sat down in her favourite chair on the front veranda and waited for the first guest to arrive. It was Oriente. Bianca offered her a drink, which Duarte, the houseboy, brought back from the pantry. The two women were sipping their drinks and chatting when Philippe and Ferdie arrived within a minute of one another. No fool, for all her blandness, Oriente noticed that her hostess did not offer either man a drink. Instead, as soon as each of them had settled down into the chair of his choice, Duarte padded into the room. Bianca, in anticipation of the sybaritic sophisticate she would soon evolve into, made all her servants wear black shoes with rubber soles so that they would not make any more noise than a cat walking on marble as they served her and her guests.

Silent as a thief, Duarte presented each man with his drink of choice, chilled white wine for Philippe and a Bloody Mary for Ferdie, leaving Oriente to conclude accurately that each man was already so much a fixture in the Calman household that the houseboy knew what they would want to drink without them having to ask. Oriente knew that this observation had ramifications but, starved of sufficient knowledge to know what those were, she pushed it to one side, together with the vaguely disquieting sensation that her presence might be useful rather than desired.

'Shall we?' said Bianca, jumping to her feet and leading them all into the dining room.

Once the hostess had seated everyone around the table, and Duarte had served the cold vichyssoise, she moved to test the water and see if Ferdie was really as 'sweet' on her as she sensed. Leaning towards her daughter Antonia, seated between Bianca's least favourite child, Pedro, and Ferdie, she said: 'Darling, you mustn't forget to tell you father about your day at school. He'll be so proud of you.' Beneath the table, however, a message of another sort was being conveyed at the same time, for while she was speaking, Bianca purposely - but delicately enough for it to be construed as accidental - brushed her right knee against Ferdie's thigh.

Having done so, she pulled back, turned her attention to Ferdie and said: 'One's children give one such pleasure. Don't you think kids and a good marriage are the best things in life?'

'After work,' Ferdie laughed.

'Of course, for a man, after work,' Bianca tinkled with all her renowned charm, stopping short of flirtatiousness. Then she leaned in towards Ferdie, touched him on the left arm between his wrist and his elbow and, once more fleetingly brushing her knee against his thigh as if by accident, said: 'Do you think we have a budding romance here? Look at how taken Philippe is with Oriente.'

Ferdie swallowed his soup, smiled and said in what was patently a *double entendre*: 'I see every prospect of a budding romance.' With that, he brushed his knee past Bianca's thigh.

Instantaneously, she felt a surge of sexual excitement. 'It would be so wonderful,' she responded, 'if their budding romance could bring them the happiness they deserve, wouldn't it?'

'I can think of nothing else I'd like more for them than to see them achieve the happiness they deserve.'

'Nor me,' Bianca said huskily and sexily.

With that, Ferdie slipped his left hand under the table and caressed his hostess's thigh while changing the subject of conversation to politics.

Later, as he was bidding goodnight to Bianca, Ferdie said right in front of Bernardo: 'Would you mind if I telephoned you tomorrow to ask your advice about something personal?'

'I'd be delighted,' Bianca said.

Because Ferdie had a justly deserved reputation for never looking at married women, it never occurred to Bernardo that his guest might actually be making a play for his wife right under his nose. Bianca, however, knew - or, at any rate, hoped that she knew - differently.

The following morning at eleven o'clock, the telephone rang. Before she even picked it up, Bianca was certain that it would be Ferdie. Sure enough, it was.

'I thought about you all last night,' he said.

Why Ferdie, you devil, you,' she said lightly and flirtatiously.

'I'm falling in love with you, Bianca. Would you like that?'

'I can't think of anything I'd like more,' said Bianca, surprised at how quickly her little plan had worked, her voice a sensual combination of self-possession and throatiness that had never failed to inflame men.

'I have to be honest with you. I don't believe in extra-marital affairs. Never had one. Never will.'

'I wouldn't want one myself.'

'We need to spend some time together, alone. Can you get away for the day tomorrow? We can go to my place in the country. I'm in the middle of doing it up, and I need some ideas now that Amanda's no longer handling it. If you tell Bernardo that I need your help, will he let you come?'

'Why don't you ask him yourself? He's far more liable to say yes to you than to me.'

'Done. I'll phone him right now and ring you back.'

While she waited for Ferdie to call her back with the news that Bernardo had agreed to their assignation, Bianca could hardly believe the dramatic turn events had taken. Ferdie was all but proposing to her – or at any rate, he was subtly informing her that what he wanted was marriage. Shocked though she was, Bianca could hardly contain the feeling of jubilation that sprang up within her. Could this really be happening? Could Ferdie – Ferdie Piedraplata, for goodness sake – really be offering marriage? All Bianca had ever wanted was to be a peripheral member of Mr and Mrs Ferdie Piedraplata's circle. It all seemed almost too good to be true.

Bianca had never spent any real time alone with Ferdie, so the following day was going to be important as well as instructive. On the way to his country house, they sat in the back of his Rolls Royce, the glass panel separating them from his chauffeur safely raised to preserve privacy.

From the moment she stepped into the car, Ferdie took charge. His personality seemed to fill every available iota of space, even more than it had at her house. While Bianca herself had a strong personality, by the time the car stopped outside the house, which I M Pei had built on the island a hundred metres from the old presidential retreat, the price she must pay for their relationship to progress from friendship to intimacy was clear. Bianca would have to concede all control to him. She could already tell that Ferdie Piedraplata was the sort of man whose need to command was so great that even the more extreme forms of Latin American machismo paled into insignificance beside it.

To someone as used to having her own way as Bianca was, this was a departure from the norm, but she rationalized that it would be a welcome relief to have someone else orchestrating life for a change. After all, Ferdie had already indicated that he was in the market for a wife, not an affair, so if they got along well, he would give her everything she had ever desired, and more. So why place obstacles in his path when, with a bit of compliance, he might offer her even more than Philippe could? After all, she asked herself, had not all her efforts been a quest for what Ferdie had, was and represented? As she set foot inside the I M Pei extravaganza, she made a mental note to surrender her will to Ferdie's.

Without realizing the enormity of what she was doing, Bianca even lay down what she thought to be a reasonable condition for swapping a life with Bernardo - or one with Philippe - for a life with Ferdie. Since she did not love him, Ferdie must fulfil the reason why she was entering into this relationship: he must make all her worldly dreams come true.

As Ferdie showed her round the house, Bianca was careful to play true to the role she knew would win his heart. Being a firm proponent of the view that men preferred to earn the regard of a woman to having her serve it up to them without effort, she did not to let on to him that she was eyeing his country house with a view to being its future chatelaine.

Even though she rightly suspected that he was showing it to her with that objective in mind, he would have to voice his intentions in clear and unequivocal terms before she would even acknowledge that marriage might be a possibility for them. He would, in short, have to win her. With that in mind, Bianca gave helpful but noncommittal pointers about how to finish the décor that, she could tell, would have been exquisite, had Amanda been given the chance to complete the job.

While this ostensible advice session was taking place, Ferdie was steering her, as she suspected he would, to the master bedroom. This in itself was an exciting prospect. As she looked around the room and saw an imperial-sized four-poster bed but no other furniture whatsoever, Bianca relieved tension by quipping: 'I think you'll need a bit more furniture than that to give this room the elegance its proportions deserve.'

Ferdie smiled and shut the door without locking it. Then, his face a mask of desire, he stepped up to Bianca and kissed her for the first time.

No man had ever kissed her quite like that before.

His tongue felt as if it were made of jelly. The sensation was utterly alien to her. Bianca could not immediately decide whether she liked it or not and, thrown by a sexual situation she had never envisaged, responded as best she could, trying to mask her uncertainty and anxiety while at the same time intent on enjoying to her fullest capacity what was happening between them.

Unfortunately, as the moment dragged on, and Ferdie's tongue did not lash her with desire but retained its gelatinous quality, she became at a real loss as to how to respond. She was, after all, used to men who were voracious, whose tongues were instruments of desire. But his seemed to be all sensuality. Whether there was fire there remained to be seen, but she had never expected to find herself in the position with any male of the species where she was unsure of how to respond. Or indeed, unsure of why he was performing as he was.

Just as Bianca was wondering whether Ferdie had judged their first foray into the physical a success or failure, he answered the question for her in the most unexpected way: 'Will you marry me?'

'Marry you?' Bianca said feebly, lost for words for one of the few times in her life.

Ferdie smiled indulgently. 'Yes, marry me.'

Bianca gesticulated speechlessly.

Ferdie started to laugh. And laugh. And laugh. He laughed until the tears ran down his cheeks, and still he laughed some more. Bianca, catching his mood, also began laughing, until they both fell onto the bed together. Gradually, their positions shifted. Bianca was on her back, Ferdie on his stomach, beside her. There was a pause, and he said: 'Well?' She nodded her head to indicate yes, and they made love for the first time.

For Ferdie, it was everything he had ever wanted from lovemaking.

For Bianca, however, it was even less satisfying than having sex with Philippe. Despite the fact that Ferdie was a devastatingly handsome man, and she had believed that she would thrill at his touch, she discovered the unwelcome fact that, for her, there was no chemistry between them. This, of course, was not something she could do anything about: one's body knew the truth. And there was something about the quality of Ferdie's skin that she did not like. Something about his scent. Something about the way he felt to the touch. Technically he was all enthusiasm and no finesse.

All emotion and no technique. On the other hand, if having sex with him were the price she had to pay to become Mrs Ferdie Piedraplata, international socialite, she would not only pay it but put a happy face on it too. Who knew? Maybe she would even learn to enjoy it.

Bianca believed that she would always be happy and that she would always be able to make others happy. She therefore intended to make Ferdie Piedraprata happy the way she had done so with Bernardo and Philippe. Not because she loved him, nor even wanted him, but for the simple reason that she wanted to be Mrs Ferdie Piedraplata. To have all that Mrs Ferdie Piedraplata had. To be all that Mrs Ferdie Piedraplata was. And to live the life of Mrs Ferdie Piedraplata. Of course, if she could have obtained all Ferdie was offering without being his wife, she would gladly have taken it, kept Ferdie as a friend and remained with Bernardo. Life, however, was not like that. She could not have the benefits of being Mrs Ferdie Piedraplata without being married to Ferdie Piedraplata. And since she could not be Mrs Ferdie Piedraplata without him - and since he was offering her a world beyond anything she had ever wanted, even in her most unguarded moments -she would, of necessity, make him happy.

That, at least, was her plan.

Part Two

Chapter Nine

Switzerland: Easter Sunday, 1969. The sun was dancing on the surface of Lake Geneva as Ferdie and his niece Magdalena walked, past the borders separating the flagstone path from the lawn, down to the shore.

'Switzerland is so beautiful at this time of the year,' remarked Ferdie. 'The one thing I miss in Mexico is the changing seasons. The chill in the air. Invigorating days like this. They remind me of my youth in Romania.'

'I wouldn't knock all that warmth and sunshine if I were you. You have no idea what it's like spending month after month longing for a warm day.'

'It's difficult to believe that you're now a young woman.' Ferdie said. 'It seems like just the other day that you were christened.'

'Tempus fugit,' Magdalena laughed. 'But time has treated you kindly, Uncle Ferdie. You still look young. Calorblanco is flourishing. Banco Imperiale is expanding...'

'You are coming to the opening on Wednesday evening, I hope.'

'I wouldn't miss it for anything.'

'Your mother is my eyes and ears in Europe. You know that, don't you?'

'Of course, Uncle Ferdie. Grandpa was always going on and on about how important it was that we stick together as a family and trust no outsider.'

'Papa did sometimes get things wrong. I suspect his experiences in Romania during the war had something to do with it. I never agreed with his scepticism about Raymond and Philippe, but there was no point resisting him, especially when it became apparent that he was dying. He

136

was also wrong about Amanda, as it has turned out.'

'How do you mean?'

'He practically made me promise on his deathbed to stick with Amanda no matter what. He thought the world of her and believed that I could never go wrong as long as she was by my side.'

'I gather from Mummy that Grandma backed you up when you decided to divorce Amanda.'

'She did. It turns out Mama was never as fond of Amanda as Papa was. She says she always found her a little stiff and could never be really comfortable with her.'

'That's only because you've never been wrong in Grandma's eyes. Mummy says that's the way it's been since she was a little girl.'

Ferdie took Magdalena's hand and stroked it. 'It must've been rough for your mother, not being the boy. Mama's never bothered to hide the fact that she adores me and has little or no time for your mother.'

'Mummy doesn't mind anymore. She says it was painful while she was growing up, but she's got over it now. I think because she's such a powerful businesswoman in her own right, many people treat her as if she's a man, and I don't mean that in a pejorative way.'

'She has the ability of ten men.'

'And the energy.'

'Do you like her new husband?'

'He's OK, I suppose.'

'Not a patch on your father, though.'

'No.'

'What's your father up to nowadays?'

'He's living in London.'

'Why London?'

'His half-sister Sissi lives there. She's the one who married Professor Alfred Bertram...you know, the owner of the Bertram chain of department stores. He inherited them from his grandfather and had to give up his career as a biochemist to run the business. He says he hates it, but Aunt Sissi has become one of London's greatest socialites and loves all the kudos that goes with being married to the chairman of the board of Bertram Limited. She's always entertaining royalty and lives in the gossip columns now that Uncle Alfred's business profile has raised her social one as well. Uncle Alfred says if it amuses her, that's fine by him. Daddy's working for them now. Do you remember their daughter Delia?'

'Yes, I do. Vaguely. She was a pretty little thing, wasn't she? Small and dark.'

'She's tall and dark now. Thin as a rake and very popular with the boys. She's at RADA studying to be an actress and has just become engaged to a young actor called Charles Candower.'

'Never heard of him.'

'You will. He's very blond and very handsome and has star quality stamped all over him. They mix with a very smart set because Delia went to Benenden with Princess Anne, and they're the greatest of friends.'

'You young people are really growing up. You're all developing lives of your own.'

'It's your life that concerns me, Uncle Ferdie, if I may be so bold. It was wrong of Amanda to adopt Anna Clara without your permission, but couldn't you have forgiven her? Everyone always thought you were so happy together.'

'It's too late now. She's in Mexico getting the divorce, and I've met someone else I want to marry.'

'Does Mummy know?'

'Not yet. Give me a chance, for goodness sake. I only got here late last night,' Ferdie said jocularly.

'Who is she?'

'She's the ideal woman. I've known her for some time but only as a family friend. Amanda was never crazy about her so I only saw her at friends' houses. But it gave me an opportunity to size her up as a human being. She's warm-hearted and generous-spirited with a magnanimous personality. A real family woman. Great with her kids. Great with her husband. Great with her friends. A gracious hostess and good fun. You'll love her. She's got a great sense of humour and is game for anything. She'll be a good mother to Manolito, and I like her children. I can see many happy years of family life ahead of us.'

'But she's married?'

'She's in the process of getting a divorce. Her husband - a nice guy, actually - has been seeing another woman for some time now. A few weeks ago, matters came to a head between them when she returned home from a day out with me. I'd taken her down to Sintra to show it to her. With her husband's approval, I hasten to add. When she got back she found a shirt of his rolled up in the laundry basket smeared with lipstick and a book of matches from the Fountainbleau Hotel in Miami with a girl's name and telephone number written on it. Bernardo had stayed there only a few weeks before, poor schmuck. Imagine being caught out like that. You can't help but pity him. She asked him to leave their home immediately and has filed for divorce on the grounds of his adultery.'

'Does he know about you?'

'No. I mean, he knows me, but doesn't know that Bianca and I are planning to get married.'

They reached the shore. Ferdie started throwing pebbles into the lake in a manner reminiscent in Magdalena's eyes of a young and carefree man.

'Try to throw the next on into that ripple,' Magdalena said, getting into the spirit of things.

The pebble sailed out of Ferdie's hand in the direction of the everexpanding ripple just as Clara's butler came running towards them. 'A long distance call for you, sir. From Mexico.'

Ferdie smiled, thanked the butler. 'That will be Bianca,' he said to Magdalena. 'She's helping me finish Sintra. She's been having a hell of a time finding certain things. But she's such a wonderful woman, she won't settle for anything less than what I want. The pains she goes to are heartwarming. They show me I've made the right choice. Third time lucky, as the saying goes.'

With that, Ferdie disappeared into the house, built in the style of the Second Empire. He did not emerge for another twenty minutes. An hour later, Magdalena, Ferdie and Clara were sitting on the terrace waiting for the managing director of Calorblanco Switzerland to arrive when the butler came out yet again to announce another telephone call from Mexico. 'That will be Bianca again,' Ferdie said proudly, walking back inside to take the call. 'Tell your mother about her, and I'll fill her in on the rest of the details when I get back.'

Fifteen minutes later, Ferdie returned.

'Madgalena tells me you're getting married,' Clara said.

'Yes. She's the most amazing woman, Clara. You'll love her when you meet her.'

'What's her name?'

'Bianca Calman. Her father is Harold Barnett, the British aristocrat who has a surveying practice in Mexico City as well as a finger in one or two pies with Julius Finkelstein.'

'Bianca Calman,' Clara echoed in disbelief. 'Not Bianca Calman whose house Philippe Mahfud took me to last year when I was in Mexico?'

'It must be the one and the same. There's only one Bianca Calman...of that I am sure,' Ferdie said, radiating pride.

'But surely Philippe's been having an affair with her.'

'No. They're just good friends.'

'*Puhleeeze*,' Clara drawled sarcastically. 'You're sounding like a spokesman for MGM commenting on the relationship of Elizabeth Taylor and Richard Burton during the making of *Cleopatra*, and we all know how penetrating that friendship was.'

'Seriously,' said Ferdie pleasantly, well used to his sister's frankness, 'they're really only friends. Everyone in Mexico has known of those rumours for ages, but he's just a family friend. In fact, it's through Philippe that I got to know Bianca. He used to take me with him when he dropped in to see the family... after Amanda and I hit the buffers, of course. And it really was a family gathering every time: Husband...children...the whole shooting match.'

'Where there's smoke, there's fire,' Clara said, clearly not convinced by her brother's disclaimer. 'I've found that adage to be only too frequently true.'

'Not in this instance, I can assure you. I've even talked it out with Philippe, man to man.'

'What does that mean?'

'I asked him outright. It was the second time he took me to her house. We were on our way home and I said to him: "You know what all Mexico says about you and Bianca. Is there any truth in it?" He assured me there was not.'

'For God's sake, Ferdie, you're a grown man. Of course he was going to deny it to you. Would you tell him if you were having an affair with a friend's wife...right under his nose? Of course you wouldn't. No man...no gentleman...would. I saw them together with my own two eyes, and I have to tell you, it was my impression that there was something between them. No man and woman can have that level of understanding without intimacy. Have you ever asked her?'

Ferdie shifted uncomfortably. 'There's never been any need to. I'm confident that Philippe told me the truth, and the question has never arisen between Bianca and myself... at least not directly. It did come up obliquely, though. The first time I took her to see Sintra, I told her I'm not the sort of man to have affairs, and she said she'd never have one either. So I suppose she did confirm to me in a roundabout way that she and Philippe were not having an affair.'

'Ferdie, you're my brother, and I love you, but I have to tell you...not for the first time, as you know only too well...you give Voltaire's Candide stiff competition when it comes to *naïveté*. I don't suppose it matters, though, whether she and Philippe did have an affair or not. All that matters is that she makes you happy.'

'And that she does,' Ferdie said, closing the subject as the butler led Hannes Veitbech, the managing director of Calorblanco Switzerland, out onto the terrace.

While the meeting was going on, Magdalena, who had been a silent but avid listener to the conversation between her mother and uncle, withdrew into the house. To kill time until the meeting was over, she telephoned a friend.

Unusually for most private homes of that time, Villa Favorita had two telephone lines, the second of which Clara had installed so that she and Ferdie could speak at length when he was in Mexico and they had business to discuss without inconveniencing the other members of the household. Ten minutes into the telephone call, Magdalena heard the other line ring. She ignored it, safe in the knowledge that the staff would pick up the call. It was with a mixture of amusement and incredulity that she saw her uncle walk past her on his way to the library. Their eyes locked.

'Bianca again,' he said, a bright smile on his face, pride emanating from every pore. 'She's having a problem with something to do with Sintra and needs me to steer her through it.'

By the end of that first day of Ferdie's stay at Villa Favorita, the pattern of calls from the absent Bianca had been set. For the remainder of his eight-day visit, the only variable within the pattern was the quantity of communications emanating from his new love. Every day she telephoned at least four times, more usually six - and one day, nine. Nor was the telephone the only vehicle for her ministrations. Telegrams, still a feature of life at that time, showered down upon the object of her desires at least once a day, and more usually three or four times.

Although Ferdie was clearly pleased by all this attention from the woman he had described as 'perfect', Clara could no longer stand it by the day of the official opening of the new Geneva Headquarters of Banco Imperiale Geneva. 'Ferdie,' she said over breakfast in her most sisterly way after the latest telegram was delivered on a silver tray by the butler, 'don't you think it's a bit excessive for any woman to bombard a man with telephone calls and cables the way this woman is doing?'

Ferdie laughed good-naturedly. 'She loves me. No one's ever put me first the way she does, except Mama. Don't be jealous just because you don't have someone going to such lengths for you.'

'I wouldn't want it,' Clara replied. 'I'd be too nervous. Normal women don't behave like that. Only geishas go to such extremes to please a man. It's disturbing, Ferdie, and I wouldn't be fulfilling my duty as your sister if I didn't point that out to you.'

'No, no,' Ferdie said, waving Clara's concerns aside. 'This is how she is. She's the kindest, most generous, most unselfish woman I've ever met.'

'That surely isn't the Bianca Calman whose house Philippe took me to. Admittedly, she was a charming and gracious hostess, and admittedly she made a great show of how feminine a personality she is, but no woman would fail to recognize the steel underbelly of that butterfly. And that ostentatious love of luxury: everything calculated to impress and bedazzle in that garish house of hers. I ask you, Ferdie, can you be blind to how phoney the place is, and what it reveals about the character of the woman whose home it is? Please, Ferdie, please...don't rush into this marriage. I have an awful feeling you're going to live to regret it.'

'I've asked her to meet me in Paris the week after next. Come, spend a day or two with us and get to know her better. You'll change your mind, I'm sure.'

'Do Philippe and Raymond know about your marriage plans yet?'

'No.'

'Do you have any objection to my telling them?'

'No. In fact, it will make things much easier for me if the news comes from you. Even though I'm sure there's never been anything between Philippe and Bianca, there's little doubt in my mind that he's always carried a torch for her.'

The most important aspect of the reception that evening at the Banco Imperiale's new Geneva headquarters turned out not to be the president of Switzerland and his minister of finance. Nor was it the Dom Perignon vintage champagne or the Beluga caviar served in antique Russian silver pots containing two kilos apiece, or indeed any of the other myriad indices of serious wealth that were the specialty of Ferdie Piedraplata and the Mahfud brothers. It was not even the guests, who were the targets of the arrangement, even though they consisted of a cross section of the new international elite which was emerging upon the world stage. The inclusion of such names as Greek shipping tycoons Aristotle Onassis and Stavros Niarchos, heiresses such as the American Duchesse d'Uzes and the Dutch-Egyptian Baronne Marie-Helene de Rothschild; the art collector Baron Heini Thyssen-Bornemisza and his beautiful Brazilian wife Denise, the son and grandson of Manny Silverstein's Romanian patrons King Carol II and King Ferdinand, the exiled King Michael, with his wife Queen Anne and her Bourbon-Parma great aunt Zita, last Empress of Austria, supplied only a sideshow to the main action of the night.

This took place right after Ferdie, the senior business partner and Clara, his official hostess, led the president and finance minister into dinner in the boardroom, followed by Philippe and Raymond Mahfud and the twenty-four most prominent guests. Sitting with the president on her left and Philippe on her right and following protocol, which required a change of conversational partners with each course, Clara started conversing with Philippe.

'I think the reception went with a bang. How about you?' she opened.

'I hope it will have the desired effect. The national papers, the *Wall Street Journal*, the *Herald Tribune* and the fashion magazines such as *Vogue*, *Harper's Bazaar* and *Women's Wear Daily* all sent their correspondents, and they seemed complimentary about the guests and the headquarters. If we get the publicity I expect, we should be on a roll.'

Clara smiled and decided to plunge in headfirst.

'Thank God Ferdie's health hasn't been affected by the break-up with Amanda.'

'I can take some of the credit for that,' Philippe said, making the fishing expedition Clara was embarking upon easier than she had anticipated. 'I've kept him busy. Immersed him in family life, in fact. He's spent practically every evening and most weekends with me at Bernardo and Bianca Calman's house. I figured that what he'd miss most is family life, so I've made sure he got even more of it than he had when he was married to

Amanda.'

'That was very clever and thoughtful of you, Philippe,' Clara said. 'It's had the desired effect, even if it's also had another, more unexpected outcome. Ferdie's fallen in love with Bianca Calman and wants to marry her.'

Although Philippe's lack of surprise made Clara aware that her guard really had to be up, it was his response that truly astonished her. 'I know. Bianca told me the day before I left Mexico.'

At that moment, Clara realized that her brother's junior partner and his future wife had most definitely once been lovers and most likely still were. After all, she reasoned, what married woman would confide in her future fiancé's business partner that she had accepted his proposal before her divorce arrangements had even been concluded? Except, of course, if she were already having an affair with that same business partner. There could only be one explanation for such an intimate confidence. Bianca and Philippe had been, and undoubtedly still were, lovers. Clara could see that Philippe really had no other course of action open to him than to step aside and let Ferdie have the woman he had chosen. Her brother was not the sort of man to forgive someone for taking what he wanted or for besting him or indeed lying to him, thereby allowing him to make a fool of himself. Ferdie was too proud, too self-willed and emotional to cope with having Bianca in his life as his junior partner's wife.

Clara knew only too well that Philippe Mahfud's professional success depended upon keeping her brother happy. Without the Piedraplata family money and Ferdie's energy and contacts, there would be no Banco Imperiale. Without Banco Imperiale, there would be no Mahfud fortune. The Mahfud brothers would be reduced to what they had once been: a tiny insignificant bank in Beirut but with a reputation for having fallen out with one of the richest men in the world. Hardly an enviable position to be in.

'She seems a lovely woman,' Clara observed, deliberately veiling her true feelings behind the remark's ambiguity.

'Oh, she is,' Philippe said, his face a beacon of adoration. 'I don't know what I'd have done in Mexico without her.'

'Hopefully nothing will change between you when Ferdie marries her.'

Philippe laughed shyly and blushed, his swarthy skin turning deep purple. 'I don't suppose anything much will change,' he said, providing Clara with all the confirmation she needed of the danger she and her brother would be in if this marriage were to go ahead.

'You can all be one big happy family,' she said disingenuously.

Philippe blushed again, nodded his head. 'I suppose so,' he said.

'Life is so unpredictable, isn't it?' Clara said, placing her right hand on Philippe's left arm. 'Who would ever have believed nine months ago that Ferdie and Amanda would be divorced and we'd be sitting here speaking about him marrying Bianca Calman? I thought that if anyone were going to marry Bianca, it would be you. You both seemed so...well, how shall I put it?...sympathique. But there we have it. Handsome Bernardo couldn't keep his zip up. Amanda, silly girl, went and alienated Ferdie's affections. Now Bianca has captured Ferdie's heart, and you, whom I thought would have been the one she would have turned to, have been a loyal friend to both her and my brother. It quite reaffirms one's faith in humanity.'

Chapter Ten

For most of us, reality never exceeds our dreams, but there are a lucky few whose reality exceeds any dream they might ever have had.

Bianca became one of those privileged rarities when Ferdie slipped a ring on her finger and turned her into more - much more - than the reigning queen of Mexican Society. For the first time in years she no longer suffered from the ennui her perfectly planned and predictable life had induced in her. She now had to fit herself in with the plans of a husband to whom a typical day was an alien concept. Indeed, the only predictable aspects in Ferdie's way of life were the constant mobility, the complete unpredictability and the infinite luxury with which they went from one place to another.

But what a way of life it was. The following Easter was spent in the Caribbean, cruising on Marjorie Merriweather Post's ocean-going yacht, the *Sea Cloud*. The largest sailing ship ever built, it was chartered by Ferdie to celebrate, as he put it, a 'quintet of happy events'. Julio had made the Dean's List at Harvard University, where he was studying business admin- istration. Pedro was accepted by Columbia University, where he would study history; Antonia had started at her English school, St Mary's Ascot, and Manolito was turning three, while Ferdie and Bianca were marking their first six months of marriage.

To assist them with the *Sea Cloud* celebrations, Ferdie and Bianca asked eighty friends and relations, including his mother, her parents, Raymond and Begonia Mahfud, Philippe of course, two exiled kings and their queens, four princely couples including the Serge Obolenskys, Bill and Babe Paley, Mainbocher and his life companion Douglas Pollard, the legendary Margaret Duchess of Argyll and three brace of movie stars to sail with them throughout the Caribbean, stopping at ports in Aruba, Trinidad, Grenada, Guadeloupe, Martinique, Barbados, Puerto Rico, Santo Domingo, and Montego Bay, Jamaica.

To Bianca, this was an occasion to relish. Playing hostess to the world's leading socialites meant that she was not only Mexico's première socialite, but she was now also one of the world's elite. If, however, Bianca needed confirmation of her new position, she had to look no further than the latest activity planned by Ferdie. No sooner was the *Sea Cloud* cruise over and her feet on dry land than she was preparing to leave Mexico for the summer. Her new husband always based himself in London for that season, and, in deference to the change in wives, he was transferring his allegiance from the Ritz Hotel to the Dorchester, where he had booked the penthouse suite adjoining Elizabeth Taylor and Richard Burton's.

Inevitably, the two glamorous couples met one another and struck up a casual friendship. 'What a pity we didn't know you at Easter,' Bianca said, the first time they had drinks in the Taylor-Burton suite. 'We took over the *Sea Cloud* for a fortnight's cruise of the Caribbean.'

'I know Jamaica well,' Elizabeth Taylor said. 'I went there with my last husband. We were great friends of Ernie and Betty Smatt. Do you know the Smatts?'

'I think we met them,' Bianca said. 'We stayed on for a few days afterwards as guests of Bill and Babe Paley at Round Hill.'

'Jamaica's so beautiful,' Ferdie said, 'but nothing like Mexico. You must come and visit us, if ever you're in our neck of the woods. And in the meantime, come and stay on the boat we've chartered for the summer. It's moored at Monte Carlo, and we plan to spend most of August there.'

'Maybe we can link up with you down there on the *Kalizma*,' Richard Burton said. 'That's our yacht. We combined the names of our daughters Kate, Liza and Maria to come up with it. Not bad, eh?'

'It's a lovely name,' Bianca agreed. 'God knows what we'd call ours if we were lucky enough to have one of our own.'

'We never will,' Ferdie says categorically. 'I believe in chartering. We've taken the *Auriole* for the summer. It's a two-hundred-and-forty footer, built between the wars for one of the Guinnesses and is both comfortable and good value for money. Maybe if I were in acting instead of business, it would make sense to have my own boat, but with the demands made upon my time, I can't justify tying up so much capital.'

'Moreover, Ferdie's sister and mother would demand their pound of flesh,' Bianca said, betraying the first hint of anything untoward in her relationship with her husband.

'They'd only be using what was rightfully theirs,' Ferdie said, reprimanding Bianca in a tone that conveyed that his mother and sister might be contentious subjects. 'All our businesses are family concerns,' he explained, looking at Richard Burton instead of at his wife.

'We know all about family ventures,' the actor boomed theatrically. 'Don't we, Elizabeth?'

She smiled sweetly.

'I hate to break up a good party,' Ferdie said, standing up, 'but we're due to have dinner at nine o'clock, and we don't want to be late.'

Bianca leaped to her feet and, ensuring that her neighbours wouldn't confuse Ferdie and herself with just another *nouveau riche* couple with money to throw around, said in a charmingly conspiratorial tone: 'We must be on time. You know how royalty hate it if you arrive after them. And if we don't behave ourselves, the Queen might just lop off our heads.'

Bianca could tell from the tinkling laughter of the world's reigning movie queen that her comment had achieved its desired effect. The fabled Burtons would thereafter never be tempted to dismiss Ferdie Piedraplatas and his wife as just another obscenely rich couple. Not when the Queen of Hollywood and her consort knew that the Piedraplatas moved in royal circles.

Although the actor and actress never did make it down to Monte Carlo, that did not detract from the fun Ferdie and Bianca had that first halcyon summer. There were a series of cruises: the shortest being a day, the longest, a week. Once, they took a group of friends out to sea for lunch, stopping off for dinner in St Tropez. Another time, they took the boat out for a few days, stopping off for lunch at the Hôtel du Cap in Cap d'Antibes, followed by dinner at an amusing little restaurant in Ramatuelle, with lunch the following day at a seaside bistro in St Tropez, before heading back to Monte Carlo. On a longer jaunt, they crossed the Mediterranean and stopped off in Tangier and Marrakech, where King Hassan of Morocco received them and their ten guests and the three elder children at the palace for dinner. After this regal meal, they set sail due east along the North African coast to Libya. There, the Crown Prince received them at his palace in Tripoli before they set off, with their guests, on a desert safari in a fleet of Land Rovers, laid on by the Libyan royals, to marvel at the ancient ruins of Leptis Magna and Carthage. Suitably edified, they returned to Tripoli, where the Crown Prince and his brother joined Ferdie, Bianca, their guests and children for dinner onboard the *Auriole*. It wasn't long afterwards that Muammar Gaddafi overthrew King Idris and his sons were no longer in a position to entertain such international socialites. 'It's wonderful being married to a man who knows everyone,' Bianca commented to her favourite child, Julio, while walking on deck one moonlit evening.

That first summer of her entry into paradise, Bianca was discovering that the big boat crowd - Ferdie taught her never to say 'yacht': it was a dead giveaway of what he called being *'nouveau'* - formed a clique all its own. Access required a combination of factors: name, fame and fortune.

Whether it was Prince Johannes von Thurn und Taxis dropping in from his palace in Germany for a few days cruising or the movie producer Sam Spiegel, with his motley crew of aspiring actresses and rich backers, pulling alongside and sending over an invitation for dinner, there was always someone rich, famous and entertaining to entertain - and to be entertained by.

Some of the big boat crowd also owned villas, and Bianca decided the most elegant way to lead one's life was to have your own villa, where you slept and which you used as your base while making maritime forays. When you didn't have to be at sea, she discovered, you should stay on dry land and reduce your chances of developing sea legs. One of the few downsides to the super-rich lifestyle, Bianca had already concluded, was that she could not abide the sensation of stepping ashore for lunch or dinner and feeling as if the earth were swaying in time to the rhythm of the seas. She therefore made a mental note to begin a subtle campaign of encouraging Ferdie to buy them a villa, possibly in Biarritz.

It was at this point that Bianca fell in love. It was not with her husband, however, or indeed with another man, but with a house.

L'Alexandrine has frequently been called the most beautiful villa in the South of France. Built in 1864 for the Grand Duke Alexander of Russia, it was Napoleon III at its best: spacious, gracious, elegant and tasteful. No expense had been spared by the Grand Duke. The villa was constructed of the finest coral-coloured stone, its floors and columns of the finest marble. The plasterwork alone took a team of masons nine months working round the clock to complete and was regarded as one of the finest examples of plasterwork in existence. The bathrooms, which were state-of-the-art for their time, were all en suite and were still as they had been when completed by the architect a hundred years beforehand.

All twenty acres of the grounds had been sculpted as if by an artist, with flowerbeds, bushes, lawns, follies, and gazebos laid out to titillate and to entice. There was a pool house and a swimming pool reminiscent of a Roman bath from Herculaneum. The lawn tennis court required the services of a full-time gardener and was illuminated by specially constructed lights made of iron in the Art Nouveau style in 1906 to resemble trees, the electric light bulbs covered by glass which had been custom-made by Baccarat.

L'Alexandrine was truly a house fit for royalty, and Bianca - who had taken to regal living with so little adjustment that a psychologist would have had a field day analysing her - resolved upon first sight of it that she would own it one day. It was, she felt, the perfect house. Having never felt that way about anything before, she knew - just knew - deep within herself that she would never be able to rest until L'Alexandrine was hers.

Whatever the price, she would pay it.

Bianca had discovered the object of her veneration by accident. She and Ferdie had been to lunch in the hills behind Biarritz with some friends. On the way back, two of their car tyres suffered punctures no more than ten feet away from the high wrought-iron gates of L'Alexandrine. The driver rang the bell, the mistress of the house, who turned out to be an avid gardener, had been watering plants nearby, so answered it herself and, seeing what she concluded were a lady and gentleman, graciously asked Ferdie and Bianca in while their driver attended to the tyres.

Before she even saw the interior of the house, Bianca was already enchanted by the property. Then Mrs Kenward-Townsend led them into the morning room and, her fate sealed, Bianca said, without any attempt at flattery: 'I don't think I've ever seen a more beautiful house.'

'Would you like a tour?' asked Hyacinth Kenward-Townsend.

'I certainly would,' Bianca said with even more enthusiasm than usual.

The elderly widow then ordered coffee for her unexpected guests before showing them round her house, describing its points of historic interest as they walked from one exquisite room to another. At the end of the tour, Bianca said: 'I'm in love with your house. If ever you think of selling, will you let me know? Not, I hasten to admit, that I'd ever do anything without my husband's knowledge or approval' she added quickly, looking directly at Ferdie, mindful of how Amanda had created in the first place the vacancy she was now filling.

'Give me your details, and I give you my word that if ever I want to sell, I'll give you first refusal. I know exactly how you feel. I've felt the same about L'Alexadrine...ever since I first saw it back in 1923 when I came to this neck of the woods on honeymoon with my late husband. You won't believe it, but I've always believed I was fated to own this house. Bertie's father had been attached to Grand Duke Alexander's staff as ADC when the Grand Duke visited England for Queen Victoria's Jubilee.

'In those days, of course, honeymoons were more leisurely affairs than they are today. We had time on our hands and a plethora of letters of introduction, one of which was to the old Grand Duke. He asked us here for tea and, as soon as I'd set eyes on the place, I blurted out to him, in much the same way that you have, how taken I was with it. He said he was finding the upkeep a great burden and said that if ever we wanted to buy it, he'd sell it to us. Bertie wasn't in favour at first...I suspect you're most likely entertaining the very thoughts he did all those years ago, Mr Piedraplata...but then Bertie was diagnosed with TB a few months later, and suddenly it made sense to move to the South of France. I've never left...except during the war years, when I went back home to do my bit.'

Three hours later the car was roadworthy again, and Ferdie and Bianca took their leave. As soon as they were in the car, Bianca, slightly afraid of Ferdie's tendency to cut people out of his life when they displeased him, slipped her hand through his arm and snuggled up to him, saying: 'I hope you didn't mind me speaking the way I did about the house. But I knew that if I didn't grasp the moment, it would never come again. I really wasn't trying to go over your head.'

'I have to hand it to you,' Ferdie responded. 'You manage to push the boundaries to their absolute limit but in such a way that I have no justification for being angry with you. You missed your calling. You should've been a diplomat or a negotiator.'

'Are you complimenting me or insulting me?'

'I'm definitely not insulting you, but it's not altogether an unalloyed compliment. I have to say that the better I know you, the more I come to see how layered a personality you are. I don't think I've ever met anyone who has such a visceral response to material possessions.'

Ferdie did not say it in so many words, but Bianca had just been forewarned that he might be coming to the conclusion that she had married him for his money. She, however, did not pick up on the implication, marking it down to his moodiness.

'Oh, darling,' she said cheerily, 'the last thing I want is to upset you. I couldn't help it if I fell in love with the house. You must admit, it is the most amazing place you've ever seen.'

'I wouldn't put it quite like that,' Ferdie said, now clearly irritated. 'I've seen plenty more fantastic places. It is exquisite, but I have no intention of buying any house in the South of France. Not now, not ever. And if I don't buy it for you, who will? I don't see your father's money extending to L'Alexandrine.'

'Ferdie, why do you always take everything so much to heart? Has it not occurred to you that this may just be a pipedream?'

'A man has to nip these things in the bud, otherwise they flower and bear fruit and the next thing he knows, he's leading a life he doesn't want,' Ferdie said defensively, removing her hand from his arm and withdrawing to the furthermost reaches of the backseat.

Like many women with a Middle Eastern heritage, Bianca seldom challenged a man directly. Rather, her tactic was to ignore the fact that something unpleasant might be happening and to plough ahead as if everything were all right. It was a technique that proved infallible when it came to taking the wind out of a man's sails, and she resorted to it now.

'I do hope Yvette doesn't have another appointment,' she said, referring to their masseuse. 'I could certainly do with a long lingering massage, and those punctures have made us late. Maybe you'd prefer to go first?'

'No, I have work to do. Those flat tyres have thrown out my whole afternoon.'

'I know, darling, I know,' Bianca said sympathetically. 'But you really mustn't let every little thing get to you. It's bad for your health and only makes you miserable, and the last thing I want to see is my Ferdie unhappy.'

Ferdie, however, would not be jollied out of his mood, and when they reached the harbour, he leaped out of the car and was halfway to the mooring before Bianca even had a chance to alight. Had she married him for love, this sort of conduct would undoubtedly have perturbed her.

Neither Bernardo nor Philippe had ever behaved like that, and if they had done so, she would have taken it adversely. But because Ferdie could not reach her heart, Bianca accepted it from him as just another manifestation of his impatient personality. It was therefore an unperturbed Bianca who made her serene way up the gangplank, where the chief steward was awaiting her arrival.

'Mademoiselle Yvette is waiting on the poop deck,' he informed her.

'Please show her to the gymnasium,' said Bianca.

With that, she made her way into the boat and to the appointed meeting place, where the Venetian blinds had been drawn, blocking out most, although not all, of the daylight. She undressed fully and slipped into a heavily embroidered silk kimono-style bathrobe, ignoring the white terry-cloth one hanging beside it. No sooner had she tied the sash than Yvette entered.

'I'm so sorry we're late,' Bianca said graciously. 'We had a mishap on the road.'

'Is Madame hurt?'

'No. Just anxious to have my massage,' she said, slipping off the bathrobe and making herself comfortable on the massage table.

Yvette opened her leather container and took out various bottles of oils. Bianca breathed in the delicate but crisp scent, relaxing before the masseuse had even touched her. This woman was the best practitioner of her art that Bianca had ever experienced and, being something of an expert on the subject, having had a massage every week of her adult life, she now surrendered herself to the delights awaiting her. In fact, Bianca's love of massage provided an invaluable insight into her personality. She loved being touched and prodded and kneaded. She was transported when a good masseuse worked her fingers over her body and through her scalp. She did not mind in the least that her hair became matted with essential oils, nor that she would have the trouble of having her hairdresser come to wash and style it. To her, the sensation of gentle fingers working their way over every external centimetre of her flesh was more than just a sensual experience. It was also a spiritual one.

'How is that, Madame?' Yvette asked as she started the massage, gently pushing her thumbs into Bianca's shoulders.

'Good...good,' she replied, almost dreamily.

The woman silently continued her circular movements.

'So have you and your boyfriend decided on a wedding date yet?' Bianca asked, her voice turning husky as she surrendered to the stimulus of those relaxing hands.

'Yes, Madame,' Yvette replied. 'We're getting married on the November 16 in a little church in St Paul de Vence.'

'Have you decided what you're going to wear yet?'

Although Yvette did not know Bianca well enough to realize that such interest in her activities was a natural part of her patron's warm and affectionate personality, it was indeed actually typical of Bianca. She seldom read books. She had no intellectual curiosity. She had no real hobbies. Her whole being was geared towards people and the rewards relating to them brought. People were her interest, her hobby and her activity, and she treated everyone with whom she came into contact with kindness and consideration. The result was that she was the firm favourite of many of the people who served her, not because she was undemanding - on the contrary, anyone who worked for her had to provide her with precisely what she required as and when she did require it - but because she was so human with them. The class barriers seemed to have been removed, and there was a natural ebb and flow that gave vitality and dignity to the relationship that employees knew to be rare.

'I've seen the most beautiful dress in a shop window,' Yvette went on. 'It's outside my budget, but I'm going to do some extra sessions and hopefully I'll earn enough to make a large enough down-payment for the shopkeeper to allow me to pay off the rest after the wedding.'

'Hire purchase,' Bianca said. 'That's how my husband got his start in the business world. How much is the shop asking for the dress?'

'One hundred and twenty dollars in United States currency,' the girl replied.

An hour later, from somewhere between sleep and complete relaxation, Bianca heared Yvette give her cue that the massage was at an end: 'Thank you, Madame. I hope you're feeling well.'

Bianca opened her eyes, adjusted her gaze to take in Yvette, who seemed like a distant shadow even though she was no more than three feet away. 'Be a dear and reach me my handbag,' she said.

Yvette brought over the large, tan, calf-leather Hermes bag from the chair where Bianca had rested it. Bianca sat up, naked, on the massage table, while Yvette fetched the terry-cloth robe.

Yvette held it up, allowing Bianca to slip in her left hand first. 'What a great lady,' she thought to herself, filled with admiration. 'None of my other ladies are so refined that they use a soft silk robe when their skin is clean, but a terry-cloth robe when their skin is covered in oil. All my other ladies either use silk, which they then have cleaned, or terry-cloth, which is so harsh to the touch unless you're covered in oil.'

Bianca, who had meanwhile been scrambling around in the recesses of her oversized handbag, pulled out a wallet, opened it, took out a note, folded it in two and said: 'Here, buy yourself something nice as a wedding present. *Yourself*, mark you. Not your husband.'

Yvette took the bill and, in keeping with the tact that made her such a good servant, tucked it away in her trouser pocket without even looking at it.

'Thank you, Madame,' she said. 'That's very kind of you. I'll treat myself to something special.'

What Yvette actually had in mind was heading into Eze with what she imagined was a five or ten dollar tip and buying herself a hundred millilitre bottle of *Moment Volé* toilet water from the Fragonard shop.

'You do that, Yvette,' Bianca said, amused and respectful of Yvette's discretion and without giving a clue as to what she knew would come.

'Now, if you'll wait a few minutes, I'll have the chief steward fetch Monsieur.'

With that, Bianca padded out of the gymnasium, knowing only too well that Yvette would look at the note as soon as she had left the room.

Sure enough, no sooner has the door shut than Yvette pulled the banknote out of her pocket. She looked at it and blinked. She had never seen a thousand-dollar bill before, and she had to look twice to be sure that her eyes were not playing a trick on her. When she accepted that they were not, she jumped - literally jumped - with joy then quickly stuffed the money away in her purse. Knowing the standard of calmness required of her, she suppressed her exuberance and composed herself once more so that when Ferdie came into the room, wearing a terry cloth robe, nothing in her obliging professional demeanour would give away what had just taken place – just in case he would not have approved of his wife's gesture.

Had Ferdie known of it, he would not have been displeased. Although he did not indulge in impulsive gift-giving with employees the way Bianca did, he was one of the richest men in the world, his worth on a par with that of Aristotle Onassis, Stavros Nairchos and J Paul Getty, and his generosity was justifiably legendary. Unlike Getty, who had installed a payphone at his stately home in England when too many guests made long-distance calls, Ferdie was genuinely munificent and only too happy to have everyone share in his good fortune. This was true both personally and professionally. Not only did Calorblanco operate an official policy of socialized education, hospitalization, medical care and hire-purchase schemes for its employees and their families but Ferdie himself could not have been more open-handed with everyone who crossed his path.

Whether it was his employees, his friends, his family, his ex-wives or his current wife, he contrived to give them more than they had ever wanted, even in their greediest moments. The result was that Bianca had a weekly allowance of ten thousand US dollars to spend as she pleased without reference to her husband or anyone else for that matter. This was aside from an unlimited dress allowance. The bills for the Fall Collection, her first as Mrs Ferdie Piedraplata, from Yves St Laurent, Valentino, Balenciaga, Ungaro, Givenchy, Balmain and Madame Grés in Paris and Scassi, Norman Norrell, Pauline Trigere, Oscar de la Renta, and Halston in New York had amounted to $241,768.91. This was on top of the $176,836.42 he had allowed her to spend within weeks of their marriage at Maximilien on a maxi sable coat, a black-diamond mink coat, a natural buff-coloured ranch mink coat, a leopard-skin coat and a chinchilla coat, and the $34,751.89 she had spent at Ferragamo at a time when Jacqueline Kennedy Onassis's total monthly clothing allowance was the supposedly extravagant and previously unheard-of sum of $30,000.

Nor were clothes and furs the only luxuries with which Ferdie indulged Bianca. The jewels she wore engendered as much comment on the international scene as those that Amanda used to wear. Only the Queens of England, Spain and Belgium, the Comtesse de Paris and the Empress of Iran had so splendid a collection, and, of those ladies, only Farah Diba's was sufficiently modern to indicate living money the way Bianca's jewels did.

Not, of course, that the jewellery collection was actually Bianca's, although Ferdie did give her a 29.63-carat flawless white D emerald cut diamond, set in platinum, as an engagement ring. He also gave her a diamond parure, incorporating a necklace that reduced into two smaller necklaces; a pair of bracelets; a dinner ring; a pair of long-drop earrings that disconnected to leave studs with five-carat central diamonds bordered by smaller brilliant-cut stones; a choker; a brooch; and a tiara as a wedding present. The breakdown value - that is, the value of the stones and metal, which was, of course, platinum - was $2.3 million so the replacement value for insurance purposes was ten times that figure. However, the rest of the jewels with which the gaping world was bedazzled actually belonged to the Piedraplata jewellery shops, a personal investment decision which Ferdie considered wise in the light of how notoriously difficult jewels were to turn into realizable cash if and when liquidity was needed. So, even though Bianca could use whatever she wanted for as long as she wanted, technically she was a walking advertisement for the shops, and this rankled with her. It should not have, however. The morning after they had returned from honeymoon Ferdie had instructed his lawyer to change his will, leaving half of everything he owned to his new wife, the other half going to his son Manolito.

Although Bianca should have been happy with the knowledge that she had married a generous man who had put her in line to become one of the world's richest widows, she had paid a high price in human terms, having sacrificed a marriage with the man she loved. Although she loved all the worldly benefits of being Mrs Ferdie Piedraplata, there were times when she missed Bernardo and all that they had shared together so much, it physically hurt her. Her character was far too strong to give way to such regrets, but the sacrifice would only be worthwhile if she could materially obtain as much as possible. Here and now. She was not Amanda. The criterion, for Bianca, therefore wasn't whether Ferdie was generous or not, or whether he was making her financially secure beyond any reasonable expectation. The criterion was what Ferdie could give. And if he didn't give willingly, she would take.

From Bianca's point of view, this new husband of hers was not be trusted. He was too capricious. She reasoned, not without a measure of justice, that no man could be relied upon who was so fickle as to reject a loyal and loving wife just because she had adopted without his knowledge or consent a baby girl he might otherwise have wanted. Ferdie's making her an equal beneficiary with Manolito in his will, therefore, did not even enter into Bianca's reckoning, not when he could ultimately spurn her for some similar little thing. It did not occur to her that what Amanda did was not everyone's idea of a 'little' thing and that Bianca only needed to respect his parameters to avoid falling into the same trap as her predecessor had done.

And so she fell into another trap instead by embarking upon a campaign to convince Ferdie that she should stop wearing the glittering array of jewels available on loan from the Piedraplata jewellery stores, complaining about how demeaning it was to have to wear 'borrowed stock' when a few nice pieces which were her own would suffice.

At first, Ferdie took Bianca's complaints at face value. 'Don't feel like that, my beloved. Half of everything I own will go to you if anything should happen to me so, in a manner of speaking, the jewels are already yours. I certainly don't intend to let you out of my clutches,' he joked, 'as long as I have breath.'

Bianca was nothing if not persistent, and when she did not breach his defences on that first occasion she returned to the task a week later. Then two weeks after that. Although Ferdie did not react adversely, neither did he oblige her with victory, so she returned to the assault a fourth time.

This was on board the Criterion, chartered from Loel and Gloria Guinness, while Ferdie and Bianca were dressing for a dinner they were hosting for Bill and Babe Paley. 'What is this, woman?' he suddenly exploded 'How dare you complain about not having your own jewels when your wedding present is worth ten times the entire value of the jewellery most rich men give their wives'? You are an ingrate and a nag,' he screamed at her from across the stateroom, not caring whether they were overheard or not, 'and I will not permit you to wear me down into doing something I have never done for any other woman and certainly don't intend to do for you. Did you enter this marriage with the value you now possess? You act as if you were born and bred to this standard of living, but I don't recollect your father or Bernardo Calman providing you with any decent jewels. Look at that emerald necklace you used to wear! Do you call that important? An item of quality? It's a piece of junk! And what about that dinky little house you and Bernardo used to call home? It may be a pauper's idea of a mansion, but it certainly isn't a rich man's castle, that's for sure. How many times can you fit it into my Lomas house? Five times? Maybe ten? And where was your country house before you came swanning into my life and started calling Sintra your country house?

Did you have one at all? Spare me the nagging, woman, before I really lose my temper and you make me do something you'll regret.'

With that, Ferdie pulled up his trousers and stormed out of the stateroom, slamming the door behind him. Bianca was mortified, not only because other people onboard might had overheard but also because until that outburst it had never once entered her mind that Ferdie might consider that he had elevated her, even though she herself accepted that he had.

Ferdie returned fifteen minutes later, an aloof expression on his face.

'Darling, I'm so sorry I upset you,' said Bianca, who was combing her hair while looking a lot less worried than she actually felt.

'Well, you did,' Ferdie said, changing his shirt to a fashionably pale green cotton one.

Intent upon mending fences, Bianca rose, walked behind him, slipped her arms around his waist and started to stroke his stomach seductively while kissing his back and pressing herself into him. He grunted then surrendered to her touch, pulling her in front of him as the tears started to spill out of her eyes. 'Just don't nag me ever again,' he said. 'It's the one thing I can't abide.'

'I really didn't intend to,' she said, lifting her face towards him as she plaintively wiped away her tears with the back of her left hand. 'You forgive me, don't you?'

'This time, yes,' he said, kissing her gently on the lips but nevertheless issuing a warning which registered with her.

The following day, Ferdie's sister Clara, brother-in-law Marchese Rodolfo d'Offolo and niece Magdalena joined the *Criterion* in Cap Ferrat. Although Clara was suspicious of Bianca's motives for marrying her brother, and her husband was of the same opinion, Magdalena was a firm admirer of her new aunt, having fallen for Bianca's charms when she went to Mexico for her marriage to Ferdie. In turn, Bianca gravitated towards the one member of the family who, she sensed, genuinely liked her. 'Come, let me show you your cabin,' she said to Magdalena, linking arms with her as if they were sorority sisters. 'I hope you'll like it. It's starboard.'

A stranger looking at the two women as they headed down the deck might well have taken them to be sisters, Magdalena having developed into a real beauty just like Bianca with long blonde hair, green eyes, classical features and a slender figure.

'So,' Bianca began conspiratorially, as if she were speaking to a contemporary, 'how's the big romance going?'

'He's sooooo gorgeous. I just wish he'd pop the question.'

Bianca, intent on solidifying her position within the family by all available means, was resolved to turn Magdalena into a friend and ally.

'We'll have to knock heads together and see if we can't devise a strategy to get you what you want,' she said. 'My own experience of men is that you can always get them to do what you want. Just cover them in lots of sweetness and light and let them know how wonderful and powerful and strong you think they are. Appeal to their better nature. Let them think you view them the way they secretly want to be viewed.'

'What do you mean?'

'There's always a way,' Bianca replied, her laughter tinkling. 'Believe me, any woman can get anything she wants out of any man, as long as he lusts after her.' Even so, after last night's little scene, Bianca wondered if Ferdie might not be the exception to the rule.

They had now reached Magdalena's cabin. Bianca opened the door and stepped aside to let the younger woman in first. 'Hydrangeas!' Magdalena exclaimed. 'I don't believe it. My favourite flowers.'

'I know,' Bianca said, quietly capturing her prize. 'You let that slip at the wedding...remember? When we were discussing my bouquet?'

Magdalena moved towards her new aunt and hugged her. 'Words can't convey how touched I am,' she said, already well on the way to falling completely under Bianca's spell.

'It's my pleasure,' Bianca said. 'I like nothing better than seeing my loved ones happy.'

'Then life must be an uphill struggle for you when Uncle Ferdie gets in one of his moods.'

In the family, Ferdie's depressive periods were always euphemistically referred to as 'moods'.

'You can say that again,' Bianca replied demurely. 'And your grandmother doesn't help. In fact, she makes things much, much worse.'

'Grandma's very possessive of Uncle Ferdie. She's never really wanted to share him with anyone. Mummy would go further and say that she's never wanted to share herself with anyone but Uncle Ferdie...and Grandpa, of course, when he was alive.'

'I know what your mother means. I don't want you to take this the wrong way, but I actually sympathize with your poor mother. I've seen your grandmother in action. It's always Ferdie who's wonderful, while Clara can't do anything right, even though your mother is far more reliable than your uncle. To a newcomer like me, it just doesn't make sense. It's as if she doesn't see either of her children as they really are. Ferdie is seen as possessing every virtue, Clara possessing none...though, I have to tell you, I've seen your grandmother change tack when she wants something out of your mother.'

'It's been very difficult for Mummy having a mother like Grandma, but she's come to terms with it and, it doesn't bother her anymore.'

'I must ask her the secret, for I have to tell you: your grandmother makes my blood boil. She's always putting me down to your father. She's a real troublemaker. I can tell she'd like nothing better than to break us up.'

'I wouldn't go that far. She'd much rather have you there so that she can snipe at you. It's all part of her game.'

'Horrid old bat...spreading poison every time she flaps her wings. No wonder your uncle has his moods. In fact, it's a wonder he doesn't have more of them, with a mother like that.'

The steward arrived with Magdalena's luggage. 'You may unpack, thank you very much,' Bianca said, once more taking Magdalena by the arm and steering her towards the deck where lunch was about to be served.

As they walked, Bianca brushed her hand gently over Magdalena's cheek. 'I'm so glad we can be friends,' she said. 'Sometimes it's a bit daunting entering a family like this, especially after having come from such a united family as my own and having had such a serene family life with my first husband.'

Magdalena's heart went out to Bianca. She put herself in the older woman's shoes and could easily imagine how vulnerable she must be at times. She decided she must put in a word on Bianca's behalf with her mother and Uncle Ferdie. This was, of course, precisely what Bianca wanted her to do, although it has to be said in fairness to Bianca that she would have behaved exactly the same way towards Magdalena had she lacked an ulterior motive, for she genuinely liked her.

Magdalena's opportunity to speak out on behalf of her ally came the following day. Bianca had just slipped down to her stateroom to change into a new swimsuit after her morning swim, and she seized her chance.

'I have to tell you, Uncle Ferdie,' she said, 'the more I know Bianca, the more I like her. She really is one of the kindest, most considerate people I have ever met in the whole of my life.'

'Your life hasn't been long enough for you to have much basis for comparison,' Clara replied sharply. 'Calculation often presents itself as thoughtfulness. I'd say the jury should remain out on dear Bianca until we have definitive proof of what her motives are.'

Ferdie looked from his sister to his niece. They could almost see the wheels of his mind turning. He seemed to be thinking that both women were speaking the truth, but only one could be right. Then he turned to his brother-in-law, shrugged his shoulders and said: 'What can a man do when he's caught between two stools, Rodolfo?'

'Seems to me it's more like being caught between three stools, Ferdie,' quipped Rodolfo.

'Or four, if you include Mama,' Clara added.

'Quite enough to send a man stark staring mad,' Ferdie replied jokingly. Five days later the family left the Côte d'Azure, Ferdie and Bianca dropping off Clara, Rodolfo and Magdalena in Geneva before flying back to London on their private jet.

For Bianca, the first real awareness of her change in lifestyle had come when she was asked which was her favourite airline. 'I don't fly commercial anymore,' she had replied. Her new husband owned a Lear jet fully equipped as if it were a flying apartment, with a sitting area with sofas, a bed and a bathroom with shower, elevating Bianca beyond first class. The Lear was actually less of an indulgence than it appeared to be. With his boundless energy and the needs of his business empire, Ferdie and Bianca were constantly on the go. As the jet hurtled through the skies, Ferdie rested while Bianca took stock of her life.

Superficially relations between man and wife had returned to normal, and each was ostensibly leading the other to believe that satisfaction reigned. Bianca, however, was now dangerously disaffected. Ferdie's outburst had put her on her guard in a way she would never forget, and as far as she could see, his capriciousness and tempestuousness made an intolerable level of circumspection an imperative for survival as his wife.

She was now painfully aware of how badly she had miscalculated her ability to 'encourage' Ferdie into giving her jewels when he did not want to. Bianca suspected that she had come perilously close to stepping over the line just as Amanda had done. Clearly the waters she had to navigate to keep her marital vessel safely afloat were treacherous. For the first time she understood how Amanda – whom she had secretly dismissed as a silly woman – came to misread the signs and miscalculated the outcome, thereby unwittingly destroying her marriage. Ferdie, Bianca decided, was too inclined to blow small things out of all proportion. He was also too intolerant. He found it impossible to accept anything he did not wish to, and that made living with him difficult.

For the first time since she had married Ferdie, Bianca felt regret. Even worse, she felt insecure and expendable: sensations that were new to her. She asked herself if this marriage was really worth the price she had paid in giving up a husband whose love was firm, constant and reciprocal for a husband whose love was predicated upon a wife's willingness to obey.

One part of Bianca wished she could turn the clock back, but she also knew that whatever Ferdie's faults might be, the marriage had been worth it. If she was honest with herself – and she was – her ideal would be to fuse Bernardo and Ferdie into one man. To have the lifestyle and stature that being Ferdie's wife brought her, but to sleep with Bernardo and have Bernardo's companionship. Or, to put it another way: to have the public face of Ferdie and the private side of Bernardo.

'But,' Bianca asked herself, surrendering to her reverie, 'even if I could return to Bernardo, would I really want to do so?' The answer, she knew, was a resounding yet painful 'no'. Not after having been married to someone as dynamic and cosmopolitan as Ferdie. Comforting and comfortable though Bernardo was, the Piedraplata way of life was something entirely different, and one moreover which had infinitely greater appeal.

Bianca sipped her glass of champagne as she looked at her sleeping husband, sprawled across a sofa in the Lear, which was now high over France heading towards London. She took another sip and let her eyes take in every aspect of this private aircraft: this rich man's toy, this affirmation of her status. It was, as the saying goes, 'beautifully appointed': all pale blues, beiges and shades of taupe. The two stewards hovering in the galley behind a drawn curtain, waiting to spring into action at the touch of a button, were the best that money could buy.

Bianca could not deny that this was more than just the way to travel:

it was also the way to live. This was truly being on top of the world, and she would not give it up voluntarily. 'Even if I put the capricious and volatile aspects of Ferdie's nature to one side, the prospect of leading the rest of my life with someone who is as personally unfulfilling as Ferdie Piedraplata is anything but tempting. Not when you've spent your whole adult life being loved and indulged, as I have, first by Bernardo, then by Philippe. I am being called upon to pay too heavy a price if I continue living this emotionally barren life.'

As she looked into the future, Bianca could see the strain of being on tenterhooks lest she say or do something which would precipitate Ferdie's fury and cause him to cast her out increasing with the passage of time. Unless she could find some way of relieving the pressure, her life would become progressively intolerable. Already, the emotional cost of living with Ferdie had been so high that her feeling of well-being had diminished to a previously unknown low. If this degeneration continued, it would only destroy her capacity for happiness: something she had entered into this marriage to increase, not decrease. Moreover, she was sure Ferdie was not the sort of man who would want an unhappy wife around him, so she would lose everything unless she found a way to remain happy.

'All these very rich men only want women who complement them and add to their lives,' she reminded herself. 'Nothing is more of a turnoff for them than a needy or insecure woman. As soon as a woman starts to cause them trouble, they replace her with a less troublesome model. With them, there's always a trade-off. They give us the lifestyle, but we must fizz in return, adding sparkle to their domestic environment. And a woman who isn't happy and fulfilled and satisfied quickly loses her effervescence and, with it, her attractiveness. Then it's only a matter of time before some more obliging woman steps into their shoes.'

There was, Bianca could tell, an even more dangerous aspect to her relationship with Ferdie. He was not your typical Latin American husband who would privately dispense with the personal services of a wife who no longer pleased him, seeking his pleasures elsewhere - usually with a succession of mistresses - but without actually divorcing the spurned spouse. Typically, the woman in question might find it galling that she had been put into a humiliating position, but at least wives whose husbands had mistresses were still wives and therefore enjoyed the social and material benefits accorded their marital status. However, as Ferdie had pointed out to her that day when he first took her to Sintra and proposed to her, he did not believe in extramarital affairs. That could therefore mean only one thing. His wife either had to keep him happy or face being cast upon the heap as another ex-wife. And that, Bianca concluded, was a fate akin to death.

The very thought of being the former Mrs Piedraplata induced such a profound sense of emptiness in her that Bianca suddenly felt the need to fill the void with food. She pressed the buzzer beside her chair. The chief steward appeared, padding in silently. Bianca motioned to him to bend down so that she could whisper. 'Some caviar please,' she breathed softly in his ear, not needing to tell him how she liked it. Madame invariably had three heaping tablespoons of Beluga on each of the four slices of freshly toasted and buttered white bread she customarily required.

While waiting for the caviar, Bianca sipped her champagne, still caught up in her thoughts. 'I have to function under the premise that, no matter how much money I spend or how many boats I cruise upon or how many times I fly in this Lear, I still need to be nurtured the way Bernardo and Philippe nurtured me. That sort of love is beyond Ferdie, and I don't see why I should go without it. I still need to go to bed with a man who genuinely appeals to me. I still need to have that man make love to me, instead of having him puffing and heaving upon me and using me as a sperm bank the way Ferdie does. I will not live without the joy that good lovemaking brings…not for one day longer than I have to. The sensual and emotional sterility to which Ferdie is subjecting me are just too high a price to pay for life's goodies and, unless I remedy the situation, I'll end up without the goodies and without the satisfaction that a good relation-ship brings.'

The solution, Bianca could see, was that she must resume her affair with Philippe. In an ideal world, of course, she would have had Bernardo as her lover, but he would never have gone for playing second fiddle to the man who had replaced him, and she would not have returned to him as his wife, even if she could have done so. That left Philippe, whom she knew she could trust. Although he was not as accomplished a lover as Bernardo, and although she desired him less than Bernardo, she did at least find him genuinely appealing and truly enjoyed going to bed with him. Moreover, he had the merit of being as comfortable as a pair of well-worn slippers. Thus, she could always address any technical imperfections that remained with his lovemaking while at the same time having the emotional benefits of familiarity. 'The best lover,' Bianca had always been fond of saying to her girlfriends, 'is the man you want to go to bed with.'

As Bianca contemplated resuming her affair with Philippe, she saw that, if he had a fault, it was that he achieved satisfaction too readily. This failing had been tolerable while she was married to Bernardo, who could always supply the leisureliness she did not get from Philippe. Now that the situation had changed, Philippe's propensity for over-enthusiasm would have to be remedied. And this time she would conduct the affair right in Mexico as she intended from now on to have regular and frequent supplements to her marital diet.

Having made up her mind, Bianca immediately felt better. Being someone who acted upon decisions, she wasted not a moment when her husband woke up.

'Did you have a nice rest, darling?' she asked, munching on the third slice of caviar-laden toast.

'Yes.'

'You know, while you were sleeping, I looked at you and thought how lucky I am to have such a handsome and adorable husband.'

'Sometimes you are almost embarrassingly effusive,' Ferdie said, his pleasure evident despite this almost gruff disclaimer.

Bianca smiled sweetly, only too aware that few men could resist a compliment, no matter how extravagant or undeserved it might be. 'It's only what you deserve,' she said. 'I just wish all our friends could be as happy as we are. Especially Philippe. Poor solitary Philippe. How's he doing?'

'He's fine. Looking forward to our return to Mexico next week, he says.'

'It will be so good to see him,' she said, the conversation going exactly the way she had hoped it would. 'I've missed my old friend, as I'm sure you have. When we return, I must put on my thinking cap and come up with a nice girl for him. He's just like a pair of old furry slippers, isn't he? So warm and cosy and dependable. He'll make some nice girl a great husband.'

'I suppose that's one way of putting it,' Ferdie laughed. 'Though it would be a brave woman who took him on. He must be the ugliest man

I've ever seen. Positively simian.'

'He is very unattractive,' Bianca said, grateful for the protection Ferdie's comment provided. 'But not all women are like me. Most are attracted to what a man can give them, while all that's ever interested me is the man himself. But you mustn't get too big-headed just because you have the looks of a matinée idol and are a tiger where it counts.'

Ferdie positively glowed.

Shifting her bottom and congratulating herself on a job well done, Bianca gave a final push. 'We've seen so little of Philippe since we married. I suspect he's nervous that you're wondering if there was ever anything between us, the way Bernardo used to do. As if a handsome devil like you would ever have to worry about a monkey like him. Poor deluded Philippe. He must be so lonely without the family life we used to supply him with.'

'You know, Bianca, you never fail to surprise me. You really are so considerate. You're right. The poor guy must be very lonely indeed. I've never considered him a threat. It's ridiculous,' Ferdie grunted disparagingly, 'that any woman who wanted me could want Philippe Mahfud. When we get back home, I'll make a point of asking him to dinner.'

'Maybe we can ask him around once a week or so, in keeping with the ritual we had when I was married to Bernardo. And maybe he can come to stay at Sintra for the odd weekend. It will be our act of mercy,' Bianca said sweetly.

'I don't want to encourage him to become an appendage to our marriage the way he was to yours and Bernardo's. All that dropping in night after night isn't my style.'

'You could've fooled me,' she ribbed him gently. 'But for Philippe's propensity for dropping in, we wouldn't be married now. I'd say we have a lot to be grateful to Philippe for. But you're right. We don't want him overdoing his visits. That's why I've suggested asking him for dinner once or twice a week, with the odd weekend at Sintra. That way we establish a formula whereby he is asked enough so that he won't feel the need to exceed his ration.'

'I hope the traffic isn't too bad,' said Ferdie, who had no reservations about changing topics of conversation when they ceased to interest him. 'I don't want to be late for dinner.'

'I can't understand what you see in that father and daughter act,'

Bianca responded, picking up the ball he had thrown to her.

'It's so unlike you to take against people the way you've taken against Burt and Sarah.'

'Should I like them just because they're the Duke of Marlborough and Lady Sarah Spencer-Churchill?'

'No. You should like them because they're genuine characters and great fun.'

'Thank you. Dinner at Blenheim Palace is not my idea of fun.'

'You know, Bianca, if it weren't for your parentage, I'd swear you were anti-British. I can't think of one British person you like...aside from your father, of course.'

'Maybe I am anti-British. Maybe I find them stuffy and pretentious and not sympatico the way I find North Americans, Latin Americans, and Europeans.'

'Well, if you can't enjoy this evening, I promise you'll enjoy tomorrow.'

The following day, September 24, was Antonia's birthday. It would prove to be a day that showed Ferdie at his very best and went someway towards illustrating to Bianca why Ferdie would still have been a man worth having, even if he were penniless.

Six months before, Ferdie had come up with the idea of organizing a special matinée performance of *Hair*, the hit musical of the time, to celebrate his stepdaughter's birthday. Without saying a word to either mother or daughter, he had cleared his plan with the Mother Superior of St Mary's Ascot, then had his London Executive Assistant book the cast and theatre and to lay on luxury coaches for all the girls at the school. The afternoon of Antonia's birthday, Bianca arrived at the theatre with Ferdie expecting to see only Antonia. Instead, she saw all the students of St Mary's Ascot, who had been bussed up from Ascot to London, each bus with its own stewardess offering the girls a selection of soft drinks and refreshments.

At the theatre, the girls were presented with an array of sweets and snacks, including cotton candy, hot dogs flown over from Nathan's on Coney Island, hamburgers flown in from Ferdie's favourite diner on Third Avenue between 84th and 85th Streets in New York, plus corned beef sandwiches, bagels, cream cheese and lox from London's East End, where there were still delicatessens and restaurants in what had once been the old

Jewish Quarter.

At twenty-five minutes past two the first bell sounded. The guests made their way to their seats, and each was given a special souvenir programme commemorating the event. Then the show itself began at two-thirty.

In the interval, everyone was once more offered whatever they wanted from what was, to English schoolgirls, a staggering choice of sweets, snacks and drinks.

After the performance, they were all bused to Claridge's, where Ferdie had booked the ballroom for them to be served the most sumptuous tea any of the girls had ever had, save those royally-connected girls who were used to having tea with Queen Elizabeth The Queen Mother at Clarence House.

At six-thirty, Ferdie stood up and, clinking his teacup to silence his chattering guests, thanked them for coming to celebrate Antonia's birthday. 'I regret that all good things must come to an end,' he said, an audible hum of disappointment echoing throughout the ballroom as the girls groaned at the end of a fantastic day, 'but we've enjoyed having you, and I hope you've enjoyed yourselves as much as we have.'

Antonia, who was sitting at the head table with her mother, stepfather and nine of her favourite school friends, got up. All the other girls rose at this cue, while Ferdie crossed over to his stepdaughter, hugged her and said: 'Well, my little treasure, do you think your friends enjoyed your birthday treat?'

'Oh, Uncle Ferdie, what you've done today is the most marvellous thing in the whole of my life...'

'It really was, darling,' Bianca interjected, touching Ferdie's elbow fleetingly. 'Thank you on Antonia's behalf.'

Antonia pecked Ferdie on the cheek before turning to brush cheeks with her mother, whose firm rule was that no lip should ever touch her face in social kissing. Antonia then turned back to her friends, whom Bianca and Ferdie could overhear saying how 'cool' they were and how lucky Antonia was to have such parents. The girls trooped out, like all well-regulated school children, in an orderly if noisy fashion, while Ferdie beamed with delight at the success his idea had been. When the last of the girls had left, he turned to Bianca and asked smilingly, 'Well, my little petal, are you ready to wend your way back to the Dorchester?'

'Yes, darling,' she said, and at that moment, Bianca came closer to loving him than she ever had before or ever would again.

Chapter Eleven

Bianca broke off from kissing Philippe. She reached over to the Louis XVI bedside table and removed the lid of the small silver pot that she always kept in readiness whenever she and Philippe were about to make love. 'My magic potion,' she called it, and there was indeed something miraculous about the effect.

As Philippe's erect penis stood upright, swaying from side to side, its proud owner lay back and anticipated the pleasures that awaited him.

Bianca decorously dipped the tip of her index finger in the unguent and removed a tiny amount, rubbing it against the tip of her thumb. 'Are you ready for our favourite pleasure?' she said.

'As always,' Philippe panted, his instrument of delight pulsating.

With her thumb, Bianca touched the back of his penis where the head meets the shaft and spread a thin film of Xylocaine Jelly around the circumference, easing the unguent up onto the head, which secreted a clear liquid of desire.

Taking time to let the anaesthetic work, she slithered on top of Philippe, still lying prone of the bed, and kissed him voraciously. He responded in kind. Fortunately for Bianca, the one thing her lover no longer needed was lessons in kissing. This activity had become a sensual experience in itself. Even without coitus it was always gratifying, but now that she had devised the way for prolonging their sexual union, kissing was – as it was meant to be – the harbinger of greater satisfactions to come.

Bianca waited until she was sure the Xylocaine had taken effect before sliding down Philippe's body, her mouth kissing him on the chest, belly, groin and testicles as she worked her way downwards, till her lips encircled the shaft of his penis. Then using her teeth, she gently nibbled it. He moaned with pleasure.

'I think my Philippe deserves a little kiss,' she said girlishly, taking care to avoid contact with the Xylocaine as she inserted the very tip of his penis between her lips, her tongue darting around it.

'There's no one else like you,' he groaned, as she took in his entire manhood, her lips and tongue playing with the base of his shaft.

Bianca was nevertheless practised in the art of never overdoing a good thing. Therefore, when she judged that he was reaching the point of no return, she paused, mounted him and, using the head of his penis as a stimulant, made herself fully ready to accommodate him.

After making love, Bianca and Philippe lay intertwined together, spent and satisfied.

Ever since resuming their affair, Bianca and Philippe had devised a post-coital ritual that was completely different from the way they used to behave when she was still married to Bernardo. In those days, Philippe had always wanted to lie back with Bianca in his arms for what he termed a 'Jewish siesta', but she had always curtailed those moments. In truth, she had not wanted the intimacy such affection created, but now that Philippe had taken Bernardo's place in her mind and in her heart, she relished these moments as much as he always had. She therefore seldom got out of bed until a good half an hour had elapsed, during which time they cuddled, talked, dozed or just rested in one another's arms.

On this occasion, they fell asleep for over an hour, Bianca only awakening when Philippe started to stroke her arm and to kiss her hair.

Looking at her watch, she sprang up immediately.

'Goddamn it!' she exclaimed, 'I was due at the hairdresser ten minutes ago. I need a manicure and a pedicure, and my hair has to be done for this evening.'

'You have a quick shower here,' said Philippe, knowing how fastidious Bianca was about her appearance. 'I'll use one of the other showers.'

'Thank you, darling. You know how I hate to go out smelling of sex. It's *soooo* tacky,' she said, stylishly emphasizing the word 'so' in the same way Magdalena did.

Philippe watched admiringly as Bianca raced into the bathroom. She was in remarkably good condition for a woman of her age, not to mention a mother of three children who did no exercise aside from the occasional game of tennis or leisurely foray into the swimming pool or sea.

He felt his desire for her return. 'I can never get enough of her,' he reflected, willing the blood away from his penis. He then ambled through his bedroom and into the passage that ran the full length of the house he had bought so that he and Bianca could have privacy when meeting. He crossed into the bathroom opposite to take a shower.

By the time he was finished, she was already dressed and ready to go.

'See you at nine tonight,' she said, kissing him gently on the lips.

He started to kiss her properly.

'Don't be greedy,' she said in a joking, mock-scolding tone. 'You'll make me late.'

Breaking away, she tore down the stairs, heading for her car, which was parked in the *porte-cochère*. Once there, she flung open the door, threw herself in, pushed the key in the ignition, turned the engine of the Mercedes Benz over, jammed her foot on the accelerator as she headed at speed towards the hairdresser, grateful that Philippe was as protective of her privacy as she was. The result was that, in a country where there were no secrets, owing to the constant presence of servants, she was the one woman who had the confidence of knowing that her affair was known to no one but her lover, because Philippe always gave his servants time off when they had an assignation.

On this most crucial of days, Bianca arrived at the hairdresser flustered. This was the fourth time in less than a month that she had been late. Such unpunctuality would once have been unusual for her, but in the last year, her timekeeping had become erratic. Sometimes, the old Bianca arrived as punctually and as serenely as she used to. Other times, such as now, she was almost frenzied. 'I'm trying to do too much,' she said by way of apology to her hairdresser. 'Honouring all my commitments is making my life a nightmare.'

'It's all right, Señora,' he said sympathetically. 'You know you can do no wrong as far as I'm concerned.'

Never had anyone uttered truer words. Bianca was, without a doubt, his favourite client, and not only because she never tipped less than one hundred dollars in US currency but also because she was always so approachable, so kind, so considerate, so human. In the past, when she had always been on time, she was perfect, but now her unpunctuality made her seem more accessible. 'Poor Mrs Piedraplata,' he thought, not for the first time, 'having such difficulty coping with all the demands made upon her now that she's become so rich.' Never once did it occur to him that she might have a lover.

Of course, there was no question of someone as important as Mrs Ferdie Piedraplata being kept waiting, and as soon as she and Jorge, the hairdresser, had greeted one another, he turned her over to his assistant to wash her hair. Then it was back to him for a blow dry and a comb-out, while the manicurist did her fingernails and toenails.

Thanks to the level of care that she received, Bianca's schedule was almost back on track by the time she was ready to depart. 'I need to use the phone,' she said.

'If you want privacy, come into the back room.'

'No. That won't be necessary. The receptionist's phone will do. But first, be a dear and fish out my wallet,' she said, handing him her handbag. 'If I do it, I'll be sure to smudge my nails. Take your usual tip plus whatever this comes to.'

While her faithful hairdresser dug around in her Hermes bag in search of her wallet, Bianca dialled a telephone number with a pencil she picked up off the receptionist's desk.

'May I please speak to Luis?' she said before replying, 'Tell him it's Señora Piedraplata.'

'She must be under a lot of pressure,' the hairdresser observed, while Bianca tapped her sandaled right foot impatiently. 'It's not like her to be so impatient.'

'I'm coming by in ten minutes,' she said mysteriously. 'Please see that everything is ready and waiting for me to collect.'

Another pause.

'It's ready?' she said, as if repeating what the other person had told her with seeming pleasure. 'Good. Please have one of your men waiting outside to load everything straight into the back of the car. I'm in a rush. Thank you, Luis.'

'The things one has to do to keep people happy,' Bianca said upon hanging up, more to herself than to anyone else, but loud enough for her hairdresser to think she was speaking to him.

With that, she stretched out her hands, took her handbag from him and headed for the door. 'I'll ring you tomorrow,' she said, which he knew meant she was not sure what her movements would be before the next appointment.

Bianca ran to her car, jumped in and drove off like a maniac, headed in the direction of *Le Français en Mexico*, the capital's finest French restaurant and renowned throughout Latin America for the excellence of its cuisine. When she pulled up in front of the restaurant, one of the kitchen staff was standing outside the front door of the converted villa. Beside him were piles of boxes. Bianca screeched to a halt, jumped out and, without even waiting for the waiter to open the car trunk as she customarily did, opened it herself.

'Please pack the things so that nothing spills,' she commanded. While the waiter was loading up the car, Bianca stood beside him, hurrying him on by beating time with her fingers.

By pure chance, as she was standing there, clearly visible from the road, Ferdie's chauffeur was driving him past the restaurant from an afternoon meeting to his office. 'Ah, there's...' Ferdie started to say then, thinking better of it, stopped.

'Sir?' the driver said, looking into the rear-view mirror to see what it was that his boss wanted.

'Nothing. It's nothing,' Ferdie replied, trusting his instincts. Duarte the driver was, after all, Bianca's man. He had once been her houseboy and now was Ferdie's driver. Indeed, one of the first things Bianca had done, upon returning from honeymoon, was to employ the three servants who had been members of her staff prior to her new marriage. In those early days, while the glow of the marriage was still fresh, she had even convinced Ferdie to enrol Duarte in driving school and pension off his old chauffeur, Mario, saying that it was inhumane to have such an old man still working. When Ferdie had pointed out that Mario wanted to work, she had considerately retorted that his great age was risking Ferdie's life and her own as well as the lives of the children, especially Manolito, who was still a toddler. Thinking how considerate Bianca was, and how insensitive it was of him not to have thought that Mario was most likely only hiding his true feelings through a misguided sense of self-protection, Ferdie had pensioned him.

Next to go was Elvira the cook, who had been working with the Piedraplata family since Manny had been alive. She had stayed on to work for Ferdie after his first marriage. Having vacated the family home so that Ferdie's new wife could be absolute mistress of her own home, Anna Piedraplata had taken Elvira's assistant to her new home. Ever eager to

175

keep her adored son happy, Anna had stated that she would 'train her up' in case anything should happen to Elvira so that Ferdie would be assured of being served food prepared exactly as he liked it. In yet another instance of the thoughtfulness for which she would become so renowned, Bianca suggested to Ferdie that Elvira train her own cook, brought from the Calman to the Piedraplata households, so that she could prepare food exactly the way he liked it and his mother's old cook could return to the employ of her former mistress.

Despite Bianca's thoughtfulness, Ferdie had been developing an increasingly strong instinct over the past year that he should not trust anything about her. Although he could not put his finger on it, he had no doubt that he had picked up on something real, and it was to test this intuition that he ordered Duarte to head for home the moment he saw Bianca standing beside the open car trunk with a uniformed waiter outside *Le Français en Mexico*.

The unworthy thought had already crossed his mind that Bianca was buying in food and passing it off as her own. In yet another of the many unsolicited displays of dedication to the domestic comforts of her husband that Bianca seemed compelled to display, she had volunteered to cook dinner for their guests that evening. She had suggested quail stuffed with foie gras, followed by chateaubriand with Bérnaise sauce. Ferdie had told her, as he usually did, that there was no need for her to do so. When Bianca pulled her disconsolate face he kissed her on the forehead saying: 'If it makes you happy playing the housewife, who am I to spoil your fun?'

As Duarte drove past the tree-lined avenues, Ferdie was thinking of the many occasions upon which Bianca had played housewife. Invariably, she followed the same pattern and withdrew for the day, her explanation being that she had to do all the shopping herself because she claimed it was 'the only way'. 'Fresh produce makes all the difference to the taste,' she would argue. 'Fresh produce and loving preparation.'

Upon her return home with boxes and boxes of produce, she would retreat to the cooking quarters, which were not so much a kitchen as a separate section of the house dedicated to food, with a room full of freezers, a sitting-room and a television room for the cook and kitchen maids to occupy themselves while waiting to cook. Bianca always banned members of the family from coming near those quarters when she was cooking, stating: 'I can't concentrate when I'm interrupted.' From time to time she would emerge and seek out Ferdie for a 'break' that never lasted more than five minutes. Even then she was truly a sight to behold: her perfectly coifed hair and perfectly made-up face set off by a crisply ironed apron from Harrods in London, her hands covered in white cotton gloves from Cornelia James, glove-maker to Queen Elizabeth II.

Now the timing of Ferdie's sighting of her could not have been more disastrous. Had he seen her standing outside *Le Français en Mexico* twelve months before, he would have thought something must have happened and that she was buying in dinner. Ferdie was not a suspicious man, but he was now convinced that his wife had never prepared any of the meals for which she had taken credit. That would certainly explain why the array of cuisine over which she seemed to possess absolute mastery was so impressive, having served superb Lebanese, Thai, Chinese, Indian, Korean, Vietnamese, English, Spanish, Portuguese and American meals all to gourmet standard.

'Christ,' Ferdie said to himself, 'things have reached a sorry pass when I suspect that my wife goes around buying in food so that she can take credit for culinary accomplishments she does not possess. But who is at fault? Bianca or me?'

Not being sure what the answer was, Ferdie took steps to preserve the element of surprise as Duarte turned into their street. 'Drop me off just before you reach the gate. I'm feeling a bit tense and the walk up to the house will do me good. Also,' he added, seeing a way to get Bianca's man out of the way, 'I want you to go to the pharmacy and buy some kaolin and morphine. My stomach's killing me. If it's Señora Verde on duty, tell her I want two bottles, but if it's Señor Montero, just get me the one. I never trust his mixtures.'

Durate slowed down and pulled the car up to the kerb.

'Right here will do,' Ferdie said, opening the door before the car had even come to a complete halt, thereby forcing the driver to stop well short of the gate.

As soon as the car had actually stopped, Ferdie hopped out and tapped the roof with his open hand. 'Now don't let them keep you waiting,' he said. 'Tell them I'm in a bit of discomfort and want to take my medicine as quickly as possible.' With that, he bounded up the driveway. As he approached his family home his golden retrievers, Spot and Dart, rushed up to him silently, their tails wagging furiously in greeting. He stroked them lovingly, and they turned around and ran off in front of him in the direction of the house.

Upon reaching the house, Ferdie did not enter through the front door, as he normally would have done. He swung to the right side, where the swimming pool, pool house and tennis court were situated. Walking briskly past them, he turned to the left, cutting through the terrace where he had deprived Amanda of all hope of reconciliation.

Up to this point, he had almost been enjoying himself. Certainly it was exhilarating to take charge and, hopefully, resolve his doubts. But, seeing the location where he had called time on his marriage to Amanda, he was suddenly deflated. The thought shot across his mind that Bianca was his retribution for having dealt too harshly - and rashly - with her predecessor. Pushing that thought aside, Ferdie squared his jaw and turned the corner. He mounted the three steps up to the veranda abutting the servant's quarters. Walking past a series of bedrooms, he arrived only too soon at the doorway leading into the servant's television room, where the set was blasting away loudly.

Normally, Ferdie would have looked in and swapped a few companionable words with whomever was there. Instead he purposefully strode up to the pantry door. This led into the kitchen, and as he reached it, a rush of adrenalin enveloped him. There, on the table, were what seemed to be a plethora of boxes of varying sizes. All their lids were open, indicating that they had only recently been emptied. Beside them was a receipt, which he picked up, his heart beating wildly against his chest.

Right there, neatly laid out before his eyes, were the chateaubriand, the gravy, the Béarnaise sauce, the stuffed quail, all ready to be heated up and passed off as the handiwork of the mistress of the house. A surge of blood hit his brain. He stormed out of the pantry into the kitchen in time to see Bianca departing through the swing doors, oblivious to his presence. He noticed she was wearing her apron. A coldness settled over him. Should he confront her now, or should he wait? 'No,' he decided, 'I won't confront her just yet. Let's spin it out a little longer.' With that, he turned around and retraced his steps until he reached the front of the house, whereupon he let himself in through the front door. 'Anyone home?' he shouted 'I'm back.'

Bianca materialized, just as Ferdie expected she would. But for the apron, she was the living embodiment of high-maintenance elegance: not a hair out of place, not a nail chipped. Images of Marie Antoinette playing at rustic simplicity in l'Hameau sprang to Ferdie's mind.

'Darling, you're home early,' Bianca said, wiping her hands in her apron as if they were slightly damp from all the cooking she had been doing.

'I'm not feeling well.'

'Oh, my poor sweetie,' she said, pulling a sympathetic face. 'What's wrong?'

'My stomach's acting up.'

'Let me get you some kaolin and morphine.'

'Don't trouble yourself. You seem to have quite enough on your plate at the moment.'

'You can say that again. Those stuffed quail are a nightmare to prepare. All those bones! I tell you, after this afternoon, I could get a job in any hospital as a surgeon. But you know how much I love clucking over my loved ones.'

Just then Manolito came running into the room with his nanny, heading straight for his father, who scooped him up and threw him in the air at the last second: a ritual that both father and son adhered to every afternoon. This was definitely not the time to alter the established greeting in favour of a confrontation with a woman whom Ferdie now despised as comprehensively as he had once desired her, so he turned his attention to the dark-haired little boy.

'Must leave my boys to their play while Mama does her cooking,' Bianca said, smiling indulgently, then walked off towards the kitchen, while Ferdie and Manolito went up to the nursery.

Ferdie was deeply immersed in a game of blind man's buff when Clara telephoned from Geneva. 'Mama left this morning for Genoa. She's taking the *Cesare Borgia* and will be docking next week Saturday at Cartagena.'

Ferdie smiled. His mother did enjoy crossing the Atlantic on passenger liners. He could picture her dining at the captain's table every evening, outshining all the other old ladies with her droll, almost acerbic, take on life and her fabulous jewels, couture clothes and furs worn whenever she had the slightest excuse. 'I'll send the plane for her,' he said then lowered his voice almost to a whisper. 'You'll be pleased to hear I've decided to divorce Bianca,' he announced.

'Oh darling,' Clara said, empathizing with her emotional idealistic brother and how he must be feeling at the prospect of a third marital break-up. 'I'm sorry to hear that. What happened?'

'I won't go into the whys and wherefores now. All I'll say is that I've seen the light. You were right about Bianca. She's not all she appears to be.'

'I'm still sorry. Is there anything I can do to help?'

'No, no. I'll be fine. It's not the end of the world. I mean, it's not as if I'm losing anyone worth having. Bianca is no Amanda. Now that I've got her number, I can't wait to see the back of her.'

'What was her reaction?'

'She doesn't know yet.'

'She doesn't know yet?'

'I haven't told her.'

'Ring me back when you do. I'd like to know how she takes it.'

'It will be my pleasure,' Ferdie said, and Clara could hear from the rancour in his voice that he meant it.

Clara wanted to ask if he'd caught her with Philippe, but she was too sensitive to her brother's feelings to do so unless he provided her with the right opening.

'Can't you give me a clue as to how this came about?' she asked, hoping to start the ball rolling.

'She's been pretending to cook meals that she buys in from restaurants.'

'I'm sorry, Ferdie,' she said, bursting out laughing, 'but I've always wondered how you could possibly have fallen for that act.'

'She's an accomplished actress and very good in bed.'

'I never cease to be amazed by how a sexy woman can deceive the cleverest of men,' Clara replied. 'Still, the important thing is that you've now seen through her before she takes you for a bigger ride than she's already been doing.'

'She won't get one penny out of me, of that you can be sure.'

'She'll still be substantially better off than when she entered the marriage...'

'She'll leave with only the jewellery I've given her as well as the clothes and furs. That's not that much...'

'It's a hell of a lot compared to what she was used to before she smarmed her way into our lives...'

'But it's significantly less than she'll want. Believe me, Clara, Bianca is the most ambitious and mercenary person I've ever met.'

'Don't gild the lily, Ferdie.'

'No, I'm serious. Now that I can see through her, I have her measure better than you do. Remember, I know her better. I have almost two years of daily contact to call upon. I'm telling you, she is the most materialistic person I have ever encountered in the whole of my life.'

'Fortunately you have good lawyers...'

'I'm not worried. Money is the most eloquent force in a court of law, as you know only too well. She won't stand a chance if she turns nasty, especially with our judges. Anyway, we have people coming for dinner this evening, and I'd better get dressed before they arrive. You take care, and I'll ring you at the weekend to tell you about her reaction.'

Ferdie hung up, went straight to his and Bianca's bedroom and undressed by his side of the bed, dropping his clothes where he stood, as was his habit, knowing that one of the maids would pick them up for his valet to decide whether they need to be laundered, dry cleaned or merely pressed and hung up. This habit annoyed Bianca intensely for she could not endure the sight of a messy room. As he walked naked towards his bathroom, he smiled to himself at the thought of how upset his wife would become over his discarded clothes.

Almost gaily Ferdie sauntered into the shower. When he had finished, he dried himself and dropped the towel on the floor, again for the maid to pick up. Then he crossed to the mirror, took out his Remington and shaved, looking at his reflection in the mirror in amazement; the glow caused by feelings of liberation at the idea of a divorce from Bianca was both palpable and discernible. Could it be, he asked himself, that he was getting used to divorce, or was he simply glad to be rid of a wife he now saw as being unutterably irredeemable? He decided he did not care what the reason was. All that mattered was that he did not care. That indifference was the liberating thing. Not caring whether Bianca lived or died, whether she sank or swam, whether she lived in penury or plenitude, was such a good feeling.

Ferdie heard the bedroom door shut. Bianca had entered the room.

Almost looking forward to plunging in the knife, he unplugged his Remington shaver and splashed cologne over his face. Then he brushed his teeth, combed his hair and stepped, stark naked, into the bedroom.

Bianca was sitting at her dressing table, a solid silver intricately carved and supposedly 'important' piece once owned by the Maharani of Baroda.

Just seeing it added to Ferdie's resolve, for he had always loathed the flashiness of it, but his wife, whose taste had always inclined towards the elaborate, was not the sort of woman who could ever have enough opulence. She had bought it from Partridge's in London, despite his objections, along with a solid silver armchair that now reposed in her study, resplendent with cushions especially commissioned from Valerian Rybar, the exotic interior designer in New York. As Ferdie thought of how ostentatious they were, antique cloth of gold embroidered in silver and studded with genuine ruby beads, he wondered how he could ever have been fool enough to stump up the $15,000 for them in the first place.

Bianca looked up from her makeup mirror. This too was silver and enormous, measuring two feet in height and one foot in width, and it also came from the Maharani's palace in India. One side of it had a magnifying glass, the other an ordinary mirror; and Bianca had been rotating between the two, looking at her image with the exactitude she brought to bear upon all areas of her life. She had just finished applying a set of false eyelashes to her bottom lids in keeping with the style of the day, and nothing less than precision would do for her.

Realizing that she could see Ferdie in her mirror instead of having to turn around, she turned back to catch sight of his reflection, regretting – as she always did whenever she saw his magnificent body – how cruel nature had been to deprive her of the means to enjoy it. Catching his eye, she smiled lovingly and said: 'Is your stomach feeling any better, darling?'

'I want a divorce,' Ferdie said lightly, hoping to avert a scene.

'What?' Bianca gasped, the colour draining from her face.

'I want a divorce,' Ferdie repeated lightly, a half-smile on his lips.

Bianca started to laugh, initially out of nervousness, but then out of disbelief. Ferdie was joking. Of course, he had to be. If he'd been serious, he'd have been screaming at her the way he always did when he lost control. His sense of humour, it had to be said, was something she had never been quite able to fathom, but since she had to put up with it, she made the best of a bad deal, coping with jokes which, in her view, were never funny.

Meanwhile Ferdie remained disconcertingly cool and contained, a half-smile still playing around the edges of his mouth. In his view, this was turning out better than he could ever have predicted. 'I'm serious, you know,' he said, still lightly enough for Bianca to continue clutching at the straw that this really was one of Ferdie's dubious jokes.

More from relief than anything else, she continued laughing, the underlying suspicion that Ferdie might be serious giving her voice a hysterical edge.

Then, without saying another word, Ferdie turned on his heel and went to his dressing room, where the valet had laid out his clothes for the evening. He sat down on his stool that had once been owned by Napoleon, slipped on first his right sock and then his left, before stepping into his underwear. In that condition, he went back into the bedroom, where Bianca was applying blusher to her cheeks. He stood behind her the way he had before, once more establishing eye contact through the mirror.

'In case you think I'm joking,' he said, 'I'm not. I want you out of this house by Sunday at the very latest.' With that, Ferdie turned and walked back into his dressing room.

Bianca jumped up, knocking her knee hard on the edge of the dressing table. She barely felt the blow in her rush to follow Ferdie into his dressing room. 'What do you mean by that?' she demanded, grabbing his arm.

'Exactly what I said. I want a divorce, and I want you out of here by Sunday. If you want to go down to Sintra to collect your clothes, you can do so. Otherwise I'll have them packed and sent to you.'

'But why on earth would you want a divorce all of a sudden? This morning when your cock was in my mouth, you were full of what a wonderful woman I am.'

'That was this morning,' he replied, resolved not to give Bianca an opening she could exploit in her attempt to persuade him to reverse his decision. 'This is now.'

'But, Ferdie, this is crazy. This morning I was your beloved wife, and now you want a divorce? I think I deserve an explanation at the very least.'

'My idea of what you deserve is not the same as yours,' he answered levelly.

'Are you telling me you want a divorce without even telling me why?'

'That's about the size of it.'

'I don't understand... What's happened?' Bianca said, breaking down and sobbing.

'Dry your tears,' Ferdie said. 'You can't move me the way you've done in the past. I'm on to you now.'

But Bianca could not stop. 'I don't understand why,' she said between sobs. 'I've been an exemplary wife to you. I have to know what's gone wrong.'

'You, Bianca,' Ferdie replied. 'You're what's gone wrong.'

'Me? How have I gone wrong? I've been a loyal and loving wife to you...and I needn't remind you that you can be a handful at the best of times.'

'Well, you needn't exert yourself on my behalf anymore.'

'But I *want* to...'

'Bianca, I can see through you. To me, you're now as transparent as glass. Shall we leave it at that?'

'What do you mean by that, Ferdie? Of course I'm as transparent as glass. I have nothing to hide.'

'Here she goes,' Ferdie said, almost amused and admiring, despite himself. Given an opening, Bianca was the sort of woman who could make a man believe the sun rose in the west and set in the east. 'My decision is final,' he continued, 'and I will not countenance another word on the subject. I suggest we behave as normal for the benefit of our guests tonight, but from tomorrow, I'd prefer it if you didn't address a single word to me until your departure. I want you out of my house and out of my life. Get your lawyers to contact mine. Now I'd be most grateful if you left my dressing room. Oh...and you can move into one of the guest bedrooms for the rest of your stay here.'

Bianca looked at him, stunned. Hardly able to believe what she was hearing, she clutched Ferdie's sleeve and opened her mouth. Before she could form the words, however, he looked down, plucked her hand off his sleeve as if it were repugnant to him and pointed towards the door. Realizing she had no choice but to accede to Ferdie's demands, she walked towards her dressing table, still reeling from the shock.

What she did understand, however, was that the impact of Ferdie's words had been horrific. Her immediate instinct was to re-establish the norm - any norm - so she returned to her dressing table and tried to apply her lipstick. This simple task, however, was not as easy as it had hitherto been; her hand shook uncontrollably. Gritting her teeth, she willed it to greater stillness as she applied her lipstick, and even though she was unable to force it to stop the quivering entirely, she was gratified to see her self-possession returning.

In the years to come, Bianca would look back on that evening in late 1970 as the worst of her life. Had she sacrificed everything to be abandoned by this lunatic who wouldn't even tell her why he wanted her out of his life? Was she to lose the crown she had striven for? To be supplanted, the way she had supplanted Amanda, by another woman, who would go on to reap the rewards of being that nutcase's wife while she was exiled to social Siberia?

Bianca knew the score. No matter how much money an ex-wife had, 'ex' meant demotion. It meant being second-class. It meant being ignored and overlooked. It meant being out in the cold, just another ordinary human being: comparable to that beggar woman who had pushed her face between the wrought-iron railings of her parent's gate the day she became married for the first time, contemplating her betters as they prepared for a feast she would never enjoy.

Bianca forced herself to put on her clothes, doing so by rote. When she had finished, she sat in the bedroom which she would have to vacate later that evening, distractedly flicking through catalogues of forthcoming 'important' jewellery sales in New York, London and Geneva sent by Sotheby's, Christie's, Phillips' and Belmont's. Although she was unable to absorb anything she was looking at, save the thought that all this was being removed from her grasp, the activity itself gave her something to do. She persisted in this activity until she saw through the bedroom window the car lights of the first guest coming up the driveway. At that point, she threw the catalogues aside, smoothed down her skirt and headed towards the drawing-room, where an unruffled - indeed, contented-looking - Ferdie was sitting with a glass of scotch in his hand.

The first guests were the Swiss banker Alfred Hister and his wife, Inge.

Bianca heard herself greet them effusively, as if everything was well in her world, and it was not about to collapse. She was surprised at her ability to give such a bravura performance - something that Ferdie had expected of her. All the same, Bianca hated feeling as if her whole being had just disappeared. At the very moment that she was observing herself giving outstanding performance, she was trying to reassert herself internally.

The next couple to arrive were Raoul d'Olivera, the Mexican minister of the interior, and his wife Gloria. Raoul d'Olivera was, as Ferdie had often said, 'someone you can do business with'. He was notorious throughout the country for the alacrity with which he accepted bribes, but he was so adept at oiling the machinery of business and of government and so careful to modulate the size of the bribe so that the pain it caused was limited that he had retained the post despite successive changes in the government.

As soon as the butler showed them into the drawing-room, their hosts both went up to greet Raoul and Gloria d'Olivera. Ferdie and Bianca both appeared so normal, so hospitable and so apparently cheerful that neither the d'Oliveras nor the Histers had any clue that something was wrong. Indeed, Bianca was responding to one of Raoul d'Olivera's stories with tinkling laughter when Philippe walked in.

Normally, Bianca was deliberately tepid with Philippe when Ferdie was present. 'We don't want him suspecting anything,' she frequently used to say to her lover; and like Bernardo, Ferdie had become firmly convinced that Philippe's much-vaunted fondness for Bianca was not reciprocated. Right now, however, Bianca needed to speak to Philippe. Even as she was speaking to her guests, her mind was racing, wondering what could have brought on this catastrophic change of attitude in her husband. Was he playing a cat and mouse game with her, the reason for his refusal to give her a reason for the divorce being that he had found out about Philippe and herself? That must be why he wanted a divorce. Try as she might, she could think of no other reason. In the meantime her lover needed to be informed about this change of circumstances as soon as possible. Bianca wound up her conversation with Raoul d'Olivera and crossed the room to greet Philippe, as if she were fulfilling her duty as a hostess and doing no more.

Philippe was already talking to Frau Hister when Bianca joined them. They were discussing orchids; after greeting him, she said: 'Ah, but if you like orchids, Frau Hister, we must get my husband to walk you down the driveway to the orchid house. I adore orchids, and we've been developing a fine collection.' With that, she linked arms with Frau Hister and waltzed her off to Ferdie.

'Darling,' Bianca said, approaching her husband with a big smile on her face, 'Frau Hister wants to see the orchids. She'd love it if you showed them to her.'

Ferdie did not miss a beat. 'It will be my pleasure,' he said, ignoring Bianca and offering his arm to Frau Hister.

As soon as she had accepted it and the two of them had headed off together, Bianca crossed the room to where Philippe was now deep in conversation with Raoul d'Olivera. 'Do you gentlemen mind if I break up this conversation for a minute?' she asked charmingly 'I need Philippe to help me with something.'

The minister of the interior clicked his heels, bowed his head and said: 'I must see what my wife and Señor Hister are up to. Do excuse me.'

'I think Ferdie might be on to us,' Bianca said as soon as the minister had withdrawn. 'He's told me he wants a divorce, but he refuses to say why.'

Philippe was surprised, but nothing Ferdie did ever shocked him. He'd grown to know him too well. If Ferdie suspected his wife and his partner were having an affair, it would be just like him to turn out his marital partner first before turning on his business partner.

'When did this happen?'

'About an hour ago.'

Philippe cast his mind back to the events of the day. That very morning, he and Ferdie had had a personable chat in his office at Banco Imperiale. Everything had been absolutely ordinary, and Philippe did not think that Ferdie actually possessed the skill to dupe him if there was a problem between them. So whatever it was had happened that afternoon.

'I don't suppose he saw you leaving my house,' Philippe offered.

'I don't know. I *never* know his movements for the day.'

'What do you want to do?'

'I don't see why I should be cast out like Amanda, but what can I do to preserve my position? Maybe I should have him committed? Do you think we could get a friendly psychiatrist to lock him up?'

'That wouldn't work,' Philippe replied. 'Clara and his mother would simply throw some money around, and then they'll all be after your blood. What we need to do is remove him from the scene in a way that leaves everything else intact. You do realize that if he divorces you, we're both done for? Ferdie's much too proud a man to give one penny of alimony to a woman who's deceived him. And I don't see him allowing me to remain a partner one second longer than it suits him. He'll set up my financial execution and enjoy it too. We're staring annihilation in the face, Bianca. You do realize that, don't you?'

'I do,' she said, turning pale again.

'Has he set a timeframe?'

'He wants me out of here by Sunday.'

'And the terms?'

'He said I'm to get my lawyer to get in touch with his.'

'He means business. Does anyone else know?'

'No.'

'Not even the servants?'

'They definitely haven't overheard anything. He told me so casually that I actually thought he was joking at first.'

'It's good if no one else knows but us.'

'What can we do?'

'I have the germ of an idea. I'll think it through over dinner and tell you afterwards. I can tell you right now, though, what we can't do. We can't see or speak to each other after tonight until our problem has been solved. No telephone calls. No visits, especially in the afternoon,' he said with a regretful smile before looking Bianca squarely in the eye and adding in very deliberate tones: 'In life, circumstances sometimes force people to do things they normally wouldn't do. Do you understand what I mean?'

'I'm not sure I do,' Bianca said, looking decidedly uncertain.

'Drastic situations call for drastic measures.'

Bianca nodded her head.

'We both accept that something has to be done to maintain the status quo, don't we?'

'I suppose so,' she said, still not exactly sure what he was getting at.

'You trust me to solve this problem in such a way that neither of us loses out?'

Bianca nodded again.

'On the face of it,' Philippe continued, 'the only solution I can think of is a permanent one.'

'Of course it must be permanent,' Bianca said, not understanding what Philippe was getting at.

Checking the room to see that no one was observing them, 'Sometimes "permanent" means "point of no return",' he said.

'There must be another way,' Bianca gasped, finally taking in what Philippe had been getting at.

'And if there isn't?'

She grimaced. 'My God, Philippe, the very idea makes my stomach turn.'

'This is not the time to fall to pieces. You've got to be strong and keep a clear head. And you must act as if everything's all right. Smile. Be brighteyed and carefree. Now let's go over and engage d'Olivera in conversation. We don't want Ferdie seeing us together if we can possibly help it. But we must talk after dinner, so find a pretext for us to be alone.'

Dinner, for Bianca, was a torment, but for Philippe, it was nothing more or less than an exercise in problem solving. If love barely existed where Philippe was concerned, friendship did not exist at all. Since Ferdie Piedraplata was nothing more than a vehicle through which he could make money, he could contemplate the removal of his senior partner with a chilling degree of dispassion. There was, in his view, only one solution to their current problem; and he and Bianca both knew it. The practicalities of removing someone permanently were not something he had ever confronted before, but Philippe, like many other bankers who invested the private fortunes of wealthy private clients, had a great many contacts from all walks of life, including the seamier side of society.

One such contact was his client Antonio Gagliari, a cousin of the famous Gambino family in New York. Gagliari liked to think that people in Mexico City considered him a businessman, when in fact everyone knew he was a front man whose business interests were the means by which his mob connections laundered some of its ill-gotten gains. In the business community, it was an open secret that he had arranged, over the years, the murder of three business associates who had tried to rip him off. However, like many a Mafioso, unless you crossed Antonio Gagliari, he was honourable, and polite and scrupulous in his dealings. His reputation, of course, had never mattered to Philippe and Raymond, or indeed to Ferdie, all of whom followed the precept that there was no such thing as tainted money.

By the time dinner was finished, Philippe had a plan. As soon as they all rose from the table, he asked Ferdie - not Bianca - if he could use the telephone. It was important that he and Bianca were not seen to be colluding with one another, and he couldn't very well use someone's telephone without their permission. Ferdie's reaction could not have been more normal. 'You old goat you,' he laughed. 'Making a midnight rendezvous with a hot little number, are you? Use the telephone in my study. That way none of the ladies can overhear you.'

More convinced than ever that Ferdie knew about Bianca and himself, Philippe headed towards the study and sat behind his host's desk. He took out his handkerchief, covered the receiver of the telephone with it and then, removing his Mont Blanc fountain pen from his pocket, used it to dial Antonio Gagliari at home.

The butler answered. 'Tell Mr Gagliari that Señor Piedraplata wishes to speak with him,' Philippe announced then waited for him to come to the telephone.

'Ferdie,' Antonio said when he picked up the receiver. 'This is a surprise. What can I do for you?'

'It's Philippe Mahfud, not Ferdie. I'm calling from his house. We have a little problem, and we need some assistance with it.'

'What sort of problem?'

'The problem isn't the problem; it's the solution. We need a permanent solution, and we need it quickly.'

'How quickly?'

'Friday.'

Antonio Gagliari sucked in air between his teeth. Philippe heard it clearly. 'I have a friend who might be able to assist you. I suggest you meet him on neutral territory. Somewhere crowded, like a busy street corner. Say the corner of Ascencion and Madrigal.'

'That will be fine.'

'Eleven o'clock tomorrow morning?'

'I'll be there.'

'Wear a white carnation in the lapel of your jacket and carry a rolled-up newspaper under your right arm. He'll approach you.'

'Ring me at home later. Say after midnight, if that's not too late for you.'

'We're night owls in this family.'

'How much will the service cost?'

'Why don't you credit an extra $25,000 to my account in Geneva, and we'll forget we ever had this conversation?'

'Thanks for your help, Antonio. It's much appreciated.'

'Think nothing of it, Philippe. We businessmen have to stick together and help each other out when we can.'

When they hung up, Philippe let out a sigh of relief. 'My God,' he thought, 'he didn't even want to know the identity of the person we're wasting.' That level of professionalism took the breath away. It was just another contract.

The delicious irony of arranging a contract on someone from the victim's own desk was not lost on Philippe. He almost felt sorry for Ferdie. Almost: but not quite. With a sense of accomplishment, Philippe walked back outside. He had always wondered if he could kill someone.

Now he knew the answer.

Chapter Twelve

Duarte dropped Ferdie off at five-forty five sharp, as was his habit. Instead of taking the car to the garage at the back of the house before having a relaxing drink in the servant's television room, he followed Bianca's instructions, issued at midday when she had sent him to Sintra to pick up a dress she wanted to wear the following evening.

His instructions were to drop Ferdie at the front door and leave immediately to collect Bianca and Manolito at the house of Señor and Señora d'Olivera. To ensure that Duarte would not dally, she had specifically forbidden him from entering the house, even to use the lavatory, telling him if he did so she would dismiss him instantly. Knowing that Bianca, for all her generosity, would carry out her threat if she ever discovered that he had deviated from her orders even slightly, the chauffeur adhered to them punctiliously, as Bianca knew he would. The virtue of having well-trained servants was that you knew precisely how they would react.

As soon as Ferdie was out of the car, he sped off. Duarte did not realize that Ferdie was now walking into a house where there were no servants at all, all of them having been given the afternoon off while he was en route from Sintra to Mexico City with the dress that Bianca had ordered him to collect. The last he saw of the Señor, therefore, was when he looked in his rear-view mirror and saw him entering the house through the front door.

Ferdie walked into the hall. The house was still, but that was not unusual. Stillness is always an overriding characteristic of big houses with a lot of staff, no matter how many people buzz around in the background.

This is one of the less renowned perks of great wealth, so even though it may not buy happiness, it can and frequently does buy a superficial calm born of a well-tended and structured environment.

'I'm home,' Ferdie shouted, the cue for Manolito to come bounding up to him. He did not know that his son was at the d'Oliveras', although he was aware that Raoul d'Olivera's driver had taken his son there, along with Bianca, that afternoon.

Nothing.

'Manolito, Papa's home,' he shouted expectantly.

Still nothing.

No Manolito, no dogs. The latter must be having a bath, Ferdie presumed, knowing Bianca's mania for cleanliness. She insisted that the dogs be bathed twice a week, which, he knew, was not good for their coats. Fortunately it was now only a matter of time before he and the dogs were rid of her. What he did not know was that she had locked the dogs in the laundry room, having given them, in typical Bianca fashion, raw prime ribs of beef to keep them quiet.

Ferdie listened carefully. He could vaguely hear what sounded like a television set playing in the nursery. 'Ah, Manolito must be up there,' he decided, and set off down the passage past his office, heading towards the stairs which led to his son's room. Ferdie's last thought was of Manolito, his last sight the Louis XIV console table with its vast arrangement of orchids, ginger lilies and cocoa leaves in the passage just past the door to his office.

No sooner had he passed that office than the hitman, wearing surgeon's gloves, stepped out of the room into the passage behind him. He knocked him out with one blow to the back of the head, delivered with Ferdie's own gun. Philippe had informed the killer where he would find it. With consummate professionalism, the assassin bent down, removed Ferdie's Gucci loafers to prevent them from scuffing the carpet as he dragged him upstairs and, careful not to dislocate Ferdie's shoulders lest the pathologist do a thorough job at the autopsy, grasped him from the front under his armpits and pulled him up the stairs to his bedroom.

Once there, the hitman hauled Ferdie up onto the bed. Placing a silencer on the gun, he stood over him momentarily then briskly put the muzzle directly onto Ferdie's ribcage over his heart. To ensure that serendipity could play no part and that Ferdie might somehow survive a bullet delivered at point-blank range into his heart, he pulled the trigger twice.

Blood oozed from Ferdie's chest cavity onto a counterpane that Bianca had ordered to be specially made at Porthault. The hitman, satisfied that he had accomplished his task, pulled back Ferdie's eyelids to check that he was dead. Then he removed the silencer, placed the gun in Ferdie's left hand and ambled out of the house so unconcernedly that an onlooker would have taken him for a lazy servant dragging his heels in the performance of his duties.

At the gate, the killer sauntered out into the street with all the casual ease of a servant going home for the evening. He continued to amble down the street until an old pink Pontiac passed him, coming to a stop. To an onlooker, the driver appeared to be offering him a lift. He jumped in, and the two men drove off, again at a slow enough pace to avoid notice.

Bianca looked at her watch. It was only a quarter past six. Her servants were off until seven. There was little prospect, therefore, of them returning before that time. She knew that on no account could she return home until after the servants had done so. How could she stretch out this visit for another hour? Whatever Gloria d'Olivera's virtues, they did not include wit or sparkle, and the conversation had been so leaden that Bianca already felt as if she were an athlete pushing a two-ton cannonball up to the top of a mountain peak.

Just then the d'Olivera butler came to inform his mistress and her guest that Duarte had arrived. 'Give him a cool drink,' Gloria d'Olivera responded, 'and tell him the Señora will be with him when we've finished out chat.'

In desperation Bianca decided she must do something to remove the possibility of any suspicion in the future that she had lingered on selfservingly.

Pressing her right hand against her temple and covering her right eye and forehead with her fingers, she said: 'You know? My head's been bothering me slightly all day. I really should've gone to bed in a darkened room... That's the only thing that works when you get a headache...but not for anything would I have missed the pleasure of seeing you here, in your own home...'

'Can I get you some aspirin?'

'That would be kind,' Bianca said as her hostess pressed the buzzer on the wall three times.

'It's tension, of course,' Bianca said. 'I don't think I'm being disloyal to my husband if I tell you something you most likely already know. He suffers from depression and he has these "turns"...'

'I'd heard that his health fluctuates...'

The butler appeared again in the doorway. 'Please fetch some aspirin for Señora Piedraplata,' Gloria d'Olivera ordered imperiously.

The butler nodded assent.

'Ferdie's started another of his depressions,' Bianca confided. 'He can be very trying when the mood takes him...the tension is probably the reason that I'm having this headache.'

'My poor friend, is there anything I can do?'

'Would it be too great a liberty to ask you if I could lie down in one of your guest rooms for an hour or so? If I could just rest for that amount of time, it would make all the difference.'

'My dear, of course you can. Come with me.'

Gloria led the way to a bedroom at the back of the house overlooking a courtyard. The minister's wife proudly indicated an imperial-sized double bed. Bianca winced, not out of pain but because the lady's taste was so execrable that even Bianca was revolted by it. The furniture staring her in the face was a caricature: an over-carved, overpainted, over-gilded, over-sized bedroom suite in a blend of the worst features of the Rococo period. 'And I thought the drawing-room was tasteless,' Bianca thought to herself, knowing that her hostess would be waiting for a compliment.

'What an inviting bed,' Bianca said in her most dulcet tones, as she congratulated herself for not actually having lied. 'I'll bet Señor Cassia made it.'

Señor Cassia was Mexico City's premier purveyor of carved furniture, most of which was crudely and hastily executed at extortionate prices for the *nouveaux riches* to procure as future antiques for their progeny.

'He did,' said Gloria d'Olivera proudly. 'In fact, he carved all the furniture in the house.'

'You mean, both the drawing-room furniture and this?'

'Oh, no, my dear. I mean the furniture in each and every room of our home, except, of course, the servant's quarters. That we got at Calorblanco,' she said with a nervous little laugh.

Bianca clutched her temple and winced again. 'I mustn't laugh,' she said. 'It makes the pain worse. But Calorblanco...that is funny.'

'Laughing hurts me too when I have my headaches. Come, my dear, lie down here,' Gloria said, making to turn down the bedspread.

'No need to bother,' Bianca said. 'I'll just lie on top of it. Will you wake me up in an hour?'

'Seven-twenty it is then. I'll have your aspirin sent in to you right now.

'If you need anything else, please don't hesitate to let me know.'

'You are too kind,' Bianca said sweetly, beaming her a tiny smile of gratitude.

As she reclined on the bed with her eyes closed, images of what was happening – or had happened – at her house flashed past her eyes. Was Ferdie being strangled? Shot? Was he being hacked to death with a machete? Try as she might, she could not put the images out of her mind.

Finally, sick to her stomach, she rushed to the lavatory and threw up. As she was kneeling on the floor over the bowl, it occurred to Bianca that this unintended proof of illness was providential. Vomiting, after all, was evidence of a severe headache. So, fastidious though she normally was, and sickened though she would ordinarily have been by what she was about to do, she allowed some of the vomit to miss the lavatory. It trickled down the front of the bowl to the vibrant green pattern of the tiles on the floor. Bianca returned to the bed and lay down again, waiting for the wakeup call. At exactly seven-twenty five her hostess knocked softly on the door and opened it quietly, saying: 'Time to get up, Bianca.'

Bianca made a great display of slowly opening her eyes, as if she had been in a deep sleep. 'Is it time already? I'm feeling much better now, though I have to warn you, I had a little accident in your toilet, and I've left a bit of a mess on the floor.'

'Think nothing of it,' Gloria said graciously.

'I don't know how I would've managed without you,' Bianca said, getting up and slipping on her red and navy Ferragamo shoes. 'Thank you so much.'

'Would you like something before you go?'

'It's kind of you, but I think not,' Bianca replied, advancing towards Gloria, who picked up the cue and started to escort her towards the front of the house. 'My husband is waiting for us. His greatest joy is playing with

Manolito. I've already eaten into an hour and a half of his time, so we mustn't inconvenience you further.'

'It's been a pleasure, my dear. While you were sleeping, I checked at the back of the house where Manolito has been playing with the cook's three-year-old son. They've been having the time of their lives.'

'I'm so glad you're like me. I always let my children play with the servants' kids. It's good for them to grow up being able to relate to all categories of citizen, I believe,' Bianca said.

Just then Manolito came into the hall with the butler. 'Mama,' he said excitedly, obviously pleased to see his stepmother. She tousled his hair and drew him to her so that she could snuggle with him while standing up. 'I hear you've been a very good boy and you've been having a very exciting afternoon,' she said, 'but the time has come to say goodbye to nice Señora d'Olivera. Now be a good boy and hold out your hand the way Mama has been teaching you and shake hands like a proper English gentleman.'

Gloria smiled as Manolito extended his little hand. 'What an adorable little boy he is,' she said.

'Yes. Daddy and I love him madly. Don't we, my darling son?' Bianca said, stroking his hair while thanking her hostess for having had them for tea. She then took the child by the hand and walked towards the vehicle whose engine Duarte had running.

Manolito, of course, was not Bianca's son at all, but she had grown to love the little boy. Moreover, the way she had come to be his 'mother' was not her fault at all, but Ferdie's. Manolito had remained more attached to Amanda than to Bianca, so he had taken steps to ensure that his new wife would become Manolito's primary mother by instructing his lawyers to inform his ex-wife that it would be in everyone's best interests if she saw her son only twice a year. Furthermore Ferdie had stipulated in his will that, if he should die before Manolito achieved his majority, his custody of the child was to be transferred to Bianca.

Now, as Bianca journeyed home with Manolito to face the outcome of Philippe's plan, her thoughts turned to Amanda and her predecessor's relationship with the little boy. If Ferdie were indeed dead, he would inherit half his late father's assets, the other half going to his widow. Amanda, as his mother, would have control over all the child's assets unless Bianca could obtain guardianship of the boy. She only hoped that Philippe had this complication under control, otherwise she could foresee

Amanda becoming a problem for the remainder of their lives.

By this time, Duarte was steering the car into the driveway of the Piedraplata family home. 'The place is crawling with police,' Bianca remarked, steeling herself against what she was about to discover. 'I wonder what's happened.'

'I don't know, Señora,' the old retainer replied. 'Everything was fine when I dropped Señor Piedraplata off.'

The driver pulled the car up under the porte-cochère, jumped out and made to open his employer's door. Before he could do so, however, a policeman beat him to it.

'What's happened?' Bianca asked.

'Who wants to know?' the policeman retorted.

'I am Señora Piedraplata.'

'I'll take you to my captain.'

'What's happened?' Bianca demanded, determined to display what she judged to be the correct level of innocent ignorance. 'I want to know.'

The policeman suddenly softened. 'The captain will tell you, Señora,' he said with a mixture of kindness and embarrassment as he escorted her into her own drawing-room.' Please wait here.'

'Where's the boy's nanny?' she asked.

'The captain will explain everything.'

Bianca took a seat in the wing armchair nearest the door, her right leg crossed over her left, swinging it nervously. Manolito sat beside her. Ominously, she noted that none of the servants were anywhere to be seen.

Before three minutes had elapsed, the captain was standing in front of an increasingly unsettled Bianca. 'What in God's name is going on here?' she asked, covering her nervousness with irritability.

'Señora, it is with a heavy heart that I tell you that your husband has been found dead with a gun in his hand...'

'What?' she spluttered, genuinely shocked despite her knowledge of what would happen and blanching without any pretence.

'I am sorry to have to bring you this news...'

Manolito started to cry. Although he did not understand what was happening, he was picking up on the tension and reacting accordingly.

'It's OK, darling,' Bianca said soothingly. 'This nice man isn't going to hurt you. He's just here to make things better.' Changing tone, she looked at the captain and continued: 'We can't speak about something like this in front of the baby. Where's his nanny?'

'She'll be with you soon.'

Bianca got up and, rocking Manolito, dedicated herself to soothing him, grateful for the distraction. Her heart was beating furiously, her hands shaking like an alcoholic's. Meanwhile the policeman hovered nearby, eyeing her up and down.

The nanny arrived. She handed Manolito over, kissed him goodnight.

'You go to sleep now, darling,' she said, 'and remember that Mama loves you.'

The captain watched the child putting his arms around Bianca and kissing her lovingly on the lips before he toddled off with the girl. Señora Piedraplata was clearly a family woman whose conduct fell outside the realms of suspicion.

'Where did he shoot himself?' Bianca asked as soon as the nurse and child were out of the room.

'In your bedroom, Señora, but you mustn't see him. It would be too upsetting for you.'

'No. I meant where on his body did he shoot himself?'

'Through the heart.'

'Are you sure he's dead?'

'You can't shoot yourself through the heart and survive, Señora. I'm sorry, but there's no doubt that he's dead.'

'He really meant business, didn't he? I suppose I always knew he might kill himself. He suffers from manic depression, you know,' she said, careful to inject the present tense the way a grieving widow might who had been surprised by a husband's tragic death. 'Up for several months and then crashing suddenly...the deepest darkest depressions you can imagine. Oh, my poor Ferdie. When did it happen?'

'The servants discovered the body when they came back on duty. They say Señor Piedraplata had given them the afternoon off.'

'That's right,' Bianca said. 'He's the most considerate employer, as all Mexico knows... If he were going to do something like that, he would never have involved anyone else.'

'So he knew you were going to be out?' the captain said, his tone slightly too official for Bianca's taste. She could see that he was used to viewing everyone connected with an incident as a potential suspect, and this did not make for a comforting experience.

'Oh, yes,' she said, dabbing at eyes that stubbornly refused to disgorge the tears that normally flowed so easily. 'He insisted I take Manolito. I went to visit Señora d'Olivera, you known, the wife of the minister of the interior.'

'That would fit in with the scenario,' he said. 'Would you like me to call your doctor?'

'That won't be necessary. I never take drugs. Not even tranquillizers. But I would like a stiff drink. Where are the servants?'

'They're being questioned separately. We need to satisfy ourselves as to what happened, and, unless they're questioned one by one, we can't rely upon their accounts of what happened.'

'Have you notified my husband's partners yet?'

'No.'

'I think you ought to. Not only are they great personal friends but my husband's death also has the potential to affect the economy of our country unless his partners can stabilize things. I'd say that ought to be a priority on both the personal and national levels.'

'Where would they be now?'

'I'll give you their numbers,' Bianca said then proceeded to do so, giving Raymond Mahfud's before Philippe's.

The captain of police telephoned Raymond. 'We'll come over right now,' he said as soon as he heard what had happened. 'My brother is with me as I speak. Tell Señora Piedraplata. She must be in a state. She was so in love with her husband.'

Making a mental note to include that comment of Raymond Mahfud's in his report, the policeman rang off. 'Is there anyone else you'd like me to contact?' he asked.

'It's OK, thank you, Captain. You have a lot to do. I'll contact the family myself.'

'If you'll excuse me, then, I'll go back to the bedroom.'

Bianca brought her handkerchief up to the corner of her right eye and dabbed at it, as if tears were forming there. Without waiting for the captain to leave the room, she walked over to the telephone on the Louis XV writing table, picked up the receiver and dialled. 'Operator? I'd like a number in Switzerland: Geneva 3642. Person to person to the Marchesa d'Offolo. My name is Bianca Piedraplata.'

The policeman left the room while Bianca was waiting for the connection, preparing herself for the exchange with the sister who was not only her adversary but who also adored Ferdie.

Clara came on the line. 'This is an unexpected surprise,' she said before her sister-in-law could say anything.

'Bitch,' Bianca thought, knowing very well that Clara had a low opinion of her.

'I have some bad news for you,' she said in a concerned tone of voice, taken aback at how pleased she was to be in the position to inflict pain upon someone whose good opinion she had formerly desired. 'Ferdie committed suicide an hour or two ago.'

'I don't believe it,' Clara said quietly.

'It's true. The police are here. They say he shot himself through the heart. I haven't actually seen him...they won't let me...but I don't think they'd say something that wasn't so.'

'Did you hear the gunshot?'

'No. I wasn't here. I was visiting Raoul d'Olivera's wife Gloria.'

'Put me onto the police. I need to know what happened.'

'They're very busy at the moment. They just told me to phone the family and let you all know what's happened.'

'Has Mama been told yet?'

'You're the first person I've called.'

'Don't tell her. Her heart wouldn't stand the shock. I'm going to try to get a flight out as soon as I hang up. I'll be with you as soon as I can. I'll meet her ship at the dock next Saturday. Please arrange for her doctor to be at the house when I get her back there. We can break the news to her after he's sedated her.'

'That old bat doesn't deserve a daughter like you.'

'Don't worry yourself with the details of the funeral,' Clara continued, doubting that a woman who was about to be divorced would wish to be bothered with organizing one for the man who about to dump her. 'I'll arrange it all when I get there.'

'That's sweet of you.'

'I'll call and let you know when I'm coming,' Clara replied, putting aside her dislike of Bianca at this most poignant of moments. 'Till then, take care. And don't, whatever you do, speak to the press. They'll only twist anything you say, and it could have devastating consequences for Calorblanco and the banks.'

'Thanks for the advice, Clara. It's so good to feel that I can rely upon you to protect me,' Bianca said, not without a measure of irony.

'As I said, you needn't worry yourself about the funeral arrangements. I'll attend to them when I arrive. Bye, Bianca.'

'Bye, Clara,' she said, hanging up, her feeling of triumph mixed with a sickened sensation. What had she got herself involved in?

Mindful of how injudicious it would be to turn for support to Philippe, Bianca's next telephone call was to her ex-husband. Bernardo had moved to Panama earlier that year and was due to be married soon, but she knew that he would come running to her at a time like this. She needed only to ask. 'Bernardo, I need you and the children to come and be here with me by Sunday at the latest. Ferdie has killed himself, and I cannot cope without your support. Can I rely upon you to make the arrangements?'

Bernardo was in the process of assuring his ex-wife that he would do everything in his power to be there, with all three children, by Sunday when Raymond, Begonia and Philippe arrived at the house. Still on the telephone as they were shown into the drawing-room by a policeman, Bianca gave them a wan little wave and a tight smile and motioned them to sit down.

When she rang off, she went straight to Philippe. He got up, hugged her. Then she broke down and started to cry.

'It's unbelievable,' Begonia said.

'I had no idea,' Raymond said.

'None of us did,' Philippe responded.

'I'm not that surprised,' Bianca said, bursting into more tears. 'Suicide is always a danger with manic depressives.'

'Do your parents know?' Philippe asked.

'Not yet.'

'I'll ring them,' he said.

'Get them to spend the night with her,' Begonia suggested. 'You don't want to be on your own tonight of all nights, Bianca.'

'That's true,' Bianca replied.

As their father had arranged, Julio, Pedro and Antonia all flew into Miami that Sunday afternoon. Bernardo was there to greet them, having arrived that morning from Panama. At six o'clock that same evening, they boarded a Pan American airways flight to Mexico City. By the time they had arrived, cleared Immigration and were waved through Customs, it was after midnight. Then it took another fifty minutes to reach the Piedraplata residence.

Bianca was waiting by the front door, dressed in a Pucci black and white trouser suit, when Duarte dropped them off.

Julio was the first one she greeted. She hugged him, squeezing him tightly in that old familiar way she had with him. It had never occurred to her that Pedro and Antonia, whom she never greeted so keenly, might notice the difference and be jealous. Where her relations with her children were concerned, their mother, who could be so sensitive to the thoughts, feelings, and needs of others, was somewhat insensitive.

'What can I say, Mama? You must be devastated. We all loved Uncle Ferdie. He was a great guy,' Julio said, making way for Antonia, who was crying.

Bianca hugged her perfunctorily, this gesture of affection so tinged with carelessness that her daughter quickly stepped aside for Pedro to have his turn.

'Mama, I'm so sorry. I know how much you loved Uncle Ferdie,' he said, in turn stepping aside quickly before his mother could chill him with a hug that invariably had all the sincerity of a greeting between rival socialites at a cocktail party.

Bernardo was now standing directly in front of her. 'I knew I could count on you,' she said gratefully, and as she hugged him, she realized for the first time ever that she was well and truly over him. It was like hugging a brother, someone you loved, wanted to see and could count upon.

Patting Bernardo on the back in a sisterly fashion, Bianca pulled away from him. 'Come, let me show you to your rooms,' she said, as gracious as ever. Bernardo instantly noticed that his former wife had changed since the time of their divorce. 'She's even more confident than she was when we were married,' he reflected, surprised that anyone as confident as she had been could have become even more so in two short years.

She put Bernardo in the guest suite, the place where she had spent the nights of exile from the marital bed preceding Ferdie's death. It was a spectacular suite, consisting of two bedrooms and a shared bathroom and sitting room, situated at the opposite end of the house from the suite she had shared with Ferdie. The children she scattered in the three remaining guest bedrooms.

'We don't need all this space,' Bernardo said, thinking he was being helpful.

Bianca, however, had a plan of her own. 'Of course you do,' she said. 'I can't have you all return from halfway across the world then squeeze you into tiny guest bedrooms.'

The real reason why Bianca needed to use up all the guest facilities in the Piedraplata family home would soon become apparent when Clara arrived in Mexico City.

Clara's flight landed on the evening of Tuesday, November 24 1970.

Accompanied by her husband, Rodolfo d'Offolo, and her daughter Magdalena, she had not expected her sister-in-law to meet them personally at the airport. Sending Duarte would have been more than enough. However, as Clara stepped out of customs, there stood Bianca, waiting patiently for them, a tight little smile conveying bravery in the face of adversity, as the porter wheeled out their baggage.

Bianca and Magdalena fell into one another's arms.

'I'm so sorry, sweetie pie,' Bianca said. 'I know how you felt about your uncle and how he felt about you.'

Magdalena started to cry. 'I can't believe it,' she said between great wracking sobs.

'I know,' Bianca said, patting her on the back comfortingly. 'That's how I feel too. We were so happy together. If it hadn't been for his damned depressions, we wouldn't be in this situation now.'

Magdalena and Bianca released one another, leaving Clara and Bianca face to face. To Bianca's surprise, Clara stepped up to her and embraced her for the first time ever.

'It's hard on us all,' Bianca said.

'You can say that again,' Clara replied, pulling away. Bianca could tell that her sister-in-law was not comfortable displaying affection towards her. But she had done so, and that was to the good.

'Bianca, you have our sincerest condolences,' Rodolfo said, leaning down to pick up his hand luggage with his left hand and Clara's jewel case with his right.

'Thank you, Rodolfo,' Bianca said, waving Duarte over to pick them up.

While the porter was loading their luggage into the trunk of the car,

Bianca turned to Clara and said sweetly: 'Where are you going to sleep tonight?'

'The usual, I should think,' Clara replied, thinking that Bianca had meant which bedroom in the Piedraplata family home did she wish to occupy. This, of course, was the same guest suite that had been allocated to Bernardo, but which all the members of the Piedraplata family invariably called 'Clara's wing'. Whenever she was visiting the family in Mexico City, Clara and her current husband had always occupied one bedroom in the suite, Magdalena another; and they had always treated the sitting room as their own private fiefdom. That way, they remained together, had their privacy, did not get in the way of the remainder of the family but nevertheless had a place in the family home: one that Clara partly owned.

'Dear Clara,' Bianca said, fixing the other woman with a gaze of concern and sincerity. 'I wish I could put you up, but my whole family has descended upon me, and there just isn't room for anyone else. I hope you don't mind. I couldn't very well tell my family they can't stay with the widow in an empty house because I have to keep it vacant for the sister-in-law when she arrives. I'll see that you're booked into the Presidential Suite at the Hotel Imperiale. You'll be very comfortable there. And, of course, the business will pick up the tab... I only bring up the money so that you'll see that I'm doing everything in my power to make life as comfortable and agreeable for you as possible at this most difficult time.'

Deciding that it was better to say nothing, Clara simply glared at Bianca, scarcely able to believe her ears. Maybe Bianca wasn't such a brainless opportunist after all. They got into the car.

'Have the police had the autopsy results back yet?' Clara asked.

'Yes,' Bianca said quietly and started to sniffle as if she were about to break down crying.

'Well...what did they say?'

Bianca's sniffles increased. 'This is so painful...' she said, trailing off.

'I know it's difficult for you, but it's also difficult for me,' Clara replied. 'He was my brother, after all, and I knew him a lot longer than you did. If I can grit my teeth and face facts, then so can you. *Courage, ma cherie.*'

Bianca looked over at Magdalena as if she wanted to be rescued. 'If Bianca finds it all too difficult to speak about,' the younger woman said 'maybe you should ask someone else, Mama.'

'I think if Bianca knows the results, she should tell us,' Clara said.

'The autopsy shows that he shot himself through the heart,' Bianca said with evident agitation, knowing that it was better if her sister-in-law heard it from her first. 'You know how thorough Ferdie was. He made sure he didn't botch the job. He shot himself twice.'

'Twice?' Clara said, shooting a look across at Rodolfo, who sat opposite her in the back of the Lincoln Continental. 'What was the range?'

'Point-blank.'

'Twice through the heart at point-blank range?'

'Yes.'

'It's not possible.'

'Anything was possible with Ferdie. He was the most exceptional human being...and nothing if not thorough. You of all people know that only too well.'

'My dear Bianca,' Clara said icily, 'thoroughness is a matter of character. Death is a matter of fact. Dead people cannot shoot themselves. Anyone who is shot through the heart once cannot shoot himself again in the same organ.'

'Why would anyone want to kill Ferdie?' Bianca asked so innocently that Clara became convinced that she must have had a hand in her brother's death.

Clara decided to play her cards close to her chest. 'You know, Bianca,' she said in an almost patronizing tone, as if she still took Bianca to be the imbecile, 'Ferdie was a very successful businessman. He must have had many enemies. Any one of them could've killed him.'

Bianca's response reaffirmed Clara's earlier hunch that Bianca might have had something to do with her brother's death. 'No,' she said, shaking her head violently. 'Everyone loved my husband. He was the most revered entrepreneur in Mexico. It's not possible. And,' she added, a triumphant note creeping into her voice, 'to show you how completely wrong you are about anyone else having a hand in his death, did you know he cleared the house of everyone before he did the deed? That's right. He sent me to Raoul d'Olivera's house with Manolito. He gave all the servants the afternoon off. He made sure the house was empty. Is that the conduct of someone who intends to kill himself or someone who sits in wait for an imaginary killer? No, Clara, your theory defames and dishonours my husband, and I will have none of it.'

'You have a unique perspective,' Clara replied witheringly, 'but I don't propose to get involved in a brawl with you.'

'It's going to be a busy few days,' Magdalena said, hoping to channel the conversation away from controversy, 'what with making the funeral arrangements and all that.'

'Your mother very kindly offered to help when we first spoke, but I've been muddling through on my own. Decisions had to be made, and I couldn't leave things until you arrived. The funeral's scheduled for next Monday. The cathedral. Three o'clock. The archbishop will take the service. Philippe and Raymond will read lessons, and so will Raoul d'Olivera. The president and two of the Orleans-Braganza princes from Brazil are coming,' Bianca said sweetly, looking at Clara.

At this point in the conversation the limousine pulled up in front of the hotel, and Clara hurtled out of the car before Bianca could even draw breath. 'A wife of less than two years and about to be divorced, and she's the one taking over the funeral arrangements of my brother? I don't think I've ever encountered such gall,' Clara said to herself, trying to shake off the dirty feeling that clung to her after this encounter.

'There'll be no need to come in,' she said to Bianca. 'You must be very tired. Go back to my family home and get a good night's sleep. And thanks for coming to meet us at the airport. I appreciate what you did,' Clara added, delivering the *coup de grâce* and hoping Bianca would understand the implications of what she was saying.

'It's so nice to be appreciated,' Bianca said warmly, 'and yes, I am very tired. I can't wait to get back to my home and collapse into my bed,' she continued, replying to Clara's pointed claim to joint ownership of the family home. 'Call me tomorrow when you surface.'

Of course Bianca had no intention of keeping someone as astute as Ferdie's brainy sister at anything less than arm's length, so, the following day, when Clara telephoned, Bianca had the butler inform her that she was not feeling well and was in bed. To maintain the illusion of family solidarity Clara in turn left an ostensibly friendly message, asking that her sister-in-law call her when she was up and about. The remainder of the day was so busy that Clara did not notice until ten o'clock that evening that Bianca had not returned her call.

The main reason why Clara had been so distracted was that word had spread in Mexico that she was in town, staying at the Hotel Imperiale, and by midday the trickle of friends and business associates had become a flood.

After that, even if Clara had wanted to get away from the many callers, it would have been difficult to do so. The Mexican custom of dropping in to pay their respects to the members of the deceased person's family – and for that family to reciprocate by showing hospitality – ensured that she was constrained to uphold a custom that also conveyed the regard in which people had held her brother. The widow, on the other hand, was not receiving callers and remained cloistered with only her children, ex-husband and parents for company, having instructed the servants to direct all callers to Clara at the Imperiale.

By the end of that first day, Bianca had established a pattern that kept Clara out of her way while allowing her to present herself as the grieving widow to a wider public. Not that Clara was starved of information on what was going on in Bianca's household. Magdalena was spending much of her time at the Piedraplata family home. Her daughter, like many of her peers in full rebellion against the authority symbolized by her parents, could see every side of every question except that of her own mother. 'I feel sorry for Bianca,' she said on the night before the funeral. 'At a time when she needs all the help she can get, not only does she have to contend with a sister-in-law who doesn't like her, but her son Pedro decides to flip his lid.'

'I'd be a lot more convinced by this grieving widow act if I didn't know that your uncle intended to divorce her,' Clara replied, well used to Magdalena's cutting remarks. 'But what's that you say about Pedro's flipping his lid?'

'He's flipped his lid. Gone crazy. Loco. We were sitting around the pool having coffee after lunch. Bianca and Philippe came out to join us. Bianca said something to the effect that Uncle Ferdie could be a real bastard at times. Pedro said he'd always liked him, and she replied: "Of course you did. He was always very nice to you. But then, he would've been. He identified with you. He felt you were both victims. But the truth is, neither of you has ever been anyone's victim." Pedro just went crazy. He accused her of never loving him. Of never loving Uncle Ferdie. Bianca started to cry, but this only made Pedro even angrier. He said: "What are you crying for? You never loved him, and you don't love me. You only married him for his money. You broke up our family so that you could social climb." Bianca started to cry even harder. Philippe tried to intercede, but Pedro wasn't having any of it. He told him to keep out of it and said to Bianca: "You can't fool me. I know the way you function. Don't think we didn't figure out what was going on between you and Uncle Ferdie this summer. You think we couldn't tell that he was getting fed up with you? He could see through you just the way I can. He knew he couldn't trust those smiles or tears of yours, and I'll bet you had him killed because he wanted to be rid of you." I tell you, Mummy, you could've heard a pin drop as far away from as Geneva when Pedro said that. Bianca looked as if he'd slapped her hard in the face. She was completely shocked and appalled...like a doe caught in the headlights of a car on a highway.'

'What did Julio and Antonia say? For that matter, what did you say?'

'Julio said Pedro should keep his voice down before the servants heard what he was saying. Antonia and I said nothing, but Philippe said: "This is a terrible accusation for a son to make against his mother. It's immoral and obviously untrue. She was with the wife of the minister of the interior when Ferdie shot himself." Pedro started to laugh and said: "You're a man of the world, Philippe. You know as well as I do, you don't have to pull the trigger yourself to kill someone. This is Mexico, man. You can hire anyone to solve any problem. Well, dearest Mama, your problem's solved. You don't have to put up with Uncle Ferdie any longer, and you've got his money, which is all you ever wanted from him in the first place. You even have the best alibi anyone in Mexico could come up with. The wife of the minister of the interior, indeed! Unfortunately, whoever shot Uncle Ferdie was too efficient, and only a fool would buy the explanation that he shot himself through the heart twice just to make sure he was dead." Bianca was wailing like a baby by this time, so Philippe said: "You don't have the right to speak to your mother like this." Pedro looked at him very scornfully and said: "You're just like my father. You'd swallow any line she comes up with. Well, work it out for yourself, Philippe. How is it possible for a right-handed man to shoot himself through the heart with the gun in his left hand? Then, to compound the impossibility of it all, he repeats the process a second time? Come on, this is bullshit. Someone killed Uncle Ferdie, and if Mama isn't behind it, she'll use some of that money she's going to inherit to get Uncle Ferdie some justice. The guy deserves it.'"

'Well, I don't believe it,' Clara said, shaking her head before continuing,' Out of the mouth of babes and sucklings...so what happened next?'

'Nothing really. Philippe took Bianca inside. Julio, Antonia, Pedro and I stayed outside, and Pedro and Julio lit up a joint.'

Magdalena, knowing that her mother disapproved of the custom of marijuana smoking, expected her to launch into her usual homily about the evils of the weed. This time, however, she totally ignored it. 'Are you telling me that Julio and Antonia didn't disagree with their brother,' she merely said, 'or argue with him or anything like that?'

'No. They just ignored it.'

'So they think Bianca killed your Uncle Ferdie too. Every word Pedro said was both true and fair. You do realize that, don't you, Magdalena? Even down to the fact that Uncle Ferdie was going to divorce her.'

'How do you know that?'

'Because, my dear child, your uncle telephoned me two days before he was murdered and told me that that was what he was going to do. He said he was giving Bianca until Sunday to move out of the house. Two evenings later, he's dead. Well, we'll just have to see what we can do about bringing his murderers to justice. One thing's for sure. This was no accident. And more than one person was involved.'

Chapter Thirteen

A rich man's funeral is always an event no matter how little or how much he was loved. It is his leave-taking of the world, the yardstick by which everyone measures him: the richer the man, the greater the event.

While Ferdie's funeral was heartrending for those who loved him, they could take comfort from the small things, even as the humblest mourner does. Whatever her flaws, Bianca's sense of showmanship ensured that the service had the flair that was already one of her most pronounced characteristics. There was only one word for the funeral: magnificent. It was a leave-taking fit for a king. The cathedral was packed. Not only was the president of Mexico there, along with five - not two, as Bianca had told Clara - members of the Imperial Family of Brazil but also people as disparate as Prince Johannes von Thurn und Taxis; Ferdie's two ex-wives, Gloria and Amanda, and just about everyone else he had ever done business with, entertained or been entertained by.

The islands of people clustered around the cathedral told their own story, but by far the largest group consisted of the workers of Calorblanco who had drawn lots for places in the cathedral in the lottery which Raymond and Philippe, in conference with Clara, had judged to be the fairest way of deciding who should be inside and who outside. Those who lost out listened to the service over loudspeakers along with the thousands of Mexico City citizens who had come along to witness the spectacle of Mexico's richest man taking leave of this world.

The Archbishop of Mexico, assisted by twelve priests, gave a rousing sermon about the transience of this world and the unimportance of its goods. This message contrasted with the splendour of his robes, but what was even more striking was that he took the mass at all, for suicides were not supposed at that time to be buried according to Catholic rites in consecrated ground. The Archbishop, however, had circumvented that troublesome point by making a passing reference to the dangers of cleaning your gun and how easy it was for accidents such as this to be mistaken for something more ominous. This remark was greeted by a collective intake of breath on the part of the richer members of the congregation, all of whom started wondering how large a donation Bianca or Clara or Anna Piedraplata had been obliged to give to the church to ensure Ferdie a Christian burial. The answer was $30,000, paid out of Bianca's own pocket.

This sum was insignificant compared with the $30,000,000 that was being paid into an account Philippe had opened for Raoul d'Olivera with the Banco Imperiale in Geneva at the same time as the minister of the interior was standing in the pulpit, reading the First Lesson from 1Corinthians: 'Though I speak with the tongues of men and of angels, but have not love, I have become as sounding brass or clanging cymbal...'

The morning after Ferdie's death, Mexico City's chief of police had arrived at the Piedraplata house to question Bianca. Not realizing that she was the prime suspect in her husband's murder, she had invited him into the drawing-room and had offered him coffee.

He had started the interview by saying, 'Señora, we're not here on a social call. We have reason to believe that your husband may not have committed suicide. We need an account of all your movements for the last seventy-two hours.'

'I don't believe this,' she said, startled by this new development.

'Where were you yesterday morning?' he continued harshly.

Harshness had always brought out the rebel in Bianca. As soon as the chief of police's tone became abrasive, she felt her blood rise. 'If you're going to treat me like a common criminal,' she said, jumping to her feet and crossing to the telephone, 'you'll have no objection if I wait until my lawyer and my husband's business partners come here before answering any more of your questions.' She called her lawyer, Juan Gilberto Macias, first. He said he would be with her in as many minutes as it would take for his driver to get him across town. He also warned her not to say anything to the chief until he arrived. Then she rang Philippe and asked him to come over with Raymond. 'I'll do better than that. I'll ring Raoul d'Olivera and get him to call his bloodhounds off the scent. Just stall for time until Raoul orders that creep to leave you alone.'

Philippe then telephoned Raoul d'Olivera, who had been waiting for this call and had already instructed his secretary to interrupt whatever he was doing if Señor Raymond Mahfud, Señor Philippe Mahfud, or Señora Piedraplata should ring him.

As far as the interior minister was concerned, this was the big one: his once-in-a-lifetime opportunity to make a killing. In a manner of speaking, he had been waiting all his professional life for this one telephone call. He had always taken bribes in the certain knowledge that one day someone would need so huge a favour that he would be able to throw caution to the wind and overcharge with the same degree of exactitude that he had limited his takings in the past. Year in, year out, he had garnered a reputation as someone with whom everyone could do business while patiently bearing in mind that his reputed lack of greed would ideally place him to demand the ultimate bribe.

Soon after the police had realized that Ferdie Piedraplata had died from a gunshot wound to the heart, the officer in charge had telephoned the chief of police, who had in turn alerted Raoul to the death. This was routine procedure. The fact that the richest man in Mexico had died from unnatural causes made it imperative that the minister of the interior and the chief of police would be involved, and, once the former was informed that Ferdie had died from unnatural causes, he instructed his subordinates to keep him closely informed. Before Ferdie's body had even been transported to the morgue, Raoul d'Olivera knew that there was little prospect that his death was anything but murder. This belief was reinforced when the officers interrogating the servants provided the information that Bianca had given them the afternoon off, claiming that it had been upon Señor Piedraplata's orders.

Raoul almost admired Bianca's audacity in establishing an alibi for herself at his own house. Clever, yes – but not so clever that she hadn't left her tracks uncovered elsewhere. Already Ferdie's lawyer, Ignacio Ribero, had provided him with the information that Bianca and Manolito were the sole beneficiaries of Ferdie's Mexican estate. That alone was motive enough for his widow to have him killed. 'Had Bianca been a truly clever woman,' Raoul reflected, 'she would have persuaded Ferdie to give the servants the time off himself. But she cleared out the house herself. In so doing, she's made it easy for any prospective prosecutor to create a strong circumstantial case against her. The question isn't whether a jury would find her guilty: it's whether she would wish to be tried for murder.'

Having a crystalline view of Bianca's predicament, the minister of the interior then ordered the chief of police himself to interrogate her. This was nothing more or less than the exertion of pressure, for who else could Bianca turn to for protection against the chief of police than his superior, the minister of the interior?

The timing of the plan was so smooth, so subtle, so sure that Raoul would have derived pleasure from its execution had he not genuinely liked Ferdie Piedraplata. Whatever his failings Raoul d'Olivera was not an evil man, nor was he a callous one. But business was business, so when the call that he hoped would change his life for all time came, Raoul answered chirpily.

'Philippe, dear friend,' he said, as if he had no clue what the other man might want from him. 'What can I do for you?'

'I've just had Bianca on the phone. She says the chief of police is interrogating her about Ferdie's suicide in a manner that makes her wonder if he doesn't suspect her of having a hand in it.'

As Philippe was speaking, Raoul remembered the gossip about him being in love with Bianca. Of course, it would make perfect sense for her to get Philippe to arrange the hit.

'Have they detained her?' he asked, deliberately keeping such things in mind.

The very idea filled Philippe with horror, as had Raoul hoped it would. 'Good God, no,' he replied. 'They're questioning her at home.'

'That's their job, Philippe. Don't you know that more murder victims are eliminated by members of their own family than by third parties? Bianca is the person who profits most from her husband's death. For what it's worth, Philippe, the police are quite rightly looking at Ferdie's death as a possible homicide.'

Philippe had to be careful – very careful. 'Raoul,' he said, 'you're a man of the world. A woman like Bianca simply isn't used to being treated like a common criminal. As Ferdie's partner and friend, I feel it's my duty to protect her now that he's no longer around to do so. I know you're a man of kindness and understanding, and I'm prepared to show you my appreciation in any way you'd like. My own suggestion is that you instruct the chief to desist from asking questions that only upset her. Put yourself in her shoes. Her husband's just committed suicide. She'd worried that people will think that she drove him to his death by making his life miserable. She's caught between the devil and the deep blue sea, so to speak. On the one hand, if she justifies his cause of death as suicide, she opens herself up to accusations of being a bad wife. On the other hand, if she argues that one of his enemies killed him, she's dishonouring his memory. I'm sure Ferdie would want me to obtain your cooperation, to ensure that his wife doesn't have to face that kind of lurid questioning, especially at a time when she's coming to terms with such a sudden and tragic loss.'

'There's also another dimension to this,' Philippe continued, without pausing for breath. 'Think of the effects such an investigation will have financially. It will be disastrous. For Calorblanco. For the banks. For the employees. For the economy. For Mexico. Ferdie's dead and gone. It's never been a secret that he suffered from depression. It's really best for all concerned that he's left to rest in peace, which is what he wanted, after all.'

'He's good,' Raoul thought. 'He's very good.' The underlying hint of the bribe was unmistakeable. 'I agree that this is a difficult time for Bianca,' he replied, 'and, of course, I feel for her as a friend. But just as I can't allow my friendship with her to influence the police investigation, equally I have a duty to consider the wider issues, and how they affect the financial security of this country.'

'The people of Mexico will be sincerely grateful to you for protecting their interests. I know how public-minded you are. I've been thinking of suggesting to you for a long time now that we establish a foundation for you to use to endow whichever charitable causes you wish to support.'

'Your idea of funding a foundation for me to benefit the deserving in this country is just the sort of public-spirited initiative that we need,' Raoul said. 'It's a brilliant idea, Philippe, but I think it would be better for the future recipients of the foundation if it's set up outside Mexico, possibly in Switzerland, which is so economically stable. That way we guard against the economic downturns which have been such a feature in this part of the world over the last decade.'

'Agreed. I'll get in touch with my people in Geneva and make the arrangements for the funds to be transferred into the name of a foundation of your choice...'

'I suppose you'd prefer that we keep the existence of this foundation and the donations it makes to the needy secret?'

'Of course,' Philippe agreed. 'We don't want the taxman getting in on the act and taking his slice of a cake that should remain in the hands of the needy...'

'Since it's going to be doing such good work, I'd rather like the foundation to bear my name...'

'Why don't we make things even simpler? Geneva can open a numbered account with you as the ultimate beneficiary...that way you'll have absolute control over all the funds and you can be as discreet or as open as you wish with your donations...no one but you and your bankers need ever know the source of any of your donations, unless, of course, you want to go public with them... If you have a numbered bank account, all the activities of the foundation will retain the element of anonymity. As you're the only person who will have control over those funds, you'll be, so to speak, your very own, personal charitable foundation...'

'Good thinking,' said Raoul.

'Now all we have to do is agree on what the starting sum is.'

'That's right,' Raoul said, letting his words hang in the air.

'I think something in six figures would be a healthy start for all the good works you will do,' Philippe replied, jumping right in.

Raoul did a quick calculation. Calorblanco and the banks in Mexico alone were known to be worth over $400,000,000. Bianca would be the beneficiary of half of that. He had no doubt that Ferdie would also have salted away vast sums abroad. Raoul laughed pointedly and without amusement. 'My good friend, if one wishes to be charitable, one needs at least seven or eight figures. We must think of all the good we're going to do for the needy.'

'I don't know that the funds will be available for an endowment on that scale...' Philippe began, realizing that this was going to be harder than he thought.

'That's quite all right, my good friend,' the politician said with an ease that he both did and did not possess. 'We're only bouncing around ideas that have emanated from you. If something isn't to your taste, that's fine by me. I needn't remind you that everything, from the initiation of this conversation to what we're now discussing, has been at your instigation.'

Philippe was quiet on the other end of the line. Raoul, however, was used to the various techniques employed by people wanting favours. Sure enough, just before Raoul ran out of patience Philippe said, without any hint of emotion: 'I suppose the party in question could rise to the low sevens if necessary.'

'I myself was thinking more of the mid eights...' Raoul said, so lightly they might have been speaking about $50,000 US instead of $50,000,000.

Once more Philippe took his time before replying. This time Raoul almost enjoyed the delay as he savoured the moment that might lead to the big one. He could taste adrenalin on his palate. He started to beat a jaunty rhythm on his desk with his index and third fingers.

Hearing that, Philippe understood that Raoul was giving him a message – that he could either take it or leave it. His aim was now to make the best of a bad deal for Bianca 'I don't see how it would be possible to manage more than five...' he said, refusing to succumb to the pressure that his adversary was imposing upon him.

'Tut, tut,' Raoul said without missing a beat on his desk.

Philippe, realizing that he had failed in his objective, decided to let Raoul wait before he upped his offer. It would be a petty victory, but a victory nevertheless, and a man of his stature required that he win at least some of the battles in any war, whether they seemed pointless or not.

Therefore, Philippe dragged out the interval until it was almost unacceptably long before saying: 'Well, maybe she can go to eight.'

Raoul continued beating out his rhythm on the desk.

'I don't see how anyone could manage more than ten.'

'It would be a real trial if the needy had to manage on such a small endowment,' Raoul said, emphasizing his words carefully.

'Not even Onassis could manage more than twenty-five,' Philippe said in a pained tone of voice.

'But Onassis isn't the one who wants to share his wealth with the needy of Mexico,' Raoul replied, still without closing the deal.

Philippe now fell silent while he thought through the situation. There could be room for manoeuvre further up the ladder: with the president, if necessary. 'Thirty is my final offer to you,' he said, putting all his emphasis on the pronoun.

Raoul got the message. 'Done,' he said. 'You set up the deal as you suggested, with one proviso. Banco Imperiale Geneva must confirm to the Kritzler Bank in Zurich at the opening of business tomorrow that they have the sum available for account number 74963271.'

'Good,' Philippe said. Then, because he was sure the politician must be feeling magnanimous after such an astounding victory, he said: 'You know, Raoul, it would honour Ferdie's memory if you could give a eulogy or read a lesson or do whatever it is you Catholics do at funerals. I know it would mean a lot to Bianca.'

'I'd be honoured to take part in the funeral service. Ferdie was a good man, and I was genuinely fond of him. Respected him too. Tell Bianca to get in touch with my secretary, who will then make all the arrangements.'

Within minutes of their conversation the minister of interior telephoned the chief of police at the Piedraplata family house. 'How's it going?' he asked without preamble.

'We're waiting for Señor Juan Gilberto Macias. When he comes, I'll start.'

'You know, I've been giving this some thought. The more I think about how things have gone, the more certain I am that Ferdie Piedraplata did indeed commit suicide.'

'But Señor, it's not possible...'

'I knew him very well, and believe me, it's possible.'

'But how could he?'

'Stop and think about it. The man was a suicidal depressive. He wanted to die.' Then, earning the money he had just acquired for himself, he lied and said: 'I've heard him say a hundred times that he would eventually kill himself...not that I want you to broadcast that all over town. The last thing I need is to have my name brought into this mess. But what better way to kill yourself than the way he did?'

'It's a fact that suicides are very angry people. I suppose that, if he felt that his wife had let him down in some way, he could have hired someone to do the deed in such a way that he could wreak his revenge on those he thought had failed him.'

'You have more experience of this sort of thing than I do. But it has the resonance of truth, I'd say.'

'We are dealing with someone who was highly intelligent and imaginative...' the chief replied.

'And also vengeful... I'd say it's the perfect way to commit suicide, if you have all the money in the world and no one you want to live for.'

'You've saved me a lot of time and effort, Señor d'Olivera. But that's the advantage of having a boss who knows the subject we're dealing with.'

'My suggestion to you now is that you go back to her as soon as you're off the phone and tell her that you're satisfied with her reactions then leave before her lawyer gets there.'

The moment the chief of police departed, Bianca headed straight for the telephone and dialled Philippe's number.

'Well?' she said as soon as his secretary had put him on the line.

'It's done...but it wasn't cheap.'

'How much?'

'Thirty big ones.'

'That's not so much,' she said, thinking he meant thousands.

'It's a good fifteen percent of your Mexican holdings.'

Bianca felt her temperature drop as the enormity of the sum she was paying for her freedom sank in. 'But that's highway robbery,' she said.

'There wasn't any alternative. He made it crystal clear that he would step aside and watch the police do their damnedest, if I didn't agree that figure.'

Just then Juan Gilberto Macias entered the drawing-room. Bianca waved him over. 'Listen, I have to go,' she said, winding up the call. 'My lawyer is here. We'll speak later. But thanks. I really appreciate your efforts.'

'Before you go, I have one bit of good news. He agreed to read a lesson, or whatever it is Catholics do, at the funeral on Monday. You're to get in touch with his secretary to finalize arrangements. Do it today. We don't want him changing his mind. His contribution at the funeral will quieten any gossip.'

It was on the evening after the funeral, when Clara and her husband Rodolfo were changing into more comfortable clothes in their suite at the Hotel Imperiale, that they received the first in a series of mysterious phone calls. They came at ten-minute intervals. All that could be heard at the other end was someone breathing quietly without ever once uttering a word. After three hours of this, Clara instructed the hotel switchboard not to put through any more calls. Another call immediately came through. 'Hello,' she said, thinking that it must be Magdalena or someone else whom the switchboard recognized. But before she could say anything more, a man with an educated but harsh voice cut her off.

'If you value your life,' the man said, 'you'll leave Mexico tomorrow with your husband and daughter. If you don't, we can't be responsible for what becomes of you.'

'Who is this?' Clara asked.

In answer, the line went dead.

Clara promptly dialled the switchboard. 'Operator, didn't I tell you not to put through any more calls?'

'We're sorry, Señora, but it was from the police.'

'How do you know?'

'The caller said so, Señora. Besides, you can always tell when it's the police. The line has a different sound. It's like the telephone company line. You can't disconnect them, but they can disconnect you. It's different from an ordinary call.'

That night Clara immediately made arrangements to charter a plane to fly her husband, daughter and herself out of Mexico the following afternoon.

Chapter Fourteen

Flee. There was no other word for it. Along with Rodolfo and Magdalena, Clara fled to Miami, where they spent the night, before catching a connecting flight to London. Even as they were crossing the Atlantic, Magdalena still did not want to believe that Bianca could have played a part in her uncle's death. Whatever doubts Rodolfo and Clara might have had were dispelled by the threat to their lives.

The first thing Clara resolved to do after they arrived in London was to ensure that the Piedraplata family fortune was safely under her control.

Later that morning, she telephoned Hannes Veitbech, the managing director of Calorblanco Switzerland, and, after discussing the quandary with him, she decided to avail herself of the much-vaunted protection the English legal system afforded her.

Because Bianca was clearly enjoying the protection of the Mexican authorities, London seemed to be the place to spearhead any legal action Clara might undertake. All she needed to do was find a good set of lawyers. With that in mind, the first thing she did after checking into her usual suite on the fourth floor of Claridge's, was to telephone the uncle of her former sister-in-law, Amanda.

'Hello, this is the Marchesa d'Offolo. May I please speak to Lord Paulington?' she said to the refined voice that had answered the telephone.

The English custom of having well-bred young ladies work as junior secretaries until their marriages had always struck Clara as a sensible one. That way, the girls learned how to deal with a multiplicity of people in a variety of situations and to develop a sense of calm which was in marked contrast to those unmarried Latin American and Mediterranean girls for whom work was a proscribed activity.

Solicitude evident from the first word, the welcome voice of Piers Paulington came on the line. 'Clara. I am so sorry to hear about Ferdie. Dastardly business, killing himself.'

'He didn't, Piers. He was murdered. That's why I'm phoning. I need you to recommend a good lawyer. Someone unconnected with Calorblanco, Banco Imperiale or Banco Mahfud. Someone who can mount an action to protect my family's interests against the widow and our partners. Someone of absolute probity but with a killer instinct.'

'Henry Spencer's the man you need. He's sharp as a pin intellectually but a man of probity. He's the senior partner of Henry Spencer and Co in the Temple. His father was Attorney General during the reign of King George V, and the firm is sound. Solid as a rock.'

'Do you know him well?'

'Absolutely. He's a member of White's and Boodle's. I see him all the time. If you'd like, I'll ring him right now and tell him you want to see him. When will you be in London?'

'I'm here already. We arrived a short while ago. I'm staying at Claridge's,' she said then recounted how she had been forced to flee from Mexico.

No more than five minutes elapsed from the moment Clara hung up before Piers Paulington called back to say that he had made an appointment for her to see Henry Spencer within the hour.

Fifty minutes later, Clara and Rodolfo entered the central hall at New Court at the Temple, the ancient legal chamber beside the River Thames, where they were directed to the offices of Henry Spencer and Co. As soon as Clara gave the receptionist her name, she and Rodolfo were shown into the Honourable Henry Spencer's office. This *éminence grise* of the English legal profession was tall, slim and sallow, with a great beak of a nose and the manners of a courtier. Here undoubtedly was a pillar of the Establishment: a figure of rectitude. Someone you could trust. He received Rodolfo and Clara with the cultivation of a lifetime of considerate concern, and, within minutes, Clara was unburdening herself, sure that she was in safe and capable hands.

'Marchesa, this is a difficult one,' he said, peering over his pince-nez, when Clara had completed her explanation. 'I don't think there's any merit in accusing your sister-in-law outright of murder. Rather, what we should try to do is get to her in a roundabout way. Through your brother's assets. Unravelling ownership of offshore shell companies is always a difficult task. However, by the sound of it, we at least have jurisdiction, albeit in a qualified way. My advice is that I write to the executors of your brother's will, affirming your and your mother's claim to continuing ownership of your portions of all the properties and companies in which you both had a share with your late brother and asking for an account of all the assets and funds jointly held.'

'That will set the cat among the pigeons,' Clara said.

'We need to smoke them out. If there are any irregularities with joint assets, that will go some way towards contaminating her profile. Also, we want to discourage an attempt on their side to gain possession of assets that are already beyond their ambit. I'd say it's a fair assumption that someone who can kill her husband will defraud his family. It's up to us to make that as difficult for her as possible; it's been my experience that the longer someone is in possession of assets to which they have no legal entitlement, the harder it is for the legal owners to regain possession of them. We must therefore move quickly.'

'Possession being nine-tenths of the law,' Rodolfo said.

'Quite so, Marchese,' Henry Spencer said, looking from Rodolfo to Clara. 'Why don't I draft a letter this afternoon and get it sent over to you at your hotel for your approval? If it's acceptable, we can send it off first thing tomorrow morning.'

'That sounds fine,' Clara said, rising to her feet, aware that Henry Spencer would charge her for every second that she spent being cordial to him. 'Thank you very much for seeing us at such short notice.'

'Always happy to help out an old chum like Piers. I understand you're related through marriage.'

'Yes,' Clara said, the realization hitting her for the first time that, now that Ferdie was dead, Amanda, by right of being Manolito's mother, should have custody of him and thereby control of his share of her brother's fortune. During the dramas of the past few days, she had never once thought of that.

As soon as Clara returned to Claridge's, she telephoned Amanda, who was still in Mexico. Sure enough, Amanda had already raised the matter of care and control of Manolito with Bianca. She had done so the very day Clara, Rodolfo and Magdalena had fled so precipitously from Mexico. Amanda had gone to the Piedraplata family home to see Manolito and make arrangements to take him back to England with her.

To her consternation, Bianca said: 'Manolito's now my son. He barely knows you. He's attached to me, and Ferdie left me custody in his will. I believe the clause says that I am to bring him up in the event of anything happening to Ferdie.'

'You can't inherit custody of someone else's child,' Amanda pointed out sharply.

'I can, and I have,' Bianca said, dropping her voice and coating it in candy. 'It's my duty as Ferdie's widow to fulfil his wishes. It's also my duty, as the only mother Manolito knows, to protect his family life. He has his brothers and sister here. We all love him. And, what's more, I'll bring him up to be a true Piedraplata. If you have him, you'll bring him up to be a little Englishman, in defiance of Ferdie's specified wishes.'

'Bianca,' Amanda said, the blood flooding into her face, 'my custody arrangements with Ferdie were private. They have never had the force of law. You don't have a right to my child, and I want you to hand him over to me this afternoon.'

Bianca's response once more flabbergasted Amanda. She smiled kindly, brushed her hand over her right cheek and said, even more sweetly than before: 'Amanda, I respect your instincts as a mother. But you must realize that I share those instincts and feel exactly the same way as you. Let's not fight over this. Why don't we work out a new arrangement? Something that is a perpetuation of the old one but gives you more time with Manolito. Say, four times as much time as you had before? And, I have to tell you,' she said confidingly, 'you've had my sympathy and my admiration ever since I discovered the harsh deal Ferdie cut with you over Anna Clara. Now that Ferdie's dead, I think we women ought to stick up for each other, and do what's right by each other. With that in mind, I'd like to create a trust fund for Anna Clara. The trust fund Ferdie should have created. A million dollars in trust. You keep half the income until she turns twenty-five, at which point the capital and the other half of the income will go to her. It's only fair, don't you think? After all, she's a Piedraplata too. It was,' Bianca continued, scrutinizing Amanda's face for an indication of how she was receiving this offer, 'a very unfair thing that Ferdie did to you and that sweet little thing.'

'I've set my heart on getting Manolito back,' Amanda said, thinking that Bianca's reputation for munificence was well deserved, 'though what you suggest with regard to Anna Clara is very generous.'

'Don't let's fight over this. Even if I felt differently about Manolito, I'd be honour-bound to respect Ferdie's wishes where his upbringing is concerned. If you take me on, I'll have to respond accordingly. Only the lawyers will benefit, Amanda, and, after they've stripped you of as much money as they can, the custody arrangements will be no more generous than I'm proposing and will most likely be a lot worse. You don't want to fight a Mexican in Mexico, do you? Think about it. You'll be jeopardizing a large part of your overall worth against someone whose resources, compared with your own, are limitless.'

'I'll have to speak to my lawyer,' Amanda said.

'To show my good faith, why don't I say that the offer remains open for twenty-four hours? I'll have Juan Gilberto Macias draw up a draft agreement and send it over to your lawyer later today. Look it over. Speak to him. We can have this put to bed by tomorrow. Anna Clara will be secure for life, you'll have greater access to Manolito, and we'll be friends.'

'And after twenty-four hours?'

'I'd prefer not to go into that, and hope you won't want to either,' Bianca said levelly. 'And Manolito stays here till we come to a final agreement.'

The agreement, which Juan Gilberto Macias drew up that same day, gave Amanda everything that Bianca had promised. In return, it required Amanda to surrender guardianship of Manolito to Bianca along, by implication, with all his assets.

Seeing no prospect of mounting a successful challenge against the might of the Piedraplata name in the Mexican Courts, Amanda signed the document in her lawyer's office with a heavy heart the following morning.

It was only after she had returned to her hotel that she found out how utterly her successor had outmanoeuvred her. Clara telephoned her, with the eye-opening news that she had fled to London and needed her former sister-in-law's help in securing the Piedraplata family fortune against

Bianca, who had plainly had Ferdie killed with Philippe's complicity.

This call was the first time that Amanda had heard that Ferdie had died by anything but his own hand. 'You're Manolito's legal guardian,' Clara said. 'He's inherited half of Ferdie's assets. Bianca is sure to seize whatever she can, and she'll have Philippe's assistance in doing so, unless we join forces and block them.'

'How do you mean?' Amanda enquired.

'You're responsible for Manolito's fifty percent of Ferdie's assets. I'm responsible for my percentage of the companies, which amounts to another third. Bianca only has half of Ferdie's third share in the companies. If we join forces, we have more than fifty percent, so we'd have control of everything.'

'And there's your mother's share,' Amanda added.

'We'd better keep that out of the equation. She doesn't even know how Ferdie really died, and I don't want her to find out. It will kill her if she does. And you know how much she enjoys causing mischief for me.'

'But, Clara, I'm no longer Manolito's legal guardian.'

'Of course you are. Who told you that you aren't? Not that jerk Juan Gilberto Macias.'

'I signed my rights away earlier today.'

'*What?*'

After Amanda explained what happened, Clara said: 'Phone Ferdie's lawyer, Ignacio Ribero, right now and get him down to the courts. If the Deed hasn't yet been ratified by a judge, it will only have the strength of a contract and not the force of a Mexican court. We can get it overturned on the grounds of deception or some such thing. We don't have a second to waste. If the judge has already ratified it, there's no reversing that. Call him as soon as I hang up and make sure he goes right down there right now.'

Two hours later, Amanda telephoned Clarita with the news. Juan Gilberto Macias had taken the Deed of Transfer of Custody down to the court for ratification as soon as she and Bianca signed it. It had been ratified within an hour of signature.

'I can hardly believe the speed with which Bianca has accomplished such a polished move. It's too effective to have been hatched by that birdbrain. I can't see Juan having any incentive – not even the money – to come up with a scheme like this. I detect the hand of Philippe Mahfud behind this,' Clara rightly concluded.

For her part, Amanda was also incredulous. 'What have I done?' she kept on repeating over and over again. The enormity of it was almost beyond absorption. But the deed was done, and there was nothing either of them could do about it.

Seven days later, Henry Spencer's letter arrived on Juan Gilberto Macias' desk. Upon reading it, he immediately telephoned Bianca. She referred him, as she always did then, to Philippe. 'Stonewall them,' he ordered the lawyer. 'Give them no information. Tell them that we're...that is, that you and Bianca are looking into ways and means of meeting their request for information. Tell them you'll be in touch again, when you've compiled the information.'

Juan duly responded as instructed. Henry Spencer replied within another week, making the obvious point that bankers and lawyers are obliged by law to hand over the information he had requested.

'Furthermore,' he observed, 'it will not reflect well upon Señor Gilberto Macias' clients if they continue to withhold such information.'

Once more, the ball was back in Philippe's court. This time, he instructed Juan to state that Ferdie's will had left all of his assets jointly to his wife and son and that they were under no obligation to provide information to disinterested third parties about assets that they now owned exclusively.

That letter precipitated another round of correspondence, the upshot of which was the claim that neither Ferdie's mother nor his sister had been joint-owners of Calorblanco Central America or of Banco Imperiale or Banco Mahfud. Their full and complete shareholding of the Piedraplata companies in Mexico, according to Juan Gilberto Macias's account, was limited to the Piedraplata jewellery shops. All other Piedraplata assets, save Calorblanco Europa, were, he claimed, owned exclusively by Ferdie, according to the company records.

This, of course, was untrue, and Henry Spencer had a simple recommendation for Clara. 'Sue. It's the only way to establish joint ownership. We'll put in a Statement of Claim that alleges Bianca and Philippe Mahfud have colluded to defraud you and your mother of your rightful inheritance. That has to be the way to proceed, but first I want to run it by Conkers Coningby. That's Lord Ralph Coningby, second son of the Marquess of Bankshire. Capital man. Sound as the Lutine Bell. He's the

man we must brief as your Silk. You know what a Silk is, don't you? It's a
Queen's Counsel. A senior barrister. He's in Sir Alfred Kindersley's
Chambers. You'll also need a junior. Senior barristers don't function
without them. He normally uses Adrian Clewth for matters of this kind.
You can't get better.'

To Clara Piedraplata d'Offolo, lacking in knowledge as she was,
English justice seemed to be her best hope of regaining some of the family
assets with which Bianca appeared intent on absconding. She also had
another objective: to achieve something approximating justice for her
murdered brother. In the process of a trial against Bianca and Philippe, she
intended to make the point that her brother has been murdered precisely
so that his widow and her lover could get their hands on his fortune.
Exposure of the truth, Clara believed, would lead to who knew what final
denouement.

Clara d'Offolo, of course, could not see into the future and could not
imagine how she was being set up to be skinned alive financially. Three
weeks after her initial conversation with Henry Spencer, full of hope for
a just and successful outcome to her noble legal undertaking, she boarded
a Swissair flight at Geneva Airport to keep an appointment with Conkers
Coningby and Adrian Clewth in the presence of Henry Spencer in
London at His Lordship's chambers.

As Clara approached the chambers of Sir Alfred Kindersley QC in
Brick Court, around the corner from Henry Spencer's offices in New
Court, and saw Lord Ralph Coningby's name inscribed beside the oak
door leading into the foyer, she even felt warm and cosy. There was
something curiously, homely even, about all those figures of power and
influence and ability in the English legal system being located in nearby
buildings.

As Clara sat down in the large Victorian reception room, with the
carved stone fireplace, waiting with Henry Spencer and Adrian Clewth for
Conkers Coningby to receive them, she would have been alarmed at how
closely located everyone was in the case of d'Offolo versus Piedraplata and
Mahfud. However, Clara did not know that Bianca's QC was none other
than Lord Ralph Coningby's Head of Chambers, Sir Alfred Kindersley
himself.

Blithely unaware of what she was letting herself in for, Clara even
allowed herself to enjoy a foretaste of victory as her legal team confidently

predicted a favourable outcome during the conference that she was of course paying through the nose for. Henry Spencer had come accompanied by one of his associate solicitors, being too grand to take notes himself, as well as a clerk, so she was paying four separate professionals and one employee for the labour that any one of them could have accomplished blindfolded. As Clara would later on state, her education in real life began that day.

Bianca meanwhile was also busy with her lawyers, signing the completion papers on the purchase of L'Alexandrine in the South of France.

Chapter Fifteen

L'Alexandrine: April 1 1972. It was one of those bleak, cold and wintry afternoons that explain why so many of the International Set traditionally decamp from the South of France to the West Indies between November and April. Outside, there was a constant but light drizzle, unrelieved by a single burst of sun above the low-lying clouds. Julio and Pedro were sitting on the enclosed back veranda, their feet up on ottomans, smoking: the former Balkan Sobranie, the latter Moroccan Black. They were both dressed in the finery of the day, as befitted American college students: velveteen bellbottom trousers, ruffled shirts, string ties. Julio's hair was fashionably long, as were his shapely chin-length sideburns, while Pedro's was shoulder-length, his sideburns more reminiscent of a Victorian gentleman's than a flower child's.

Antonia joined them, flopping down wordlessly onto one of the vast over-stuffed chintz sofas that would become one of the hallmarks of their mother's many houses. At fifteen, she was still young enough to be heavily influenced by her mother's taste, although today she was being granted her liberty and was bedecked in typical English teenage fashion: a pale blue crushed velvet skirt with matching bolero and contrasting long-sleeved, high-necked ochre under-blouse from Biba, all set off by boots from Susan Small on London's King's Road, that had caused her mother to comment: 'Why can't you young people have more elegance?'

As Antonia sat down, Julio offered her a cigarette from his distinctive black and gold packet. She shook her head. Suddenly Manolito burst into the room, running ahead of his nanny. As a foil to their current style, and an indication of the aristocratic heritage to which Bianca was now laying claim, he was dressed like Little Lord Fauntleroy: green velvet knicker-bockers, green velvet jacket, white lace jabot, finest white muslin shirt, neatly tucked in vertical rows and shiny black patent leather shoes.

He jumped into Antonia's lap, and she ruffled his hair, saying, 'You made a very good ring-bearer, baby brother.'

'I wish Mama had married Uncle Philippe instead,' he said plaintively.

'Don't worry, baby brother,' Pedro said. 'This won't last.'

'I hope it doesn't,' Antonia agreed. 'I can't see what she sees in Ion. Uncle Philippe would be a much more appropriate stepfather.'

'She daren't marry Uncle Philippe. Not with Uncle Ferdie's sister suing them both in the English courts claiming that they've made off with $200,000,000 of the Piedraplata family fortune.'

'Why are you always so negative about Mama?' Julio asked.

'The truth obliges one to speak as one finds,' Pedro said.

'Come on. She's not as bad as you make out.'

'I'm not the one who says that Mama had Uncle Ferdie bumped off because he was going to divorce her, so why am I being held responsible for just repeating what everyone else is saying?'

'You always go too far, Pedro, that's your trouble.'

'No, Julio, my trouble is I call a spade a spade, and your trouble is you want to bury your head in the sand and pretend that nothing's happened.'

'You'd better put that joint out before Mama comes down.'

'It's cool, man. I'll light a few joss sticks. She won't smell a thing.'

Pedro was taking one last toke when Ion Antonescu joined them on the veranda. He sniffed and then sniffed again.

'Pedro,' Antonia said, coming to Pedro's rescue before their new stepfather could say anything, 'I told you not to light those foul-smelling Turkish cigarettes. They really stink. Light some joss sticks…and choose jasmine.'

'No, man, that's too feminine. I'm gonna use sandalwood.'

'Whatever they are, I'd suggest you light them before your mother comes down,' Ion Antonescu said helpfully, trying to adopt a middle course between complicity and authority. 'There's a strong scent of marijuana here, and you know how your mother deplores drug-taking.'

'The guests will be here at seven, no?' Julio said, deliberately changing the subject.

'Yes.'

'So how does it feel to be a married man?' Julio asked jocularly.

Ion Antonescu pouted. He was a tall and handsome man with charming manners and the flaccid expression of the weak. Romanian by birth, French by nationality, homosexual by inclination and an art dealer by trade, Bianca had met him nine months previously, exactly two weeks to the day after she moved into L'Alexandrine. The occasion was a dinner party hosted by her immediate neighbours, the renowned American advertising guru Ruth Fargo Huron and her airline chief executive husband, Walter Huron, who had been only too relieved to have this effete but genuinely nice man squire his wife at social events for several years. No one at that dinner party, not even the Hurons themselves, would ever have expected that a walker of such renown could ever be of marital interest to any woman.

Bianca, however, was on the lookout for someone with whom she could enter into a *mariage blanc*. As Pedro had rightly surmised, she needed something to throw Clara and the many Mexican socialites who insisted that she had arranged Ferdie Piedraplata's death off the scent. Ion Antonescu could not have appeared at a better time. Moreover, he and Bianca clicked, which was hardly surprising considering how worldly and gregarious they both were.

The day after their meeting, Bianca telephoned Ion and - killing two birds with one stone - asked him if he could advise her on purchasing art for L'Alexandrine. Naturally, he was agreeable. Two days later, over lunch in St Paul de Vence, the initial impression of compatibility was reinforced by a most companionable and enjoyable time. By the end of the meal Bianca was mixing business with pleasure - something she would do time and again in the years to come - by agreeing a commission rate that was mutually satisfactory: ten percent of the purchase price on any works she bought at auction upon his advice, ten percent on any works he obtained through other dealers on her behalf, but his full profit on any pictures or objets d'art he found on his own.

Having hooked her red herring with the prospect of large

commissions, Bianca immediately threw herself into the project that was then dearest to her heart: doing up L'Alexandrine. Within weeks, she and Ion were travelling to and from Geneva for art sales at Christie's; to Paris for the auctions and to see dealers; to Rome, Florence, Copenhagen and Frankfurt. Ion was making money hand over fist, while Bianca was thrilled to acquire items she would never otherwise have had the acumen or knowledge to acquire for L'Alexandrine: much-needed pictures and trinkets, such as a Faberge Easter egg and four bejewelled picture frames, containing signed photographs of Tsar Nicholas II, Tsarina Alexandra; the Grand Duchess Xenia and the Dowager Empress Marie Feodorovna from a member of the former Imperial Family of Russia.

During this time, Ion came to know Bianca well. Whenever she popped over to France, she saw him on an almost daily basis. Although under constant pressure from Clara's lawsuit against her and Philippe and not one to endure her suffering silently, she was nevertheless an excellent companion. Indeed, she was some of the best company Ion had ever had, and that was really saying something, as he was well used to glamorous and entertaining women. Day in, day out: she would recount the latest developments, sometimes with humour, sometimes poignantly but never dully. The common thread of her complaint was that Clara was crazed with grief and trying to blame Philippe and her for something that wasn't their fault. 'The idea of us running off with $200,000,000! How can anyone run off with that amount of money? Can you imagine how much it would *weigh?*' she would frequently joke.

From Ion's point of view, Bianca Piedraplata was the ideal woman to have on his arm. She was beautiful, stylish, warm, witty and a big spender.

She was consummately glamorous, and her life had all the elements of grand theatre. Certainly, her forays into the law courts, while traumatic for her, were fascinating to him. Although Bianca's complaints about how the lawsuit was ruining her life were constant, they were delivered with such verve and vivacity that they never became tiresome. Indeed, her demeanour always had such a dimension of theatricality, and the cast of characters in her life were so rich and so glamorous, that the saga became more - rather than less - entertaining for Ion the more he knew of what as going on.

Whenever Bianca wasn't discussing the lawsuit, she remained equally interesting and was even more effervescent and charming. With her captivating manner and the lavish and intoxicating way of life she was building with his help, Ion began to feel as if he were creating Nirvana in the South of France. As they grew closer, he found that he faced a choice: either wind down his other clients and friends when she was in town or incorporate her into his social life more than he had done so to date. So, gingerly at first, without knowing that Bianca had plans of her own where he was concerned, Ion asked her to various dinner parties and luncheon parties with other friends and clients and, in so doing, played right into her hands in both a personal and a social context. As these were precisely the people she wanted to meet, Bianca now found herself in the fortunate position of getting even more out of the relationship than she had wanted.

One evening, they were at Ruth Fargo Huron's house for dinner when their hostess said, only half in jest: 'If I didn't know better, I'd swear you two were enamoured of one another.'

Ruth's comment provided Bianca with the perfect opening. She alluded to it on the way home. 'I suppose I am enamoured of you in a nonsexual way,' she remarked. 'You're such wonderful company and such a decent guy that I feel utterly safe with you. In truth, you're the only man I'd marry if I had to get married again.'

Ion blushed, cupped Bianca's fingers, raised them to his lips and, in real aristocratic fashion, kissed the air immediately above them, lips brushing against hands being deemed a vulgar practice in aristocratic circles. The subject suitably introduced, Bianca was soon suggesting, ostensibly as a joke, that they enter into a *mariage blanc*. This sort of union, of course, had always been a respected feature of life in the highest social circles, and the banter between Bianca and Ion gradually progressed to the point where they started to speak about it seriously.

Meanwhile, Bianca's relationship with Philippe had been going from strength to strength. Whenever she was in Mexico, he visited her every evening and spent the night with her until two o'clock, at which time he got out of bed and drove to his house. In New York, they also maintained a modicum of discretion, in case Clara had private detectives on their trail. Philippe booked a small apartment beneath Bianca's at the Waldorf Towers, which he never used except to change his clothes. Those cautionary devices aside, they were solidly a couple and thought of themselves as such.

Philippe remained as besotted with Bianca as he had ever been. Her feelings for him, meanwhile, had deepened thanks to their more fulfilling sex life and the tremendous wealth that he had engineered for her to acquire. Although she did not possess the passion for him that she once had for Bernardo, in her mind he was her man: her only man. The fact that their financial interests were uniquely tied up only served to preserve both her interest and her fortune, which was actually more than the $200,000,000 Pedro had claimed it to be. The figure that Bianca had positioned herself to inherit was nearer $270,000,000. Already, in the short space of time since Ferdie's death, Philippe had increased it to well over $300,000,000. He, naturally, benefited from this, to the tune of some $15,000,000. He and Bianca were now partners in business as well as in bed and in crime. With Bianca's money to invest, Philippe could finally give free rein to his business ideas, and in so doing he was discovering that he was as gifted financially as Ferdie had been, albeit without Ferdie's flair for the unusual or the altruistic.

Life, of course, was not perfect. The complications caused by Clara's lawsuit meant that Bianca and Philippe had to assume a level of subterfuge that Bianca had hoped to leave behind her forever now that she was a widow. Instead of which, she was being confronted with the need to divert suspicion and wagging tongues away from her relationship with Philippe by marrying a man who neither the English nor Mexicans could prove was the 'beard' he was. So she proposed to Ion, he accepted her, and together they planned their wedding.

Bianca had intended no irony when she chose April Fools' Day for wedding to Ion Antonescu. It was simply the most convenient date. The children would be at home for the holidays. It was a good time for Philippe to be away from Mexico; and Ruth Fargo Huron had agreed to steal five days away from her advertising agency in New York to fly to Nice and act as matron of honour for her newest best friend.

Despite Bianca's intentions, however, the occasion was so laden with paradox that it was almost satirical. The bride, still not confident enough of her social standing in the South of France to call the shots, behind her carapace of easygoing deference had allowed Ruth Fargo Huron to choose her own matron of honour's dress. Ruth chose an Adolfo lace dress in beige too similar in colour, texture and style to Bianca's dove-grey Valentino guipure suit for anyone to feel anything but acute embarrassment - especially Ruth Fargo Huron, who prided herself on her impeccable social habits – when both bride and matron of honour appeared before family and friends for the civil ceremony at the local *Mairie*. That, however, was only the first of the day's embarrassments. The sight of Bianca being ushered down the small pathway which served as the *Mairie's* bridal aisle on the arm of her eldest surviving son, Julio, to meet Ion, who was standing beside his best man, Philippe, was too much for her second son. Pedro squirmed, bent his head towards his sister's ear and whispered loudly enough to be overheard by the friends in the aisle behind them: 'Uncle Philippe's not only the best man. He's the only man. You should've seen him coming out of Mama's bedroom this morning. This whole thing's too bizarre to cope with. I need a joint.'

What struck Pedro after the ceremony was the marked lack of joyousness on the part of all the assembled guests. It was as if everyone was singularly aware that the whole arrangement was a sham. Everyone, that is, except Ion Antonescu, who beamed proudly and swanned around, having bagged a rich widow as his bride. Meanwhile, the other guests milled around outside the *Mairie* waiting for the wedding photographs to be taken on the front steps. As Ion slipped from person to person, accepting congratulations that no one meant, Bianca looked vaguely uneasy but ignored her new husband's antics until the photographer's assistant came up and said he was ready to take the pictures. She immediately marched over to her new husband and brought his peregrinations to a sudden end by peremptorily grabbing him by the sleeve and frogmarching him to the top step. 'Time to pose for the pictures,' she commanded. 'You can talk all you want at the reception.' After the photographs had been taken, the assembled company broke up.

The family returned to Bianca's true love, L'Alexandrine, and while the children lounged about on the enclosed veranda smoking, she headed upstairs to change into one of the amazing couture numbers that Yves St Laurent had created specially for her.

The reception itself proved to be a rerun of the wedding ceremony.

Once the guests had arrived and the event was in full swing, the prevailing atmosphere among them was anything but celebratory, and, indeed, if anything, the tone had deteriorated from silent bemusement to open questioning. Everywhere Julio, Antonia and Pedro went, they caught snippets of conversation from the guests, all of whom were openly speculating about the reasons behind this marriage.

Julio and Antonia, being more accepting by nature than their more spirited brother, were less disturbed by what they were overhearing, although they too felt sullied that their mother's private life was being discussed with such embarrassing openness. But Pedro, acutely aware of Bianca's true motive for marrying Ion, was positively furious with her.

This was reflected in his demeanour, which, to even the most unpractised eye, was awkward in the extreme. As her second son skulked from group to group, alternating charm with sullenness, Bianca kept an eye on him, fearful that he might say something that would embarrass her in front of these new, socially desirable friends whom she hoped would form the basis of her circle, her ambition still being to become a leading light of the International Set.

Bianca found it impossible to feign pleasure in the company of her second son for any length of time. Usually she ended up saying or doing something that antagonized him and fed the deep-seated hostility Pedro had held towards her ever since, as a little boy, he realized that he came a poor second to his elder brother Julio in his mother's eyes. The sad truth was that Pedro had always rubbed Bianca up the wrong way. The consequence was that he had long ago become firmly convinced that his mother despised him, which was not strictly fair, for while their person-alities were mutually antipathetic, she did have strong maternal feelings for him.

This being Bianca's wedding day, and Pedro suffering from the unloved child's natural tendency to want love even when he knows it would not be forthcoming, he walked up to his mother towards the end of the evening and asked her to dance. 'Madame Antonescu,' he said humorously, bowing deeply, 'May I have the pleasure of the next dance?'

'*Avec plaisir,* Monsieur,' Bianca said, smiling sweetly and putting her hand through the crook of his arm. Together they stepped into the ballroom, where the Confrey Phillips Band, one of the British Royal Family's favourites, was playing a version of the Beatles' 'With A Little Help From My Friends'.

Pedro twirled his mother around the dance floor, enjoying what seemed to everyone to be a happy moment. As the music came to an end, he raised her hand and kissed it, Continental-style, his lips touching her skin. 'Only peasants connect their lips with the flesh on a lady's hand,' Bianca said without even thinking. 'And I do wish you'd stop trying to draw attention to yourself with this flamboyant conduct,' she continued. '"Madame Antonescu" indeed!'

'Ashamed you're married to a fag instead of someone who can give you a straight fuck?' Pedro retorted, stung by the unfairness of his mother's response, when all he was trying to do was be as gracious as possible under difficult circumstances.

Immediately Pedro could see he had gone too far. 'You seem to have lost your mind,' Bianca snapped back, her expression diabolic. 'Keep this up, you little shit, and I'm going to have you locked up on the grounds of insanity.'

'I bet you'd do it too, even though you know I'm the sanest of your children, certainly the most clear-sighted.'

Very aware that they were being watched, Bianca ran her hands through Pedro's hair, a smile on her face, then said quietly: 'I don't care how open you keep your eyes, as long as you keep your mouth shut. I can do without the rumours you're helping to spread about me. Do I make myself clear?'

'Excuse me for having been decent enough to come over and ask my mother to dance and for calling her by her new married name,' Pedro replied bitterly. 'Ungrateful cunt,' he muttered as he walked away, just loudly enough for Bianca to overhear.

The party ended at eleven o'clock, when the last of the guests left with Ruth Fargo Huron and her husband Walter.

'Now for the interesting part,' Pedro remarked with mischievous amusement to Julio and Antonia. 'Will the newlyweds drift off into the night to share their own special cloud, or will our new stepfather have to play with his own dick while dear Mama and Uncle Philippe do their Anthony and Cleopatra act? Which do you think it will be?'

'Why don't we wait and see?' Antonia said.

'We'll have to, unless you have some inside information on the bedroom Mama has allocated Ion. Does he have his own?'

Julio and Antonia looked befuddled. 'So you don't know either,' Pedro said. 'This is developing into an interesting evening.'

'Nightcap, anyone?' Philippe asked, as if he were head of the house.

'I think it's time for bed,' Bianca retorted. 'Manolito has to be on a plane in the morning, and I have to be up early to see him off. And we're off on our honeymoon tomorrow, though Philippe is keeping our final destination a secret from us. So shall we?' Bianca said, looking at Ion, who bid everyone good night and followed his new wife out of the room.

Ion also shared the children's curiosity about where he would sleep that night. He knew this was not a marriage in the full meaning of the word, but good form had prevented him from enquiring about the location. Trusting to Bianca's good taste, he had steered clear of the subject, but now that he was ascending the stairs, he wondered where the staff had unpacked the overnight case he had sent over earlier that day, along with the suitcases he was taking on his honeymoon. A honeymoon he was sharing with his wife's lover and Philippe's sister Rebecca, whom neither he nor his new wife had yet met.

'I thought we'd put you in the bedroom opposite mine,' Bianca said as they reached the top of the stairs, 'if that's agreeable with you.'

'I'm sure it will be,' Ion said before he had even seen which room was being allocated to him. He was, of course, familiar with the layout of the house, and indeed with all the rooms, having acquired furniture and objets for them, but he was still not sure which room she was referring to, and he was too restrained to indulge in vulgar curiosity.

Bianca took his arm and led him into the large bedroom opposite her suite of rooms: that is, the medium of the three sizes of L'Alexandrine's many bedrooms. This startled Ion, who had expected that he would at least receive one of the huge bedrooms. His disappointment, however, was quelled somewhat by the furnishings. The focal point of the room was a bed that had once belonged to the Empress Marie Louise. The armoire had also belonged to Napoleon's second wife, but the chest of drawers, writing desk and armchairs had all come through a descendant of Prince Eugene de Beauharnais, the Empress Josephine's only son who subsequently became the Duke of Leuchtenburg after the collapse of the French Empire. The furnishings were covered in the most exquisite iceblue silk, embroidered in gold thread with Napoleonic bees. This theme was picked up in the heavily flounced curtains of the same ice-blue material. From Ion's point of view, however, the *pièce de résistance* was not any of the furnishings or even the landscape by Sisley, the pastel of a ballerina by Degas or the erotic charcoal of Paul Roche by Duncan Grant but the exquisite Corot landscape above the writing desk. Even if the room had been smaller, its appointments could not have been bettered. Ion made a snap decision not to let this surprising turn of events bother him. Nevertheless, he also made a mental note of it.

Ion had actually detected something about Bianca Barnett Calman Piedraplata Antonescu that few others had ever had the opportunity to note. For all her generosity, she could be unexpectedly - and counterproductively - mean. This, of course, was a trait about which Pedro could have written epistles, for Bianca's generosity was something she doled out, either to obtain an advantage or, in his fairly partial opinion, to bewitch those she wanted to have in her thrall.

His head whirling with the implications of his new lodgings, Ion said goodnight to his wife with a chaste peck on the cheek and was about to accompany her into her bedroom when she held up her hand and said:

'You are such a dear, but there's no need. Goodnight and sweet dreams.'

Within minutes, he heard Philippe's footsteps in the passage as he headed into Bianca's suite of rooms. He needed little imagination to envisage who was consummating his marriage for him.

The following morning, the new Madame Antonescu got up at nine o'clock to say goodbye to Manolito. He was flying from Geneva to London on Swissair with his nanny to link up with Amanda, who was due to take him back to Mexico with Anna Clara for a holiday in the sun.

Part of Amanda's custody agreement with Ferdie had required him to provide her with the use of two Mexican houses: one in Mexico City and another in the country. Although owned by Ferdie, these houses had been chosen by Amanda and were maintained, fully staffed and furnished, all year round, in perpetual readiness for her imminent arrival. No one was allowed to live in them except Amanda and anyone of her choice, and she could, any anytime within her lifetime, elect to change the locations of either house. In other words, she had two fully staffed, well maintained and fully furnished Mexican houses at her disposal, for the remainder of her life. And Amanda had chosen well. The country property, which was a five-minute drive from Sintra, had one of the largest and most beautiful gardens in Cuernevaca, while the villa in the city was an eighteenth century Spanish nobleman's hacienda in San Angel two cobble-stoned streets away from the Piedraplata family home. It was to these houses that Manolito and his nanny were now heading.

Manolito was now six years old. Although he called Bianca 'Mama' at her suggestion, he called Amanda 'Mummy' as he had always done. He loved both women. In reality, he now had two *de facto* mothers. This did not present a problem for him, because both women treated him well.

While Amanda's feelings for him were purely maternal, and her consequent conduct was as nurturing as a loving mother's could be, Bianca's treatment of him was also good, even though her detractors would say that her motives were mixed. Undoubtedly, she was genuinely fond of the little boy, who was cute and lovable; but Amanda and Clara were not alone in asking whether she would have been so interested in Manolito, had control of his inheritance not been the benefit of his guardianship.

There was, undoubtedly, an element of truth in this rather jaundiced view. They also believed that Bianca, being farsighted, understood that the little boy would come of age within a few short years and would then have the freedom to do what he wished with his vast fortune. As Bianca's and Philippe's financial interests were tied up with Manolito's, the only way she could keep a measure of control over his fortune was to gain and keep his trust. In their view, her objective was therefore to create a personal relationship and a professional structure of such soundness that Manolito would have no incentive to alter anything, once he turned eighteen.

Of course, Manolito was oblivious to everything except that Bianca was warm and loving towards him, which was only conducive to his ultimate feelings of well-being and love. Even Amanda had to concede that her Nemesis indeed performed as a good stepmother would, and that Manolito was, as a consequence, flourishing under her care and control.

Nevertheless, there were significant gaps in the child's upbringing, as Amanda discovered on the third morning of their arrival in Mexico. They were walking past one of the large Calorblanco shops housed in a seventeenth century palace in the old centre of the city. 'You know, darling,' Amanda said, intending to reinforce the loving feelings the little boy had for Ferdie, 'your Daddy founded this company. Do you know what that means?'

Manolito looked up at her quizzically. 'That means that Daddy started the company that owns Calorblanco. You see this shop. Your Daddy, Grandma and Aunt Clara owned it. They owned all the other Calorblanco shops in Mexico. One day a large part of that will be yours. It is a great heritage, and you should be very proud to be a part of it.'

Manolito looked blank. 'Hasn't Bianca told you anything about your Daddy...about what a special person he was?' Amanda asked, careful to keep all accusation out of her voice. 'It's OK, honey, you can tell me.'

'Mama never talks about Daddy,' Manolito replied.

'Come,' Amanda said on an impulse. 'Let's go into Calorblanco. I'll show you. Your Daddy's portrait is in all the shops as the founder. In all the clinics. The schools. All the Calorblanco properties. His portrait always hangs above Calorblanco's emblem of the white flame. It was the wish of your Grandfather. He was a wonderful man. So kind. So decent. He was proud of your Daddy, because your Daddy had amazing ideas and brought them to life in a way that benefited the life of thousands of people, rich and poor alike. Let Mummy show you.'

Taking Manolito by one hand and Anna Clara by the other, she walked into the first Calorblanco store she had been into since leaving Ferdie. This one she knew especially well. She headed for the north-east side, but when she reached the spot where Ferdie's portrait had once been, she saw a head and shoulders colour photograph of Bianca glamorously bedecked in a parure of emeralds and diamonds. Beneath the lavishly carved gilt frame, where once there had been a bronze plaque commemorating the occasion upon which Ferdie had opened the shop, there was a new brass plaque that stated simply and sparingly that it was a likeness of the chairman of the board, Bianca Barnett de Piedraplata, taken by Antony, Earl of Snowdon. Amanda was pleased to see that Bianca had resisted the temptation to point out to the ignorant that the photographer was the husband of the Queen of England's sister Princess Margaret. She grimaced, however, at the showiness above the frame, for there, for all to see and be impressed by, was the company emblem of the white flame topped by a coronet, which, if Amanda's genealogical memory was correct, had the number of points assigned to an English baron. 'She doesn't even have the good grace to let poor Ferdie keep recognition for his accomplishments,' she involuntarily observed. 'And she calls herself a lady. What a piece of work she is...and such a phoney too! She's not entitled to a coronet, and neither is that father of hers who can't even speak English properly.'

With that, Amanda shuddered, took Manolito by the hand and walked out into the blinding Mexican sunshine.

'I didn't see Daddy's picture, but I saw Mama's,' Manolito murmured.

Chapter Sixteen

From the outside, the High Courts of Justice on The Strand look like a vast complex of buildings covering what would be in New York an array of several Avenue blocks. As you step in off the street, there is the vast central hall, as long and wide as a football pitch, off which runs a rabbit warren of cold stone corridors leading to the panelled courtrooms. It is very easy to get lost, even if you know the place quite well, so Henry Spencer took the sensible precaution of having his clerk meet Clara and Rodolfo outside the main entrance on The Strand.

Clara and Rodolfo pulled up in the Piedraplata Rolls Royce promptly at nine-fifteen on the morning of the Wednesday following Easter for the second day of the trial. The Rolls was one of the few family possessions that she had managed to retain, having taken it out of storage shortly after arriving in England after Ferdie's death. Thereafter, she 'declined' - to use her word - to return it to the storage facility where Bianca would undoubtedly seize it, as she had seized so much else. It was, Clara recognized, a small victory, but it was a victory nevertheless, and she needed to see that she was making some headway against her sister-in-law and Philippe Mahfud.

The case had begun the day before, on Tuesday, April 24 1973, and it had gone well. The morning had been taken up with legal arguments before Mr Justice Landsworth, during which Clara and Rodolfo had sat in the same row of benches no more than three feet away from Bianca, resplendent between her new husband Ion Antonescu and Philippe Mahfud, who Clara had no doubt was still the man in her life.

After lunch Conkers Coningby had opened the case for the Plaintiff by calling Clara to the stand. His examination of her had been brilliant, eliciting answer after answer that drove home the point that Bianca and Philippe were opportunists who were seeking to deny the documentary evidence. Clara had been a good witness too. Lucid. To the point. Calm.

At four-thirty sharp, while Clara was answering a complicated question about the way her shares and her mother's had been registered in the various Calorblanco subsidiaries, Mr Justice Landsworth had looked at his watch ostentatiously, peered down at Conkers Coningby, held up his hand to Clara and said theatrically: 'Counsel, I take it there will be no more questions after the Marchesa has answered this last one, and we can call it a day till ten-thirty tomorrow morning?'

'My Lord,' Conkers Coningby had said, nodding his bewigged head and rushing Clara through her answer before being excused from the witness box with the warning that, as she was still under oath, she could not discuss the case with anyone, including her own legal representatives.

Conkers escorted Clara out of court, repeating as they went the judge's warning about not discussing the case. 'But of course, we can discuss anything else,' he said, and waiting until they were in the icy, tiled corridor which held the chill and fear of centuries of trials, said pointedly to Rodolfo, 'I take it this isn't being too much of a strain.' Clara rightly took this to be his way of circumventing the judge's dictat while conveying approval for her performance. Realizing that he might also be hinting that he could speak openly to Rodolfo, who could then pass on his comments to his wife without any of them fearing breaching the judge's interdict, Clara excused herself and went to the ladies' room.

'You can be proud of your wife,' Conkers said as soon as she had walked off. 'She's acquitting herself admirably.'

'It's difficult for me to judge...but if you say so.'

'It's always a pleasure to look across a courtroom and see furrowed brows,' Conkers said. 'Did you see how the other side's expressions became increasingly worried the deeper we probed into the Beneficial Ownership question?'

'At one stage, it looked as if Sir Alfred wanted to throw his pitcher of water at his instructing solicitor,' Adrian Clewth said with some amusement.

Conkers laughed. 'That wouldn't have gone down well with old Landsworth.'

'I should say not,' Adrian Clewth agreed, his face contorted with pleasure as the two men guffawed. The real reason for his disapproval was that Bianca's instructing solicitor was none other than Mary Landsworth, a partner in the firm of Darter and Co, and the wife of Mr Justice Landsworth.

Clara rejoined the men while their banter continued. 'I didn't think it was a good idea for Mrs Antonescu to be poking Sir Alfred with a ruler to capture his attention,' Adrian Clewth said, reminding Clara for all the world of a schoolboy speaking about his headmaster. 'Especially when her solicitor was sitting right beside her and she's meant to convey all instructions through him. I thought Mr Justice Landsworth was going to chew her head off.'

Conkers Coningby laughed. 'He very nearly did,' he said, mimicking him in adolescent fashion, '"Mrs Antonescu, will you please desist from paying such strict attention to Counsel's sleeve and provide instructions in the conventional manner..."'

Just then, Bianca, Philippe and their legal teams stepped out of the courtroom into the passage. Sir Alfred led the way. He walked up to Conkers Coningby. 'I say, old boy,' he murmured. 'Could we have a quiet word?'

'Excuse me,' Conkers said to Clara and Rodolfo and left them with Adrian Clewth. 'They're old chums,' the latter explained for the benefit of these foreign clients who might consider it odd that their Silk was going to have a *tête-à-tête* with the opposition's Silk. 'Most likely they're arranging a game of golf for the weekend or some such thing.'

'As long as their friendship doesn't affect Lord Ralph's ability to prosecute my case, that's fine,' said Clara.

'Heaven forbid,' Adrian Clewth said. 'All good barristers leave their personal feelings out of their cases. It's the only way the system can work. That, and Chinese walls.'

'Chinese walls?' Rodolfo said.

'Chinese walls. The system whereby each barrister erects a wall of probity around himself, so that no other barrister has access to him or his information, save those on the same side as himself. The British legal system couldn't work without Chinese walls. Not when members of the same set of chambers are pitched against each other. It's a question of integrity. Barristers have to be men of the utmost integrity.'

'You mean barristers from the same chambers oppose each other?' Clara said.

'Absolutely. There's nothing exceptional about Sir Alfred and Lord Ralph being from the same set of chambers.'

'You mean that Lord Ralph and Sir Alfred share the same chambers?' Clara said slowly and deliberately, hoping that by accentuating her foreignness she would conceal the degree of perturbation she was experiencing.

'Absolutely. Nothing at all unusual about that.'

'So who's senior?' Rodolfo asked, coming to Clara's rescue.

'Sir Alfred. It's his chambers. Lord Ralph is second in order of precedence. Not that that means anything in terms of his success rate.'

Clara saw Conkers Coningby heading jauntily back towards them, a smile on his face. 'Thanks for putting us straight on your fascinating legal system,' she said, wrapping up the conversation before her Silk had a chance to overhear what they were speaking about.

'Did Sir Alfred have any settlement offers to make?' Clara said.

'We should be so lucky,' Conkers said. 'We're in for the long haul here.'

'He made that clear?' Clara said.

'With people like Sir Alfred, it's not what they say so much as how they say it. He's a master of inference. I don't know if that answers your question. He certainly didn't actually say it, but one can read between the lines. Tomorrow's another day, though, so why don't we all get a good night's sleep and meet at nine-thirty in the cafeteria for some coffee and a conference? My Clerk knows where it is. He'll meet you on the pavement and escort you in, won't you, Rowbotham?' With that, Conkers Coningsby led the way downstairs, robes billowing magisterially.

Clara knew she was being reassured, and she hoped that her failure to be fully mollified by the reassurance was simply over-scepticism, but she had a nagging feeling that something was going on which she did not understand. She would see how correct her intuition had been the following morning.

Conkers Coningsby and Adrian Clewth were already ensconced upon opposing wooden benches when Rowbotham escorted Rodolfo and Clara to the Formica table where they had scattered their papers, Styrofoam cups of very bad coffee and paper plates holding Danish pastries that looked as if they were left over from the Viking invasions.

Conkers and Adrian stood up as the Silk greeted them. 'So sorry you can't partake until you've finished your evidence, Marchesa,' he said. 'But the Marchese can join us if you don't mind sitting over there.' He pointed to an adjoining table. 'Here, have some coffee and pastry. We're already stuck in. This promises to be a sticky day.' Where his conduct had inspired confidence yesterday, it now created anxiety.

Once more dogged by doubt, Clara sat down and tried as best she could to follow the legal complexities that Conkers was addressing supposedly out of earshot. 'What I don't understand,' Rodolfo said, 'is how the Beneficial Ownership is such a problem now, yet it wasn't last Thursday when we had that conference at Henry Spencer's Chambers, nor was it yesterday afternoon outside Court when you thought it was plain sailing.'

'Good point, Rodolfo,' Clara thought, smiling to herself.

'I'm afraid we can't speak about this in front of your wife,' Conkers replied.

'I'll go and sit down over there, then,' Clara said, pointing to a table at the opposite end of the room.

'Capital idea,' Conkers said and waited while Clara walked off. 'The thing about cases is that they develop in unexpected ways,' he continued. 'What you don't think is going to be a problem can suddenly become one, while what you anticipate as being a difficulty, doesn't materialize as such.'

Having concluding his rather patronizing discourse, Conkers returned his gaze to Adrian Clewth, and continued to preach about the choppy seas ahead, making a great show of flipping through one massive legal textbook after another.

Seeing the futility of staying with them, Rodolfo rose from his seat. 'I think I'll join my wife,' he said.

I do apologize not to be able to give you more of my attention,' Conkers replied, 'but as you can see, we're pretty busy.'

Rodolfo nodded his head politely.

'I wish I could shake off the feeling that something's going on behind the scenes that we're not privy to,' Clara said as soon as he slipped in beside her.

'Maybe he's trying to justify his vast fees,' Rodolfo said. 'Men often make things seem more difficult than they are to confuse ladies into thinking they're working harder than they are.'

'Maybe,' Clara said. 'This sort of production doesn't inspire confidence, though.'

When court reassembled at ten-thirty, she re-entered the witness box.

Mr Justice Landsworth leaned over and said smilingly: 'Marchesa, you will remember that you are still under oath.'

'Thank you, My Lord,' Clara said and turned to face Conkers.

'Now, Marchesa,' he began, his thumbs stuck in the sides of his black gown. 'Yesterday you were telling us about how the Beneficial Ownership papers came to be signed.'

'That's right.'

'Am I right in thinking that a consideration would have been Foreign Exchange Control Regulations?'

Clara could barely believe what she had just heard. What business did her own Silk have bringing up the fact that she, her mother and her late brother might have been circumventing foreign exchange control regulations? Surely he had to realize that you do not prosecute a case by stating that your client might be bending inconvenient laws for her own financial benefit?

'I don't understand the question,' Clara said, stalling for time while she thought up an answer.

Conkers looked rather irritated, as if his prey were avoiding his trap.

'That's perfectly all right. We understand that English is not your native tongue, so I'll repeat myself: were you and your mother and brother trying to get around various countries' Foreign Exchange Controls by establishing a series of interlocking Nominee and Beneficial Ownership Agreements for your family companies?'

'Is this man crazy?' she asked herself. 'Just who is he representing? Me or Bianca and Philippe?'

Clara, however, never buckled under pressure. Instead she felt a sense of calm settle over her. 'Lord Ralph,' she said icily, 'my mother, my brother and I were each other's Nominees and were the Beneficial Owners of our family companies because they were family companies. They were owned by all of us. My brother and I had equal shares. We took the very best legal advice available and allowed ourselves to be guided by those experts, some of whom, I venture to say, might even be your colleagues.'

'Thank you, Marchesa,' Conkers said, looking mollified. 'That will be all from me. But please remain standing as Sir Alfred would doubtless like the opportunity of asking you one or two questions.'

With that, Conkers sat down and busied himself with his papers, once more behaving in a manner that suggested to Clara that she was now on her own. Sir Alfred stood up. He was a short, amiable-looking man with a complexion that proclaimed a love of port. 'Marchesa d'Offolo, you've told this court that the documents relating to Beneficial Ownership confirm that you owned an equal share of Calorblanco and Banco Imperiale with your brother and that your mother owns a share equal to that of your late brother. Is that correct?'

'Yes.'

'The documents also show that you were your brother's Nominee and he was yours. That is correct too, isn't it?'

'Yes.'

'So, in the event of the demise of one, the other's share fell into the lap of the remaining sibling?'

'Yes.'

'Is not such an arrangement unorthodox?'

'I don't know what you mean by "unorthodox". When you're dealing with multinational companies, you can't have parochial arrangements. As I said to Lord Ralph, we took top legal advice. Everything we did was in accordance with the laws of the countries in which we function.'

'You are aware that it is our client's case that the system of Nominees was purely a device to avoid Foreign Exchange Controls in case one of you got in trouble as you moved money from country to country without the permission of the states involved, and that the system of Nominees was never intended to indicate true ownership?'

'You're very naïve if you think we could've moved large sums of money from country to country undetected and without the knowledge of the said countries' banks.'

'Of course, you would say that, wouldn't you? The fact is, the system of Nominees could just as easily be read as your brother being the true beneficial owner of the companies. The paperwork, to the contrary, is nothing but a dodge concocted by dishonest business people to subvert the laws of various governments and to deprive a devoted widow of her rightful inheritance.'

In response, Clara just stared at Sir Alfred.

'Cat got your tongue?' he said with vicious glee. 'Well, I can understand your reluctance to reply. You don't have very much sympathy for your sister-in-law, do you?'

'No, I don't suppose I do.'

'Don't you think that someone who has lost her husband in the awful way your sister-in-law did would warrant sympathy from her unfortunate husband's only sibling?'

'I think any sister would find it very difficult to sympathize with a sister-in-law who cleared out the house of all staff so that her brother would be there alone, only to be discovered an hour or so later with two bullet holes through his heart.'

'Your dissatisfaction is not really about money, isn't it?'

'It's really about how my brother died. Money plays a part, a small part, but the larger issue, so far as I'm concerned, is how my brother can be said to have committed suicide in circumstances which make it clear that he could not have killed himself.'

'Marchesa,' Sir Alfred said, 'am I right in thinking that the Mexican police investigated your brother's death?'

'Yes.'

'What was their conclusion?'

'That he had committed suicide, but this was preposterous since no right-handed human being can shoot himself once, much less twice, through the heart with his left hand.'

'Of course we all sympathize with the distress of a sister whose brother died in horrific circumstances,' Sir Alfred said, trotting out the odious hypocrisy for which the British legal profession is so famous, 'but the death certificate clearly states that your brother died by his own hand, doesn't it?'

Clara remained silent.

'I've asked you a question,' he barked. 'You are obliged to answer it. What is your answer?'

'Yes,' Clara said, her expression one of supreme distaste for the man who was asking her these questions.

'Incidentally, Marchesa,' he said, as if he had just remembered something, 'your correct title is Marchesa d'Offolo, is it not?'

'That's correct,' Clara said.

'You're quite sure?' Sir Alfred said.

'Yes.'

'Your husband is a marchese?'

'Yes.'

'"Marchese" is Italian for what we would call a marquis in Britain, I believe.'

'Yes,' Clara said, seeing where Sir Alfred is heading.

'You would have this court believe you are a woman of credibility, I take it?'

'That's right.'

'You wouldn't claim to be something you're not, would you?'

'Obviously not, Sir Alfred.'

'You are not a marchesa in your own right, are you?'

'No.'

'I take it that the reason why you are Marchesa d'Offolo is because you married the Marchese d'Offolo.'

'That's right.'

Looking triumphant, Sir Alfred waved a piece of paper. 'How very peculiar, then,' he continued, pressing home his point, 'that the Italian authorities state that there is no citizen of Italy by the name of Rodolfo d'Offolo who is a marchese and that you are nothing but Signora d'Offolo. It would appear that even your claim to being the Marchesa d'Offolo is without merit. That will be all, Mrs d'Offolo.'

Smiling dismissively, Sir Arthur looked over at Conkers to see whether he wished to re-examine his witness.

Conkers got to his feet. 'I know this is difficult for you, so I'll limit myself to one question only. Why do you believe that Madame Antonescu is entitled to only a minority share of your family's assets?'

'Because that's the way my father set up the companies. That's the way my brother and I ran the companies. And that's the way it is, both morally and legally.'

'Thank you,' Conkers said, smiling wanly at Clara as he turned to the judge to dismiss Clara. Realizing that he had no intention of addressing the issue of her title and that he was therefore prepared to allow the judge to accept Sir Alfred's contention that she was a phoney, she said: 'Before you sit down, Lord Ralph, possibly you, as an aristocrat who presumably knows something about the way titles work here and elsewhere, will give me the opportunity of explaining to the court that there are Papal titles and Italian titles. The Vatican is a sovereign state, and the Pope is the elected monarch of that state. As such, all Papal titles have as much force and validity as any other title granted by a monarchy. I don't suppose Sir Alfred considers himself a fraud when he's in Italy just because his title is English, and what applies to him applies to me. My husband is a Papal marchese. His title has as much official recognition as Sir Alfred's, or indeed, yours. While it is true that Italy voted to become a republic in 1946, and it withdrew official recognition of all Italian titles at that time, it did not abolish foreign titles. I trust this addresses the issue of my correct style and title.'

'Thank you for that explanation, Marchesa. You have saved me the task of asking you a question upon which I had no instructions, but which I would have liked to have addressed myself,' Conkers said smoothly and, turning to the judge, bowed his head and said: 'That will be all, My Lord.'

'Thank you, Marchesa. You are excused,' said Mr Justice Landsworth, looking at the clock obsessively as Clara stepped out of the witness box.

'And now, if it's agreeable with Counsel, I suggest we break now and return at ten-thirty tomorrow morning.'

Both Silks stood up and, in unison said 'My Lord,' with an exaggerated respect that struck Clara as ludicrous theatricality.

'Everyone be upstanding in the court,' declared the Clerk of the Court stentoriously, maintaining the tone set by the Silks.

At that, everyone stood up. Mr Justice Landsworth rose with a flourish, swishing his robes as if he were a drag queen sashaying across the stage of a dingy nightclub in Lower Manhattan. All the members of the legal teams bowed exaggeratedly towards the departing judge as if they were Catholics genuflecting before an altar dedicated to the Holy Trinity.

As soon as the door to the judge's chambers swung shut, Conkers turned around to Clara. 'I thought that went jolly well,' he said within earshot of Bianca and Philippe, who were sitting side by side no more than four feet away from his client. 'Well done, Marchesa. You certainly gave as good as you got.' With that, he laughed appreciatively.

Before he had even finished laughing, Sir Alfred tugged Conkers' sleeve. 'I'll catch up with you later,' he said.

This was just a bit too cosy for Clara, who felt a surge of anger well up within her. 'It's so refreshing to see how civilized the English legal system is,' she said, removing all trace of anything but approval from her voice. 'There you are with Sir Alfred, such good friends, representing sworn enemies like my sister-in-law and myself.'

'It's the civility of it all that makes this the best legal system in the world,' Conkers said, unaware of the irony and failing to appreciate that Clara was being sarcastic. 'I know you're smarting under the lash of Sir Alfred's tongue. All his victims do. But don't underestimate the power of a reasoned argument. He may be all thunder and lightning and insinuation, but that doesn't necessarily sway judges the way it does juries. I think you'll find at the end of the day that our way is the winning way. What say you, Clewth?'

'I'd say so,' Adrian Clewth agreed, nodding his bewigged head as he gathered up his papers and stuffed them into a well-worn brief case that he then proceeded to put underneath the table where he was sitting.

'You're surely not leaving those there?' said Rodolfo.

'There's no danger. The court will be locked within minutes. No one will have access until tomorrow morning.'

'But what happens if we come back later than the other side?'

'Oh, they'd never look at our papers. It just isn't done.'

Rodolfo shot Clara a doubtful look. Was he being overly suspicious or was Adrian Clewth being incredibly naïve? Clara agreed with her husband that these English legal practitioners were expecting reasonable people to suspend an unreasonable degree of disbelief in the probity of humankind but indicated by the flicker of an eyelid that he was to leave the subject alone. The British system, she concluded, certainly was bizarre.

But was her trust in it misplaced?

That night, as Clara and Rodolfo were dining together in an exclusive little restaurant in Knightsbridge, Mary Landsworth was introducing Bianca Barnett Calman Piedraplata Antonescu to her good friend Clarissa Coningby. 'Lady Ralph Coningby, Madame Antonescu,' she said in those braying tones for which the upper-middle classes of the day were renowned. 'I know you ladies have a lot to talk about, so I'll leave you to it while I circulate.'

After the usual niceties, Clarissa came straight to the point. 'Mary tells me you want to sponsor our little cause,' she said brightly and appreciatively.

'It's such a worthy one,' replied Bianca, careful to present herself as the quintessence of benevolence. 'You and Mary should be congratulated for starting it up. I was amazed to discover the trouble you've been having with funding.'

'Not everyone cares about Distressed Gentlefolk,' said Her Ladyship plaintively, 'especially when you narrow it down, the way we have, to the widows and orphans of judges, barristers and solicitors who have fallen on hard times.'

'I'd have thought you'd get a lot of support from the legal profession,' Bianca said astutely, getting to the heart of the matter.

'To an extent, we do. They're always happy to lend us venues such as Lincoln's Inn or Gray's Inn for our fundraising efforts, but the legal profession in this country is not rich the way it is in America. By the time you've bought the wine and laid on food, you're lucky to break even, much less make a profit.'

'I know from experience of my own country how difficult fundraising can be,' said Bianca, who had never done a stroke of charity work in her life. 'That's why, when I saw the brochure for the Distressed Legal Gentlefolk Society in Mary's waiting room, I decided to offer my support.'

Bianca had actually noticed it on her second visit to Darter and Co's offices, around the corner on Chancery Lane from the High Courts of Justice in The Strand. It was prominently displayed on the coffee table in front of the large red Chesterfield sofa in the waiting room, where it had been laid out beside the latest copies of *Tatler* and *Harper's & Queen*. This had been done by Mary Landsworth's secretary on her instructions.

Rightly concluding that the brochure was bait, Bianca had sweetly asked Mary for a brief explanation of the Distressed Legal Gentlefolk Society as she was ushered into her office. Mary had launched into an enthusiastic explanation about its aims, stressing its nobility of purpose, as if these relics of prosperous legal practitioners could ever qualify, in real terms, as hardship cases, and had given her client a brochure to take home so that she could familiarize herself with the work they were trying to do.

Back at the Dorchester, where she and Philippe had the old suite she and Ferdie used to share, while Ion was in the suite beside it - the one that Elizabeth Taylor and Richard Burton used to occupy in those days – Bianca discussed what to do about the Society with her lover. 'Of course, your solicitor's doing nothing less than subtly soliciting your support for a cause she has control over,' Philippe observed. 'Presumably its true purpose is to advance her career and that of her colleagues by currying favour with their superiors in the legal profession. I gather the English legal profession is like that. It's an old boys' network. They all know one another and further one another's careers with the proviso, of course, that you play ball with them. Not only does she have her own career to consider - and the best way of getting work and becoming an eminent solicitor is to obtain good results by befriending judges, with the possibility of even ending up as Solicitor General - but her husband's a judge. As you know, the other co-founder, Lady Ralph Coningby, is married to a Queen's Counsel, who's a hotshot barrister. Both husbands are tipped for high office, which means that they're moving heaven and earth behind the scenes to achieve their goals. It is said that Mr Justice Landsworth aims to become Lord Justice Landsworth, a Court of Appeal Judge or a Law Lord, while Lord Ralph Coningby hopes to move up the scale from being just another Queen's Counsel to a judge and preferably a senior one at that. And how, my dear, do you think they'll get there? I'll tell you. They'll earn and peddle influence. That's how it's done in England.'

'You make it sound even more underhand than the Mexican judiciary,' Bianca said.

'It is. The way barristers' and judges' careers are advanced in England is shrouded in secrecy for the simple reason that the legal profession doesn't want to create influential judges and advocates whom it can't control. The ultimate goal of the legal profession in England isn't the administration of justice. It sees to it that the justice system is administered by tame judges and lawyers who protect the interests and the power of the legal profession.'

'Are you saying that the real pay-off isn't money - it's power?'

'That's right. And I'll tell you how they do it too. Promotion from a junior barrister to a Silk, or from a Silk to a judge, and from the more junior levels such as District Judge through the more mundane levels such as Circuit Judge to the senior levels such as High Court judge, comes from secret meetings of the most senior members of the legal profession. Ability has little or nothing to do with advancement. Playing ball with the powers-that-be is the only way a barrister will move up the professional ladder. It's also the way he wins his cases. Most judgements have little or nothing to do with the merits of a case. They're determined by who is most in favour with the Judge. That's why I directed you to Mary Landsworth. She has what the English call "impeccable connections", which means that she knows which strings to pull. My take on what's happening is that she's giving you a message: "Support my charity, and I'll go that extra mile for you." Your father was right to despise the English, Bianca. They're real hypocrites. My advice is to ring Mary Landsworth up tomorrow and tell her that you're very moved by the objectives of her charity. You want to become a supporter and so you'll make an initial donation of £20,000. Then dangle a carrot in front of her. Say you'll endow her society to the tune of £20,000 per annum over the next five years, as long as she keeps you abreast of her plans for the charity. Lay on your own brand of heartfelt moralizing with a trowel. She'll like that.'

'Do you really think they're as bad as that?' Bianca asked.

'Worse, my darling, worse.'

Philippe continued to call the shots behind the scenes and advised Bianca to wait until her next meeting with Mary before implementing his suggestion regarding her endowment of the Distressed Legal Gentlefolk's Society. Bianca did as he suggested, and thereafter the matter of her future endowment of the charity remained a tantalizing possibility to keep Mary dangling on the line that he had hooked her upon.

Throughout this crucial period, Philippe continued to nurse the rod, waiting until the week before the trial was due to begin before he deemed the time appropriate for Bianca to reel in the fish. He chose the moment carefully, tipping her the wink as they were leaving Mary's Chancery Lane offices late in the afternoon after they had gone over their witness statements with her. It was with real pleasure that Bianca heard herself saying: 'You know, I'm so impressed with the work your Distressed Legal Gentlefolk Society is doing that I'd like to donate another £20,000 immediately. But I don't want to do it in my own name, as it might create the wrong impression. Would you mind awfully if I got one of my Isle of Man offshore companies to make the donation?'

'That's very generous of you, Bianca,' Mary said, pushing her spectacles back onto the top of her head and failing, as she did so, to conceal the look of pure glee that lit up her horsy features. 'We have a great deal of expenses and we have been rather concerned that we might sink instead of swim.' With that, her lips rolled over teeth that a Derby winner might have envied.

Although Bianca was pleased with Mary's response, Philippe was not. He rightly decided that she was dropping a major hint that the more Bianca could pay the better. He rightly suspected that Mary milked the charity financially under the guise of 'legal costs' and 'expenses' to divert funds to herself. He therefore stepped into the breach he detected. 'Bianca was telling me yesterday,' he said to Mary, 'that she really wants to provide you with an endowment of £50,000 in addition to her previous donation, but she needs to meet your co-founder to make sure that she's the sort of person she can trust.'

The co-founder, of course, was the key: she was none other than Clarissa Coningby, whose husband, Conkers Coningby, was Clara d'Offolo's barrister. Bianca was awestruck at Philippe's daring. It had never have occurred to her that Mary would find it acceptable for her to make an approach to Clara's barrister's wife through her. Bianca remained motionless, not even daring to look at Mary lest she jeopardize the delicate negotiations. She need not have worried, however.

'I'll give her a ring this evening and set something up,' Mary said, taking the bait. 'Shall we say at my house as soon as possible?'

Philippe's resourcefulness was rewarded, as he knew it would be. Mary Landsworth not only arranged the meeting between the wife of Clara's barrister and Bianca at her own house, while her husband was also there, but also did it during the trial itself, despite the fact that her husband was judge in the case.

That was how Bianca, with Philippe at her side, found herself attending a drinks party at the end of the second day of the trial. While Mary Landsworth was in her drawing-room, setting up the pay-off by introducing Clarissa Coningby to Bianca and Philippe, Mr Justice Landworth made sure that he stayed in his study.

It was, of course, no surprise to either Mary Landsworth or Clarissa Coningby that Bianca, who stood to lose hundreds of millions if the verdict went against her, agreed to donate the munificent – to them – sum of £50,000. They were pleasantly taken aback, however, when Philippe offered them a further £20,000 on the grounds that he too was moved by the plight of all those distressed legal gentlefolk.

'I'm sure,' he said to Mary and Clarissa, ensuring that each party would get what they wanted, 'that you wouldn't want anyone misinterpreting our support for your charity by linking our donations to the case, and in the circumstances I feel the most judicious course of action is to wait until the verdict is in before we transfer the money. In the meantime, we can give you post-dated pledges, if you feel the need for such assurances.'

'Oh yes,' said Mary. 'Do give us the pledges. I'll have the charity's secretary draft something.' Clearly she trusted Philippe as little as he trusted her.

The following morning the various parties assembled in the High Court for the latest instalment of what became, to Clara, a Kafkaesque affair. As the trial ground to its inevitable conclusion, she became transfixed by the grotesque and ephemeral way in which the matter was being conducted. Even though she did not yet know what the outcome would be, she had a hunch it was going in Bianca and Philippe's favour, so when the Defence rested and Mr Justice Landsworth began the preamble to his verdict, she was not surprised that his tone was heavily slanted in favour of the defendants.

What did come as a surprise, however, was when Clara discovered by pure chance, several years later, how the verdict had been arrived at through influence peddling and bribery. When she stumbled upon this information, conveyed to her through Conkers Coningby's ex-son-in-law, she could only mirror Philippe's estimation of how cheaply English justice sold out the interests of those who sought legal redress within its system.

By the time Clara learned how Bianca and Philippe had achieved their victory, over two and a half decades had elapsed, and Lord Justice Landsworth had reached the position on the bench he had always aimed at. Dame Mary Landsworth was one of the most eminent solicitors in the land and a figure who featured on so many government-affiliated boards that she was known as the 'Quango Queen'. Conkers Coningby had died a High Court judge, halfway up the ladder he wished to scale, but bitterly disappointed that his only daughter had married the son of a grocer.

Only Sir Alfred Kindersley remained a feared and fearsome advocate, caring nothing for advancement as a judge but coining money as few other English barristers had ever done. He lived as high off the hog as only someone with no style and little taste could, swanning around the most famous restaurants with the latest of his mistresses, all of whom had to sign confidentiality agreements. That way, none of the tabloids would get to publish their recollections of the whippings that she had administered to this most eminent of English barristers, stripped of his robes and kneeling, his neck encased in a dog collar, as the blows rained down on his pink behind and spotty back until he ejaculated with the invariable cry of 'Mother'.

Part Three : Philippe

Chapter Seventeen

The month following the end of the trial was a time of great uncertainty, for Clara had that length of time in which to lodge an appeal, and the defendants had no guarantee that, if she did, the Court of Appeal Judge would be as amenable as Mr Justice Landsworth had been.

However, Clara did not know the full extent of Conkers Coningby's complicity, nor did she know about the party that had taken place at Mr Justice Landsworth's house during the trial. She consequently decided that there was little point in pursuing justice through the courts and instructed Henry Spencer not to file an appeal.

'But we stand a good chance on appeal, Marchesa,' he advised, which Clara rightly took to be an invitation to spend more of her money.

'I'd rather get on with my life than prolong the distress of seeking justice for my brother through your courts. I've got the message. There is no justice here. But one day my sister-in-law and that partner of my brother's will make a mistake, and when they do, I intend to be right there, ready and waiting, to get a fairer approximation of justice than I'll ever see in any court of law.'

'It's your decision, of course, and I respect it, but Conkers feels we stand a good chance of reversing the judgement on appeal. He's even informally looked up some helpful case law.'

'My mind's made up,' she said simply, and that was the end of the matter.

Bianca was with her gardeners, tending to the azalea bushes, when the butler came outside to inform her discreetly she was wanted on the telephone.

'Mary Landsworth here. I have good news. The Marchesa isn't filing an appeal.'

Bianca was genuinely puzzled by her sister-in-law's conduct. If the roles had been reversed, she would never have thrown in the towel. Bianca was a fervent believer that persistence wins the day – or, at very least, sours your adversary's victory.

'Does that mean that the case is closed, once and for all?' she asked, needing to be reassured that the danger had passed.

'The judgement is now set in stone,' Mary said.

'I can't tell you what a relief that is,' Bianca said, meaning every word. 'Clara would have completely destroyed my reputation if she'd won that case. As it is, she's hopelessly sullied it in Mexico. Every time I'm there, I have to rise above the sniggers and whispers that accompany me everywhere I go. People have no idea how painful it is to be suspected of something you didn't do.'

Any public appearance she made in Mexico was accompanied by a palpable ripple of speculation about what had really happened to Ferdie. Try as she might, Bianca had found it impossible to ignore. To someone for whom social approval was as essential as oxygen, this notoriety was an exquisite torment, especially when she contrasted it with the days when Ferdie was still alive and she was fêted everywhere as the socially eminent Mrs Piedraplata. If it were up to her, she would never have gone back to Mexico once the sneering had started, but being one of the richest women in that country with vast financial interests there, she had been obliged to maintain a public profile for the duration of the legal proceedings and act as if nothing was happening. All the same, she made sure that she visited only when she had to and stayed for the barest minimum length of time.

'You don't deserve being vilified the way that sister-in-law of yours has been pillorying you,' Mary observed sympathetically.

'I know,' she agreed, Mary's expression of faith mingling with the joy that suddenly welled up within her at the prospect of finally being able to enjoy her status as one of the richest women in the world without being crucified on the cross of public humiliation. All that delicious money she had inherited from Ferdie was now hers and hers alone. For the first time in her life she had the liberty and the means to satisfy her every urge and desire. It was a truly liberating sensation, and the headiness of it was positively intoxicating.

'You know, Mary,' Bianca said, 'I'm grateful for your help in getting that woman off my back. To show you my appreciation, I'm going to get Asprey to make you a copy of that Verdura brooch of mine that you admired the other evening when we had dinner at the Caprice. And I'm going to donate another £100,000 to your Distressed Legal Gentlefolk Society. Truth be told, I'd like to give it to you outright as a present, but I wouldn't want to do anything that would embarrass you or give people the wrong impression if they found out about it, and I'm pretty sure you would prefer it to go to the charity.'

'You're so kind and sensitive. If anyone deserves a smoother ride, it's you, Bianca. Thank you so much for your expression of appreciation. I'd love a copy of the brooch. It will be a most welcome personal token.'

At the start of dinner that evening, Bianca laid the first brick in the new courtyard of her life. 'You know, Ion,' she said, having discussed her plans previously with Philippe, 'I've become increasingly aware over the last few months of how unfair I've been to you. I've presumed far too much on our friendship in having asked you to give up so much for me for so little in return. I've been thinking a lot about whether it would be fair to you to continue as we've been going, and I've come to the conclusion that the greatest favour I can do you...and the most sincere expression I can convey to you of the real affection I have for you...is to set you free. For that reason, I'd like us to get a divorce. I want you to know,' she continued, reaching out and touching Ion's hand, 'that I appreciate what a devoted and wonderful companion you've been, and I hope that we'll always remain the very best of friends.'

Knowing that he had outlived his usefulness, Ion had been expecting this, but he was still astonished at the speed with which his wife had moved.

'I'm happy to have been of service,' he said and arched an eyebrow, his expression registering some of what he was now thinking.

Bianca, hypersensitive as always to the reactions of others, took immediate steps to remove any sting from the situation, especially as she and Philippe were both of the opinion that it would be far too dangerous to fall out with him. 'Oh, darling, I wouldn't put it like that,' she replied soothingly. 'You've been the most devoted friend any girl could want, and I hope none of that will change. To show you how sincere I am, I want you to continue finding things for me in the same way as you did before our marriage. I also want to continue your allowance for the next ten years, and would love it if you'd consent to a lump-sum settlement as well. Would you do that and make me happy?'

'What sort of a lump-sum settlement?' Ion asked, mindful that Philippe's hooded eyes were boring right through him.

'I asked Juan Gilberto Macias what a generous settlement would be, and he said $250,000. But because I love you so much and I'm confident that we'll always remain close, I want you to have the maximum I can afford: $500,000.'

Once more Ion raised an eyebrow, this time in surprise at the amount she was offering him. Obviously, his role had been more crucial than he had realized. 'I don't know what to say,' he said, intending to be gracious.

Philippe assuming that Ion was trying to raise the stakes, jumped in protectively. 'Bianca is being very generous, Ion,' he said quietly 'Half a million dollars for a short-lived marriage...many wives get far less from their multimillionaire husbands after twenty years...'

Before Ion could reply, Bianca, compounded the comedy of errors by adding: 'I love you, Ion. You're one of my best friends and always will be, I hope. I don't want you and Philippe to get into a wrangle over anything and certainly not over money. I know how exquisite your taste is, and what the price of things is nowadays. I want you to be in a position to leave this marriage with good memories, and to buy yourself a few mementos. If I scrabble around, I'm sure I can manage $600,000, and that's the amount I'd really like you to have. Will you accept it together with all of my thanks, and will you promise me that we'll always remain friends and that you'll come for dinner at least once a fortnight?'

'Of course I will,' Ion said, raising Bianca's hand to his lips and kissing the air between them.

'That's settled, then,' Philippe said.

'Shall I move out tomorrow?' asked Ion, ever the gentleman.

Immediately after the divorce, Philippe, who had been waiting years to make the woman of his dreams his wife, swung into action, arranging for a Reform rabbi to marry them at the Synagogue in St John's Wood, London. 'Let's keep it small,' Philippe suggested and made it plain to Bianca that the only guests he wanted were her three children and Manolito, together with his brother Raymond, sister-in-law Begonia and sisters Hepsibah and Rebecca.

This marriage meant almost more to Philippe than the fortune he had acquired by fair means and foul. As a result, the ceremony was tremendously moving, and there was no doubt in the minds of any of the guests that this was a union to which both bride and groom were committed for the remainder of their lives. Everyone was struck by the passion emanating from Philippe. 'He really loves her,' even Hepsibah observed to her sister, having taken an instant dislike to Bianca the moment she first met her.

After the ceremony, Philippe ensured that the romance of the occasion continued in true style by taking over the Brasserie at Claridge's for the wedding breakfast. Aside from the family and Walter and Ruth Huron, who flew in from New York for the reception, their guests consisted exclusively of members of the legal profession. Mr Justice Landsworth popped in for forty-five minutes during the lunch recess of his trial. His wife Mary arrived and left with Lord and Lady Ralph Coningby, and Juan Gilberto Macias flew in from Mexico especially for the event. During a short speech, in which Philippe thanked everyone for coming, he raised his glass to Bianca and put into words what his every action had been conveying: 'To the woman of my dreams.' No one present doubted the sincerity of that statement, although Hepsibah could not resist remarking to Rebecca: 'I can see what he sees in her, but what does she see in him? Their relationship just doesn't make sense to me.'

Of course, neither Mahfud sister knew anything about the ties binding the happy couple to each other. This was only the fourth occasion upon which Hepsibah had met her, although Rebecca did accompany Philippe on Bianca's honeymoon with Ion, at which time she formed the opinion that she was a charming but trivial personality with, as she put it, 'all the emotional depth of a powder compact.'

Although Hepsibah and Rebecca succeeded in keeping their opinion of Bianca from Philippe, they were less successful in keeping it from their new sister-in-law. 'I don't think your sisters like me,' Bianca remarked to her new husband.

'Of course they do. They even said how glamorous and elegant you are.'

'Now that really convinces me they don't like me,' she shrewdly observed, looking at Philippe's plain and dour sisters, neither of whom was wearing any makeup, one in a plain bottle green dress, the other in an equally style-less dark blue dress, each costume topped off with a well-cut wig whose uniformity of colour announced their commitment to their Orthodox faith.

Thereafter, Bianca's new sisters-in-law would never fail to make her skin crawl for they had committed the cardinal sin of failing to like her, to succumb to her charm and warmth and to reflect back to her the opinion she wished them to have of her. Although she was hereafter as careful as they were to keep her true feelings from their brother, Bianca marked them down as adversaries to be avoided, resolving there and then to do all she could to loosen Philippe's ties with them.

Such problems, however, were very much in the future in those early days of the marriage. From the start of the marriage, Philippe seemed to be calling the shots, while Bianca played the traditional Middle Eastern role of the obliging wife. Although she would have liked to continue basing herself at L'Alexandrine, her new husband had decreed otherwise. 'The South of France is not a practical place for us to live. Ideally, we should live between New York and Mexico. L'Alexandrine we can use as our summer house.'

Careful though Bianca was never to defy Philippe in public, in private it was another matter altogether. 'Never,' she declared in no uncertain terms as soon as the dreaded word 'Mexico' was uttered. 'If you want to live there, you'll have to do so on your own. I will never live there again.'

'I don't know what you have against Mexico. If I can move into Ferdie's house in Mexico City and into Sintra and treat them as my own, why can't you? I don't like having to go there on my own.'

'I will never live in Mexico again,' she repeated with a decided and emphatic vehemence. 'I hate the place and will only ever go when I absolutely have to.'

'Come on, darling, it isn't that bad. I like it. The children like it...'

'Then they can live there if they want, and so can you.'

'What's the point of keeping two properties fully staffed for your use all year round if you hate the country they're in so much?'

'If I ever severed my ties with Mexico, Amanda would use that as an excuse to revise the custody arrangements with Manolito,' Bianca replied. 'I have to have an official residence there, at least until he achieves his majority. You know that only too well. If it weren't for that, I can tell you, I'd never set foot in the place ever again.'

'Julio and Pedro tell me they want to live there when they've finished college. To them, Mexico is home.'

'It used to be for me too, but no longer. Home is now L'Alexandrine, though I suppose I'll have to expand my horizons to include New York as well.'

'Why don't you fly there next week and find us an apartment?' suggested Philippe, conceding defeat.

'Living in New York is fine by me. I'll speak to Ruth and see who she recommends as a realtor.'

Of course, Philippe did not need to explain to Bianca why it was important that she use a top realtor. She now knew that in New York the only way to buy into a really good building was to do it through good connections. And good connections could always be obtained if you paid a high enough price. As Philippe and Bianca both needed a good address – he for professional reasons, she for social ones – the best way of achieving what they wanted was by using a top realtor.

However, neither Philippe nor Bianca knew one, but Ruth Fargo Huron did. She unhesitatingly suggested Ruby Leighton, a well-known professional who had achieved the then almost unheard-of accomplishment of being listed in the *Social Register*, despite being Jewish. Through a combination of energetic effort and savvy, she had carved herself a niche in the New York property world and could now provide access to the best apartments in the best buildings in the best locations in Manhattan.

Wisely, Ruth Fargo Huron had warned Ruby Leighton that Bianca had an atavistic approach to property. 'She is as passionate about houses as most people are about their husbands and children. Bear that in mind when showing her around.'

As luck would have it, Ruby did not have to heed her warning, for Bianca fell in love with the first apartment the realtor arranged for her to see. It was a twenty-four room duplex on Fifth Avenue overlooking Central Park in the upper Seventies. It had the most incredible rosewood panelling in the drawing room and library; and intricately carved sandstone fireplaces in both drawing-room and dining-room. These had come from one of the Richelieu *chateaux* at the turn of the twentieth century, when Grace Vanderbilt was refurbishing her palatial New York residence. The apartment also had two separate servants' bed-sitting rooms, with adjoining bathrooms, on a lower floor, so Bianca would be able to have live-in help without using up any of the seven bedrooms with en suite bathrooms in the main apartment.

'I love it,' she said at the end of the viewing, as decisive as ever when she saw what she wanted. 'We'll take it.'

Ruby Leighton noticed she had not even bothered to ask the price.

Bianca, however, was about to get her first lesson in the intricacies of purchasing property in New York and to discover that her cosmopolitanism was not quite at the peak she thought it was. 'I wish it were that easy,' said Ruby, 'but this is New York, and no one can just buy an apartment in a co-op...especially a co-op in one of the most desirable buildings in Manhattan...without first being vetted and approved by the management committee.'

'You mean to tell me that we have to be *approved* before we can buy it?'

'Yes, and that will apply to any other apartment you might like.'

'I've never heard of such a thing in my life,' Bianca exclaimed, her South American pride offended by such a humiliating system. 'What nerve.'

Ruby, however, was amused. 'Don't worry,' she said. 'You'll pass with flying colours. I'll see to it. I know two members of the management committee. One is in the *Social Register* with me and the other would like to be, so he's as obliging as can be. I think he thinks that by being nice, we'll spread the word to the compilers of the *Register* that he ought to be invited to be listed.'

Ruth Fargo Huron had mentioned that what made Ruby Leighton one of the finest realtors in town was a unique combination of savvy, charm and good connections. As she talked, Bianca could see what her friend had meant.

'All you have to do,' Ruby continued, 'is turn up to the meeting of the management committee on time, bring your husband and to dress as sedately as if you're being tried for murder.' Bianca blanched. Wondering what she had said wrong, Ruth continued as if nothing were amiss. 'Basic black dress. Nice string of pearls...not too big, not too small. Nice pearl stud earrings. Light makeup. Hair not too elaborately styled. And a darkblue or grey tailored suit for your husband, with a plain white shirt and the tie of a good club like the Union if he's a member, otherwise something very conservative from Hermes. You want to give the impression that you're people of means but not flashy. That will convey the message they want to hear, which is that you'll fit in with the other residents and cause no trouble. Management committees are terrified of people who are famous or flashy. They think the former will attract the press, which is the last thing they want, and they're convinced the latter will have loud, all-night parties that will give the other residents a hard time and the building a bad name. There are sound financial reasons for those concerns, I can assure you, because if a building gets a reputation for having a bad resident, no one wants to buy into it, and all the other resident's find that their property values are adversely affected as a result.'

Armed with that advice, Philippe flew up from Mexico especially for the meeting with the management committee, during which he and Bianca did exactly as they were told. Ruby proved to be as good as her word, and by the time the apartment was theirs, she and Bianca had become fast friends.

Ruby, in fact, would prove to be quite a catalyst in Bianca's life. It was through her that Bianca became friendly with Valerian Rybar, the interior designer who had been married to Guinness heiress Oonagh, Lady Oranmore and Browne and whom Bianca had patronized in a limited way while married to Ferdie. Now she discovered that they had much in common, including an Ottoman heritage, a love of social life and tastes that inclined towards the exotic and the extravagant. As her 'style' would become one of the major features of her life, its importance was not to be denigrated, trivial though it might appear to be, to those with more substantial matters to which to dedicate their lives; and her relationship with Valerian Rybar became one of the most compelling in her life.

It began as it would continue; within an hour of their meeting it was apparent that most - if not all - of Valerian's more outlandish innovations appealed to Bianca. Encouraged to greater heights by her receptivity, he poured forth the most amazing ideas for the Fifth Avenue apartment.

Within weeks she had not only commissioned him to 'do up' the place but they had also become so friendly that they were meeting for lunch and cocktails two or three times a week.

Within six months, Valerian Rybar and Bianca turned a conventional pre-war apartment into a riotous meeting of East and West. The drawing room and the library became a blaze of overstuffed sofas, covered in the finest hand-woven antique Ottoman fabrics, which were then engulfed in masses of cushions, also of antique Ottoman fabric. The dining-room's walls were covered in antique hand-woven fabric, this time from the days when Bulgaria was part of the Ottoman Empire, although the dining table and chairs were genuine Hepplewhite and therefore as traditionally English as it was possible to be. The European accents were furthered by a unique combination of Old Masters and more contemporary painters.

There was a magnificent Tintoretto over the fireplace in the drawing room, a Picasso from his Blue Period over the fireplace in the dining-room and a stunning Corot over the fireplace in the library. Dotted throughout the apartment were works by David, Van Dyck, Rubens, Gainsborough, Modigliani, Dufy, Miro, Jackson Pollock, Roy Lichtenstein, Velazquez, Augustus John, and Sir Gerald Kelly. Pride of place in the entrance hall went to two massive oil sketches that the eighteenth-century English master Sir Joshua Reynolds had given to Lady Gordon: one of Charity, the other of Justice. These had originally been displayed in the staircase hall of the Earl of Winchelsea's country house, Haverholme Priory, a century before. Their companions, Faith and Hope - as Bianca and Valerian knew only too well - reposed in the English residence of a famous British aristocrat whom she had met once.

As with so much in Bianca's life, the creation of this Fifth Avenue extravaganza was fostered by her determination to forge a well-cut future enhanced by a well-constructed past. Many of the items were found by Ion Antonescu, who had been in Europe ferreting out treasures, as he had done with L'Alexandrine, from the homes of the nobility or from the auction galleries and dealers at the commission rates agreed with Bianca at the time of their divorce.

While Ion searched, and the apartment was taking shape, Mr and Mrs Philippe Mahfud lived in the old apartment at the Waldorf Towers that she and her late husband used to occupy whenever they were in New York.

During this period, Ruth Fargo Huron helped to introduce Bianca and Philippe to her social set by hosting a series of luncheons and dinners for them. Word soon spread among this moneyed group that there was a new couple in town. 'I can't get over how easy New York is,' Bianca observed to Valerian one day while they were choosing fabrics over lunch at Mortimer's. 'We've only been here for a few months, and already we're inundated with invitations.'

'That, darling one, is because Ruth and I have been spreading the word among the movers and the shakers.'

'In Mexico or the South of France, social circles are so much more restricted. People won't invite you to anything unless they've met you several times through friends, and you've known them, or the person who's introduced you, for an eternity.'

'New York doesn't work like that. Success is the only criterion. If you have something to offer...if you're beautiful or elegant or well connected or rich, Manhattan's yours for the taking. And,' he laughed wickedly, 'we've been telling all and sundry how divinely elegant and entertaining and rich you are.'

'Well, you know, darling, I'm the new kid on the block. I don't really know how this great city of yours functions,' replied Bianca, always one to disclaim knowledge she possessed if it served to make others feel good.

'Take Ruth, for instance. It required a series of dexterous manoeuvres to work her way up from being just a partner in an advertising agency to being the pre-eminent socialite she now is.'

'How did she do it?' Bianca asked: so eager to catch a glimpse of the Holy Grail that she almost choked on her asparagus salad.

'Well,' drawled Valerian, sitting back in his chair and enjoying the power that gossip gave him, 'it took her about ten years. First, she met John Lowenstein...he's in public relations...and got him to get her on a few lists...you know, parties given by places like Sotheby's and Tiffany's and Belmont's and Bergdorf 's. That's how she met Walter Huron...at a party at Bergdorf 's. So, she meets him and dates him then she marries him. That was a big step up, because he's a serious player in the airline industry, while she was...without being bitchy...just another middle-class success story. He catapulted her onto another level entirely. Then through him she met Aileen Mehle...that's Suzy Knickerbocker the society columnist...'

'I know who Suzy is. In fact, she was at a luncheon Ruth had for me three weeks ago...'

'Did you like her?'

'I thought she was charming.'

'She is. But then, you're just the sort of person everyone here wants to be charming to. A genuine British aristocrat with style, money and...'

At those words, a warm glow suffused Bianca. It was so reassuring that all her new friends here accepted that she was an aristocrat whose adventurous father had gone to Panama to oversee the family fortune there before moving on to Mexico.

'It's sweet of you to make me sound so desirable. But how did Ruth parlay being just another rich man's wife into the social leading light she now is?' Then, in case Valerian realized that she wanted to know the strategy so she could replicate it, she added as a disclaimer: 'It's always so interesting to hear how one's friends function.'

'Well,' Rybar said, licking his lips gleefully with his tongue. He did so love it when his audience yanked him back onto the path of revelation.

'Let me see...where as I? Ah, yes. The upward trajectory. Well, my darling, she did it the way everyone else does it. Through the charity world.'

'You mean things like the Cancer Society...'

'Good God, no,' Rybar said, a look of genuine horror settling on his face. 'Cancer and those other diseases kill more than just people. They kill social aspirations as well, unless you combine one of the fashionable charities with them. The only causes that count in New York are the arts. You know, things like the Metropolitan Opera or the ballet or the Philharmonic or one of the museums. Ruth started out by supporting the Met and the Museum of Modern Art and has ended up on the boards of both institutions. Of course, it's cost her...or rather, Walter...dearly. They say the Met's cost him $3,000,000 and the Museum of Modern Art closer to $7,000,000. But I'm sure he and Ruth think its been worth the price, because they're now powers to be reckoned with socially...which was not the case before she first took to charity.'

To Bianca $10,000,000 did not seem too high a price to pay to fulfil her ambition of becoming one of New York's most powerful socialites.

Later that evening, after Philippe had returned from the office, she recounted her conversation with Rybar. 'Maybe it would be good for the bank if I got involved with a charity or two in New York,' she concluded.

'Bad idea,' Philippe said. 'We don't need any more invitations than we have, and the whole venture would be counter-productive and could impact adversely upon my business. If you start supporting charitable causes too actively, people will interpret your efforts as a sign of weakness. They'll say: "Oh, we thought Mrs Philippe Mahfud was this fantastically rich widow who's married to this fantastically rich banker and is a figure to be reckoned with socially in Europe and Central America. Why would someone who is so grand need to be scavenging around in the dustbins of New York society, trying to make her mark through charity work? We thought she was already established. She can't be, if she's trying to establish herself here the way all the other climbers have done. "You see the logic? Your actions will diminish the regard people have for us and will ultimately undermine our reputations. No. All we need to do is behave in a Latin American, European or indeed a Middle Eastern way. Go out and about. Accept the best invitations, and reciprocate when the apartment's ready. The way you entertain, I promise you, everyone will beat a path to our door.'

'Do you really think so?' Bianca asked, mentally allocating some of the sums she had set aside for endowing charities to the buying of lavish presents for all her new and future friends. It was something for which she was already acquiring a reputation. As far as she was concerned, everyone loves a giver, and she was going to show New York what she had already shown Mexico and the South of France: when it came to giving, she had no equal.

'If we have two large parties a year here, the way you used to when you were married to Bernardo,' Philippe replied, 'and a series of intimate dinner parties, you'll have New York eating out of your hand. And that's before we take a box at the Met and entertain friends there or take a table at the fancier charity balls and take along a group of friends. Just you wait and see. I give you two years before you're right up there with Ruth Fargo Huron and all those other *grandes dames*.'

Deferring to her husband's wisdom, Bianca turned her attention to generating as much publicity for herself as she could. This she did under the guise of assisting Valerian Rybar, but he was not deceived. 'If it would help your future commissions, I won't mind if you get this apartment featured in one of the better magazines,' she had offered. He saw only too clearly, however, that this new friend and client was trying to use his connections to raise her profile and promote herself into becoming a more visible figure in New York society, but as his interests coincided with hers, he was pleased to assist. Over the next weeks, therefore, he ensured that he trooped the features editors of *Vogue, Architectural Digest, Interiors, House and Garden, Town & Country* and *Harper's Bazaar* through the apartment, pointing out to them that it was not yet finished but would be in a few more weeks. As Rybar had expected, all the magazines wanted to do spreads, to include several pages of photographs and an article about the amazingly rich Mr Mahfud and his elegant wife.

When Bianca referred the offers back to Philippe, he was much less enthusiastic than she had hoped he would be. 'Publicity is a double-edged sword which too frequently draws the blood of those who use it,' he said.

'We don't want to become like some of those new friends of yours, who are always in Suzy's column. But just this once might be useful, so long as we choose the right magazine.'

'Once?' said Bianca, a pained look flickering across her perfectly formed features. The thought of all that delicious attention disappearing before her very eyes was enough to bring her close to tears.

'Once. We don't need to be famous in the street so long as we're known in the right drawing-rooms and boardrooms. Those are the only places fame counts. Everything else is bullshit.'

Recognizing the wisdom of what he was saying, even if the sillier and frothier side of her personality would have dearly loved to avail herself of all that unnecessary attention, Bianca cheered up at the thought of achieving recognition from the people who mattered to her, if only this once. 'Which magazine do you think we should go for?' she asked.

'That is not my province. I don't know enough about it to make an informed decision. Why not discuss it with Valerian? He'll be sure to steer us in the right direction.'

'Why not Ruth or Ruby? Surely they know the scene better. Ruth is one of the most successful advertising executives in the country, and Ruby one of Manhattan's top realtors. They'll know more than an interior decorator.'

'I doubt it. He's terribly social and besides, this feature will be useful to him only if it brings in commissions for him from the very sort of people we want it to reach. If we ask Ruth or Ruby for advice, they may think we're desperate for advancement, and we'll lower ourselves in their eyes.'

So Bianca turned to Rybar, who advised over lunch at Mortimer's that she choose Town & Country.

'Why *Town & Country*?' she asked. 'I thought you'd suggest *Vogue* or *Harper's*. They certainly have a higher circulation and are more famous.'

'Yes,' he said, betraying how fully he saw through Bianca's motives in allowing the feature, 'but you're not a dress or jewellery designer, and neither am I. *Town & Country* is the magazine that all the people with serious money read. It might not be as big as *Vogue* or as chic as *Harper's*, but its target audience is precisely the sort of people I want to reach, and, I daresay, are also potential clients for your husband's bank.'

So *Town & Country* it was.

Sure enough, when the article was published, Valerian Rybar was proved right. That one article went quite a way towards enhancing the Mahfuds' reputation. Invitations flooded in, and by the end of the year, Bianca considered herself to be well on the way to being one of New York's social luminaries.

There were, however, two social sets in New York. These functioned in separate orbits and overlapped only occasionally. The more visible set was the *nouveaux riches*: the more eminent and prestigious, the Old Money set. Many of the *nouveaux riches* employed press agents who planted information about them in the gossip columns, fame being the yardstick by which they could measure their success. Old Money, on the other hand, wouldn't condescend to employing an agent, with the result that the *nouveaux riches* were more visible. That, of course, did not mean that Old Money did not live equally interesting lives, or that joining their hallowed ranks had lost any of its desirability. It simply meant that it was harder to scale their walls, and once in their compound, the way to lose your place within it was to make yourself too available to public inspection via the press. Publicity was seen as a cause for sympathy, not for celebration.

As Philippe had shrewdly discerned, the fact that he and Bianca did not seek publicity led observers on the social scene - and the social scene proliferated with observers - to categorize them as being more Old Money than *nouveaux riches*. Bianca further enhanced this perception in clever ways. One was the judicious use to which she put Clara and Rodolfo's title. Without ever letting on that her sister-in-law would sooner kill her rather than speak to her, she frequently let slip that 'my brother-in-law's a marquis'. She also said, from time to time, 'My father was a real British gentleman.' Both claims were hard to verify but credible, so she got away with them.

Within a year of being in New York, Mr and Mrs Philippe Mahfud were under the impression that they were accepted everywhere – as she would put it – 'as Old Money'. She was out every day for lunch, and when Philippe was not away on business they were out every evening with the likes of Mr and Mrs Donald Trump, Mr and Mrs Walter Huron, and Mr and Mrs P Adolphus Minckus, the real estate developer who would shortly change wives by marrying the former Miss Cyprus, Stella Reocleous.

It was an interesting, glamorous and busy life, but she was still not quite where she wanted to be, although she would never let on to anyone, not even to Philippe. As far as she was concerned, her position in New York was on a par with her position in society when she was married to Bernardo. Having experienced the sensation of being the Empress of Mexico while married to Ferdie, she would not be satisfied until she had replicated that position in her new habitat. Only when she was wining and dining *en famille* with Jackie Onassis and Maurice Tempelsman, with Paul and Bunny Mellon and Brooke Astor, would Bianca feel that she was where she truly deserved to be. In the meantime, it was consoling to see that people considered her to be a luminary of New York society. To them, she was already what she wanted to be; and, as perception was more than half the battle, she counted herself a partial, although by no means a total, success.

If Bianca did not actually possess the stature she was perceived as having, the opposite was true of the younger generation of her in-laws in Ferdie's extended family. Their positions within the top drawer of English society became firmly established during the seventies. Ferdie's niece Magdalena became engaged to Lord John Witherton, second son of the Duke of Arlinton, whom she married in 1975 as the second of four husbands, while by 1979 her half-first cousin, Delia Bertram, had become quite a celebrity in her own right as a result of her equestrienne activities, her close friendship with Princess Anne, and her husband, the film star Charles Candower, whose motion picture, *Return to Castle Howard*, was one of the greatest hits of the decade.

Bianca, who believed in using whatever was at hand to further her cause, frequently interwove the connections and accomplishments of

Ferdie's relations into her conversation, taking care never to mention that she was *persona non grata* with them. But it was when she was tooting her own daughter's horn that she enjoyed the full benefits of name-dropping.

'The only thing that impresses me is sincerity,' she loved to say. 'I've brought all my children up to think the same way, and they do. Take my daughter Antonia. One of her little school friends is Princess Caroline of Monaco. I've made sure she's treated Caroline the same way she's treated all her other friends, with the result that she and Caroline have become fast friends and she's always staying at the palace in Monaco. Caroline is such a sweet unspoilt girl, and Antonia doesn't have an affected bone in her body. Of course, Caroline doesn't look a thing like her mother, but she's every bit as pretty and down-to-earth as dear Grace, who couldn't be sweeter to Antonia when she stays at the palace in Monaco. I make sure we hold up our end too, by having Caroline to stay at L'Alexandrine as much as possible. It's so easy for royalty to feel that they're being used. One does have to keep things on an equal footing, otherwise one loses the human element of the relationship, don't you think?'

As the decade progressed, and Antonia and Caroline left school and drifted apart, Bianca still continued to drop the princess's name whenever she could. She even did so to Moussey Najdeh, Antonia's first serious boyfriend after school, and made sure that Caroline and her husband Philippe Junot were put on the guest list when Antonia married the handsome heir to one of the Middle East's great fortunes in November 1978.

By then the Lebanese civil war was raging, but that did not affect the Najdeh family fortune to any large extent, although it did mean that the family had to flee their country and take refuge in Paris, where they bought a superb *hôtel particulier* that once belonged to the Ducs de la Rochefoucauld on the Avenue St Germain. After marriage, Antonia took up residence there with Moussey, his parents giving them the top floor as their own apartment.

As far as Bianca was concerned, her daughter could not have married better and never ceased to let people know how happy and rich Antonia was. She beat that drum with as much frequency and regularity as she beat out her elder son's accomplishments. 'I'm so proud of my son Julio. He's such a good boy. So responsible. He graduated *cum laude* from Harvard before transferring to Oxford to take his doctorate in philosophy. Poor boy. He's had to sacrifice it all to go into the family business. He's now managing director of Calorblanco. It hurts me to see someone so young and talented burdened with so much responsibility, when all he really wants to do is become a Don in Philosophy at Oxford. He's been offered a place there, you know, but fate has decreed another, less academic path for him to follow, so he makes the best of it. And he's married such a nice girl and given me such a beautiful granddaughter. She's named Biancita in my honour and looks just like me too.'

In fact, Julio's marriage was a sore point with his mother, although she was too proud and too smart to let anyone know. When he returned to Mexico in 1977, to take up his position in the family firm, he promptly fell in love with his secretary. This was a girl who was the antithesis of every ambition his mother had for him. She was middle-class. She was Catholic. Worst of all, she was of Spanish origin, or, as Bianca put it:

'*Verrrrrry* Mediterranean-looking.' Caring not a jot that she was pretty, bright and sweet natured, Bianca saw only her daughter-in-law's swarthy complexion, aquiline features and the brown down that covered her arms.

Because Julio was her favourite, Bianca trod softly from the very outset. She kept her disapproval to herself and instead attacked the problem sideways when it became apparent that Julio was serious about her. 'Are you sure she wants you for yourself?' was the first question his mother asked him when he declared his love for her.

'What sort of question is that, Mama?' Julio said, his face flushing perceptibly.

'Well, you're my son, and I love you and need you to be sure that this girl wants you for yourself and not because we have a lot to offer in worldly terms.'

'Mama, she wants me for myself. Of that I'm sure. But if it makes you happier to put her to the test, I'll let her know I have no money in my own right.'

'You do that,' Bianca said and hammered home the point on several occasions in the twenty-one months that elapsed between that conversation and Julio's marriage to Dolores Gonzalez Irigoya.

The marriage was a happy one; and Bianca was pleased, despite the child's maternity, when Dolores gave birth to a baby girl who bore an uncanny resemblance to her blonde, green-eyed grandmother. She was even more delighted when Julio and Dolores named the baby Bianca in her honour. To her regret, however, she saw very little of the baby, because Julio and Dolores lived all the time in Mexico, in a villa which they rented near the Piedraplata family home.

As for Pedro, his relationship with his mother had degenerated to the point where there was virtually no contact between them. They did not speak by telephone or write letters to each other. On the odd occasion when they were thrown together, mother and son either had a blistering row within the first ten minutes or spent the whole time avoiding one another. This, however, did not worry Pedro. He had never liked his mother, even if he had always wanted her love, while she had never liked him, even though she claimed to have feelings of love for him. In truth, Pedro was alarmed by his mother. He considered her to be one of the most poisonous and dangerous people he had ever known, despite the fact that she had used her considerable influence to settle him in a life of some security. He was in charge of public relations at Calorblanco or, as Bianca phrased it when offering him the job: 'You may as well get paid for your gift for dramatics.' Pedro had taken the job, not because it interested him but because it gave him unparalleled freedom. Caring little for the things of this world but hungry for spiritual knowledge and experience of life, he took full advantage of this sinecure by seldom showing up for work. Instead, he continued to live at the Piedraplata family home, which Julio had vacated upon marriage, and spent his days with his friends, either exploring the countryside or just sharing time with them. Sometimes, they smoked a joint or two, as many others of their generation did, but Pedro's bent was so intellectual that he would never try anything stronger. This, however, did not stop Bianca from describing him - even to her friends - as 'my problem son with a drug problem'. This gained her sympathy from her friends while having the desired effect of neutralizing any comments Pedro might make about her, for, whenever they had their spats, as he would still throw in her face his belief that she had played a part in the death of his beloved stepfather.

On Wednesday, July 27 1983, Bianca arrived in Mexico City with Philippe for a six-day stay. She had not been to that city in over three years.

As soon as she arrived at the house, she saw that Pedro had changed the arrangement of the furniture in the family room, the dining-room, the pool house and his own bedroom. As soon as Pedro walked through the door, Bianca was waiting for him with a face like thunder. 'What is the meaning of altering the furniture in my house?' she trilled, her voice ringing out as she emphasized the word 'my'.

'I thought you wouldn't mind since you're never here and I live here all the time. I only wanted to make things a bit cosier.'

'Cosy? You and your cottage mentality. God knows where you get it from. It must be the Calman blood coming out...'

'I'd have thought it far more likely that it's the Barnett blood,' Pedro retorted, 'considering that Grandpa was a working-class bloke made good.'

'Your grandfather was never working-class,' Bianca spat, her face contorted with rage. 'You're always putting me down and everything to do with me. He was a *gentleman*.'

'Oh, he was a gentleman all right. But he was a working-class gentleman who made his way up in the world.'

'How dare you disparage my father to me?'

'You know, Mama, it's one thing to go around posing as an aristocrat in public, but do your lies have to take over all our lives and crowd out the truth? Can't there be room for posturing and for the facts as well?'

'You snivelling no-good drug addict...you haven't been in this house more than ten minutes, and you're already being rude. The problem with all of you druggie types is you have no gratitude. You feel *entitled*...'

Pedro looked at his mother. Despise her as he did, he really did not want to get caught up in another row. 'You know what's true, Mama,' he said. 'I *don't* want to argue with you. You're my mother, and I'd really like to get along with you. The problem is, you've never liked me. You've always sniped at me and used me as your whipping boy. Well, I'm sick of it. If we can't get along, why don't we just call a truce and fill the vacuum with good manners? Don't you think that would be more constructive?'

Just then Julio and Dolores walked in with little Biancita, who promptly started to cry at the sound of raised voices. 'Come to Granny, darling,' Bianca said, stretching out her arms to the little girl who barely knew her. She clung to Dolores' knees as if she were lashed to a mast.

'Now see what your brother's done?' Bianca said to Julio. 'Typical. Just typical.'

'Yes, it's all my fault,' Pedro retorted. 'It's always my fault.'

Since Dolores, in Bianca's mind, was not truly a member of her family, she did not behave the way she would have done had she been alone with her children. 'I don't know about you always being at fault,' Bianca replied. 'No one's ever persecuted you, so the very suggestion is indicative of paranoia. Don't tell me,' she went on, turning for support to Julio, 'that I now have to contend with paranoia on top of all your brother's other mental problems?'

'You really are the most poisonous viper,' Pedro retorted scornfully. 'Slithering everywhere, leaving a trail of venom wherever you go.'

Bianca retaliated by slapping Pedro hard across the face. He glared at her with an expression of absolute loathing. 'Defiant, are we?' she said then slapped him again even harder.

Without making a sound, Pedro grabbed his mother by the shoulders and started to shake her like a rag doll, her head going back and forth 'Get him off me! Get him off me!' she screamed.

Julio intervened. 'Come on, Peds, stop it,' he said, grabbing Pedro in a bear hug from behind. 'You've got to stop it. Control yourself, man. She's our mother.'

Pedro finally released Bianca by shoving her halfway across the room. She toppled over a table, in tears. Julio crossed over and put his arms around her. 'It's OK, Mama,' he said. 'You're fine. It's nothing.'

Bianca buried her head in his arms then, stiffening, she turned to Pedro. 'You beast,' she said. 'No one's ever laid a finger on me before and you will not get away with it.'

'What're you gonna do? Call the police?' Pedro taunted her, knowing very well she would pick up the implication.

Bianca shot him a look of unadulterated ferocity. 'You think you're so clever. But you're not as clever as all that.' Then she turned to Julio.

'Darling,' she said, 'do make Dolores and the baby comfortable. If you'll excuse me, I'll just disappear for ten minutes. But before I go, tell me what your plans are for later today and tomorrow.'

'We thought we'd spend the afternoon and evening here with you. Tomorrow morning, I have an important meeting at the office, and Biancita's swimming coach is coming at ten-thirty to give her a lesson, but maybe we can go to Sintra and have a late lunch there after we're through.'

'That sounds lovely,' Bianca said, making an effort to appear composed but not succeeding entirely as she headed towards her bedroom, shaking from nervous strain. At the doorway, she said turned to Pedro. 'And you?' she demanded. 'What are your plans for the morning?'

'I'm going to watch Biancita have her swimming lesson.'

'And when do you propose to depart from this house?' she inquired archly.

'About ten, I suppose,' he said, his face flushed and not entirely in command of himself yet.

'I see,' Bianca said neutrally and stepped out of the room.

Forty minutes later a refreshed Bianca, dressed in a simple but elegant cotton trouser-suit, came back downstairs and rejoined her sons, daughter-in-law and granddaughter. As usually happened after one of Bianca's and Pedro's rows, everyone, including the participants, acted as if nothing untoward had happened. The only indication that something was wrong was the fact that not a word was exchanged between mother and second son. This made conversation an intricate exercise, especially in such a small group. On the surface, it might seem to an onlooker as if a slightly odd conversation was taking place, but underneath there was a tolerance of the intolerable, a well-rehearsed play, with each participant knowing his or her part. In fact, only Dolores was uncomfortable, unused as she was to such tension, but Julio whispered reassuringly that everything would be OK and that she was just to ignore the tension and stay with the baby, who was proving to be a welcome distraction.

At eight o'clock the next morning, Bianca, who seldom rose before ten, was up and dressed and sitting by the pool, having her coffee and reading the newspapers, when the butler came in to tell her that there was a Dr Melhado at the front door asking for her. Juan Gilberto Macias was with him.

'Show them both in,' she said.

Juan entered ahead of the doctor, and she extended her hand in greeting without bothering to get up. 'Hello, Juan!' she announced in a tone of voice that he knew meant business.

'Good morning, Madame Mahfud,' he said, addressing her in the French manner as she had instructed him to do since her marriage to Philippe. 'May I present Dr Melhado?'

Dr Melhado stepped forward and bowed slightly, as if he were in the presence of an august personage.

'I take it Juan has explained everything to you, and you've both made all the arrangements?' she asked.

'Yes, Señora,' he said, bowing again.

'You brought along assistants?'

'Four, Señora.'

'Well, get them in here, and let's get this over with,' Bianca said without further ado and rose from her chair.

Dr Melhado withdrew, and she stepped in closer to where Juan was standing.

'He's good?' she inquired. 'You're sure?'

'The best in town,' Juan replied.

'This isn't my province, after all.'

'He is the very best.'

'Good, good,' Bianca said, nodding as Dr Melhado returned with four assistants in white coats. She held up her hand to tell them to stop and crossed over to where they were standing. 'Follow me,' she said, 'Although you'll understand if I don't stay to watch.'

With that, Bianca led them to Pedro's bedroom door. 'He's in there,' she said and walked off as Dr Melhado stooped down and removed a syringe from his medical bag. He attached a needle to syringe, pushed it into a bottle of liquid, pulled it out, held it up and squirted it into the air. He then nodded to his four assistants.

At that signal, they burst into Pedro's bedroom, where he was still sleeping, and jumped on him, holding him down while Dr Melhado pushed the syringe into one of Pedro's buttocks.

'What the fuck...?' was all Pedro managed to get out as the men in white coats pushed his face sideways onto the pillow. One of them held up his left arm, wrapped a plastic tube around it, making a tourniquet, and extended it for Dr Melhado, who, finding a vein, plunged a second hypodermic full of liquid into Pedro's arm.

Within seconds, Pedro was out cold. The assistants then ran outside, brought back a stretcher and, placing the young man upon it, carried him out of the house and into the ambulance, parked out of view around the back. The whole exercise had taken less than ten minutes.

At ten-forty five, Dolores telephoned. 'Biancita is asking where Tio Pedro is.'

'The sweet darling,' Bianca responded sweetly. 'Tell her he's not well.'

'What's wrong?'

'Nothing for you to bother your pretty little head with, my dear,' she said kindly.

'Will he be well enough for the trip to Sintra?'

'I shouldn't think so, but that needn't stop us from going there and enjoying ourselves.'

'Can I have a word with him?'

'That won't be possible, dear, but I'll be sure to pass on your best wishes.'

At midday Julio, Dolores and Biancita arrived at the house, expecting to link up with Pedro and Bianca. 'Hi, Mama,' said Julio. 'You're looking as chic as ever. I'll only be a second. I'm just going to call in on Peds before we go.'

'He's not here,' Bianca said neutrally.

'Where is he, then?' Julio said, plainly perplexed.

'He's in hospital.'

'Hospital?' Julio asked, as if he were reading from a script he did not understand.

'Darling, poor Pedro's finally lost his mind,' she said, the sweetness trickling off her tongue like sap oozing down the bark of a tree. 'This morning he went completely crazy. Fortunately, I had Juan Gilberto Macias here with me, and he was able to arrange for a doctor to give him the help he needs.'

To Julio, this was an ominous development. Much as he loved his mother, he also loved his brother. He was not blind to either of their faults, and while he would have been the first to agree that Pedro did sometimes fly off the handle and say things which were injudicious about their mother, he also knew that Bianca had a Machiavellian streak, even if he were loathe to admit it to anyone, even to himself.

Speechless from shock, as well as afraid of what to say, Julio just stood there looking at his mother. 'I know,' Bianca said. 'It's difficult for you. It's difficult for me too, darling. Whatever our differences, Pedro is also my son, and I love him. I'm just glad Antonia and Manolito aren't here for this.'

'Where is he?'

'He's been taken to Santa Maria Hospital. He'll be fine. Don't worry. All he needs is a few weeks' treatment, then a period of convalescence. I blame the drugs.'

'Mama, Pedro doesn't do any more drugs than most people of our generation.'

'Don't tell me you're following in his footsteps now. If you say it, I don't think I'll be able to stand it...'

'Mama, everyone under thirty-five has smoked pot. It's no big deal. Come on. Loosen up a little. Maybe Pedro and you have issues, but he's not a drug addict...'

'If drugs aren't the problem, then we're left with a son who tells the most vicious lies about his mother and who assaults her when he's called to order. I'd say that leaves him in a far worse light than us laying the blame at the doorstep of his drug taking. You weren't here for what happened this morning...'

'What happened?'

'I can't speak about it. It's too awful. I'll never be able to speak about it. Not even to you. And if I can't speak about it to you...you can imagine how dreadful it was.'

'I'll call in and see him this evening, when we get back from Sinitra.'

'No visitors for a week, the doctor said.'

'A week?' Julio said incredulously. 'I'm afraid I don't get it. Don't you think this doctor is blowing things out of proportion?'

'No. I don't. In fact, I think his response has been very measured, considering your brother's conduct and problems.'

To say that Julio was disconcerted by this turn of events would be to underestimate the turmoil he went through over the next few days. His mother, on the other hand, could not have been more serene. She had given her orders and, used as she now was to being obeyed, expected Dr Melhado to follow them to the letter. Indeed, she was so confident of the doctor that she left Mexico with Philippe a couple of days earlier than planned, flying out on the Lear.

No sooner was she airborne, however, than Julio telephoned Dr Melhado. 'I'm coming to see my brother in an hour,' he informed him.

'This afternoon won't be possible, Señor Calman,' Dr Melhado said smoothly.

'Ten o'clock tomorrow morning, then,' Julio said in a voice that would brook no opposition.

'Your mother...' Dr Melhado started to say.

Julio cut him off. 'My mother is out of the country, but I'm here, Dr Melhado. Until a week ago, she hadn't been to Mexico for nearly four years. She might not be back for another four years. I'm managing director of Calorblanco. I live here. Tell me,' Julio said, his voice hardening, 'has my brother been legally committed?'

'Your mother didn't want a scandal...' he started to say.

Once more, Julio cut him off. 'So you're holding him unlawfully. Look here, Dr Melhado, you don't have to be caught between a rock and a hard place. You can release my brother tomorrow...send in a bill to Calorblanco for a stay of however long it is you wanted to hold my brother for. I'll see that it's paid. You don't even need to say anything to Juan Gilberto Macias, if you don't want to. I certainly won't. This was nothing but a family squabble, and I can't have my brother held in a hospital because he and my mother had a quarrel. I don't propose to go into the ins and outs of their relationship with you, but I will say there are at least two sides to every story, and I cannot believe that my brother did anything to warrant being held incommunicado in a psychiatric hospital against his will.'

'I suppose you could have a point,' Dr Melhado said. 'Maybe your mother overreacted when he assaulted her. She was worried he was going to kill her, but when we went to get him, he was sleeping peacefully in his bed.'

'When was that?'

'About nine o'clock in the morning.'

'Dr Melhado, I was there when my brother and mother had their altercation. She assaulted him, not once but twice after goading him, as has always been her wont with him. It was only after she'd slapped him across the face for a second time that he grabbed her shoulders and shook her. He wasn't trying to kill her but to stop her from assaulting him again. Now, we can do this easily, as I've suggested, or you can force me to do this the hard way and turn up with a battery of lawyers, which will do your reputation no good and might result in charges being filed against you for kidnapping and false imprisonment. Now which is it going to be?'

'I'll see you tomorrow and have a bill ready for the three-week stay your mother planned.'

'That's better,' Julio said then added as an afterthought: 'Incidentally, Dr Melhado, if you're thinking of calling Juan or my mother to tip them off, I wouldn't suggest that you do it. You might find that you've bitten off more than you can chew. Understand?'

'I understand perfectly, Señor Calman,' said Dr Melhado.

'Now let me speak to my brother.'

'He's under sedation and can't speak.'

'He'd better be unsedated by tomorrow morning when I come to pick him up,' Julio answered angrily, 'or there's going to be all hell to pay.'

Slamming down the receiver, Julio telephoned Antonia, who was at L'Alexandrine with Manolito, to tell her what their mother had done.

'This time Mama has gone too far,' Antonia said.

'I think she's trying to give Pedro a scare,' said Julio, who never failed to incorporate his mother's point of view into every question.

'Julio, mothers don't go around having their sons committed illegally just because they don't get along. You've got to speak to Granny about this.'

'I don't want to get more involved than I already am. Pedro can tell her when he comes out. I'm going to fetch him in the morning and take him to Sintra for a few days.'

'Ring me when you get to Sintra. Manolito's out at the moment, but I'll make sure he's here so that we can speak to both of you.'

The following morning Julio rose bright and early. He took Biancita for a swim before breakfast. He and Dolores were still struggling to come to terms with the full horror of what his mother had done, and they spoke about it some more over their breakfast grapefruit. The conversation then switched to the logistics of getting to Santa Maria Hospital and Sintra and back with Biancita, the nanny, all the paraphernalia they would have to take, plus Pedro and themselves. They decided the only practical solution was to use separate cars, so Pedro opted to drive his two-seater convertible Mercedes Sports while Dolores would take the Range Rover with the nanny and Bianca and everything else.

After breakfast, Dolores and Julio loaded up the cars. Just as they were about to set off, Biancita asked her father if she could travel with him.

'Sure, sweetie pie,' he said, and transferred her car seat from the back of the Range Rover into the front seat of the Mercedes Benz. They then set off in convoy, with Julio and Biancita leading the way and Dolores and the nanny following.

At exactly nine-fifty seven, Julio turned into the driveway of Santa Maria Hospital. 'Darling, you put the car seat back in the Range Rover while I go inside and fetch Pedro,' he said to Dolores.

Less than ten minutes later, Julio returned with his brother. Dolores noticed that Pedro was visibly shaky, as if he were still drugged from his stay at Santa Maria. But there was no doubting the look of happiness and relief on his face as he eased himself into the front seat beside Julio, having first stopped to give Biancita a big kiss.

Once more, the family set off in convoy, this time headed towards Sintra. They were no more than two miles away from the country house when a goat ran across the road. Julio swerved to avoid it. The car left the road, hit the bank and flipped over onto the driver's side. Dolores, being right behind, saw exactly what happened. She jammed on her brakes, jumped out of the Range Rover and ran towards the overturned car. Its horn was blaring in an awful symphony of despair. By some miracle, Pedro, who had been wearing his seatbelt, was still alive. He crawled out on his belly onto the road. Julio, however, had taken the full force of the impact. He looked dead. The right side of his forehead was crushed, his arm pieced by a piece of metal. But he wasn't dead, as they discovered when Dolores passed her compact under his nose and the mirror misted up. After what seemed an eternity but was a mere twelve minutes, the ambulance arrived and Dolores piled in with Julio for the journey to the Cuernevaca General Hospital while Pedro followed in the Range Rover. After a flurry of tests, including the most sophisticated brain scans the Mexicans were capable of doing, they determined that he had serious brain damage and would either die of them shortly or remain in a persistent vegitative state. Not content to take the word of Mexican doctors, Dolores and Pedro arranged for an air ambulance to fly Julio to the Forth Worth Hospital for Neurosurgery in Dallas, Texas. Waiting there to greet them four hours and thirty three minutes later was Rufus Rutherford, the eminent brain surgeon who Raymond and Begonia had contacted as soon as they had received word of the tragedy. Eight hours later, when Dr Rutherford had done all he could, he gave Pedro and Dolores the grim news. If – and it was a big if – Julio survived, he would be like the living dead, with no recognition, no cognitive or motor skills. His brain had been so severely damaged that there was no more medical science could do. His life, to all intents and purposes, had ended. The halcyon days for the family were over forever, and, with them, had gone the one person Bianca loved more than anyone else on earth. It was a loss from which she would never recover.

Chapter Eighteen

Moussey Najdeh was making love to his wife Antonia when the telephone on their bedside table at L'Alexandrine started to ring insistently. Blotting out the sound, he continued the rhythmic thrusting that had Bianca's daughter moaning ecstatically beneath him. However, the telephone persisted in its belligerence, becoming impossible to ignore.

Moussey and Antonia both knew that Louis, the butler, would never put through a call to them at this hour of the afternoon unless it was extremely important. Slowing momentum, the young man looked down at his wife, whose eyes were now open.

'Shall I or will you?' he asked.

By way of answer, Antonia stretched out her hand and picked up the receiver. 'What is it?' she said, doing her best to keep the irritation out of her voice.

'It's your brother in Texas,' the butler said with the easy but respectful familiarity a good servant manages to bring to his relationships with employers. 'You need to take this call.'

Without even knowing which brother was on the line, Antonia was now ready for something momentous. Not even that warning, however, could have prepared her for the news that Pedro conveyed. She listened for a moment and then let out a scream 'What is it?' Moussey demanded, now deeply alarmed.

Hurling the telephone at Moussey, Antonia screamed again, as if by doing so she could somehow defend herself against what she had just heard.

She then crawled under the sheets and stuffed the corner of a pillow into her mouth while Pedro told Moussey about the accident that had just effectively claimed Julio's life. He did not, however, tell him that his mother had ordered him to be locked up, nor did he say that none of this would have happened if it hadn't been for her actions.

When Pedro finished the tale, Moussey said: 'Does your mother know?'

'No.'

'Do you want us to tell her or will you?' Moussey said, knowing the state of his brother-in-law's relationship with Bianca.

'I never want to speak to that cunt again until the day I die,' Pedro said by way of reply. 'But for her, Julio would still be fine.'

Deciding not to pursue that line of reasoning until they met face to face, Moussey tried to keep with the matter at hand.

'Is she still in Mexico?' he asked.

'No. She left yesterday. She's in New York. If I remember correctly, she's supposed to be leaving for L'Alexandrine tomorrow. You call her and give her the news of her handiwork. God, what did we ever do to deserve a mother like this?' Pedro added bitterly.

'Hang on, Pedro. Antonia wants to speak with you,' Moussey said, handing her the receiver.

For a further ten minutes, between bursts of sobbing, brother and sister talked together, with Pedro filling Antonia in on how the accident had happened.

When they rang off, Antonia did not even replace the receiver but dialled her mother's New York number immediately. As luck would have it, she was at home, finalizing arrangements with her secretary for an evening at the opera in November. To her, this was a very important occasion, being in honour of P Adolphus Minckus and his wife of one year, the former Miss Cyprus, who had recently become, in New York parlance, her 'newest best friend'.

The last thing on Bianca's mind was anything familial. She was absorbed in her social campaign and was approaching the coming evening as if she were Napoleon on the eve of Austerlitz. She had shrewdly assessed that the real estate tycoon and his new wife would be her vehicle to the upper firmament of European aristocracy. This group continued to elude her just as surely as New York's Old Money did, so the importance of Mr and Mrs P Adolphus Minckus' to her life could not be exaggerated.

Bianca's priorities, at this juncture of her life, were plain. She had no major projects, such as houses to furnish or lawsuits to contend with; and her priorities had shifted away from deadlines and the discipline imposed by externals to the fulfilment of her own personal desires. This, of course, was a perk of being rich and established, which effectively meant she had only herself and her desires to think about. By nature, however, she was someone who needed goals, and she still craved the excitement of accomplishment, so the social world had become even more important to her than it had previously been. It is fair to say, therefore, that at this time the only world of any importance to Bianca was the social one. And the word on the social circuit was that P Adolphus Minckus had bought Belmont's, the prestigious firm of auctioneers, which ranked alongside Sotheby's and Christie's as the Big Three, in order to provide his socially ambitious wife with an *entrée* to the Old Money set.

Bianca could readily see that this was a brilliant strategy and secretly wished that either she or Philippe had thought of buying the auctioneer's first. Ownership of Belmont's allowed one to acquire a supreme international social position while at the same time increasing one's wealth.

For the socially ambitious New York resident with new money and age-old social aspirations, America's Old Money circles would be forever closed, just as they had been for Philippe and herself. Not even the acquisition of Belmont's, that patrician American and European firm of venerable lineage, would open the doors to New York's crusty Old Money crowd, even though some of its members might well resort to trading off some socializing with the Minckuses in return for any items they might have for sale being pushed through the auction house with discounted commissions.

The European Old Money set were another matter entirely. Belmont's, which was staffed almost exclusively by European aristocrats and royals, was virtually a refuge for the scions of the ancient European families. These men and women occupied positions in the company ranging from porters to chairmen, with every sort of art, antique, clothing and luxury goods expert in between. It was not their professional positions that interested Bianca or the Minckuses, however. It was their social positions. By buying Belmont's, Bianca discovered, Mr and Mrs P Adolphus Minckus had bought Belmont's address book and all its society connections.

P Adolphus Minckus' acquisition of Belmont's was a stroke of genius. If the Earl of Iroton wanted to keep his job as chairman of Belmont's, London, he would have to open his heart, hearth and social life to Mr and Mrs P Adolphus Minckus and their friends. The same was true of the other chairmen, Prince Tomislav Kropotkin in Geneva and Ambassador David van Alyn in New York, not to mention the myriad lords, ladies, princes, princesses, dukes, duchesses, marquises, marchionesses, earls, counts, countesses, barons and baronesses who proliferated throughout the various branches of that august establishment and whose livelihoods would hereafter depend on keeping P Adolphus Minckus and his startlingly blonde wife happy.

As far as Bianca was concerned, the opportunity to slip into the European Old Money set on the Minckus's coattails was too good a temptation to pass up. In furtherance of her campaign, she had already cast aside the former Mrs P Adolphus Minckus and taken Stella to her bosom, generously hosting two dinner parties in honour of her and her ageing husband in New York and earning their undying gratitude in the process. Her newest best friends were even due to join her for a two-week stay at L'Alexandrine, starting in the middle of August, during which time she would take them cruising around the Mediterranean on the *Auriole*, the 214-foot 'boat' she and Philippe were chartering from a Greek shipping tycoon.

Bianca was enjoying planning her own social campaign with Mary van Gayrib, her New York personal assistant, a forty two-year-old WASP whose whole family had been in the *Social Register* since its inception, when Antonia's call came through. Mary answered.

'I need to speak to my mother,' said Antonia, usually the soul of politeness and tact, without preamble.

'Oh, hello, Antonia,' Mary responded graciously. 'How are you?'

'Terrible. I'm sorry to be abrupt, Mary, but I need to speak to Mama.'

'She's desperately busy tying up loose ends before she goes to Europe and has instructed me to take all messages...'

'I need to speak to her. Now. Tell her it's a matter of life and death.'

'Bianca, Antonia needs to speak to you urgently,' Mary announced.

Bianca looked up from the menu she was arranging and pouted. She took the receiver. 'Antonia,' she began impatiently, 'I'm in the middle of...'

'Mama, the most terrible thing has happened,' Antonia said then broke down sobbing loudly.

Knowing how even-tempered Antonia usually was, her mother realized at that instant that something was seriously amiss. 'Calm down. Whatever it is, we can fix it.'

'No we can't,' Antonia replied, howling like an injured animal.

Bianca felt her blood pressure rising. She did so hate scenes and uncivilized behaviour. No matter how important something was, people should always retain their composure. 'Antonia,' she snapped. 'Get a hold of yourself. You're not some Lebanese peasant from Tripoli. I can't very well help you if I don't know what I'm dealing with.'

'Julio's brain-dead, Mama.'

At those words, Bianca felt herself go colder than she had ever been in her entire life.

'*This cannot be happening*', she heard herself whisper.

'That's not possible,' she said, numb with disbelief. 'I saw him only yesterday.'

'There was an accident. Julio swerved to avoid a goat that ran out into the road. His Benz flipped over. His skull was crushed. Pedro and Dolores flew him to Forth Worth and he's just come out of brain surgery. The doctors don't expect him to live, but even if he does, he'll never be the Julio we know and love. They've done all they can for him but the brain damage was extensive and irreversible. He'll be in a persistent vegitative state for the rest of his life. But Pedro's all right. He crawled out of the wreck, and he's fine, aside from a few bruises and scratches.'

'What do you mean, Pedro's all right?'

'They were driving to Sintra together. Dolores and Bianca were behind them in the Range Rover with the nanny. They saw everything.'

'Are they sure Julio is really...you know...?'

'Yes, Mama, he really is...'

Bianca started to sob with quiet intensity. Unlike Antonia, she did not howl, but in its quietude her grief was even more violent.

Mother and daughter sobbed together for some minutes, while Mary, who was not sure what was happening or what she should do, hung back to give them space.

Suddenly Bianca said with absolute loathing in her voice: 'I blame that shit of a brother of yours for this, that's who I blame. God only knows why he was going to Sintra with Julio. I should've crushed his skull between my legs while I was giving birth to him. He's been the cause of nothing but trouble and grief all his life. But for him, none of this would be happening.'

'Now come on, Mama,' Antonia said, 'Pedro may be many things, but he loves Julio every bit as much as you or I. I don't see how you can blame him for an accident.'

'But I do, my child,' Bianca retorted. 'I do.'

The day after the accident Antonia, Moussey and Manolito flew from Paris by Concorde, arriving in Dallas on the following afternoon. After visiting Julio and seeing for themselves the utter hopelessness of the situation, they boarded the Lear, which Philippe had instructed to fly down to that ill-fated city to meet them and take them back to Mexico City, Bianca having flown in on it the evening before.

A week later Bianca, Pedro and Dolores returned home with Julio, who was taken by ambulance directly from the airport to the intensive care unit of the Juarez General Hospital. There at the hospital awaiting their arrival were Antonia, Moussey and Manolito. As the family met the doctors and nursing staff now assigned to the case, it was immediately apparent who was calling the shots: Bianca. Within an hour, the siblings departed from the hospital, leaving Bianca there, at her insistence, alone with the second son she had now lost. It came as no surprise to Antonia, Moussey and Nanolito when Pedro announced that he was moving into Julio's house, partly to comfort Dolores but also to avoid his mother. His family, who had learnt how his mother had arranged for him to be locked up in Dr Melhado's psychiatric clinic while visiting Julio in Dallas, tacitly supported his decision.

'And now she's turning her beady eye on Dolores,' Pedro said, filling them in on the latest developments.

'Your mother has taken over all the medical arrangements,' their sister in-law said, as they sat drinking long glasses of ice tea in the garden of the house she and Julio had rented, away from the grandeur of the Piedraplata family home.'Every idea of mine has been vetoed.'"You're too young to have an opinion. Yesterday she even went so far as to reject my suggestion that Julio should have his favourite picture of Biancita and myself beside his bed. She said it would be insensitive in case he should wake up with memory loss and get upset when he becomes aware that he can't remember his wife and child. But the neurosurgeon said there's no chance of him ever waking up or remembering anything, and I don't see why I can't honour my own husband and the father of my daughter by showing the world that we exist and care about him. The way she's acting, you'd think she was the wife, and I was just a passing ship in the night. Surely I have a right as Julio's wife and the mother of his daughter to have a say in my own husband's bedside arrangements? Your mother's taken over, and the only voice that's allowed to be heard is her own.'

'That's Mommie Dearest for you,' Pedro remarked, while neither Antonia nor Manolito said a single word in Bianca's defence.

'Maybe we should say something to Aunt Bianca,' suggested Moussey. In truth, he had just gained an insight into his mother-in-law's conduct that left him decidedly nervous about getting on her bad side. It had formerly been inconceivable to him that any woman could lock away her own son on trumped-up grounds simply to bring him into line. Now that Bianca seemed to be indulging that same streak of wilfulness at the expense of Dolores' rights as a wife, he felt it was his duty to take his sister-in-law's side, irrespective of the consequences.

'You say something if you want,' Pedro said,'but it won't do any good. I've learned the hard way how that woman functions. To me, she's as transparent as glass. She brooks no opposition to the implementation of her wishes, which is why I don't for one second believe that she really wants Julio to be cared for at L'Alexandrine once he's out of intensive care. If she'd really wanted that, she'd be getting it, instead of allowing him to return here and remain in hospital here, where you and Biancita can visit him. She just wants you to believe that she's given way to you on an issue of importance to her and to yourselves, when in fact she was doing no such thing. My experience of Mama is that no one ever gets their own way with her...unless, that is, their way coincides with hers. Believe me, she was just letting you think that she's sacrificed her way for yours.'

Despite Pedro's warning, Moussey did speak to Bianca on Dolores' behalf when he got back to the Piedraplata family home. Her reply, however, was brief but devastating. 'It's out of the question. But even if I had been minded to accommodate that Roman Catholic whore, what Julio told me before I left Mexico week before last would be enough to prevent any mother from polluting her son's bedside.'

At a loss for words, Moussey looked embarrassed.

Antonia came to his rescue. 'What are you talking about, Mama?'

'Don't tell me Julio didn't tell you how he caught Delores in bed with another man and planned to divorce her? That whore only married my darling son for our money,' Bianca said and started to cry.

Antonia shot Moussey a look of astonishment. Julio had said nothing to her. For a split second she wondered if maybe her mother were lying but naïvely discounted the possibility on the grounds that such conduct at a moment like this would be beyond even her. Maybe Julio said something to Moussey or to Pedro, she thought. Men sometimes didn't like discussing sexual matters with their sisters. Especially sexually embarrassing matters.

'Mama, it's OK,' she said, giving her mother the benefit of the doubt and rushing to embrace her. 'Here, let me comfort you.'

'It's not OK,' Bianca said between sobs. 'Julio would never have had that accident if he hadn't had so much to worry about. Between Pedro and that adventuress Dolores, the poor boy must have been distracted beyond belief. Do you know what his greatest fear was?'

Antonia shook her head no. Moussey, finding himself in the middle of a maze, looked on, paralysed.

'The impending divorce. He didn't want to lose Biancita. You know how much he loved her. He was so worried that Dolores would get custody. He said he didn't want to live a life without his one and only daughter. He also said that he didn't want her having a mother figure like Dolores. He was terrified that she'd emulate her mother...become like her.'

'I don't know what to say,' Antonia responded, stunned by this new revelation.

'What's happened is too awful for words. But you must both promise me you won't breathe a word of this to either Dolores or Pedro. Since Julio didn't say anything to you, I don't want them knowing that I know. That's very important. If they know that I know, it will split the family apart, and I don't want that. Do you promise?'

Antonia nodded soberly.

Bianca then turned to Moussey to obtain his consent.

'Of course, Aunt Bianca.'

'Do you know if Manolito knows?'

'I don't think that's very likely, if I didn't know,' Antonia said.

'Then make sure you don't inform him,' Bianca said. 'Aside from anything else, we don't want him being educated too graphically about such matters at his tender age.'

Antonio and Moussey nodded in agreement. 'You see, my darlings,' she then said, going in for the kill with a degree of calmness that only added to her portrayal of sincerity, 'the fact is that Julio suspected Dolores of having more than one affair. In fact...I don't know how to say this...as a mother, I find it almost inconceivable...but Julio believed that Pedro and Dolores have been lovers for some time. That's why he set the trap when he caught her out with that other man. He was trying to catch her with Pedro.'

'That's not possible,' Antonia said, less accusing her mother of lying than dismissing the accusation.

'I'm not saying they are lovers, though you notice how quickly he's moved out of this house and into hers. It's what Julio suspected, that's all I'm saying. And I'll tell you something even worse. He said he wondered if Biancita was really his. He said the dates from conception to delivery didn't quite fit. If you remember, he was in Connecticut for three crucial weeks nine months before Biancita was born.'

'Mama, this is too unreal to be true. Biancita is the spitting image of you.'

'That's what I said when he brought up the question of the baby's paternity. "Oh, she's your granddaughter all right," he said, "of that I have no doubt. She looks too much like you to be anything else. But I do question whether she's my daughter or Pedro's." Of course no mother wants to hear things like that...' Bianca purposely let her words trail off to break the pace and give herself time to think.

'How could he have even suspected something like that? Pedro would never betray us,' Antonia said. 'Julio ought to have known that.'

'I'd only speak for myself, if I were you. Pedro's done many things over the years that I've kept from you. But he's your brother, and I don't want to come between you, so I'll keep my counsel.'

Antonia's mind was spinning. Stranger things had happened, she told herself. Dolores and Pedro were awfully close and always had been. No mother, not even Mama, she concluded, could lie about something like this - not at a time like this. 'The torment poor Julio must have been going through, to think that Pedro might be Biancita's father,' she said.

'You know what your brother was like,' Bianca continued, knowing that she had won her daughter over. 'He loved Pedro, and he loved Biancita, so whether he was her father or uncle didn't make that much difference. What did matter, though, was Dolores' betrayal, and the example that darling little girl would have if she were brought up by her mother. Of course Julio didn't blame Pedro. He felt Dolores had seduced his brother...the whole situation is too awful for words.'

'Does Grandma know?'

'I hope not, and I don't want to take the chance of her finding out. The shock will kill her. You know how she loves Pedro and will never hear a word against him. No, I think it's better we keep this one away from her.'

An unspoken distance now crept into relations between Antonia and Moussey on one side, and Pedro and Dolores on the other. This breach was further solidified after Julio's removal from intensive care, which in itself was such a dreadful occurrence for all concerned that it needed no embellishment to qualify as a genuine tragedy, for they had to face the hopelessness of the situation all over again. Julio would never recover. He was as good as dead. Bianca being Bianca, however, she could not resist the opportunity to exploit the situation and undermine her daughter-in-law while furthering her plans for Biancita under the guise of assisting her.

The family had gathered back at the Piedraplata family home after Julio's move into the wire-laden, machine-filled room that would hereafter be his world. The air was heavy with grief and shock and disbelief. Bianca and Pedro had even suspended hostilities and refrained from making adverse comments about each other for the first time in years as they circulated in the drawing-room, speaking to loved ones and the many friends who had dropped in to pay their respects and say goodbye to Bianca before her departure for abroad.

Out of the corner of his eye, however, Pedro saw his mother walk over to Dolores, who was standing speaking to his grandmother, Leila Barnett. Bianca was suddenly all sweetness and light, kissing the unfortunate

Dolores and smiling at her while she spoke.

'Darling girl, my heart goes out to you,' she announced sweetly. 'I shudder to think what it must be like to be an effective widow at twenty-five. I know we've had our differences in the last few days, but I don't want you to think we as a family are abandoning you now that Judio is no longer consciously with us. You must believe me when I say that I will do everything in my power to see that you have as comfortable a life as possible. It's the least we can do, isn't it, Mama ?'

'Yes,' said Leila Barnett. 'You're family, Dolores, and we never desert our family. Ever.'

'You're right, Mama,' Bianca said brightly then continued as if what she was about to say had come as a sudden idea. 'I want to send you and your sister and mother for a month's stay at the Botkin Institute in Santa Barbara. It's the best health farm in the world. They'll pamper you and treat you kindly and gently help you over this terrible period. The worst is yet to come. I know. I've lost a husband and a child before, so I know the grief of loss. Once life returns to a slower rythym after this period of frantic activity stops, the reality of your loss really hits you. That's true, isn't it, Mama?'

'It is,' Leila said quietly, remembering the many months of anguish she spent alone after Bianca's father had died.

'That's settled then. Speak to your mother and sister and give me some dates. I'd suggest you leave sometime next week.'

'But what about Biancita?' Dolores asked.

'Don't worry about her, darling girl. I'll take care of her. She can come and stay with us at L'Alexandrine while you're getting over the worst. Antonia and Moussey will be there with me and, truth be told, it will be nice to get to know my granddaughter a little better.'

Dolores did not know what to make of the offer. She looked from Bianca to Leila and back, her expression one of perplexity.

'I won't take "no" for an answer,' said Bianca, her voice the quintessence of concern. 'You're my daughter-in-law, and I need to do what's best for you. Isn't that so, Mama? Go on. Tell her. It's our job to take care of her now that Julio's not able to do so.'

'It can't do any harm, child,' Leila said, smiling. 'Go on. Take a break. You deserve it after all you've been through. If you don't like the Botkin Institute, you can always leave.'

'Or go anywhere else you and your mother and sister please,' Bianca interjected brightly. 'If you miss Biancita, I can always send Antonia over in the Lear with the little treasure, and you can see her.'

Convinced, Dolores walked right into the trap. 'OK...fine,' she said. 'Thanks. That's really sweet of you, Madame Mahfud.'

'Think nothing of it, darling girl,' Bianca replied, smiling sweetly. 'It's the least I can do.'

Twice during her stay at the Botkin Institute, Dolores telephoned her mother-in-law at L'Alexandrine to tell her how much she missed her daughter and to ask that the little girl be sent over to her.

The first time was at the end of the fourth day of her stay there. 'Of course I'll send her over with Antonia to see you for a few days if you're desperate,' Bianca responded, 'but she's just settled down here, and I fear it will unsettle her if she goes back and forth. Why don't you wait a few days and see how you're managing? I know you're recovering from Julio's loss, but you must realize that so is she.'

'I suppose you're right,' Dolores agreed dejectedly. 'Let me speak to her.'

'If she were here, I'm sure she'd like nothing better, but she's gone into the village with Antonia and Moussey. She's taken a real shine to the market,' Bianca said, smiling affectionately as she played the part of the indulgent grandmother, then looked through the open window at the swimming pool, where Biancita was laughing uproariously as Moussey and Antonia threw her back and forth in the water.

The second time Dolores called, Bianca, still preached concern. 'I'm sure you don't want to undermine your child's progress in getting over her father's accident,' she added this time, 'just to satisfy your own emotional needs. Being a mother myself, I know how tough it is the first time you're separated from your child, but it's our duty as mothers to place our children's welfare above our own, don't you think?'

'I suppose so,' Dolores replied wanly.

'I knew you'd see it my way. Julio always said what a wonderful wife and mother you were. In fact, maybe it would be a good idea if we just left things as they are and didn't run the risk of upsetting her with a telephone conversation. It might be kinder all round if you saved it all till you see her again.'

'Two weeks is a long time...' Dolores started to say.

'Exactly,' Bianca cut in. 'I knew you'd see my point. Two weeks is a long time to a little girl, and since she's out of her normal environment and hasn't associated the new one with missing you, it might be too hard on her. You know, darling girl, Julio was right. You really are an exceptionally thoughtful person. Which is all the more reason why you must try to forget about all your troubles and just relax while you can.'

Meanwhile Antonia and Moussey took care of Biancita at L'Alexandrine. She was an enchanting little girl. With the looks of her grandmother, the disposition of her mother and the personality of her father, she had the adults – Bianca included – falling over themselves to be with her. However, none became more attached to Biancita than Antonia. What added poignancy to the time spent with her niece was that Antonia had suffered two miscarriages in the first two years since her marriage. Sir Egerton Pickering, the eminent gynaecologist, had warned her that she might never be capable of giving birth to a live baby owing to a weak cervix. 'The only chance you'll have of carrying a child even close to term is if you were to lie flat on your back from the moment you discover you're pregnant until you give birth, hopefully eight months later,' he had said. 'Well, if Sophia Loren can do it,' Antonia had replied 'I don't see why I can't.' 'Each case is different,' Sir Egerton had observed. 'While you must not lose hope, you must prepare yourself for every eventuality. In obstetrics, nothing is ever quite as straightforward as the public believes.'

Meanwhile Dolphie and Stella Minckus were having the time of their lives at L'Alexandrine. With the self-discipline which had largely accounted for her worldly success, Bianca made no concession to the appalling grief she was suffering or, as she put it to Stella Minckus when the former beauty queen had offered to cancel the trip: 'If there's no way around grief...and there isn't when you lose your favourite child...you may as well distract yourself and do your level best to give your friends a good time. So come, and we'll act as if life were still normal.'

The splendour of L'Alexandrine would have impressed anyone, but what really sprinkled stardust in the eyes of the socially ambitious Mr and Mrs Minckus was the assemblage of Old Money personages Bianca served up with the meals. Unknown to them, the irresistible lure of Belmont's was casting its magic. Mary van Gayrib, Bianca's New York PA, had been working the telephone lines behind the scenes, asking all the local and visiting grandees to lunch or dinner or for a day's cruising, always with the specification that the occasion was 'in honour of Mr and Mrs P Adolphus Minckus to celebrate their recent acquisition of Belmont's'.

Bianca had managed yet again to kill two birds with one stone. She had made the Minckuses believe she was a fully paid-up member of the Old Money set while at the same time luring into her world many of the people she had wanted to entertain for years. Most of them had never previously so much as bothered to acknowledge her across a room; but now, thanks to her magical connection with Belmont's, they found themselves suddenly seduced by the charm and splendour of her way of life. Bianca could sense that finally, after all those years of patience - all those years of putting up with second-class people whom she had been obliged to pretend were first-class - the ice was melting, affording her access to the grandest harbour of all. She only hoped that all she would need to do now was keep up the momentum, entertaining and charming the way she customarily did, for these social acquaintances to become friends. Through them, she would be able to establish her status as one of the world's pre-eminent socialites. Then, and only then, would she be able to sit back and enjoy all she had.

Dolphie and Stella Minckus left France at the end of August, bedazzled, as all the others had been, by Bianca's European lifestyle. Stella was even resolved to use her as a role model for what a great lady should be, quite unaware that, to many of the Old Money crowd, Bianca was the living embodiment of vulgarity.

For her part, Bianca was sorry to see Dolphie and Stella Minckus go, not only because they were a welcome distraction from her grief but also because she did not want to be alone with the family for the five days that separated their departure from the arrival of Walter and Ruth Fargo Huron. Five days without the protection of guests at this crucial time, when she was only halfway through implementing her plans regarding Biancita, would expose her to too many questions about Dolores and Pedro from Antonia and Moussey. She therefore made sure Manolito was around as much as she could engineer, stating, on more than one occasion: 'I'm going to miss you so much when you go back to school in September.'

Surprisingly for someone who had not desired a fourth child since her teens and who had only fostered Manolito as a way of gaining access to his share of the Piedraplata family fortune, Bianca's statement to Manolito had more than an element of truth to it. The irony was that her motives for the relationship also supplied the reason why it had flourished in human terms. Driven as it was by the financial need to keep the young man fond of her, she had developed, over the years, into a loving and considerate mother figure. Indeed, she had a better relationship with him than with either Pedro or Antonia. With the Piedraplata heir, she was constrained at all times by the need to gain and keep his love if she wanted to continue having a say in the disposal of his fortune, especially after he achieved his majority. It would only take a few acts of callousness of the kind she had employed over the years with Pedro and Antonia to chill relations between them, but Bianca was too intelligent for that. If Amanda was given a reason for reopening the question of guardianship on the grounds of negligence or abuse, she might regain both custody and control of that half of the Piedraplata inheritance.

Even at the best of times litigation remained a fearsome bugbear to Bianca, although she was always very careful not to reveal her fears to anyone but Philippe. She still had a deep-seated fear, which Philippe's reassurances had never been able to dissolve, that the Mexican judiciary might be waiting stealthily for just such an eventuality as a legal battle over guardianship to reopen the casebook on Ferdie's death, so she always moved warily when dealing with Manolito or Amanda.

Had Amanda even the slightest inkling how much Bianca feared Mexico she would have instituted proceedings to reverse Manolito's guardianship immediately. But Bianca had been careful never to reveal her fears to anyone but Philippe. Meanwhile Manolito, blissfully ignorant of the fears of either woman, was due to fly out of Biarritz on the last day of August, with Biancita, Antonia and Moussey leaving three days after. The plan was - or so they believed - that he would meet Amanda and Anna Clara in London, while his stepsister and brother-in-law would fly on to Mexico to return the little girl to the mother, who was impatiently awaiting her return.

The night before their departure, Bianca put the next stage of her real plan into action. She began by telephoning Mexico City to speak to Dolores. The timing of the call was all-important as she had to prepare the ground with an unsuspecting Antonia and Moussey then ensure that it was not possible to revisit the subject until after Manolito's departure.

Fortunately the members of her family were seldom alone together.

Every day there was a luncheon party or a dinner. Whatever the event, the family was constantly surrounded by 'friends' of one sort or another. This made for a stimulating and distracting time, but it did not encourage personal conversations of any depth. This, of course, was the norm for those who lived in the social world, and the members of Bianca's family were all used to it, the way most social people are. Indeed, Bianca preferred it that way.

These highly socialized and regulated circumstances gave her almost total control over how long a conversation of a personal nature with a member of the family would last, where it would take place...and what its likely outcome would be.

Progress had been tricky because Bianca could not afford to have Manolito around when she discussed the subject of Biancita with Antonia and Moussey. She did not want him to hear something that might make him question how she had come to be his legal guardian.

Being clear about what she needed to do, Bianca telephoned Dolores from the privacy of her bedroom. 'Darling girl,' she said in her sweetest, most considerate tone of voice, 'How are you?'

'I'm well thank you, Madame Mahfud. I'm writing you a thank-you note for sending us to the Botkin...'

'Now, now, darling girl, there's no need for you to do anything as formal as that.'

'How's Biancita?' Dolores then asked.

'I can't hear you,' Bianca suddenly interjected, actually hearing her daughter-in-law perfectly. 'Dolores...? Dolores?'

'I can hear you. Can you hear me?'

'Dolores...? Dolores...? If you can hear me, please ring back immediately. We seem to be having trouble with this phone.'

With that, Bianca hung up. Within a minute, the telephone rang. She let it ring. Louis, the butler, answered it, as he had been trained to do, Bianca being particularly insistent that no one should answer the telephones but Louis. 'It's so common to answer one's own phone,' she was often heard to say. She waited until Louis buzzed her to pick up the receiver. 'Madame, it's Señora Calman calling from Mexico.'

'It's about time,' she said, knowing that Dolores could not overhear her until Louis switched the line over. 'The poor child has been here for a

306

month, and her mother hasn't even bothered to speak to her once. Just give me a moment to compose myself before you put her on. I'm so upset I can't tell you. She can phone to ask for more money, as she has done on two separate occasions already, but she hasn't wanted even once to speak to her own daughter. What sort of woman is she, I have to ask myself.' Then, slowing her breathing, she said: 'OK Louis, you can put her through now.' Somehow Bianca always found it easier to believe her own stories when she felt the servants had already been persuaded to accept them as true.

Giving the butler time to put down his extension, Bianca waited before speaking. 'Hello, Dolores,' she said. 'How are you?'

'Is that better, Madame Mahfud?' Dolores asked in all innocence.

'Yes, darling girl. Thank you for phoning back. Listen, Dolores, there's a slight problem. Biancita's picked up an ear infection in the swimming pool, and the doctor says she runs a danger of perforating her eardrum if she flies. I don't suppose you want her to run the risk of endangering her hearing for life, do you?'

'No. Of course not.'

'That's settled then. I'll keep you posted on her progress, and when it clears up, I'll send her back.'

'When do you think that will be?' Dolores said desperately, the pain of not seeing her child cutting through the telephone wires.

'Maybe next week. I don't suppose you'd like a word with her?'

'I'd love it, but it might upset her,' replied Dolores, having absorbed Bianca's lessons too well.

'You're quite right, darling girl. Of course it might. So silly of me not to have thought of that. You see, Julio was right. You really are the most thoughtful girl.'

As soon as she hung up, Bianca headed downstairs, looking for Antonia. She expected to find her by the swimming pool, but Louis said she was upstairs, in Biancita's room, so she returned upstairs.

Bianca entered the bedroom to see Antonia and Moussey playing horsy with the child. 'What a picture this makes,' she said, smiling with satisfaction. 'A real family picture. Happy and loving. If only Julio could be here to see this.'

'Hi, Mama,' Antonia said, while Moussey whinnied his greeting.

'You'll never believe who just phoned.'

'Who?' Antonia said, smiling indulgently at the way her mother always made you ask for the information she was dying to impart to you.

'This poor child's mother. She's asking if we can keep her for another week or two. I said yes, of course, but it's a bit rich, don't you think? That your poor brother isn't even properly cold in his grave and already she has no time for his daughter?'

'Did she give a reason?' Antonia asked.

'She said she has "things to do",' Bianca said acerbically. 'Although I don't suppose it takes much imagination to guess what those things are. What are we letting this poor child in for, if we send her back to a mother who doesn't even speak to her for days on end and, when the time comes for her daughter's return, wants to delay it? That sort of conduct doesn't strike me as particularly responsible or loving, but maybe this is a conversation we should be having when the darling little tyke is out of earshot.'

For the remainder of the evening, there was no possibility of having a personal discussion with her daughter and son-in-law, as Bianca had guests in for dinner and took pains to keep the last couple entertained until Manolito had gone to bed.

As planned, the young man left the following morning to take a scheduled Air France flight from Nice Airport to London Heathrow. That same evening she planned to bring matters to a head over dinner. She, Antonia and Moussey would be dining *en famille* with Philippe, who had arrived that afternoon and would leave on the Lear two days later for Mexico with his stepdaughter, son-in-law and granddaughter.

Bianca waited until Louis had cleared the soup plates before introducing the subject of Dolores and Biancita. 'What are we going to do about my precious little granddaughter?' she asked. 'Her mother clearly has no interest in her, and if we let her out of our hands, God knows what fate will have in store for her.'

'Have you thought of taking her in and raising her as our own?' asked Philippe, who loved both Bianca's children and Biancita as well.

'No, no, no. I couldn't go back to all the fuss of child rearing. But it's sweet of you to think of that, my darling,' she said, blowing a kiss down the length of the table to him. 'Isn't your Uncle Philippe the most wonderful man on earth, Antonia?'

'After Moussey, Mama,' Antonia said, well used to her mother's reliance upon flattery and sudden switches of mood.

'You two could take her in, you know,' Bianca said, bringing her plan to the boil. 'After all, you might never have a child of your own, and she is your brother's daughter...though quite which brother seems to be a mystery. Maybe you'd both like to talk it over and let us know what you think?'

'I don't need to discuss it, Aunt Bianca,' Moussey said. 'I know my mind. I'll have her, if Antonia will.'

'I *certainly* will have her,' Antonia said, 'if that's the only way she's going to get a loving and stable home.'

'Good. That's settled, then,' Bianca said. 'What a relief. Now I suppose I'd better go to Mexico with Uncle Philippe and iron out the details with Dolores. I daresay it's money she's after, so let's see how many pieces of silver it will take before she sells us our own flesh and blood back. I tell you, children: the longer I live, the more I realize how terrible some people can be. At least we'll rescue that little treasure, and you two will have your own daughter. Well, we'll happily pay the price, whatever it is...even if it includes having to go back to bloody Mexico.'

'I don't know what we'd all do without you,' Philippe said, suffused with admiration for his caring and capable wife.

As soon as dinner was over, Bianca headed straight upstairs to her bedroom and called Juan Gilberto Macias to instruct him to prepare draft documents for Dolores to sign, relinquishing custody of Biancita. Then she discussed with Philippe the financial question of how much to offer her daughter-in-law. He suggested $200,000: a figure she considered might be too small. 'How's she going to fight for more?' Philippe said, not for one minute questioning the veracity of his wife's claims. 'She's a whore and a negligent mother. She's lucky to get that.'

On the way to Mexico in the Lear, Philippe worked on his latest deal for Banco Imperiale involving some Colombian drug barons, while Bianca worked on her strategy. Between bouts of calculation, she looked at movies and flicked through her favourite magazines: *Town & Country*, didn't bother even to glance at *Time* or *Newsweek*, but as the jet approached Mexico City airport her mood changed, and she became perceptibly agitated at the mere thought of being in Mexico again.

The element of surprise being crucial to the success of their plan, Bianca and Philippe had not told anyone except Juan Gilberto Macias that they were arriving together, so Pedro was profoundly shocked when his mother walked into the house with his stepfather. 'What are you doing here?' he asked, so stunned that there was no trace of hostility, just surprise, in his voice.

'I have business to attend to...if you have no objection to me being in my own house,' his mother spat out, still intent on presenting herself as the aggrieved party.

'So how goes it, Uncle Philippe?' Pedro said, ignoring his mother's barb.

'Fine, my boy,' he replied, pleased as ever to see his stepson. 'Maybe we can go fishing this weekend.'

'Sounds good to me,' Pedro replied, walking out of the room.

'I'm going up to the bedroom to freshen up and make a few calls,' Bianca said to Philippe.

'I'll be in the study,' he said. 'Let me know how it goes.'

Hating being in this country and in this house, she walked up the stairs to the bedroom she used to share with Ferdie and now shared with Philippe. She picked up her own personal telephone and dialled Dolores' number. 'Hello, my dear,' she said, her voice far more neutral than it had been since Julio's funeral. 'It's Julio's mother here.'

'Hi, Madame Mahfud,' Dolores said, responding not to her mother-in-law's present tone of voice but to the solicitous one she had grown used to in the last six weeks. 'How are you? Is Biancita better now?'

'She's quite well, thank you,' Bianca replied. 'But rather than talk to you on the phone, why don't I come over and see you?'

'You mean, you're here in Mexico? You brought Biancita back to me yourself? I didn't expect that you'd do it yourself, I have to confess. How thoughtful you are, Madame.'

'Shall we say in fifteen minutes?'

'I can't wait,' Dolores said excitedly. 'Oh, the sheer joy of seeing my darling baby again.'

'Fifteen minutes, then,' Bianca said, still neutral but pleasant, and rang off.

Dolores was standing by the front door, watching for the car, hoping to get a glimpse of Biancita as Bianca's black Lincoln Continental came up the driveway. She bounded down the steps of the house so that she would be beside the car when it stopped, searching for Biancita. Not seeing her, she concluded that her daughter must be sitting in the back seat out of view. In her mind's eye, could see her sitting like a proper little lady, emulating her elegant grandmother.

Then the car stopped, and Duarte opened Bianca's door for her to alight as Dolores looked into the car and could find no trace of her daughter. For a split second, Dolores wondered if her eyes were playing tricks on her. Nonetheless, Dolores stepped forward to kiss her mother-in-law in greeting.

Bianca deftly avoided the kiss, however, lowering her head in such a way that Dolores would not think anything of it. She wanted to give the younger woman no warning of what was to come, so greeted her charmingly if distantly. She then led the way into the house she had never been in before, all the while being mindful that she must be careful not to compromise herself in front of the staff. She had learned her lesson well on that score, from the fallout following Ferdie's death. 'I'm absolutely shattered after that long flight,' she said in a pleasant and neutral tone of voice as Dolores followed her into the sitting-room, 'and dying of thirst. My throat's so parched I won't be able to utter one word until you've got the maid to bring me a long cold glass of Coca-Cola.'

'So was the flight OK? Is Biancita OK?' Bianca asked. 'I didn't expect her back so soon. I thought her ear infection would take longer to clear up than this.'

'That drink,' Bianca said lightly and waved Delores away to order it from the maid 'I can barely swallow.'

As soon as the younger woman was out of the room, she set off in the opposite direction to explore the interior of the house Julio had lived in.

Dolores came back to find that her mother-in-law had disappeared from view. 'Madame Mahfud,' she shouted.

Silence.

'Madame Mahfud, where are you?' she sang out.

Upstairs in the master bedroom, Bianca heard Dolores but did not respond. She was viewing the bed where Julio had slept, tears welling up in her eyes. 'At least I will always have a part of him in Biancita,' she thought, consoling herself. 'And she'll be brought up *my* way. To be one of us. Instead of being a peasant like her mother.'

'Madame Mahfud, where are you?' Dolores' voice rang out again.

'I'll be right down,' Bianca replied and went to look at Biancita's nursery. 'Decorated in typical middle-class fashion' she thought disdainfully, a little shudder of distaste running through her delicate sensibilities. Now she was ready to return downstairs.

Dolores, meanwhile, had started to ascend the stairs. Their eyes locked as she reached the landing.

'Shall we go into the drawing-room?' Bianca said, starting down.

'Julio was so happy here,' Dolores said, meeting her mother-in-law halfway. 'I know this house may not seem like much to you, but to us it was our bit of heaven.'

Dolores could have sworn Bianca gave her a funny look as she overtook her and once more led the way in a house that was not hers.

They then reached the drawing-room, and Bianca headed for the chair she had earmarked for herself, indicating one beside it for Dolores to sit upon, as if this were her house and not her daughter-in-law's.

'Now, my dear,' Bianca said acidly, reverting to the person Dolores had known before Julio's accident, 'why don't you save your Pollyanna act for someone less gullible than I? I know all about your antics. Julio confided in me completely before the accident.'

'I don't know what you're talking about, Madame,' Dolores said, failing to understand her mother-in-law's implication.

'Of course you do. You really mustn't take me for a fool, Dolores. It won't work.'

'I honestly don't know what you're talking about,' she said, starting to cry.

'Oh dear,' Bianca said lightly. 'Tears. The oldest trick in the book. The last refuge of the guilty.'

'What are you talking about?' Dolores said through her sobbing. 'What was there that you make sound so bad, for Julio to confide in anyone...?'

'It makes me feel dirty just repeating what I've been told...'

'Who has told you what?' demanded Dolores, her tears turning to anger as she began to sense the direction in which the conversation was heading.

'Come, come, you don't expect me to reveal my sources, do you? Suffice it to say that you deceived me at first, but my eyes are open now, and I can see right through you.'

'I really have no idea what you're talking about, Dolores replied, giving Bianca her first glimpse of the brain she had beneath her loving exterior.

'Are you going to deny that Julio was going to divorce you?'

'Divorce me? This is crazy. Julio and I were closer than ever.'

'According to my sources,' Bianca said, 'you were just as close to his brother and the man he caught you in bed with.'

'Madame Mahfud, I don't know who's been feeding you these lies, but I can assure you, that's all they are...lies. I mean this is just too ridiculous for words. Me sleeping with another man? With Pedro? For Christ's sake, Pedro is Julio's brother.'

'Precisely,' Bianca said. 'Now listen here, my dear, I don't expect you to confess. Your type never does. But my daughter Antonia and I now have your number, and we're not allowing little Biancita to live here with you. You will either relinquish custody to me voluntarily, and I will hand her over to Antonia for her to bring up in a proper manner, or I will fight you in the courts. I don't suppose you're so deluded that you think you'll stand a chance against me. Aside from the fact that I have far more money and influence than you, I will also hire private detectives to dig up every bit of dirt there is on you.'

'I don't have any dirt,' Dolores said angrily.

'You're a bright girl. Bright enough to have ensnared a young man from a rich family after working with him as his secretary. Do you think your word, and the word of one or two of your common little friends and relatives, will carry more weight than mine, my family's, various private detectives and functionaries? Come, come, Dolores. Think for a minute. Do you really want to put yourself through that?'

'And if I agree?'

'I'll give you $200,000 outright. To do with as you please. On one condition.'

'And what's that?' Dolores said bitterly, knowing what it was before Bianca even replied.

'That you relinquish all rights to Biancita in perpetuity.'

'You're doing to me what you did to Manolito's mother.'

'No, dear girl, I've learned from that mistake. Which is why you have to relinquish *all* rights.'

'And if I don't?'

'You won't get a penny, and you'll never see Biancita again. Ever. I'll make sure of that.'

'Why are you doing this to me? You know that I loved Julio and would never have cheated on him. You can't seriously believe those lies?'

'Oh, but I do believe them, dear girl. And if you oppose me on this, everyone in Mexico will know about your sexual antics by the time I'm through with you. Take my advice and make things easier for yourself. You're beaten, so admit defeat. Take some spoils from the victor. Move on with your life. As the ex-wife of my son and with the nest egg I'm offering you, you'll make yourself another good marriage in a year or two. The alternative is to fight me and see me destroy your reputation and any possibility of a resurrection from the ashes. Think about it while you go into the kitchen and get me another Coke then come back and give me the answer that will enhance all our lives.'

Dolores rose from her seat, picked up Bianca's glass and headed towards the kitchen. Bianca Barnett del Rio Calman Piedraplata Antonescu Mahfud had touched yet another life and taken from it what she wanted.

Chapter Nineteen

It would take years before the full effect of Julio's living death became evident to those who had been closest to him, but even in the months following the tragedy, the changes were nevertheless already painfully apparent. Bernardo became seriously depressed, and gradually, over a period of two years, his business collapsed. To her credit, Bianca came to his rescue without once being prompted by Antonia, and he moved back to Mexico from Panama with his new wife, after Bianca bought their old marital home and gave him the use of it, rent-free.

Dolores, stunned by the loss of Biancita and unable to marshal enough resources to fight the woman she believed to be invincible, also sank into a deep depression, seeking refuge in sleep; and when she could sleep no more, in the oblivion that drink afforded her.

Pedro lay low, simmering with even greater hatred against his mother than before but careful not to give her any reason to have him committed again. He could often be found at Dolores' house, the same house Julio had rented for her and Biancita, and to which she clung, as if by so doing, she were keeping herself in contact with the husband and daughter she had lost. Whenever Pedro was not there, he made a point of having her over to the Piedraplata family home, where he still lived, until it became like a second home to her. This Bianca knew because she telephoned Duarte once a week for him to keep her informed of her son and daughter-in-law's comings and goings.

The older woman haunted their lives, not only because of what she had done but also what they feared she could still do. Only Antonia seemed to have escaped relatively unscathed; and while it took her five years to get over Julio's loss, she now had his daughter to console her.

Also badly shaken by the loss of his eldest stepson, Philippe threw himself into his work, dissolving the business partnership with his brother and going his own separate way. Soon his New York banking concern attracted the interest of Continental Express, the credit company, which had made no secret of its desire to acquire Banco Imperiale New York.

If Philippe's pain was alleviated by his business activities, his wife's response was less straightforward. Frequently, she would be with friends, laughing and talking as if she did not have a care in the world and had never even seen the face of loss. Once she was home, however, and in the privacy of her own environment - an environment that she controlled as carefully as ever - Bianca would cry and cry and cry, sometimes for an hour or more. The staff noted that she always did this when she was alone: when no one in the family, no friend, not even Mary van Gayrib, could see her. It was as if she wanted the release of tears without the comfort of family or friends. Meanwhile the servants and household staff acted as if they had seen and heard nothing.

Yet Julio's accident also had an energizing effect upon the already energetic Bianca. It was as if she had woken up to the fact that she too would one day cease to exist consciously: that her time on this earth was fleeting and limited.

The fact of the matter was that Julio's situation, together with the paradoxical way in which she approached it, showed that Bianca was storing up problems for herself. Her great wealth and the influence it brought in its wake had weakened rather than strengthened her character over the ensuing years. Furthermore, that wealth could not buy her the protection - against adversity, against conscience - she had hoped for.

Feeling entitled to the gratification of her every desire and whim did not leave much room for the spiritual lessons that Bianca needed to learn. Her failure to confront her guilt would play a significant part in her failure to deal constructively and comfortably with the loss of her adored son.

Instead Bianca's grief became an internal running sore which could be neither cleansed nor healed, but which continued to eat away at her, year in, year out, while she focussed her energies with even greater ferocity than before upon her quest to become one of the world's leading socialites.

Even Manolito, who was only seventeen when Julio's accident took place, would find himself marked for life by his elder stepbrother's living death. The unexpectedness of it all had torn away the blanket belief in the benevolence of fate that is the natural effect of wealth upon anyone who has spent his years cocooned against the harsher realities of life, as this young man had. True, he had grown up hearing rumours about how Bianca had killed his father. True, he knew that his stepbrother Pedro hated her, and that she in turn despised her youngest son. True, his mother Amanda Piedraplata had nothing good to say about her – although she equally was careful not to say anything bad, limiting herself to the oftrepeated comment that 'there's only one Bianca, and we can all be thankful for that'. But as he grew older he was also mindful that the life he led as a member of the Mahfud family was so much more extraordinary and extravagant, so much more seductive and fascinating, than that which he lived with Amanda and Anna Clara. Sure, he loved his mother and little sister, but Bianca had also been a good mother figure to him. Bianca's seductive powers had had him in their thrall since his earliest childhood. With that extraordinary woman, anything and everything had seemed possible, and he had liked the sensation of empowerment, of being a master of his own fate that came with being a member of Bianca Mahfud's family. However, Julio's accident broke the spell. Thereafter, Manolito would always see that great wealth and a powerful personality, for all the freedom and possibility they brought, only allowed you to shape your life in a limited manner. This was a chastening and maturing lesson for him to learn, and, coming at the impressionable age that it did, it sobered him up in a way that no amount of lectures from Amanda could ever have done.

The first sign of Manolito's newfound maturity came when he turned eighteen and came into his inheritance from Ferdie. He was now conservatively worth some $350,000,000. The immediate dilemma was what, if anything, he should do about this vast fortune. Should he continue having his trustees, Philippe and Raymond Mahfud, handle his money, or should he move it out of their hands and into the care of someone else?

'I'd leave things as they are,' Amanda said. 'Investing the money of very rich people is Raymond and Philippe's business. That's what private investment bankers do. And since one is your guardian's husband, and they were both your father's partners...and have done well with your inheritance to date...I'd let sleeping dogs lie.'

'I thought you might want me to move the money,' Manolito said, looking relieved.

'Darling, I have nothing against Raymond and Philippe and never did. I always liked them, and I learned a long time ago not to believe everything one hears.'

'So you don't believe Daddy killed himself?'

'Darling,' Amanda replied, 'everyone except Bianca accepts that your father cannot have committed suicide.'

'You know what Pedro says, don't you?'

'Let's just say that I've heard what Pedro thinks, and it accords with what many other people have always suspected.'

'But you don't think she...?'

'Darling, you really don't want to burden your young head with these old thoughts. All I will say is that you should make sure you never give Bianca power of attorney over one penny of your money. And make sure you make a will that leaves not one penny of your money to her or to her children.'

'So what should I do?' Manolito asked.

'The first and most important thing is that you make a will. Uncle Piers thinks you should go to Sir David Napley. He's a top solicitor and has the distinction of being someone Bianca does not know.'

'Gosh, Mummy, you sound pretty serious about this.'

'Sex and money bring out the worst features of the human being, Manolito. There's no use pretending otherwise. People, whom we all think are nice and kind and decent, can resort to the most debased forms of behaviour to get their hands on money or the sexual partner of their choice. As your mother, I wouldn't be serving your interests if I pretended otherwise. All that money Ferdie left you makes you too vulnerable, and only the truth will offer you a measure of protection against the darker side of human nature. That, my darling son, is the price you will have to pay, all your life for the privilege of great wealth.'

'Will you come with me to David Napley?'

'Yes.'

'I'll leave everything to you and to Anna Clara.'

'If you do that, you must leave her share in such a way that she cannot touch the capital until she is thirty-five.'

'I'll leave Uncle Philippe as the executor.'

'No. You mustn't. No one connected to Bianca must have anything to do with your estate.'

'But I'll need a competent executor.'

'If you know in your heart of hearts that you can trust us, name Uncle Piers and me. He's honourable and should you pre-decease him - which seems very unlikely as long as Bianca and her children can't profit from your death - we'll find someone else reputable and reliable who will protect Anna Clara's interests when Uncle Piers passes away.'

Three days later, Amanda and Manolito arrived at David Napley's offices where they were received by the slight dapper solicitor. Having listened to their requirements, he said: 'What you need is a simple, straightforward and ironclad will which can stand all interference from third parties. It shouldn't take more than a few hours to draw it up. I can have something for your consideration by the end of next week.'

Amanda, whose solicitor had taken three months to draw up her will and had charged her accordingly, was so impressed by his honesty that she suggested to Manolito, right in front of Sir David, that he make him an executor. 'It's not good policy to have a solicitor as an executor,' he said. 'We are obliged to see that no corners are cut, and this can hamstring a beneficiary, driving up the cost of probate.'

David Napley then proceeded to draw up a will in the succeeding days that was a study in brilliant simplicity. Manolito left everything to his mother, Amanda, and his sister, Anna Clara, in equal shares. If one of them predeceased him, her share would go to the other, but if they both predeceased him, or died with him, half his money was to be left to Clara d'Offolo and Magdalena, and the other half split between two charitable foundations, both named the Ferdinand and Manuel Piedraplata Foundations, which were to be set up and administered - one in Britain, the other in Mexico - for adoptive parents and children. Sir David was named the overall administrator.

Traditionally, there was little overlap between Manolito's two families. When he was with Bianca he never saw Amanda and Anna Clara. However, he did see his stepbrother Pedro and Julio's widow, Dolores, when he was in Mexico, where he spent much of the Christmas and Easter holidays as well as a large part of the summer holidays with Amanda and Anna Clara. The year of his majority, he exercised his newfound freedom and financial power by opting to take them skiing in Gstaad over Easter instead. It was only when Manolito had booked them into the Palace Hotel through his mother's travel agent that he discovered from Antonia that she, Moussey and Biancita were also planning to be there as guests of Bianca and Philippe, along with Dolphie and Stella Minckus and the Duke and Duchess of Oldenburg.

This was a departure from the norm for Bianca, who preferred the richer air of St Moritz, but she had been propelled into a change of venue by Stella Minckus, whose personality was well on the way to fossilizing into imperious snobbishness. The former Miss Cyprus had affected not to hear what her friend had said when she had asked her to come to St Moritz for Easter. 'What a marvellous invitation, Bianca darling! We'd so love to stay with you at the Palace Hotel in Gstaad. We just adore Gstaad with all its unpretentious Old Money people. So unlike that ghastly *nouveaux* St Mortiz, where you see half the people you spend all year avoiding in New York. Did you know, that awful Ruby Leighton practically lives there every winter, from November to the week after Easter? And the Manny Greenbaums and the Morty Bachmans are there every year for Chanukah and Passover, without fail. Dolphie and I went there the first year we were married, and they all stuck to us like glue. I couldn't shake them off for the next two years, either in Switzerland or back home.'

As the words tripped off Stella's increasingly over-refined tongue, Bianca remembered the stories circulating around New York about how Stella had dropped all her old friends and replaced them with what she considered to be Top Drawer Europeans as soon as she had access to Belmont's invitation list. Fortunately for Bianca, she had qualified, in Stella's eyes at least, for inclusion in that regal circle by virtue of being a British aristocrat with international dimensions. She was therefore not about to lose face in this mutual exploitation called friendship - or her place on the Belmont's invitation list - by defending St Moritz. So Bianca ordered Mary van Gayrib to cancel the Palace Hotel in St Moritz and book them suites at the Palace Hotel in Gstaad instead.

Manolito was having lunch at the Eagle Club with Amanda, Anna Clara and their ski instructors when Antonia, Moussey and their guides walked in. 'That's Antonia and Moussey,' Manolito said to Amanda. 'Shall we ask them to join us?'

'I don't see why not,' said Amanda.

'I'd love to meet them properly,' Anna Clara added, having never had the opportunity before, although she did know Pedro from having seen a lot of him in Mexico.

Antonia and Moussey and their instructors were happy to join them and had just ordered lunch when Amanda, who had just finished her coffee, went to the ladies room to repair her makeup prior to her group departing once again for the ski slopes.

Like in a Feydeau farce, no sooner had she disappeared from view than her successor as Mrs Ferdie Piedraplata walked into the club with Stella Minckus and the Duchess of Oldenburg.

'Hello, my chickadees. Hello, everyone,' Bianca said brightly, as Manolito and Moussey tried to stand, waving them back into their seats.

'Just came over to say hi and to introduce Manolito to the Duchess of Oldenburg. She's heard a lot about you, haven't you, Graziella?'

'Your mother's very proud of you,' said the Duchess.

Manolito got up, kissed Bianca and Stella, whom he knew well, and said 'How do you do, ma'am?' to this representative of an old European ruling family. His stepmother then put her hands on his shoulders and affectionately pushed him back into his seat.

'And who is this beautiful young woman you're with?' Bianca said, knowing very well who she was from the photographs in Manolito's room. 'I must warn you, young lady, that it will take a very special woman to be good enough for my son.'

Anna Clara blushed.

'This is Anna Clara, Mama,' Manolito said rather awkwardly.

'My, what a beauty you've grown into! I remember the afternoon your mother and I met up in the Pierre Hotel in New York shortly after you were born. Well, little acorns do grow into fine oaks, and you certainly have. Incidentally, Manolito, maybe you can drop by my suite early this evening. Juan Gilberto Macias is in from Mexico, and I think it's time you addressed the issue of your will.'

Manolito looked sheepish. Bianca, who seldom missed a nuance, realized that this was a more important topic to him than she had anticipated. How silly of her, she decided, to have listened to Philippe and let things slide in the run-up to his eighteenth birthday. Doubtless that wretched woman Amanda had already been bending his ear. 'Well, we'll see whose will prevails,' she thought to herself, slapping a smile on her face.

'Sir David Napley has already drafted it,' Manolito said, wiping the smile right off it again.

'And you didn't consult me?' she replied, clearly hurt.

'I didn't want to bother you. You're so busy.'

'You know I'm never too busy for you,' she said lovingly, stroking his cheek and masking her disappointment as she continued. 'I'm just amazed that neither you nor Uncle Philippe has said a thing to me.'

'He didn't have anything to do with it.'

'I'm not following you, darling,' she said, and Anna Clara noticing the glint of steel behind the seductively pleasant manner. 'Uncle Philippe manages everything for all of us...'

'I'm not moving any investments from him. Mummy just thought that I should have a will now that I've achieved my majority, so she took me to a solicitor in London, and he arranged it all.'

'Good...that's good,' Bianca said, and Anna Clara could almost reach out and touch the look of furious frustration her brother's stepmother was trying to mask. 'As long as it's all arranged. One can never be careful enough on mountains. Avalanches and all that...' Bianca looked at the Duchess. 'Manolito is now custodian of a great fortune,' she continued, 'and it is my duty, as his mother, to see that he lives up to his responsibilities.' Turning back to Manolito, she said, 'Think of all the poor people whose livelihoods depend upon our welfare. Dying intestate is simply the worst. It causes such a mess, then the various governments get involved and before you know it, you've lost half your money, and poor innocent people are out of work in their thousands... Well, we must be off. Shall we see you at six, Manolito, for a quick glass of champagne? If you want to come, Anna Clara, do please feel free to join us.'

With that, Bianca sailed off, turning heads as she walked through the room in regal fashion. Before she had even taken her seat, Amanda reappeared.

'You'll never believe who was just here,' Anna Clara said.

'If you're going to tell me that Antonia's mother is here, I can see her over there,' she said neutrally, seeing no reason to embarrass Antonia by being disparaging about her mother.

She remained standing.

'She stopped by to say hello,' Moussey said.

'What a sweet gesture,' Amanda said, with just the faintest trace of irony to give away her true feelings. 'Now, kids, what's on the agenda for this afternoon?'

That evening, Manolito went up to his stepmother's suite alone: his sister, who had taken an instant dislike to Bianca, having refused to attend with him. She and Philippe were on their own, and the three of them sat on the matching sofas facing each other in the sitting-room, each prepared for what they anticipated would be an awkward encounter.

'Darling, would you like a little caviar with your champagne?' Bianca said sweetly, immediately working to put her stepson at his ease. 'No? Oh, come. One slice of toast with some butter and a great big dollop of Beluga will help the Cristal go down so much more easily.'

'You've convinced me,' Manolito said, immediately feeling more relaxed and leaving her, in true Latin American style, to prepare the caviar, which she always did for them.

'So what's this I hear from your mother about making a will without telling us?' Philippe said, to the point as always.

Manolito cleared his throat. His unease returned in even greater force than before. Suddenly, he felt almost a traitor. Silence hung in the air.

Philippe and Bianca, who were used to applying pressure upon others by refusing to rescue them from the ensuing silence, just looked at him. After what seemed like an eternity he said: 'Sir David Napley did it when I was in London for my birthday.'

'That was quick,' Bianca said sharply.

'Commendably so,' Philippe said, taking care to remove any sting from her words. 'Presumably Amanda organized it for you.'

'Yes,' Manolito said, feeling as if he were caught between the devil and the deep blue sea.

'That's as it should be,' Philippe said more benignly than he felt. He was a past master of using principle pragmatically and knew only too well that by praising Manolito he would gain more trust from the boy than by undermining him.

Bianca, who also understood the merits of keeping Manolito on

323

friendly terms, poured a look of radiance over her face that was sorely at odds with the glint in her eyes. 'Absolutely,' she said. 'That's as it should be, considering the relationship between Amanda and yourself...though you would've thought she'd have had the courtesy to consult us, considering we've done far more for you than she's ever bothered to do.'

'I didn't mean to hurt you...' said Manolito, suffused with guilt.

'Of course not, my darling boy,' Bianca said, rushing to put her arms around him. 'I know you'd never do anything to hurt your Mama deliberately. I don't feel hurt by you. I feel hurt by Amanda.'

'You should lodge a copy of the will with the bank,' said Philippe, keen to know its contents.

'I'll get Mummy to arrange for Sir David to send you one,' Manolito agreed, seeing a way out of personally telling them what it said.

'So are you going to tell us how you intend to dispose of your assets in the unlikely event of your death?' Bianca said lightly. 'Or are we going to have to be kept in the dark till Sir David Napley sends us a copy of the will?'

Manolito, feeling like an ingrate on top of a traitor, tried to retrieve the situation. 'It's very simple, actually,' he said. 'Mummy and Anna Clara are my main beneficiaries, but if anything happens to them, Aunt Clara and Magdalena inherit a half of the estate, with the other half going to a charitable foundation, to be set up on my behalf in the name of my father and grandfather.'

'That's all very well, but it doesn't seem like a good plan to me, son,' Bianca said sweetly. 'What if something should happen to Clara and Magdalena? Surely you're not leaving things in such a way that they can dissipate your poor father's fortune on those husbands of theirs.' Then, looking at Philippe, she said, 'Do you remember how poor Ferdie used to grind his teeth at those gigolos Clara was forever picking up? I understand it's a case of like mother, like daughter.' Turning back to Manolito, she continued: 'What number husband is each of them on?'

'Aunt Clara is still married to Uncle Rodolfo...'

'That's a miracle. Maybe the Pope will make him a saint...'

'And Magdalena just got married for the third time.'

'To another penniless lord?'

'He's an artist and a very nice guy,' Manolito answered, intent on ignoring the innuendo. 'Much nicer than her previous husband, who couldn't accept the fact that their son was born with a harelip.'

'The sins of the mother are being visited upon that poor child.'

That was too much for even Manolito. 'What sins can Magdalena have possibly committed?' he demanded rather sharply.

'Not Magdalena, silly,' Bianca said airily, shifting the meaning of what she had said from daughter to mother. 'Clara's sins have been visited upon Magdalena. The Bible says that the sins of the parents are visited upon the children even to the third and fourth generation, and, while the Bible does get some things wrong, it didn't get *that* wrong. Poor Magdalena. She was always such a sweet and pretty child. Is she still?'

'Yes,' Manolito said, taking a sip of his champagne, relieved that Bianca had not intended to attack Magdalena through her child.

'So you're leaving half your father's money outright to that sister of his, whom he deliberately cut out of his own will, and to her daughter?'

'I think it only fair,' Manolito said. Bianca could now see that he harboured secret - and dangerous - sympathies for the aunt who had lost the struggle for the Piedraplata family fortune.

'At least you're doing the right thing by Amanda and Anna Clara,' Bianca replied, furious that Amanda had trumped her but intent on masking it. 'That's lovely, darling. A son should take care of his mother and sister, though I'm surprised that you've ignored your other mother and sister. But no hard feelings. I suppose you think we already have enough so leaving us anything else would be superfluous. Although I have to tell you that I don't see it like that. In fact, I'm rather hurt that you haven't realized that making a will is about more than the disposition of assets. It's also about bequeathing people you love some physical proof of your love. By leaving neither your sister Antonia nor myself anything, it's as if you're declaring that you don't really love us. It's the thought that counts, after all, not the money.'

'I'm sorry, Mama,' Manolito said, perilously close to tears, Bianca having succeeded in making him feel even more of a heel than even he had anticipated. However, Amanda's wary voice still sounded in his thoughts, and he heard himself saying, much to his surprise: 'I'll change the will. I'll leave you and Antonia and Pedro proof of my love in the form of a rare orchid each. That way no one can ever say that I didn't even mention you in my will, and honour will be maintained all round.'

Bianca and Philippe were nonplussed. Taking advantage of their unexpected reaction, Manolito drained the champagne from the flute, put it down on the coffee table, leaped to his feet and, rushing over to his stepmother, kissed her. Before she had a chance to catch her breath, he had kissed Philippe on his cheek as well and was out the door.

It was only afterwards, when he was taking the elevator down to his floor, that Manolito realized how maturely he had handled the situation.

In fact, he was astonished that he had actually beaten Bianca at her own game, for it was clear to him that she had been angling to get him to change his will in favour of Antonia and herself. While he did not actually wish to believe that Amanda was right about Bianca being a murderess, and while he did not want to accept that it would never be safe to leave even one penny to either her or any of her descendants, on a deeper level he had already accepted that fact and would therefore never leave either of them so much as a penny.

Manolito was now taking his rightful place upon the stage that the Piedraplata family fortune had created for him. How he performed as he entered adulthood became important, not only to his immediate family but also to the thousands of employees whose fate his conduct might one day affect. The three years between the ages of eighteen and twenty-one were relatively carefree for him. He had gone up to Trinity College Cambridge to read History. Once his gap-year came to an end, he commuted between his room at the university and a flat in London, which he had bought for himself in Hereford Square near South Kensington. It was a bachelor pad but not a typical one, for the area was grander, the rooms bigger and the furnishings more elegant than your average university student's. Manolito, however, was purposefully low-key at college, so none of the students at Cambridge knew about the vast fortune he had inherited. He preferred it that way too, for he wanted to be known and liked for himself. Like his older stepbrother Pedro, he was only too aware that many people who attached themselves to the very rich had base motives. Unlike Pedro, however, who had given up the struggle for independence by embracing his mother's wealth while despising the methods by which she had acquired and retained it, Manolito was quietly resolved to keep his integrity.

Manolito's life now followed an agreeable rhythm. He saw Amanda and Anna Clara - who lived in London during term time - at least once a fortnight, usually for dinner, but sometimes for lunch or tea and occasionally for the theatre, the opera, or a concert at the Royal Festival Hall. He saw little or nothing of Bianca or Philippe until the holidays, which he still split between the opposing branches of his family, usually spending his time with the Mahfuds in Europe or America, before decamping with Amanda and Anna Clara to Mexico. As he matured, Manolito grew closer to Amanda and Anna Clara, so that the axis of his interest was shifting away from the fascinating world of his stepmother to the less complicated and more straightforward one of his adoptive mother.

Nevertheless, he saw no reason to choose one over the other, having always taken separate loyalties for granted. To her credit, Amanda did nothing to undermine his fondness for his other family, recognizing that to do so would hurt him and the other innocents, Antonia included, more than Bianca, while his stepmother's occasional barbs at Amanda's expense only had the effect of pushing Manolito even closer to the very camp from which she was hoping to keep him.

This process was also facilitated by an unexpected source. Once Dolores found out that he had gone behind Bianca's back to draw up his will, she tried every time she saw him to get Manolito to agree to intervene on her behalf with his stepmother for Biancita's return. She never seemed to understand that he could not do so; and the efforts of Amanda and Anna Clara to get her to accept that no one could do anything to change matters, only drove the young mother to greater fits of despair and ever more frenzied requests for intervention, until Manolito was reluctantly compelled to tell her that he would have to stop seeing her unless she desisted from pressuring him. It did, however, start him thinking about how Amanda must have felt when she was forced into giving up custody of him; and the more he thought about the pain that such a loss must have caused a mother, the more he loosened his ties to Bianca. Loosened - but not broke.

The problems of Dolores aside, family life in Mexico was, in Manolito's eyes, as close to absolute harmony as it was possible to have, for Amanda, Anna Clara, Pedro and Dolores were all supportive of the other, each of them wished the other well, and each of them was basically a peaceable and loving human being. It was less exciting but ultimately more fulfilling than the aura of endless but impersonal possibility that pervaded Mahfud family life.

It was in 1988, at the beginning of his third year at Cambridge, that Manolito met Leila Al Musmahri. An exchange student from Boston University, Leila was at Cambridge for only one term. She was not particularly beautiful, nor was she even especially captivating, at least not upon first acquaintance. What she did have, however, was a quiet intensity that became exceedingly appealing the more Manolito, who was used to intense women, grew to know her.

He began spending more and more time with Leila. They went out for supper, as friends, and often stayed up half the night talking about the important issues of the day. Leila was very politicized, her background being in its own way as exotic as Manolito's. She had been born in Libya to the wife of an army officer who was imprisoned for two years by Colonel Gaddafi following his coup against King Idris in 1970. When the Libyan leader concluded that General Al Musmahri would not be a threat to the new regime, he released him and two years later sent him to London as a diplomat. Leila was sent to school at Lady Eden's in Kensington, and later on to Benenden in the Kent countryside, but not before she had obtained a unique perspective on world affairs. Her father played host to sundry Libyans, Palestinians, Irish Republicans and Eastern Europeans. Then, in her third year at Benenden, he defected and sought political asylum in Britain. His circle suddenly enlarged to include Americans, pro-Palestinian Jews, West Germans and exiled Eastern Europeans, as well as various British politicians and industrialists. Leila consequently had an overview of world politics that few young people have ever enjoyed, and this was enhanced when the family moved to Boston, Massachusetts in 1985. There, they settled into a comfortable but by no means lavish lifestyle, her father having taken up a post as a Middle Eastern expert with Boston University.

Gradually Manolito found himself falling in love with Leila, and she with him. It was not sudden, but, when it happened, it quickly became earth shattering for both of them. Within a month of first sleeping together, Manolito proposed one night as Leila snuggled in his arms after making love.

'But Manolito, we're so young,' Leila observed, looking up at the strong line of his jaw.

'Is that a yes or a no?' he laughed, peering down at her with the quiet and relaxed intensity so characteristic of his personality.

'I suppose a...yes,' she teased.

'I'd better ask your father for his permission.'

'I think you'd better meet him before you do that,' Leila joked.

'True. Shall we tell Mummy?'

'Will she approve? I mean, I am Libyan and...'

'Listen, Leila, just because your country has a leader who's unpopular in the West doesn't mean you have to slink around apologizing for who you are. The Libyan people are from an ancient culture. Think of Carthage and all the Roman ruins, and it puts the newness of Western civilization into perspective.'

'But wouldn't your mother prefer a nice blonde English girl?'

'Not my mother. She won't give a toss as long as she thinks you're a decent person and you have a good character and will make me happy.'

'I find that difficult to believe, knowing how prejudiced the English can be against Arabs.'

'Trust me. My mother is not like that.'

'What about your stepmother?'

'She'll be OK too. She's half-Palestinian herself, her husband is Iraqi, and my stepsister is married to a Lebanese. So we've already got quite a Middle Eastern cabal in our family.'

As Manolito had envisaged, neither Amanda nor Bianca objected when he telephoned and told them he had met the girl he wished to marry, although both of them cautioned him against making such a commitment too soon. Manolito, however, was firmly convinced that he had met the right girl and foresaw a lifetime of happiness and adventure with Leila, especially as he knew for a fact that she had no idea of how rich he was. Indeed, her first hint of the family's extensive wealth only came when she stepped into the entrance hall of Amanda Piedraplata's house in Cadogan Place in Chelsea. Although Manolito did not know it at the time, his money was the one thing Leila did not want. Indeed, she was bowled over in the most negative sense possible by the sumptuousness of the place, despite the fact that Amanda was in relative terms the poor relation in the both Piedraplata and Mahfud families. As Leila's eyes swept the entrance hall and the adjoining passage, lined with ancestral portraits on the walls and fine console tables beneath them, she could see that this was patently the house of a lady of means and taste. The portraits were a titled roll call of Amanda's aristocratic forebears. And when Leila walked into the first of the two reception rooms off the passage it was impossible to sit upon a chair that was less than two hundred years, while the sofas were all overstuffed Colefax and Fowler, their very contemporaneousness adding to the aura of wealth and elegance.

Leila took one look at the grandeur that was her future mother-in-law's way of life and promptly recoiled. 'Can I fit into this world?' she immediately asked herself and experienced a palpable feeling of relief once the visit was over, and she stepped back out onto the street with Manolito.

'I had no idea your family was so rich,' she said.

'Is that a problem?'

'I don't know.'

Manolito laughed. 'You know, I've spent years hiding the amount of money my family has so that people will want me for myself,' he said, hugging Leila and kissing her lovingly on the back of her neck, 'and when I finally meet someone who does, she thinks it's a problem that we have too much money. In fact, you'd probably like me if I even had less.'

Leila smiled and nodded, but the fact was that if she married Manolito, she would be entering a world whose rarefied air she had no wish to breathe.

It took Manolito two months to convince Leila that she could be happy as the wife of a rich man. He also made a clean breast of the degree of his family's wealth, rightly figuring that she deserved to know what she was getting into. What he did not tell her - at least not then - were the stories circulating about his father's death. However, he did take her to L'Alexandrine to present her to Bianca, who endeared herself to Leila by being as lavishly welcoming as only Bianca could be and by referring to her at all times as 'cherie'.

It was a combination of love for Manolito and the open arms with which Amanda and Bianca greeted Leila, together with the way they took their way of life for granted, that finally convinced Leila that she could marry Manolito without losing her ability to function in the real world as well.

Once Leila made that decision, she and Manolito boarded Concorde and flew to New York, where they caught a connecting flight to Boston and turned up on her parents' doorstep, unannounced, to seek their approval for the marriage, which they gave without reservation. The young couple then flew back to the United Kingdom two days later to plan their wedding in London three months hence.

Once more Manolito showed the basic soundness and maturity of his character, as well as how the influences in his life were changing, when he took his mother's advice and appointed Lady Katharine Anderton, one of the Queen's cousins, to arrange the entire wedding, from the sending out of the invitations to the decoration of the going-away car. This choice removed the financial responsibility from a family that could not afford such an affair while removing all possibility of the wedding being arranged by Bianca, who would never have resisted the temptation to turn the proceedings into anything but a spectacle for the amusement of her international friends.

Kate Anderton had the simplest of briefs: send out two hundred invitations to the wedding, which would take place at the Catholic Church in Mayfair's Farm Street, decorate the church on the day and organize a champagne reception and dinner dance at Mossiman's in Belgravia. It was the sort of arrangement any experienced party planner could do with her eyes shut.

The wisdom of appointing an outsider to organize the wedding became apparent during the reception at Mossiman's. Pedro was standing talking to Amanda and Dolores upstairs when Bianca walked in with Antonia and Moussey. Dolores, seeing Antonia, walked straight up to her and said: 'Isn't Biancita coming?'

'Oh, hello, Dolores,' Bianca said before Antonia could reply. 'How are you?'

'I've asked you a question, and I want an answer,' Dolores said, ignoring Bianca.

'Darling girl,' Bianca said, sweetness itself, as a relieved-looking Antonia stood back and left her mother to deal with this awkward situation. 'Biancita has school. One can't disrupt a child's education for the convenience of the adults.'

'So she's not coming,' Dolores said, crestfallen.

'It would appear not,' Bianca said in her most honeyed tones.

'One of these days you're going to get your comeuppance, you poisonous bitch,' Dolores hissed, 'and I only hope I'm around to see you squirm when that day comes.' Then she spat squarely in Bianca's face.

'You snivelling little whore,' Bianca responded angrily, grabbing a damask napkin from the arm of a passing waiter and wiping her face with it before throwing it onto the floor at Dolores' feet. 'I'm going to make sure that my granddaughter never catches sight of your perverted face again, if it's the last thing I do.' With that, she stormed off in search of the ladies' room to clean herself up and retouch her makeup.

Dolores ran back to Pedro and Amanda, who had been observing all that had happened. 'Good shot,' Pedro laughed. 'What did the bitch say to you to make you hit her full in the face like that?'

'No,' Amanda said, reaching for Dolores' hands and cupping them in her own. 'Don't tell us. It will only upset you, and we don't want to blight Manolito's big day any more than it already has been by that woman's presence.'

Dolores, however, was too keyed up not to recount what had happened, and she had just finished doing so when Bianca rejoined Antonia across the room.

'Wait here,' Pedro said. 'I'll only be a minute or two.'

With that, he headed towards his mother and sister, who had each taken a flute of champagne from a passing waiter. 'Hello, Mama. Hi, Antonia,' he said, leaning in to peck his sister on her cheek.

'To what do we owe this honour?' Bianca inquired archly.

'Hi, Peds,' Antonia said fondly, glad, despite herself, that her brother had come over to speak to her.

'How long are you here for?' Pedro asked his sister.

'We leave tomorrow.'

'Where for?'

'Cyprus. We've built this fabulous house on the beach, and we're sitting out the civil war there, along with half of Lebanon, it has to be said. You should come and see us there some time.'

'Maybe I will.'

'Just make sure you don't bring that whore along with you,' Bianca spat out.

'She's not a whore,' Pedro said to his mother. 'I don't know what you have against her, but it certainly doesn't warrant you treating her the way you do.'

'The only thing that can be said for you as opposed to your brothers,' Bianca said, 'is that you don't marry your waifs and strays.'

'And what does that mean?'

'It means precisely what I said. At least you don't marry the waifs and strays you bed.'

'But Julio and Manolito have?' Pedro said, keen to see what worm lay under this particular rock.

'Exactly.'

'But I thought you liked Leila,' Pedro said.

'And why would you think that?'

'Don't you always refer to her as "cherie"?'

'No, that's "Sherry" as in Sheherezade, you idiot,' Bianca retorted. 'You know, the little Arab waif who kept her head and captured the Sultan's attention with her inventiveness.'

'It has to be said, Mama, that if anyone ever had an aptitude for spreading venom wherever she goes, it is you,' Pedro said.

'And I'm as pleased to see you too,' Bianca answered sweetly.

'Give me a ring in Mexico next week and let's talk,' Pedro said to Antonia, pecking her on the cheek before turning on his heel and returning to Dolores and Amanda.

'Pedro,' Amanda remarked after he related Bianca's putdown of Leila to them, 'your mother is such a snob that the only sort of wife she'd want for any of you is the daughter of a duke.'

'I'm going to tell Manolito,' Pedro said.

'Wait until the end of the honeymoon,' Dolores advised, echoing Amanda's sentiments.

Pedro consequently waited until the end of the honeymoon, when he was driving Manolito and Leila from Sintra to the airport for the return trip to London, to reveal the true meaning of Bianca's supposed term of endearment. Manolito turned purple with embarrassment, but it was Leila's reaction that showed Pedro how wise his brother was to have chosen a girl of such calibre.

'I don't see why you all put up with her bizarre conduct,' she declared.

Manolito waved his hand in a gesture as if to say: 'What can we do?'

'She's my mother,' Pedro said, coming to Manolito's rescue. 'I don't like it, but I don't see what choice I have but to accept it.'

'She's been a good stepmother to me,' Manolito said. 'And you have to take the rough with the smooth.'

'No, you don't,' Leila said. 'If life has taught me one thing, it's that you have to separate the wheat from the chaff. I don't mean to cause you problems, Manolito, but as long as we're married and I'm your wife, I don't want that woman to set foot in our house. And I will never go to visit her in any of her homes.'

'What about Sintra and Mexico City?'

'Those are not her homes. They are your homes. So I'll come to them as long as she's not around.'

Finally, someone in Bianca's family had drawn the line with her, although it took several months before she got wind of Leila's refusal to tolerate her presence any longer. Bianca's reaction, however, showed why she was such a brilliant adversary. Instead of being upset, as everyone in her family had expected her to be, she responded with apparent indifference. While she was still fond of the boy, she was not about to let herself become upset because Manolito's first loyalty would henceforth be, as Bianca put it, 'to his penile satisfaction'. All the same, beneath that glib reaction, she was hurt that someone whom she had poured such love into over the years could take the side of an interloper over his 'Mama'.

What helped to make Manolito's defection easier to take for Bianca was that it coincided with one of those worldly coups that had become such a feature of her existence. The reason why Bianca no longer needed Manolito was that his money was no longer the crucial part of the Mahfud financial empire it had once been. In monetary terms, he was just another client, and not a very important or powerful one at that. While his portfolio was a welcome addition to the Geneva Bank's assets, in real terms it was a luxury, not a necessity, as Bianca and Philippe would soon be rich beyond their wildest ambitions.

In the months after Manolito's honeymoon and before Bianca discovered that she had been shelved by Leila, Philippe had been working on a deal which the *Wall Street Journal* would subsequently label as 'classic'.

He had finalized plans to sell Banco Imperiale New York to Continental Express for $2.7 billion: a phenomenal amount of money for that time. The sheer magnitude of it was enough to put Manolito and Leila's actions into perfect perspective for Bianca. Why concern herself with small fry, Bianca reasoned, when she need only think of the influence that she would acquire once the world awoke to the fact that Philippe Mahfud had sold his bank to Continental Express for one of the largest sums of money ever exchanged between two financial institutions of their kind and that she was now the consort of one of the richest men in the world? Everyone knew that money was power. And money brought influence in its wake. And so it was, within days of discovering that Leila Piedraplata had banished her from her life, that Bianca woke up in her Louis XVI bed in her Fifth Avenue apartment to discover that she and Philippe were the new financial stars of the international firmament. The Wall Street Journal, spread out beside her breakfast tray, told of 'the deal of a lifetime' with a photograph of Philippe and the glamorous Mrs Mahfud beside him in all her exotic glory.

In further confirmation of the fact that Mr and Mrs Philippe Mahfud were now the luminaries portrayed by the *Wall Street Journal*, by midday, several newspapers and magazines had telephoned asking for interviews with Bianca as well as with Philippe. Although she would dearly have loved to oblige them, her husband refused to allow any, stating, in that age-old refrain of his: 'For people like us, publicity can only be detrimental. No interviews.'

Disappointed though Bianca was to miss yet another opportunity to make her mark on the world, she was not surprised by Philippe's interdict. As friend after high-calibre friend, such as Stella Minckus, Ruth Fargo Huron, and Graziella Oldenburg, telephoned to congratulate her on this latest step up the ladder, she convinced herself that her husband's approach to publicity was the right one, and the way this exclusive circle was conducting itself was far superior to the grubby attention of journalists. But if she were honest with herself, oh, how she still yearned for the widespread recognition that newspaper and television fame would bring. She could see herself walking down Fifth Avenue, turning heads the way she now did but with the important difference that people would now stop and look, saying 'There goes Bianca Mahfud,' instead of simply wondering who was this superbly elegant woman. Recognition was a powerful motivator, especially to someone who had everything else.

But rather than dwell on yet another series of wasted opportunities for real fame, Bianca pushed the wonderful image of herself as a household name to the back of her mind. Even the limited amount of publicity from the Wall Street Journal would advance her ambitions; and, she had to admit, she was getting where she wanted to be on life's ladder. This afternoon, for instance, she was due to have lunch at the Minckus apartment on Fifth Avenue. The guest of honour was Jacqueline Kennedy Onassis, whom Dolphie and Stella were courting, in the hope that she would one day allow Belmont's to sell her artefacts the way Christie's had sold the Duchess of Windsor's. Although Bianca had met the fabled former First Lady once before, it had only been in passing – Philippe had stopped to speak to Maurice Tempelsman, Jackie's boyfriend, whom he had recently met through business, as he and Bianca were leaving Elaine's after dinner one night. Bianca hoped that this second meeting through Stella Minckus would be the beginning of a more enduring relationship. Bianca was still struggling to rise above the glass ceiling separating the grandest dames from the merely *grande dames* in International Society. The real International Empresses were Jackie and Brooke Astor in the US, and Diana and Queen Elizabeth II across the Atlantic. Everyone else was in another, less stellar, category. Bianca needed to look no further than Brooke Astor to see that one only needed vast wealth, a good name and good connections to be right up there with the best of them. And if Bianca had learned one thing in the years she had been living in New York, it was that the power of determination allied to the power of wealth created an unstoppable momentum, once you were allowed to initiate the process. This, unfortunately, was something Philippe had not permitted her to do.

As far as Bianca was concerned, her ambitions had now crystallized, and she knew precisely what she wanted to be. She wanted to be another Brooke Astor. If Brooke could become one of the leaders of Society, so could she. All she needed to do was find the way.

Normally, Bianca walked the two blocks from her apartment to Stella's whenever she was lunching there, especially on a day like today: crisp and beautiful, with the sun shining and the air crackling in anticipation of the autumn. Like most New York residents, she had developed the habit of using her feet for short distances. For her, it was an uplifting experience to dress to the nines and walk down Fifth Avenue, turning heads at the age of nearly sixty. She loved the impact she still created. That, she told herself with more accuracy than modesty, was star quality, and no one could take it away from her. The energy. The vibrancy. The luminosity. When she walked down the streets of New York, the reaction of strangers told her she had still not lost her touch.

Today, however, she would have to forego the pleasure of turning heads, in case there were reporters camped outside her building. Philippe did not consider it appropriate that the newspapers should have the opportunity of capturing his wife 'walking the streets'. It would, he said, 'convey the wrong image'. So Bianca had to forego a pleasure she had never let anyone know she enjoyed. Not that she would let such a tiny little inconvenience mar what was, for her, one of the most perfect days of her life. Even if the notoriously reserved Mrs Onassis was not forthcoming, and she did not manage to make her into a friend, Bianca had quite enough in her own right to crow about. She had officially joined the billionaires' club. Hereafter, thanks to the Wall Street Journal, the world would always know that she, Bianca Barnett Calman Piedraplata Antonescu Mahfud, was a member of the most exclusive and desirable club in the world.

As Bianca exited from her building, she was bursting with well being. Although scrupulously kind to staff without exception, today she had an especially warm 'thank you' for the doorman, who held the door open for her to step out into an absence of flashbulbs. She had to admit she was disappointed that the press had not turned out in force to doorstep her, but she did not allow such a paltry disappointment to lift the gilt from her gingerbread and happily pressed two one hundred dollar bills into the palm of the doorman's hand. Then she climbed into the back of the chauffeur-driven Lincoln Continental stretch limousine that would convey her rather more sedately than she hoped, to Mrs P Adolphus Minckus's Fifth Avenue triplex.

As she settled back into the seat and stared out of the window as Fifth Avenue swept by, Bianca had to admit that, since she already had so much, it seemed a real shame that she didn't have the rest. Why lie to herself? She wanted to be famous. Really famous. To be a household name. To be fêted and courted and worshipped.

But, since Philippe considered personal publicity dangerous, she would simply have to do without this final coup, at least until he was dead – or she could get him to change his mind.

Chapter Twenty

The first time Philippe noticed the trembling was during negotiations with Continental Express prior to the sale of Banco Imperiale. He had been absorbed in a sheet of figures at the desk of his main office in the Principality of Andorra. This was something he often did. Like many highly successful businessmen, he trusted no one and had always functioned under the premise that he should keep as much as possible of his plans and thoughts away from his secretary, Gisele, even though she had been chosen for her trustworthiness as much as for her efficiency. 'You just don't know,' Philippe would say to himself. 'Maybe one day she'll want to jump ship and float off with a competitor. Maybe she'll sell our plans to a competitor, thereby giving him the edge. You just don't know.' Philippe therefore always tried to keep a crucial piece of every puzzle to himself until such time as he had to divulge the information to Gisele.

The telephone rang. It was Gisele. He reached for the telephone without looking up. He wanted to finish the line he was working on before his train of thought was severed by this latest interruption. He clamped the receiver to his ear. 'One minute,' he mumbled. Gisele knew this meant he was finishing off something, so she waited silently and patiently for his cue to continue.

Philippe wrote the final figure, looked up, catching sight of his left index finger as his line of vision settled upon the view of the Pyrenees in the distance. That, he always said, was one of the beauties of having an office in the tax-free haven of Andorra.

'What is it?' he asked quietly.

'It's Madame, sir,' Gisele said.

'Put her through.'

As they were speaking, Philippe looked, transfixed, as his index finger danced around while he held his hand in the air. 'It must be the stress,' he murmured to himself. Thereafter, he noticed that the index finger of his left hand trembled intermittently but gave it no more thought than he had given that first glimpse. Negotiations with Continental Express were intense and fraught, and it was only to be expected that, in a man of his age, there would be the occasional visible manifestation of the pressure he was enduring.

Once the deal was done and Continental Express bought Banco Imperiale, the pressure was eased off. The trembling continued, however, gradually spreading to the other fingers on his left hand.

'It's obviously the after-effects of the strain,' Philippe thought, and was soon launching himself back into a new venture, this time shoring up Banco Imperiale Geneva, which had not been bought by Continental Express, with a view to making it attractive for takeover by another financial institution.

Eight months after the sale of the New York bank, the unexpected happened when Continental Express sued Philippe in New York City for breach of contract and for misrepresentation. The gist of their case was simple, even though the *Wall Street Journal* and the *Financial Times* in London made it sound complex. They were claiming that he had padded the accounts to achieve a spectacular sale price and that he had, moreover, taken clients with him whom they had bought with the bank, having received ironclad guarantees that they would remain with Banco Imperiale NY. This lawsuit would have been devastating to Philippe's reputation had he not fought it with the vigour that he did. He hired the toughest lawyers he could find: Gassman, Ginzberg, Strelnick and Houghton. They were renowned financial specialists, with a gift for 'turning water into wine – an old Jewish trick not limited to the boy from Bethlehem', as Philippe put it. He also hired John Lowenstein, the famous public relations consultant whose services his wife had been dying to avail herself of for years.

To Bianca, with her frustrated aspirations for public recognition, the employment of John Lowenstein was almost too bitter a pill to swallow. She had been obliged to stand by throughout the years she had been living in New York, as Lowenstein pushed her friends Ruth Fargo Huron and Stella Minckus through the social columns to the forefront of the public domain, making them celebrities, while she had remained a socialite known only within the narrow confines of a select social circle.

'Let John use me,' Bianca suggested to Philippe, hoping to achieve her aims on the back of Philippe's need. 'We could form a pincer approach, so to speak, to defeat your enemies. Me in the social columns: you on the financial pages. Take a leaf out of Dolphie's book. Look at how he has used Stella to enhance his stature and Belmont's. You don't seriously believe Dolphie would have John Lowenstein on a retainer, at the prices he charges, to promote Stella, if his business interests weren't also benefiting, do you?'

'It won't work,' Philippe said, too quickly, to have truly considered all the sides of the question. 'You're too precious for me to run the risk of hurting you. And, believe me, Bianca, adverse publicity will hurt, even if it's only your vanity.'

'Let me worry about my vanity and you worry about Continental Express while John Lowenstein uses all the ammunition we can put at his disposal,' she said sweetly.

'No,' Philippe said stubbornly, his bottom lip protruding the way it did whenever he had made up his mind and pressure was being applied upon him to change it. 'I can't run the risk of dragging you into this.'

'I'm not some little china doll to be kept safely on the shelf, you know,' she said. As Bianca uttered these words she realized, for the first time in all the years they had been together, that when she could have been acquiring fame, his claims of publicity being bad for business and potentially damaging to their professional and social positions had been nothing but an elaborate charade. He didn't want the world viewing her as special, because he was afraid that if it did, she would become too independent. And then he might lose her.

'No, you're not a china doll,' Philippe replied, as if in confirmation of her observation. 'But you're even more precious than the most precious china doll to me, and I must protect you against anything bad happening.'

'Well, I wish you wouldn't,' Bianca snapped.

Philippe looked stricken. His left hand started to tremble even more than it had before. He opened his mouth to say something, thought better of it, and before she was even aware of what she would say, Bianca had jumped into the breach. 'I'm getting sick of being mollycoddled by you in this way,' she said. 'It's demeaning. And I wish you'd get that damned hand of yours looked at. That bloody tremor is getting worse than ever. You're starting to look like a shaky little old man, and that, I have to tell you, gives your opponents the scent of blood far more than anything else you can think of.'

Goaded by Bianca, Philippe made an appointment to see his doctor in New York. The diagnosis was Multiple Sclerosis. At first, Bianca did not fully appreciate the severity of Philippe's condition. Nor, in fairness, did he. Neither of them was the type to face bad news head-on. Each of them thought that by dodging the issue, it would go away. But it did not, and within a year the trembling was worse than ever, despite medication.

It was at this juncture that Bianca took things into her own hands. Acting upon the philosophy that there is no point in having influential and well-connected friends if you do not use them, she telephoned Stella and Ruth and discovered that the man they regarded as the world's Multiple Sclerosis expert worked a few blocks away on 77th Street near Fifth Avenue.

'Make an appointment with Dr Eli Wiseman as soon as possible,' she instructed Mary van Gayrib, without even bothering to tell her husband what she was doing until Mary had confirmed a date and time.

Far from resenting the steps Bianca had taken, Philippe was delighted and made no secret of it. In fact, he even boasted, as he recounted the tale to Gisele: 'I'm the luckiest man alive to have a wife like Madame. She's more capable than ten Roman legions and does not shy away from taking charge when the occasion demands it.'

Dr Wiseman's suggestions were basic enough. Philippe was to avoid stress, and he was to take his medication regularly, rather than when he felt the need for it. 'You will never derive the cumulative benefits of the medication if you imbibe it intermittently,' the doctor explained. 'It is designed to be administered on a regular basis. Without that regularity it cannot do its work, and the symptoms of the disease will not be kept at bay but will continue to encroach with the steadiness and rapidity they have displayed since your initial diagnosis. MS is no respecter of persons,

Mr Mahfud. All the money and success in the world won't help you if you don't start to show the condition the respect it deserves.'

As Dr Wiseman had noticed during that first meeting, Philippe was in many ways the worst person to have fallen victim to a disease like MS. He thrived on stress and had never been the sort of person who could conquer discomfiture. This latter trait had been the secret of his success in business and had also accounted for the great gaps within his personality. Despite being one of the most successful businessmen on earth, Philippe had never stretched the limits of his personality, withdrawing instead into a world of his own creation where he could function comfortably without the need for painful personal growth. He was someone who had always found it easier to escape the demands of small talk, casual friendship and normal socializing by retreating into his office and coming up with schemes for making yet more money. The acquisition of wealth had long been more about entertaining himself than it had been about what money could or could not buy, for he had passed the stage where his money could be spent. Money had become nothing but a yardstick of accomplishment and the means by which he was able to have the world adjust to him, rather than vice versa. In so doing, he had been able to remain fundamentally a child. A ruthless child, admittedly, but also one who could be sweet and kind and loving and who, to those close to him, had a vulnerability that made his limitations excusable, even appealing at times.

This self-indulgence might have been the source of much of his success, but it also became the cause of the rapid decline in his health. It wasn't long before Philippe disregarded Dr Wiseman's advice concerning the regular intake of his medication. 'The damned tablets either make me nauseous or befuddled,' he complained, 'and I can't afford to be either.'

At first, Bianca tried to get him to follow the specialist's regimen with wifely concern. 'You know what Dr Wiseman told you. You've got to take your tablets regularly. Why not try them for a month and see if there isn't an improvement?'

Philippe, however, could last no more than two days before abandoning the discipline of regular medication. After enduring weeks of watching him ignore the doctor's sensible advice, Bianca could stand no more. 'I have to tell you I'm getting fed up with your childish attitude,' she snapped. 'Dr Wiseman says the reason why your limbs are stiffening and shaking is that you refuse to do anything to suppress the natural progression of the disease. If you persist in this folly, you're going to end up unable to get out of a chair without help, and soon you'll be unable to walk unaided. Do your really want to have to use a Zimmer frame or a wheelchair for the rest of your life?'

'I'll be OK,' Philippe said. 'All I need to do is win the case Continental Express have brought against me.'

'If I were you,' she said, 'I'd settle it.'

Philippe looked incredulous. Even though the MS had started to affect his facial expressions, Bianca could see the passion that illuminated his irises. 'Having MS doesn't mean I've become a loser,' he insisted. 'I'd sooner die than settle that action.'

Fortunately Continental Express settled the lawsuit, having come to the realization, as Gassman, Ginzberg, Strelnick and Houghton buried them under a mountain of paperwork and John Lowenstein further immersed them under a welter of favourable newspaper coverage generated by a book he had arranged for a friendly journalist to write giving the Mahfud side of the argument, that the cost would ultimately wipe out all the financial benefits of any success they might achieve.

Left to his own devices, Philippe would have continued to go into the office every day, return home every evening, have a quiet supper; go to bed early and get up the following morning. Then he would resume plotting and planning and scheming his way towards the creation of yet another vast fortune, in an effort to give his life definition and to take his mind off what was happening to his body. However, he could no longer be left to his own devices. He needed help to walk, and he could not write anymore. He therefore became more reliant upon his assistants.

Gisele especially took the brunt of the responsibility, and gradually, as she had to do more and more for him, he found himself sharing his plans and dreams with her in a way that he never would have done in the past.

During this period of decline, Philippe kept his spirits up the only way he knew how. He dedicated himself to a new moneymaking project. This one, he knew, would have to be the climax of his financial career, so he set about making it as glorious as possible. Readying Banco Imperiale Geneva for an even more impressive and lucrative takeover than anything that had gone before, he cultivated rich clients even more avidly than he had done in the past. Using his Mexican connections, and that country's proximity to neighbouring cocaine-rich Colombia, he pushed the already murky dealings of international banking further into the mire. Like many, if not most, successful bankers, he had never been overly concerned with the provenance of a fortune. As long as someone had a large enough amount to invest and thereby boost the desirability of Banco Imperiale Geneva for takeover, Philippe would court their business – no questions asked. This was true even when it was apparent that the money was tainted, that it was being laundered unlawfully or being diverted by officials of foreign states. It was only a matter of time before the word spread in the reputable and disreputable segments of the financial community alike that the man to turn to when you had nowhere else to go was Philippe Mahfud. To those members of the financial community who valued probity – or, at any rate, the appearance of it – he now became a figure to shun. But to those who admired results – to the Manuel Noriegas and the Pablo Escobars of this world, or to the bankers who wanted an 'introductory fee' for laundering drug and blood money while keeping their own hands clean – he provided the solution to their problems.

From Philippe's point of view, this could not have been a more ideal time to build up quickly the most successful investment bank in the world. Aside from the billions of dollars of drugs money to be laundered, the Soviet Union was in the process of collapsing. The staggering wealth of that vast country was falling into the hands of a tiny minority of state officials who exploited the breakdown of the old order and the creation of a market economy by siphoning off billions of dollars. They cut deals with their cronies and either sold off or acquired state property, state enterprises and state assets.

Long before the world woke up to the existence of a new category of crook, and the Russian Mafia became a byword for unbelievable corruption and unimaginable wealth, Philippe Mahfud was the man these new billionaires banked with. Men such as the politician Yuri Vitsen, with his army of relations feathering their nests to the tune of hundreds of millions of dollars apiece, or Boris Budokovsky, the businessman who shot from penury to billionaire status within two years, needed accommodating banks such as Banco Imperiale Geneva where they could safely 'lodge' their assets. So they beat a well-worn path to Philippe Mahfud's office door at the Banco Imperiale Geneva, where the distinction between nominee and beneficial owners was negligible, and the difference between desirability of clients was measured purely in the size of the fortune to be banked. In Philippe, they had their ideal banker, for the idea of turning away billions of dollars of investors' money for any reason at all, was truly incomprehensible to him. He felt it his duty as well as his right to accept all clients, irrespective of the source of their wealth. To him, it seemed perfectly ludicrous that morality should be mixed up with banking. 'All dollar bills are green,' ran Philippe's philosophy, 'irrespective of whose fingers have touched them.'

Philippe nevertheless knew in his bones that he would not want to bring the game to a close until he had achieved his objective of selling Banco Imperiale Geneva for the highest price ever paid for a private bank. The problem there, of course, was that his health and the erratic state of the international financial community meant he could not be sure that he would actually be able to pull off this feat. Like many other outstandingly successful businessmen, Philippe was a gambler at heart, and, like all gamblers, he was transfixed not only by winning but by the prospect of losing. To people like him, victory without the possibility of loss was as dull as the idea of a woman without the scent of danger.

Multiple Sclerosis, however, was not Bianca or the banking world. It was not a tiger he could ride, and by 1993 he was fighting a losing battle with it. His mobility was so seriously impaired that he had to move the headquarters of Banco Imperiale Geneva to his Andorra tax haven in the Pyrenees between France and Spain allowing him to commute easily by helicopter between L'Alexandrine and his office in the principality.

Of course, there was never any prospect of moving from Geneva to Andorra without all the trappings that went with the billionaire lifestyle.

Neither Philippe nor Bianca was one for self-sacrifice, so he bought a palatial, rose-coloured, eighteenth-century stucco villa a stone's throw from the Presidential Palace, which he then turned into Banco Imperiale's new headquarters. Commuting between L'Alexandrine and Andorra offered only a temporary solution, however. Philippe's decline, exacerbated by his refusal to take his medication correctly, continued rapidly, and by 1994 he needed nurses in attendance around the clock. It was at this point that Bianca suggested turning the top two floors of the Banco Imperiale Building in Andorra into a home from which he could function. 'My darling,' she said sweetly, her tone warming Philippe's heart as completely as it would have chilled her son Pedro's, 'I know you live and breathe work, and I would never want you to give up anything that brings you such pleasure, but we do have to consider your well-being. It makes more sense for us to live above the bank and for you to run the business from home than for you to commute to the office from L'Alexandrine.'

Being a logical man, Philippe saw the sense of his wife's suggestion and authorized her to turn the top two floors of the Banco Imperiale Building into an apartment for them to live in. Bianca promptly commissioned Valerian Rybar and Ion Antonescu to transform the place into an Andorran version of their New York apartment and their Geneva house. Refurbishment began within six weeks. The schedule of works was intended to last six months.

Two weeks before the commission was completed, however, Bianca came home to L'Alexandrine from a luncheon party at Ruth Fargo Huron's house with shattering news. 'I sat beside the American ambassador,' she informed Philippe, who was sitting, shakier than ever, like a wizened old man in a gilt Louis XVI armchair, his legs covered in a ranch mink blanket. 'She informs me that there is trouble brewing in the US over money laundering. They're going after the Nigerians and the Russians. All the bankers who have been assisting them to divert their national assets are going to be blacklisted unless they assist the American government in tracing their assets.'

'This is serious,' Philippe remarked. 'I'll be destroyed unless I provide them with assistance. But if I do, my clients will desert me in droves unless I can find a way to prevent them from finding out that I've cooperated. But you know what that damned Freedom of Information Act is like. They force you to sing, then they list you as a canary.'

'What will you do?' Bianca asked.

'Get in touch with the Secretary of State and provide them with as much information as they need to keep off my back while cutting a deal with the authorities that will assure us anonymity.'

'And if you don't play ball?'

'They'll blacklist me, and there goes any chance of selling Banco Imperiale Geneva.'

'I do wish you'd get yourself out of the line of fire,' she said passionately. 'The stress does your health no good, and, if I could take some of the heat for you, your enemies wouldn't bother with me the way they would with you.' For some time now, Bianca had been using Philippe's increasing infirmity, and the wifely concern she expressed as a result of it, to lay the ground in the hope that he would use her as his trusted right hand so that she could become both the financial and a social queen bee.

'That might be a solution further down the line, but it's not the answer to our immediate problems,' Philippe said, careful to leave open a door he had no real intention of using.

'But surely there must be something I can do right now to help,' replied the picture of wifely solicitude.

'There is,' her husband replied disappointingly. 'Get in touch with Valerian and the architect. We're going to need the best security system in the world just in case word leaks out that I've cooperated with the Americans. You know what they're like. Between their open-government policy and their naïve insistence on always occupying the moral high ground, someone's bound to find out. We'd better be prepared, or I'm a dead man.'

'This has the potential to turn very nasty,' said Bianca, sounding more worried than she actually felt.

'You can say that again. But don't worry, Gisele will find the best security advisors, and we'll make sure they design an impenetrable defence system which doesn't intrude on the homeliness of the place.

Once the Russians and my Latin American friends find out that I'm providing the Americans with information about their financial activities, they'll put out a contract on my life. You'll be in danger too, Bianca. We've got to act right now. Security must be in place before the Russians get wind of any cooperation I give the Americans.'

Faced with a new and unexpected problem, Bianca immediately saw the one benefit that would accrue should Philippe be liquidated. She would be free to achieve the desires and aspirations that Philippe had always thwarted. This glimpse of a bright new life quickened her pulse and made Bianca realize that widowhood had an attractive dimension, but it did not stop her from doing all she could to keep Philippe alive and as healthy as she could. She duly got in touch with Valerian and Ion and set about altering much of their handiwork to accommodate a bewilderingly sophisticated security system.

Bianca was astonished at the speed with which one of the finest non-governmental security systems in the world was put into place. Titanium shutters, which went up and down at the touch of a button in the control room, were created for the windows and doors of their apartment.

Together with the reinforced steel that lined the floors and the roof of the apartment, the shutters could seal off each room within seconds, so that the whole apartment became impenetrable. Smoke alarms, sound sensors, cameras, surveillance and recording equipment covering every area of the apartment and the two access points from the bank downstairs were also installed. No one could either gain entry to the building or leave it without the consent of the guards, who materialized, like magic, from Israel.

Heading the team of bodyguards was Erhud Blum, a retired senior operative of Mossad. He assembled nine of his former combatants into what he called the 'finest security force in the whole world outside of Israel'.

Thereafter, neither Philippe nor Bianca would ever spend another moment in the Andorra apartment without being observed except, of course, when they used their respective bathrooms. In deference to their need for privacy, these two rooms were the only ones which did not have surveillance equipment, but this lack was compensated for by the titanium doors which, when operated in conjunction with the shutters on the windows, sealed off both rooms. Access to them from the outside would therefore become impossible without the cooperation of the parties locked inside the bathrooms or of the head of the security team himself. Not even the nine operatives had the code that allowed the doors to be opened. Only Philippe, Bianca and Erhud Blum possessed this information.

The security system in place, Bianca and Philippe then moved into the apartment that was henceforth to be their primary base. 'What a relief it will be that we are no longer sitting ducks for the Russian Mafia and the Columbian drug barons,' she said to him the first night they spent under their new Andorran roof, 'and that we will never have to worry about security again.'

Within weeks, however, Philippe noticed that this sentiment sat at odds with her conduct. In the last week alone, she had spent three days and two nights at a stretch at L'Alexandrine. 'What's up with you?' he asked, having missed her. 'Is Andorra our new home or isn't it? Are you afraid of sleeping here with me, or is there another reason? You're not worried we're going to be shot in our bed, are you?'

'My desire to be at L'Alexandrine has nothing whatever to do with fears of assassination,' Bianca replied crisply. 'Much as I love you and want to be with you, I can't stay cooped up in a cage. L'Alexandrine is my home and always will be. I don't mind sleeping in Andorra with you, but why should I stay here during the day while you're working, when I can just as easily be at L'Alexandrine enjoying the benefits of those surroundings?'

'But it's a security risk for you to be there on a daily basis with only one bodyguard to protect you. What happens if the Russians or Colombians decide to kidnap you in order to get at me?'

'Darling, you worry too much. The Russians and Colombians don't know anything about the assistance you're giving the Americans, and even if they do find out, they won't be interested in little old me. It's you they want. My one bodyguard is all I need. I'm not worried and I'd advise you not to worry about me either. Worry about yourself, because I don't think I could survive if anything happened to you,' she said lovingly, knowing that a kind word not only turns away wrath but also takes the wind out of a man's sail.

Although the sexual side of their marriage was long dead, the relationship still appeared to be strong. Philippe craved as much as ever his wife's presence: her touch, her scent, the feel of her body next to his. From her point of view, however, the twitching which was an inevitable part of multiple sclerosis meant that she could never get a good night's sleep in bed with him. Now that the sexual side of their marriage was dead, Bianca failed to see why she should inconvenience herself, so for the last two years she had been sleeping with him less and less frequently and now used this move to stop sleeping with him altogether.

Bianca, however, took care when vacating the marital bed to resort to the subterfuge of getting Philippe's doctor to advise her to do so on the grounds that his movements were disturbing her sleep and affecting her health. 'Dr Wiseman has suggested that I have my own bedroom near yours,' she said to sweeten the pill of withdrawal, 'but to show you that this is just a temporary change of habit, I won't even get Valerian to do it up for me. I'll use the main guest suite until things change and we can sleep together once again.'

What this meant, in reality, was that Bianca had no intention of becoming apartment-bound by her invalid husband. Now that he was sliding towards total infirmity and death, Philippe's pride prevented him from admitting that the woman he had so revered was capable of abandoning him under the guise of her health. It took a very different sort of man from Philippe to conclude that the oasis he had been drinking from was a mirage. Ferdie had been that sort of man; Philippe, and Bernardo before him, were not.

And Bianca knew it.

As Philippe's health deteriorated, Bianca found it easier and easier to spend as much time away from him as she could engineer. Added to the boredom of being with the infirm, she had developed a real and sincere antipathy towards his condition. She had always despised ill health even more than she abhorred weakness, and she secretly feared catching Multiple Sclerosis, even though the doctors had assured her on countless occasions that it was non-communicable. Still she withdrew even more from Philippe, both physically and emotionally, and felt fully justified in protecting herself against this dreadful and incurable disease.

By this time, Bianca had resumed the tenor of her life as it had been while Philippe was healthy. If one of her New York friends was having a dinner party that she wanted to attend, she would cross the Atlantic in the Lear and soak up the pleasures of Manhattan and the Fifth Avenue apartment. Her New York home remained one of the great loves of her life, on a par with L'Alexandrine and socializing, and she never returned to it or to the social scene without her heart skipping a beat of pleasurable anticipation. Paris also became a centre of activity now, and she frequently took the Lear there for some appointment with a friend, whether it was luncheon, a dinner party or one of those balls where the majority of the guests boasted monarchist names such as Bourbon-Parma, Lubomirski, and Polignac, and the inevitable guests of honour were the uncrowned queen and empress of France: Son Altesse Royale Madame La Comtesse de Paris and Son Altesse Imperiale La Princesse Napoleon. She never ceased to thrill at the old-world glamour and the magnificence of it all, and each time she saw an assemblage of the grandest of the grand, Bianca experienced an ecstatic rush of pleasure.

For Philippe, this was an acutely painful period. As he had spent most of his life jumping through hoops to avoid the unpleasant realities of life, however, this facility rescued him from the recognition of what was going on in his marriage, even if it did not alleviate his loneliness and feelings of abandonment. His powers of reasoning remained sharp, and his business acumen was not affected by the progress of his condition. He was therefore still able to work on building up Banco Imperiale Geneva for takeover, albeit from the confines of the Andorra apartment. This quest for the deal to crown all deals occupied his days and nights and much of his thoughts, while Bianca drifted in and out of the apartment for a few hours every two or three days.

Even that limited contact was a sacrifice for her, because she vehemently hated the sensation that she was walking into a prison as she entered the premises. And each time she left, she experienced the sense of release that comes with escaping from prison. There was something about enduring invalidity that made daily existence with Philippe seem like working her way through sludge. This feeling of enervation intensified rather than lessened over the months until she found herself thinking, as she walked into Philippe's bedroom: 'If only Philippe would die and release us both from the prison his illness has made of our lives.'

Then in 1998, a few months after Bianca actively began wishing Philippe would die, Dr Wiseman, conscious that his patient's condition had deteriorated to the point where his concentration was being affected, made a recommendation that would speed up Philippe's demise. 'Madame Mahfud,' he said to Bianca on one of his monthly visits to Andorra, 'you must prepare yourself for the possibility that your husband might become incompetent in the not too distant future.'

'But he's in the middle of preparing the biggest deal of his life,' Bianca objected.

'Then you'd better get him to speed up negotiations.'

'What sort of time frame are we dealing with?'

'It could be months, or it could be a year or two. The one thing your husband has on his side is his fine mind. I'd go as far as saying I've never had a more strong-minded patient than him. But even an act of will can't keep a disease like this from encroaching upon the mental faculties once the powers of concentration start to go.'

'Doctor, you know what husbands are like. The last person they listen to when the issue is their health is their wife. Why don't you have a quiet word with Philippe?' she suggested, smiling sweetly and acting rather more helpless than she actually was. 'Tell him that he must prepare himself for a decrease in his mental powers and that he should aim to conclude any projects within months rather than years. Could you do that for me?'

Dr Wiseman looked at her. She was, he felt, an astonishingly attractive woman. So feminine. So innocently coquettish. So concerned for her husband's welfare. What red-blooded man could turn down a request made in such a winning manner?

To ensure that Philippe would not detect any collusion between Dr Wiseman and herself, Bianca then left the apartment to shop in the tax-free haven of Andorra, while Dr Wiseman spoke to her husband.

'Are you sure it's the disease that's affecting my concentration and not the drugs you prescribe?' Philippe asked, clutching at straws.

'I'm sorry, Mr Mahfud, but that's the way Multiple Sclerosis progresses.'

'I was hoping it was the drugs,' he said, sounding like a vulnerable little boy.

'If you have any major projects, I'd suggest winding them up within the next few months.'

'A few months? How short time becomes when you face your own mortality,' Philippe said, tears welling up in his eyes.

'I wish there was something I could do, beyond begging you yet again to take your drugs in a more responsible fashion.'

'I will, I promise I will,' Philippe said, reminding Dr Wiseman this time of a little boy who has got into trouble and hopes, that by promising to be good, that the punishment will go away. Except, of course, it wasn't going away. Not until Philippe was dead.

Dr Wiseman looked at his patient. Here was one of the richest men on earth, yet nothing he or anyone else could do would preserve him from the helplessness and powerlessness that awaited him. Money was a truly finite entity, as limited as it was empowering. Here was a man who had once made people quake in their thousands. Now he was trembling too.

Meanwhile Bianca was winding up the shopping expedition across town. Coinciding her return with Dr Wiseman's departure, she burst into her husband's bedroom in a distracting flurry of excitement.

'Darling,' she cried, rushing up to his bed with a large box tucked under her arm, and then kissed him on the cheek, 'I went to Gucci while you and Dr Wiseman were talking, and look what I found for you. Isn't it beautiful? And so comfortable too.'

She now held up a cashmere-lined silk paisley dressing gown, the collar topstitched in the Gucci emblem. She put it on and modelled it girlishly. 'Isn't it the most beautiful shade of yellow and brown you've ever seen?' she asked. 'It will pick up your colouring perfectly. Why don't you try it on while I see Dr Wiseman out?'

'How did it go?' she asked in her most serious voice once she and Dr Wiseman had stepped outside of Philippe's bedroom.

'I think he took onboard what I was telling him.'

'This is all very ominous. I wish there was something I could do.'

'You're doing all a wife can. The important thing is to help him keep his spirits up. MS is a cruel disease.'

'What will the end be like?'

'Patients lose the ability to swallow and so can't eat. Their immune system is weakened and they fall prey to all sorts of infections and viruses. Finally, their hearts give out, or the ones with really strong hearts drown in their own body fluids. It's not a pretty picture.'

Bianca grimaced, her whole body shaking at the horror of it all.

'I only hope I'm not there to see it when it happens,' she said.

'There is one other thing,' Dr Wiseman said.

Bianca looked up at him, her beautiful eyes filled with curiosity and strength. There was no doubt in his mind that this was one woman who could cope with anything that life threw at her and remain a paradigm of desirability.

'Your husband said he doesn't like Nurse Owens. He says she's rough with him and she has no sense of humour. He feels uncomfortable around her. And,' he said, a note of amusement creeping into his voice, 'he claims that she's ugly.'

Bianca laughed. 'That, I have no doubt, is the worst of her sins. Philippe has a real thing about women's looks.'

'He seemed genuinely distressed at the prospect of being left in her care.'

'She comes highly recommended from the Van Gayribs in New York. She nursed old Mrs Van Gayrib who had Alzheimer's disease. They couldn't sing her praises highly enough. I told Philippe only last week that I'd find someone to replace her when I'm next in New York. I've taken you up on your suggestion of having brawny male assistants and am going over there in ten days to vet the men Mary's interviewing.'

'You might have trouble getting male helpers to cross the Atlantic,' Dr

Wiseman observed.

'I gather there's a queue of them willing to come.'

'How did you accomplish that? I thought all the male helpers in the world want to come to the US.'

'We're offering them deals they can't refuse,' Bianca laughed. 'Six month contracts as employees of the bank. All medical benefits thrown in free for themselves and their families for the duration of their employment, which can be renewed if they give satisfaction. Six shifts a week: $750 a shift. We fly them in as our guests, and they live here in Andorra, rent-free, all expenses paid, in a building we've leased expressly for the staff.'

'Presumably the reason why you're employing them under American contracts in America is that Andorran employment law has sharper teeth than American?' Dr Wiseman remarked.

'I honestly wouldn't know,' Bianca said. 'We're doing it purely and simply to get around the need for work permits. Can you imagine the nightmare it would be if we had to apply for four or eight different work permits every six months? This way, they come in as guests, collect their wages in New York, and we save ourselves a lot of trouble.'

'Very sophisticated,' Dr Wiseman said, smiling approvingly. 'Was this your husband's idea?'

'How clever of you, Dr Wiseman. You never miss an opportunity to assess your patient's condition,' she laughed. 'Yes, it was his idea.'

'Still no diminution in his mental powers. That's good.'

'Or cruel, depending on how you look at it. It can't be much fun for someone with my husband's mental capacities to witness the collapse of his body while his mind remains intact. And, I have to tell you it's affecting his personality. He's become even more demanding than he used to be. Everything has to be done yesterday.'

Dr Wiseman nodded his head sympathetically, bringing the visit to an end. One of the bodyguards opened the door of the apartment and shadowed Dr Wiseman into the elevator and down to the apartment's street entrance, his machine gun cocked and ready for anything.

Before the bodyguard had a chance to come back inside the apartment, Bianca had turned on her heel and was heading purposefully straight to Philippe's bedroom.

'Darling, Dr Wiseman is very concerned about your welfare,' she said.

'I know he's spoken to you about winding up your work with the bank, and I think now's the time for me to give back some of what you've given to me over the years. Why don't you appoint me chairman of the board in your place and let me act on your behalf? I'll only do what you want, of course, and refer everything to you for your consideration.'

'It wouldn't work,' her husband replied slowly and deliberately.

'Why not?' Bianca replied patiently, feeling anything but patient.

'I can't think of a worse thing to do. It would send out the wrong message to the financial community. They'll think I'm past it. All the sharks would be after the bank.'

'There's no denying it,' Bianca thought. 'This broken down old man is still a force to be reckoned with. If only he'd hurry up and die and get out of my hair, so I can live the remaining years of my life without having to waste time and energy thinking about someone who is nothing but a pain.'

'So what do you propose doing?' she asked sweetly.

'I'm going to throw bait to a few fish. Spread the word that I'm open to offers for the bank. Then I'll wait until a big enough fish swims into my waters. In the meantime, you can get me a sweet and pretty young thing to replace that ugly bitch Nurse Owens,' he said, a twinkle in his eye.

A practical nurse from Kingston, Jamaica and a devout Plymouth Brethren aged thirty-eight at the time of her employment in 1998, Agatha Wilson had been blessed with a sweet disposition, and all the adversity she had faced during her life had only made her more kindly. The sixth of seventeen children born in Trench Town, Agatha went to work as a maid at the age of thirteen. Within six months she had given birth to the first of five children, all of whom would be delivered before her twenty-first birthday. She got her big break as a nursemaid to the young wife of Nicholas Shoucaire, the Lebanese industrialist.

As Agatha's natural abilities became apparent, Odette Shoucaire promoted her as nanny to the two youngest children; and Agatha, earning more money than ever before, breathed freely for the first time in her life.

When the Shoucaires moved from Jamaica to Canada, they took Agatha Wilson with them.

Like many God-fearing Jamaicans, Agatha was both industrious and reliable. Every penny she earned, she sent back to her family in Kingston.

She took pride in the fact that her children were being sent to good schools; that they lived in a small but clean house in Havendale, a suburb, instead of the slum where she had been raised. To her, the accomplishments of her children made all her sacrifices worthwhile.

It had to be said, some of Agatha's sense of contentment lay with the Shoucaire family. Husband, wife and children were all happy and decent, and they made Agatha feel a part of the family in a way that few other employers would have done. Then in 1990 disaster struck. Nicholas Shoucaire was diagnosed as suffering from Multiple Sclerosis at the relatively young age of fifty-seven. His disintegration was even quicker than Philippe's, and when walking became too difficult for him, they sold their three-storey *maison de maître* near Nice and moved into a sprawling one-storey villa beside Walter and Ruth Fargo Huron's house near Cap Ferrat. This was shortly before their youngest child was due to go to boarding school in England, and Agatha dreaded the prospect of having to return to Jamaica once the post of nanny became redundant.

Faced with the possibility of losing their faithful retainer, however, Odette and Nicholas Shoucaire suggested that she switch roles and become his practical nurse. They therefore sent her to a practical nursing school in London for six weeks, where she learned the basics, and when she had completed the intensive course, she returned to Cap Ferrat to nurse him.

Bianca's path first crossed that of Agatha's at a luncheon party given by Walter and Ruth in 1996. She was impressed by how gently the Jamaican woman treated Nicholas Shoucaire but thought no more of her until Odette telephoned her out of the blue in 1998, just as she was about to dismiss Nurse Owens. After exchanging pleasantries Odette said: 'I'm trying to find a position for Agatha. My children are all at school and, now that my husband is dead, I simply don't have any work for her to do. I remembered that your husband has MS too and wondered if you'd be interested in employing her. She was truly a godsend with Nicholas.'

'In principle, I'm very interested,' Bianca said graciously. 'We actually need someone right now. My husband says one of his nurses is too rough with him.'

'Ruth Huron says you're a superb employer, and all your staff adore you. This is the sort of position I want for Agatha. She really is an exceptional human being, and I hope you won't misinterpret this when I say that offering her to you is about the highest praise I can confer upon you. That's how much she means to us as a family.'

Bianca and Odette arranged to meet with Agatha the following day, and the week after that, the nurse started working for Philippe in Nurse Owens' place. Agatha and Philippe clicked from the very first. 'Philippe's in love with Agatha,' Bianca frequently joked, and there was an element of truth to the statement. Both nurse and patient had complementary personalities. Each of them was hungry for an emotional attachment, and within weeks of knowing each other, they had established a genuinely companionable and emotionally sustaining relationship that only strengthened with time.

During the first months of their relationship, Philippe beavered away: setting up, with the assistance of John Lowenstein, what was little more than an elaborate scam to ensure that the financial and social columns on both sides of the Atlantic were drip-fed favourable stories about Banco Imperiale's performance with a view to enticing someone into bidding for it. However, it was a totally isolated occurrence that swung things in Banco Imperiale's favour and removed any reservations the financial community might normally have entertained about dealing with Philippe Mahfud. In August 1998 Russia defaulted on its debt, and the financial world stood transfixed, as if on the edge of an abyss, for several months.

During that period, investors with funds to invest had to find a safe haven. USNB, the mighty American bank which had the most limited exposure in Russia of all the leading American financial institutions, reasoned that Banco Imperiale was a safe haven at a time when it looked as if the extraordinary buoyancy that the financial markets had enjoyed throughout the latter part of the nineties might be coming to an end. So out of the blue, USNB tendered an offer in mid-September of $6.8 billion for Banco Imperiale. This was just the sort of deal towards which Philippe had been working ever since he had divested himself of his New York operation. Here was the highest amount ever offered for a private investment bank. Philippe, fully aware that the Banco Imperiale was not worth the price, moved to close the deal before USNB discovered how completely they had been duped or before the financial markets recovered from the Russian crisis.

Multiple Sclerosis or no Multiple Sclerosis, Philippe clearly remained as wily and astute as ever. He could see that the Russian crisis was little more than a storm in a teacup, although he was firmly of the opinion that such an overheated economy would go bust within three or four years. 'We must strike while the iron's hot,' he said to Agatha, who, having no idea what he was talking about, nodded her agreement good-naturedly. Using his health as the excuse to speed up the conclusion to their negotiations, Philippe stipulated that the deal must be signed within six weeks or it was off. Then USNB made its second mistake. It laid down the condition that it should have the right to send its own medical team to Andorra to confirm that his health was as precarious as he claimed it was. Philippe unsuccessfully tried to rub his hands with glee when that term came through. Then he had Agatha telephone Bianca at L'Alexandrine and ask her to come to Andorra as soon as possible. Wondering what the problem was, she came as quickly as she could and was more than a little irritated when she walked through the bedroom door to see her husband propped up in bed, grinning broadly. 'They've fallen for it,' he rasped throatily. 'We've got them.'

'Who's fallen for what, and who have you got?' Bianca asked, irritation tripping off her tongue with every word.

'USNB,' he laughed. 'They're suspicious about the state of my health, and they're sending their own doctors to check me out.'

'But I thought you didn't want anyone in the financial community to know your state of health.'

'I didn't before this, but now I do. Don't you see, Bianca? Their doctors will confirm that my health is so precarious that my demand to conclude the sale within an unnaturally short space of time is reasonable, based as it must be upon my fear that I might die before the deal is done.'

Philippe chuckled then started to cough, the spittle running down the side of his face, as he struggled to continue talking. 'Once the markets regularize, USNB isn't going to be quite so keen on acquiring Banco Imperiale as it now is. So we've got to move fast.'

All trace of annoyance deserting her, Bianca sat down on the bed beside him and stroked his arm tenderly. 'You're the most brilliant man I've ever known,' she said, 'and so lovable too. What would I do without you?'

'I knew you'd be proud of your old Philippe.'

'I am, darling, I am. No one else could've done this but you. Now, I must be off. Tonight I'm having dinner with the Oldenburgs, and I don't want to be late. They're having one of the Spanish Infantas, and you know how crazy everyone goes whenever any member of any reigning royal family comes to dinner.' Bianca pecked her husband on the cheek, turned to Agatha and said:

'Take good care of Monsieur as you always do.' She was out the door by the end of the sentence, having been there for less than ten minutes.

As Philippe had envisaged, USNB's doctors verified the state of his health, and it was agreed between the two sides that the purchase of Banco Imperiale would be concluded on Wednesday, October 28 1998.

On the day of conclusion, the ailing man awoke bright and early. Agatha and Eli, his favourite male assistant, helped him dress before he sat down to a breakfast of fresh mango juice, scrambled eggs, Matzos soaked in milk and butter, and coffee. The announcement of the sale was due to take place at nine o'clock New York time, which would be three in the afternoon his time.

Bianca had promised to come and share the moment of victory with him, and Philippe allowed himself to savour a delicious sense of anticipation as he shuffled towards the living room to watch his moment of glory on television from the comfort of the overstuffed sofa that Valerian Rybar had made for his stylish wife and himself.

Agatha turned on the television. Philippe used the remote control of get CNN. He squirmed from side to side in an attempt to get comfortable, before settling down to watch the financial news. So far, so good.

At eleven o'clock Agatha and Eli helped him back into bed. He rested until one in the afternoon, getting up in time to have a light lunch of mashed potatoes and smoked haddock, which the Jamaican nurse fed him, as usual, from the hospital tray beside the bed. When he had finished, he looked at the clock and registered that the time was coming up for two-twenty.

'Ring L'Alexandrine and find out what time Madame left. She's late,' he said to Eli as Agatha wiped the corners of his mouth with a Handy-Wipe before completing the job with a fine Irish linen napkin that was heavily embroidered with Banco Imperiale's emblem of the doublehead-ed eagle which the Mahfuds had adopted as their own.

Eli left the room to make the call.

'Help me up, sweetie,' Philippe said to Agatha. 'Let's see if we can't Zimmer me into the living room without Eli's help.'

His nurse pulled him up by gripping him beneath his arms. He leaned into her. 'You smell so lovely,' he said lustily.

'You're a naughty boy, flirting with me like that,' she joked.

'I wish I could do more than flirt with you.'

Agatha laughed good-naturedly. 'Naughty.'

'I used to be in my youth. I was a man of strong passions. Still am. Only thing is, the old pecker hasn't worked for years.'

'You're making me blush.'

'I love it when you blush. Come on, give me a little kiss. Just one kiss.'

Agatha smiled. What harm was there in humouring a dying old man? She pecked him on the cheek.

'No. I want a proper kiss.'

'Now, Monsieur, you don't want me to have to tell you off again, do you?' she scolded gently.

'I like it when you tell me off.'

Philippe stopped to catch his breath. They were in the passage leading from the bedroom to the living room. It was appreciably darker there than in any of the rooms because it had no windows; the security system required the doors leading off it to be kept shut at all times.

The cloakroom door suddenly burst open, and in the half light Philippe could make out a tall figure with what looked like a gun. 'Don't shoot,' he croaked, a look of absolute terror on his face, as if the bowels of hell had opened up and he had seen the fate that awaited him. 'Don't shoot. I'll give you $10,000,000 not to shoot me.'

'It's only me, Monsieur,' Eli said.

'You gave me the most dreadful fright, Eli. I thought you were a hitman,' Philippe said, shaking from terror before vomiting on the floor.

Eli and Agatha took him back into the bedroom to clean him up and change him, while the housekeeper mopped up the mess.

It was at this point that Bianca arrived. 'You'd better hurry or we're going to miss the report of your crowning glory, you fabulous emperor of finance, you,' she said coquettishly, standing well away from him for she could not abide the stench of vomit.

'I just had the most awful fright,' Philippe mumbled and explained what had happened. 'I really thought the end had come,' he said, still clearly rattled by the incident.

'Well, all's well that ends well,' Bianca said briskly, her voice displaying not an ounce of sympathy. 'So let's hurry before we miss everything.'

With that, she led the way into the living room, where the television set had remained tuned to CNN. Philippe shuffled in between his nurse and her male assistant, and they all sat down to look at the USNB-Banco Imperiale announcement, Philippe proudly taking Bianca's right hand in his left. The merest flicker of distaste passed over her elegant features, but no one caught it.

Promptly, at three o'clock in the afternoon French time, CNN ran the item along with a photograph of Philippe and Bianca taken outside L'Alexandrine ten years before. In many ways, it was the ideal photograph to use for such a story. Bianca was a study in glamour, her hair piled high on her head, her neck and earlobes ablaze with the most amazing diamond and emerald jewels. Philippe, standing slightly behind her, appeared as a short, squat, powerful man beaming with pride at the beautiful creature he called his own.

No sooner was the broadcast finished than Bianca withdrew her hand from Philippe's and started clapping. 'You make me feel so proud,' she said. 'My husband: the emperor of the financial world. This moment must make you very, very proud.'

'It does,' he said, the spittle oozing down one side of his mouth.

'You know,' she continued in sentimental vein, 'when I stop to think of the first time we met...and of all the things we've accomplished since then. We really have been an exceptional team, haven't we, my darling?'

'Yes, we have,' Philippe agreed. 'I could never have done it without you.'

'Nor me, my darling. You've been my inspiration and so much more besides.'

Philippe smiled and motioned Agatha to bring him the telephone.

'Who are you going to call now?' Bianca asked, annoyed that he was diverting his attention elsewhere.

'Raymond and Hepsibah and Rebecca, to see what they thought of our performance.'

Bianca's expression hardened. 'If you're going to do that, I'm off. No point sitting here looking at four walls while you talk to those sisters and that brother of yours.' She was about to give Philippe a goodbye kiss on the forehead when the latest item on the newscast caught their attention.

'Congress has just announced the formation of a fact-finding committee to investigate allegations of money laundering involving the Russian Mafia and banks in Europe, the Caribbean and the Americas. All the offshore banks will be targeted, and among the onshore banks whose finances are to be examined is the Swiss-based Banco Imperiale Geneva, the subject of our lead story today.'

Philippe started to gag, panic-stricken by this new development. Agatha rushed to get him some oxygen, while Bianca sympathetically stroked his hand. 'Take it easy, for God's sake,' she said. 'Otherwise you'll kill yourself.'

The nurse quickly returned with the oxygen and clamped the mask over his face. He breathed in slowly, and gradually his respiration returned to normal.

'They're going to kill me,' he said to Bianca. 'I know it.'

'Who's going to kill you?' she said, knowing very well Philippe meant the Russians. 'No one wants to kill you.'

'You don't know what they're like. Anyone who crosses them is wiped out. They're constantly gunning down businessmen in the street. They'll be sure to kill me once those fucking Americans spill the beans about my cooperation. Christ, why did I ever cooperate with them? Fucking naïve fools!'

'But you're safe and sound in here,' Bianca observed, 'surrounded by a team of the finest bodyguards Mossad has ever trained, in an impregnable fortress.'

'They'll find a way,' Philippe said gloomily.

'I'd better call the doctor and get him to give you something.'

'I can't take tranquillizers with MS, Bianca,' Philippe replied. 'My breathing is already depressed enough without drugs, which would slow it down even further.'

'Then you'll just have to get a grip on your emotions, darling,' she said gently, kissing him once more on the top of his head. 'I'll see you tomorrow. And do try to lighten up. You don't want to spoil your big day with negative thoughts.'

Philippe, however, was caught in the grip of a terror that would remain with him for the rest of his life. Thereafter, he would never walk from one room to another without insisting that his nurses, their male assistants and the bodyguards walk ahead of him. He made them look behind curtains and under furniture for gunmen who might have gained access to the premises and were lurking, ready to kill him. After the part he had played in Ferdie Piedraplata's murder, the manner of his late partner's death preyed on his mind. His greatest fear became not only that he would share Ferdie's fate but also his manner of execution.

For her part, Bianca regarded Philippe's fears as preposterous but put a tolerant face upon them until he tried to bring up the manner of Ferdie's death with her. Cognisant that their every word was being recorded by the surveillance equipment and that Agatha and Eli were both present as witnesses, she cut him short before he could say anything incriminating. 'Agatha, what tablets have you given Monsieur?' she snapped. 'He's having delusions again.'

'Just the usual, Madame,' she replied.

Bianca had always been one to recognize and grasp every opportunity that came her way, and at that moment she saw that she could turn this to her advantage. 'You know what is true,' she said decisively, jumping to her feet and turning to face her husband as she was seized by inspiration, 'it's cruel of Dr Wiseman to allow you to have delusions and hallucinations. We've all spent the last two months watching you cower in fear. It's very distressing for us and can only be worse for you. All this talk about being executed by Russian hitmen is nothing more than an indication that your drugs need to be changed. You're clearly suffering from drug-induced paranoia, and I can no longer fool myself into thinking that the signs will go away if we ignore them long enough. You're getting, worse, not better. I'm going to have a word with Dr Wiseman right now.'

Bianca reached for the telephone and called New York. She briefly explained the problem. 'I'll alter the drugs,' Dr Wiseman said. 'They're obviously affecting him mentally. We'll put him on some other medicine. They might befuddle him on occasion...at least, until he gets used to them...but that's a small price to pay for peace of mind.'

It was now only a matter of time before Philippe's greatest fear was realized, although not from the source, nor in quite the way, he had imagined.

Chapter Twenty-One

Getting rid of Eli became Bianca's first priority. As long as Philippe had such a devoted and intelligent helper, she could not take the chance of implementing the plan she had formulated. In her assessment, Agatha and the other nurses were not a problem. They were not sophisticated or intelligent enough to see through her, but Eli, she feared, was an altogether different matter. If there was one lesson she had learned from Ferdie's death, it was that one cannot be too careful around the staff. She did not propose to have a minion tripping her up.

Bianca often did her thinking while having breakfast in bed at L'Alexandrine. Everything about the setting was conducive to the smooth turning of her mind. From the priceless Louis XVI bed to the timeless beauty of the garden, there was not one item in the place that did not betoken to her the fruit of her labour. As far as Bianca was concerned, she had earned all this, and its existence not only drove her to protect what she already had but also acted as a spur for her to attain the freedom she had never had.

The decision to remove Philippe and gain absolute possession of all his wealth before doing so was not one Bianca had come to lightly or easily. She had managed to make the task easier by convincing herself that death would be a release for him. Bianca was quite open in this. 'If my poor husband were a dog,' she had often observed to friends and to Antonia and Moussey over the past few years, 'he'd have been put down long ago. Medical science has a lot to answer for. It prolongs a life that's not worth living. Poor Philippe's condition is so appalling that I find myself praying that God will be merciful and bring him the release of death.'

Having convinced herself and everyone who knew him that death would be a release for him, Bianca was able to silence her conscience with the rationale that he was going to die a slow and horrendous death some time in the future. Certainly, Bianca told herself, she was not doing it for the money. She already had more than anyone could spend in this world or the next. Nor was she doing it to get rid of an inconvenient husband, she argued, although Philippe was a burden she could well do without. Dr Wiseman, she knew only too well, would move heaven and earth to keep receiving the fat fees that were his incentive to keep his patient alive. No. She was mightily tired of having to play the dutiful and loving wife. She had an inheritance to protect, and protect it she would, not because of the money, but because of what that money represented.

Indeed, she would do more than protect that inheritance. She would enhance it and use it to realize her final ambitions before time ran out for her too. Bianca was no longer prepared to let Philippe linger on indefinitely, dissipating the quality of the remaining years of her own life when, by removing him from his misery, she could fulfil in herself in all the areas where he had thwarted her.

She was casting her gaze upon a magnificent azalea bush outside her bedroom window when inspiration suddenly struck, as it often did with her, out of a rich and determined subconscious. 'Yes,' she exclaimed. 'That's the way.'

Energized, Bianca bounced out of bed and took a quick shower after ordering Louis to have the helicopter ready within forty-five minutes. She was in a jaunty mood as she dressed: a mood that carried through to her arrival at the unaccustomedly early time of eleven-forty five in the morning, at the Andorran headquarters of Banco Imperiale, which Philippe was still occupying, by agreement with USNB, until the end of the year.

Agatha was on duty.

Bianca went straight to Philippe's bedroom, knowing that he usually napped before lunch. She opened the door to see the Jamaican nurse reading her Bible while her charge was sleeping soundly. 'One good thing about these new drugs,' she thought, 'is that they make him sleep better than he has been in years.'

As she entered, Agatha stirred. Bianca raised her right index finger to her lips, indicating to the other woman to get up silently.

'He's fast asleep,' Bianca whispered when she joined her at the foot of the bed.

Agatha smiled and nodded.

'Come outside. I need to speak to you.'

They stepped out into the corridor.

'Who's on duty with you?'

'Alvaro, Madame.'

'When will Eli be back on?'

'Day after tomorrow. Monsieur gave him time off to be with his girlfriend. She's visiting from Israel.'

'Monsieur is such a wonderful man. We're so lucky to have him in our lives. I know you share my sentiments,' Bianca said sweetly. 'Now I want you to do me a little favour. Tell Alvaro to stay with Monsieur until we get back. I want you to come with me and choose one of those vibrating gizmos that work so well on stiff necks. I slept badly last night. I'll be in the living room when you're ready.'

In response, Agatha bobbed slightly, in a motion reminiscent of a curtsey, the way the other female servants did when taking their leave of their regal Madame, and rushed off to find Alvaro. When she returned, her face was wreathed in delight at the honour of accompanying Madame on such an important and intimate mission. In acknowledgement, Bianca smiled the imperious but friendly smile that always went down so well with the staff, and they set off downstairs.

Like many simple souls, Agatha derived simple pleasures from simple things. She therefore surrendered herself to the pleasure of riding with Madame in her latest model Rolls Royce, black on the outside, beige and tan on the inside. There was, Agatha knew, something about the scent of very expensive cars that was truly a sensual delight, and she soaked up the experience while Bianca asked her polite questions about Monsieur's health and state of mind. The car pulled up outside the pharmacy where Monsieur's prescriptions were customarily filled, and the two women disembarked once the driver opened the door for them.

'Agatha,' Bianca said as soon as they were inside the pharmacy, 'I had to get you out of the apartment to warn you. You're in danger. I've discovered from one of the guards – I can't tell you who – that Eli plans to accuse you of the theft of some of my jewels so he can get rid of you and have his girlfriend employed in your place. You know how Monsieur loves you. It will break his heart if he loses you. But you also know how fond he is of Eli. I want you to help me to protect you. I'm really disappointed in Eli. I thought better of him.'

Agatha knew that every room had surveillance equipment and it was not possible to say or do anything in the apartment without the guards being privy to it.

'Madame,' she said, grabbing Bianca's hands in an act of heartfelt gratitude, 'I cannot thank you enough. You have saved my life. My family blesses you. You are a good woman. Monsieur says it all the time, and I now know to what extent he is right. I will do anything you ask of me. But what can I do?'

'I think it's time for us to give Eli a dose of his own medicine. Take this ring,' Bianca said lightly, opening her handbag and taking out a dinner ring with a central stone of a Kashmiri blue sapphire that was over fifty carats in weight. 'Slip it into your pocket now. Make sure you don't take it out until you're in Monsieur's bathroom. Hide it away in there. Then, after Eli comes back on duty, wait until you are both next bathing Monsieur. Slip the ring into Eli's pocket when he's helping you get Monsieur out of the bath. Make sure Eli and Monsieur don't see what you're doing. And you mustn't do it anywhere else in the apartment except in Monsieur's bathroom, otherwise the surveillance cameras will pick up what you're doing and you'll get into real trouble. Once you've done it, telephone me and tell Louis: "This is Agatha. Is Madame planning to come to see Monsieur today? He misses her and wants to see her." That will be our code for me to swing into action and nail that treacherous little so-and-so before he implements his plan against you. God knows what mischief he and his girlfriend will get up to if we allow them to prevail.'

'Oh, Madame, I don't know how I will ever be able to thank you,' Agatha said.

'You can thank me by swearing to Jesus that you will never repeat one word of this conversation to anyone. Not even to your minister.'

'I swear, Madame.'

'Good. Now let's go back,' said Bianca, all pretence about having a pain in the neck discarded.

Two days later she was with the head gardener by the swimming pool at L'Alexandrine discussing the hydrangeas when Louis came out with the portable telephone on a silver tray. 'It's Agatha, Madame.'

'Thank you, Louis,' she said, gesturing to him to wait. Picking up the receiver, she looked up at the sun. 'Agatha, what can I do for you?' she said, slightly annoyed that Agatha had asked for her instead of sending the message through Louis, then listened as the woman recounted the prearranged signal confirming that the ring was safely in Eli's pocket.

'Don't tell Monsieur that I'm planning to come to see him today,' she said, keeping up the pretence nonetheless, 'just in case he gets overexcited and fights the urge to rest, but I'll be over to see him as soon as I finish here.'

These paltry little victories - the fruit of the skirmish rather than the fruit of the war - were always more exciting for Bianca because there was no downside to them if they went wrong. The big projects, on the other hand, always carried with them an element of risk that made their execution too exciting to be pleasurable. As a result, she preferred her little schemes to the larger ones.

'Louis, see that the helicopter is ready in twenty minutes, will you, please?' she said, handing the receiver to the butler. 'I'm going in to see Monsieur. He misses me,' she said with girlish delight, as if she were a fifteen year old going to see a boyfriend.

That morning while getting dressed Bianca had deliberately chosen a trouser-suit in anticipation of Agatha's telephone call. Over her right shoulder she had slung a shahtoosh shawl that she kept in place with a massive *en tremblent* brooch of diamonds and Burmese sapphires. Leaving nothing to chance in case an observant servant should remember what she was wearing in the way of jewellery, she purposely did not wear any rings, with the result that once Bianca received the awaited call she had to go back up to her bedroom to put on her rings. These she now slipped on:

her 'everyday' engagement ring and her wedding ring on the left hand, while the right hand remained bare. She then left the bedroom playing with the borders of the shahtoosh shawl, thereby obscuring her naked right hand in a way that would not be memorable to anyone but would nevertheless conceal the fact that she had no ring upon it.

Bianca continued to play with the shahtoosh shawl the whole way to Andorra in case the pilot should notice what rings she was wearing; and when she arrived at the bank and took the elevator up to the apartment, she made sure that at no time was her right hand visible to the surveillance cameras.

Once in the apartment, she headed straight for her husband's bedroom, where Eli and Agatha were on duty. She greeted them as if this were just another visit on just another ordinary day. She crossed over to the sleeping Philippe and gently kissed him on the cheek, still twirling the shahtoosh around her right hand, for Bianca was only too aware how absolutely vital it was that no one should catch sight of the fact that she had entered the Banco Imperiale Headquarters Building without the sapphire ring that Agatha had slipped into Eli's pocket.

Having set the stage, Bianca now needed to get her accomplice away from it, so she said: 'Agatha, could you please get me a glass of iced tea? But I don't want one of those bottled jobs that Lipton's makes. I want you to make me a proper cup of tea, then put ice and lemon and sugar in it. Is that understood?'

'Yes, Madame,' the nurse replied humbly.

As soon as Agatha had gone out into the passage Bianca left Eli alone in the bedroom with Philippe and went into the bathroom. Once there, she urinated, making sure to do so loudly enough for the surveillance team to pick up what she was doing on the monitors. She then took her engagement and wedding rings off her finger, placed them loudly on the marble counter of the basin before picking up the engagement ring alone, this time dropping it into the basin with a real clatter so that the surveillance team would conclude from the sounds she was making that she had removed three rings. Then she said, for the benefit of the audiotape: 'That blasted sapphire is nothing but a wretched nuisance.'

Next she turned on the taps, which were not of the golden variety so favoured by the *nouveaux riches* but were sedate burnished steel of the highest quality, specially made by a firm in Italy to her specifications. She then washed her hands at a leisurely pace, taking care to leave the rings on the side of the basin, and, after drying her hands, returned to her husband's room to sit by his bed. Philippe stirred.

'Hello, my darling,' Bianca said as she bent over to soothe his brow. Philippe muttered something that she did not understand.

'I'll turn Monsieur,' Eli said. 'It will make him more comfortable.'

'Thank you,' Bianca said. 'Maybe he'll go back to sleep for a bit.'

'He's been sleeping much better now that he has those new drugs from Dr Wiseman,' Eli informed her to her annoyance, as if she needed him to tell her what she could see for herself.

'I know. I detect an improvement in his concentration too,' Bianca said sweetly.

'I can't agree, Madame. I've never seen him so befuddled as in the last few weeks, not even when he had those tablets which disagreed with him.' Eli's contradiction reinforced Bianca's conviction that she was right to get rid of him. 'Well,' she said evenly, enjoying setting the trap for an adversary who did not even know he was prey, 'we can't expect miracles, Eli. There have to be times when he's a bit spaced out from all the drugs Dr Wiseman's giving him to keep him alive. No?'

'True,' he said.

'And I still maintain I see an improvement in his concentration now that Dr Wiseman has changed his regimen,' Bianca replied as Eli finished settling Philippe.

'Oh, Eli, can you do me a favour?' she said lightly when he had done so. 'I've left my rings in the bathroom. Please fetch them for me.'

The helper headed for the bathroom and into the trap. He returned with Bianca's wedding ring and 'everyday' diamond engagement ring: a 32.6 white emerald-cut diamond set in platinum which Harry Winston had sold Philippe on their third wedding anniversary. 'You only need look at Mama's left hand to see whether she has you rated as Grade A, B or C,' Pedro once observed, neatly summarizing how Bianca ranked people socially, 'Or whether you're even no category at all, which is when she shows up in her "every day" engagement ring.'

'Thank you,' Bianca said sweetly, slipping the rings onto the wedding finger of her left hand. Then she extended her right hand and wagged the ring finger at Eli.

He stood there, puzzled, wondering what the hell was going on.

'Come on Eli, I'm too old for these games,' Bianca said.

Philippe stirred and tried to sit up.

Eli moved to help him up.

'What's happening?' Philippe asked.

'Eli's playing a little game with me, which I'm not sure I like,' Bianca said through gritted teeth.

'I don't know what you mean, Madame,' Eli said, rearranging the sheets around his employer.

'I asked you to get my rings, by which I meant all three of them. Will you please go and get me my sapphire ring when you've finished with Monsieur?'

A look of bewilderment passed over Eli's face as he finished tucking Philippe in. Having done so, he ambled into the bathroom, perplexed at how he could have missed the ring. He looked for it. It was nowhere to be seen. Confounded, he surmised that it must have fallen off the counter. He got down on his hands and knees to look for it on the floor. Then he sensed another presence in the room.

Looking up, he saw Bianca standing in the doorway, her hand on her hip, her ring finger flashing at him ominously.

'It doesn't seem to be anywhere, Madame. Are you sure you wore it?'

'I'm positive, Eli,' she said.

'It doesn't make sense.'

'Let's not worry about it, Eli,' she continued neutrally. 'We have a superb security team. Erhud will be sure to find it, wherever it's got to.' With that, she crossed to the telephone beside her husband's bed. She picked up the receiver and rang Erhud Blum's extension. 'Can you come up, please?'

The head of security literally ran up the stairs and into the bedroom, almost knocking over Agatha, who was returning with Bianca's glass of iced tea on a silver tray. 'My sapphire ring's gone missing,' she said. 'I had it on when I arrived. I sent Agatha downstairs to make me some proper ice tea, left Eli with Monsieur when I went to the bathroom, took off my rings when I was in there to wash my hands, forgot them, came out, asked Eli to go back in and get my rings. He returned with only my engagement and wedding rings but not the sapphire. He says he can't find it, so we need your skills.'

'Will everyone stay where they are?' Erhud said, a worried look furrowing his brow, as he headed into the bathroom to examine it himself. Of course, the ring was nowhere to be seen. Estimating that it must be worth hundreds of thousands - if not millions - of dollars, he carefully scoured every surface, opened every drawer and went down on his hands and knees before satisfying himself that it had not fallen on the floor. He then looked a second time in the drawers, and when he still could not find it he walked back to the bedroom. 'Madame, are you sure you took it off in the bathroom?' he asked, confident that Eli could not have stolen the ring.

'I'm positive,' Bianca replied serenely.

With that assurance, Erhud returned to the bathroom and pulled out every drawer. He tipped out the entire contents of each drawer himself, rifling through every item and looking into the structure of the furniture to see if it had got stuck between a drawer and the furniture. Only when he had satisfied himself that the ring had not been hidden or fallen anywhere in the bathroom, did he go back into the bedroom.

'Madame, I'm sorry, but...' Erhud started.

'You can't find it. Well, there's only one thing left for you to do. You must search us before calling in the plumbers to see if it got knocked into the drain.'

'Search you, Madame?' Erhud asked, as if Bianca had suggested something so incredible that he had not heard correctly.

'Yes, of course you must search me. You surely don't think that I'd want you searching any employee of ours without first submitting myself to the same procedure, do you, Erhud?'

Before the words were properly out of her mouth, Bianca stretched out her arms, with her legs apart. 'You can search everywhere except the feminine regions. Agatha will do those for you, in your presence,' she said, as if this were an unnecessary process which would never yield results from either herself or Eli.

Seeing the sense in Bianca's thinking, Erhud searched her. Then it was Eli's turn. He presented himself with less alacrity than she had done, his sense of dignity offended by this procedure. Nevertheless, he had to follow Bianca's example, so he stood facing the Head of Security with legs astride and arms outstretched.

Erhud flashed Eli a look of apology then brushed down the male assistant's arms and inside his legs before patting his way down the outside of his body. Suddenly, he hit something. 'Those are my keys,' Eli said and pushed his hand into his pocket.

'Don't do that,' Erhud ordered briskly.

Eli pulled his hand out of his pocket quickly. Without waiting a moment, Erhud pushed his own hand into the pocket and removed its contents. Sure enough, there was a set of keys – but also Bianca's sapphire ring.

Having been woken up by the commotion, Philippe had been witnessing this scene with growing dismay. Now he started to cough and splutter. 'I don't understand this,' Eli said. 'It doesn't figure.'

'Madame, this is a matter for the police,' Erhud said, ignoring him.

'I think not,' she responded authoritatively. 'That would only upset my husband and, whatever his faults, Eli has been very good to Monsieur. But,' she continued, turning to face the unfortunate assistant, 'I want you on the next flight out of Toulouse. I don't care where you go, but you're to leave the principality today, and you must never return. If you do come back, I promise you, I'll press charges and have them throw away the key. Save the surveillance tapes, Erhud, in case we need to use them.'

'Madame, I don't know what happened...' Eli started to say.

Bianca cut him off. 'I do. Your greed got the better of you. I forgive you, but I never want to see your face again. Oh, and incidentally, Eli, you won't be getting any severance pay. I don't believe in rewarding people who take advantage of my husband's kindness. Please see him out, Erhud.'

Erhud stepped up to Eli and grabbed him by the arm to carry out Bianca's order.

'Eli,' Philippe spluttered. 'I want to say goodbye to Eli.'

'Let him,' Bianca said sweetly.

Eli crossed over to the bed, where Philippe was sitting up, his eyes filled with tears. 'I'm going to miss you, Eli,' he rasped.

'I'm going to miss you too, Monsieur. I'm sorry things have ended like this. I hope you believe me when I say that I don't understand how that ring got where it did. It must have fallen off the bathroom counter into my pocket when I went to fetch Madame's other rings.'

'I'm sure it did,' Philippe said, patting his favourite male assistant's hand with his shaking ones.

'God bless you, Monsieur,' Eli said, kneeling beside Philippe.

'You too, Eli. You're a good boy. You've been good to me, and it's been a real pleasure having you here.'

'For me too, Monsieur,' Eli said, as Bianca motioned to Erhud to move him along.

Erhud stepped beside Eli and nudged him to stand up.

Eli turned to face Bianca. 'Thank you, Madame, for not calling the police. The disgrace would've been more than my family could bear. You must believe me when I tell you that I didn't take your ring.'

'Eli, if it makes you happier to hear me say I accept that there might well be another explanation for what happened, I'll say it. But there's no way we can keep you here after what's happened today. You do understand, I hope.'

'God bless you too, Madame. You're a good woman, and I wish you a long life and health.'

'You too, Eli,' Bianca said benevolently. Then Erhud gripped him by the arm and frogmarched him out of Philippe's bedroom as the old man broke out into loud sobs.

As soon as Eli had been escorted off the premises, Bianca was on the telephone to Mary van Gayrib in New York, getting her out of bed. She recounted the tale of how Eli had been caught stealing her sapphire ring then said: 'Find another male helper and make sure this time that he's honest. He doesn't have to be bright. In fact, he can be dumb as they come. But he has to be honest. I'd prefer one of those country bumpkins who are new to town or an out-of-towner who hasn't been polluted by the sophistication of New York City the way Eli was. Those city slickers are a bit too streetwise for comfort, and I don't want Philippe going through what he's just been through again.'

'I'll get on the case right now,' said Mary.

'Goodness,' Bianca then emoted, as if she were surprised. 'I've just realized the time. I am so sorry to have called you so early. I fear I got quite carried away in the heat of the moment.'

'I understand,' Mary said. 'It's important that we replace Eli as soon as possible. I don't mind. Really, I don't.'

'You're a star,' Bianca said warmly. 'I don't know what we'd do without you, my friend.'

'Let me see what I can come up with,' Mary said.

Two hours later she telephoned Bianca to inform her that she had found a replacement from her pool of rejected interviewees. 'He's a very personable guy. From London. Ontario. Born in 1962. He's married with three kids, all adopted. He was a Royal Canadian Mounted Policeman until he was invalided out with a defective ankle. He moved to Long Island last year to be near his wife's mother, who had a stroke and has since died. When I interviewed him four months ago, I thought he had too much family baggage and might come to regret working in Andorra.'

'What sort of person is he?'

'If you mean, does he have street smarts like Eli, the answer's "no". But he is like Eli in that he wears his heart on his sleeve. He told me the first time around the reason why he wanted the job was that the family had gotten itself into a financial hole as a result of his mother-in-law's illness. His wife had to stop working, and they were mortgaged up to the hilt. I just hung up from him. He says their financial plight is even worse than it was before, though his wife has started working again. In other words, he's keener than ever to take the job.'

'How long does he want to come for?'

'For the full six months. He seemed thrilled when I told him that we'd fly his family to France for a week's vacation at the end of his contract if he gives satisfaction. I think that perk, together with the salary of $750 a day, is what has him chomping at the bit.'

'You're sure he doesn't have the smarts to devise the same sort of plan that Eli did?' asked Bianca, sounding terribly, terribly concerned.

'To be frank, Bianca, he looks a bit of a loser. The sort who's a little bit too soft for his own good.'

'How does that square with him being a Mountie?'

'You'll see what I mean when you meet him. He's all heart and muscle. But I don't think he'd challenge Donald Duck in the brains department.'

'Well,' Bianca said, careful to sound just the right side of doubtful but secretly optimistic that he might serve her purposes, 'if you think he'll do, I'll rely on your judgement.'

'He says he can be in France on Wednesday. Will that be OK?'

'Yes. We'll just have to manage as best we can till then.'

In the days between Eli's departure and Frank Alderman's arrival, Bianca implemented the next phase of her operation with an efficiency and a resolve that would have impressed Philippe, had he known about it and had he not been the intended target.

His will, unchanged since the early days of their marriage, left his widow two thirds of his estate with the final third being divided between his brother and two sisters. Bianca had always shied away from confronting Philippe about changing it because he was so devoted to his siblings. Her viewpoint was that Philippe's fortune would never have been the size it was, had it not been for her contribution in the form of the Piedraplata fortune and the opportunities that that had given him, together with her social skills and the cachet being her husband also provided. 'Without me,' she rationalized, not without a degree of merit, 'he might now be worth $40,000,000 or $50,000,000 at a push. So any sum in excess of that left to his family, or anyone else for that matter, is money that should rightfully be coming to me.'

Bianca had long since resolved that, when the time came, she would do all in her power to have Philippe alter his will to reflect what she regarded as her rightful share of his fortune. Well, the time had come. Philippe must change his will and provide her with what was rightfully hers.

Knowing that he would never do so willingly, however, she now set about rectifying what she perceived as an injustice. She waited until Philippe was reasonably lucid, early one afternoon five days after Eli had left. 'Darling,' she said, 'I've had an idea. Knowing how devout you are, I thought a worthy testament to your accomplishments, character and love for our people would be for me to endow a College of Jewish Studies in your name after your time comes. What do you think?'

'It's a wonderful idea,' Philippe said, the light of gratitude and love burning in his eyes.

'Would you prefer the college to be at Yale, Harvard or Tel Aviv ...indeed, anywhere else you can think of?'

'I'd like Tel Aviv,' he said. 'How precious of you to think of this, Bianca.'

'You know me. Always trying to make the world a better place for my loved ones,' she trilled with absolute conviction.

Philippe did his best to smile: something his wife hated when he tried. Invariably, spittle always drooled from the corner of his mouth. This, however, was not the moment to give way to revulsion, so she reached for a tissue and wiped the fluid away gently, calculatedly radiating a beatific glow of adoration as she did so while thinking what a relief it would be to be finally free of him forever.

'Darling, one thing concerns me,' Bianca said quietly when she had finished her wifely ministrations. 'You know what Hepsibah and Rebecca are like. They're always accusing me of attention seeking. I think it's so unfair, especially as Rebecca took against me through no fault of my own when she accompanied us on my honeymoon with Ion,' she continued, shrewdly alluding, in a way that only Philippe would pick up, to the fact that it was thanks to him and his idea to get rid of Ferdie, that she had been forced to go through the farce of marrying a homosexual. 'Well, I don't want any more trouble from her or from Hepsibah. And, while you love them and are quite right as a loyal brother to defend them against criticism from any source, you must admit they will stop at nothing to embarrass me. Well, I don't want to be put in that position when I no longer have you here to defend me. They'll be sure to say that you didn't approve of the idea of the College of Jewish Studies...and that I'm just promoting myself...unless it's in your will.'

'I'll change it, Philippe said, recognizing the validity of Bianca's point. 'Arrange it for me with Gisele.'

'I don't think it warrants having Juan fly all the way from Mexico just to add a codicil, do you? Why don't I simply get the lawyer down the street to prepare something, then he can pop in one day and have you sign it. That way, we'll get this sorted out with a minimum of fuss. I can see it now: the Philippe Mahfud College of Jewish Studies. What a worthy memorial to my great, great husband.'

Philippe laughed as best he could, although his attempt sounded more like a grunt. As Bianca stilled the shiver of distaste that passed down her spine, he reached for her hand, wrapping his emaciated fingers around it.

With the rigidity that is a characteristic of late MS, he brought it towards his lips and kissed it. Touched despite herself, Bianca now had to suppress the feeling of tenderness welling up within her and smiled sweetly, thinking how conflicting it was to kill someone who loved you and whom you once had loved.

'You know, darling, I've been thinking that I'm not spending as much time with you as I'd like. Would you like me to move here from L'Alexandrine?' she asked sweetly, knowing only too well that Philippe would like nothing better.

'Would you?' he said, his eyes great saucers of love, reminding her in the tenderness of their expression and their complete roundness of nothing more than the eyes of the cows at Sintra, although bovines were a breed of animal Bianca had never been able to stand. Whenever she was in residence at Sintra, she always made the farm manager move them from the fields far from the house, complaining that 'they're stupid and attract flies'.

'That's decided, then. I'll move in tomorrow,' she said.

Suddenly Philippe looked startled. 'Dr Wiseman hasn't said something to you that you're keeping from me?'

'Of course not, darling, it's just that I miss being with you when I'm rattling around L'Alexandrine all on my own.'

Philippe sighed with relief. 'You don't know how happy you've made me.'

'And that makes me happier than I can say,' said Bianca, pecking him lightly on the lips.

As soon as Philippe was asleep she telephoned Maître Jean Aras, the lawyer whose offices were nearest to the apartment, to make an appointment to see him about redrafting her husband's will.

Needless to say, Maître Aras knew who Madame Philippe Mahfud of Banco Imperiale was. That was the good thing about living in a place where everyone had reverence for wealth. The greater the reputation for wealth: the greater the reverence. In Andorra, the names Mahfud and Banco Imperiale were right up there in the pantheon of the gods of Mammon, especially to someone as unreservedly bourgeois as Maître Aras.

Half the battle Bianca intended to wage with Maître Aras had therefore been won before she even made an appointment for the following day; and when she duly showed up, an unnerving and deliberate forty minutes late, Maître Aras was already worried lest a fish as big as Madame Mahfud might have escaped from his line before he had even reeled it in.

Bianca, however, placated him by explaining how she had been detained by a telephone call from 'the palace' - she did not specify which one, and Maître Aras, too discreet to ask, did not enquire. In fact, there had been no telephone call from any palace at all; Bianca had simply employed this ruse to impress him into being more malleable than he might otherwise be.

Having captivated Maître Aras, Bianca then informed him poignantly and with dignity that her husband was dying, that he wanted to change his will and that he had sent her to organize things on his behalf. She stated that Philippe wanted it done within five working days, before his health declined further. She said that he was prepared to pay the unheard of fee of $60,000 if Maître Aras prepared to his satisfaction the will that Philippe Mahfud, had dictated to her and she had written down in her own hand. 'I don't expect you to take my word for this,' she ended by saying. 'Please telephone my husband and check that I am here at his request.'

'It had not occurred to me that Madame would be anything but genuine,' Maître Aras said with Gallic courtesy.

'Still, I insist that you check. After all, we don't want you having any doubts, now do we? And since I have nothing to hide, I'd prefer that you do your own independent checks. I must warn you, though, that my husband can barely speak. Doubtless you know he has Multiple Sclerosis. Fortunately, it's not affected his mind, which remains as clear as a bell, thank God. I only tell you this so that when you speak to him you keep your questions short and simple.'

Maître Aras looked both embarrassed and grateful that this new client was insisting upon such an unorthodox but blameless course of action.

What he wanted more than anything else was for her bizarre request to pan out so that he could collect the easiest $60,000 he had ever earned in his life. He therefore did as she asked, telephoning the bank and asking to be put through to the Mahfud apartment. He was then put in touch with Erhud Blum, head of security, who proceeded to put him through to Monsieur Mahfud.

Having satisfied himself of something about which it would never have occurred to him to ask, Maître Aras turned to Bianca and said: 'Your husband confirms, as I knew he would, that you are here at his request. What are my instructions?'

'He dictated this will to me yesterday. It might look awfully short to you, but I can confirm it's no shorter than his last one. If anything, it might even be longer.' Bianca opened her handbag, took out two sheets of A4 writing paper that she had completed the afternoon before on a short visit to L'Alexandrine and handed them to Maître Aras.

Maître Aras studied the sheets. He read the instructions that Philippe wished to leave all his worldly goods to his beloved wife, Bianca, save for $20,000,000 in cash that he was bequeathing to his devoted sisters

Hepsibah and Rebecca and the sum of $1,000,000 to endow a chair of Jewish Studies at Tel Aviv University.

The endowment of a chair was, of course, entirely different from, and less costly than, the endowment of a college, but Bianca was confident that her husband would never learn of the switch.

More than ready to be hanged for a sheep as a goat, she also cut out Raymond financially. 'To my beloved brother,' the instructions now read, 'whose support and companionship have meant the world to me throughout my life, I leave all of my love, in the knowledge that he does not need anything else, having made himself, through his talents and initiative, one of Central America's richest men.'

'This seems fairly straightforward to me,' remarked Maître Aras, stating the obvious.

'It is,' Bianca agreed. 'Can you have the will drawn up and ready for signature by, say, midday next Wednesday?'

'I don't see why not,' Maître Aras said, his eyes sparkling at the prospect of having the fabulously wealthy Mahfuds as his clients.

Recognizing the glint of greed in his eyes, Bianca was very pleased as she rose from her chair and extended her hand graciously, bringing the meeting to an end. 'It's been a pleasure seeing you, Maître Aras. Shall I send our car and driver for you on Wednesday?'

'That's very kind of you,' he said, impressed with the graciousness of his new client.

'It will be our honour,' she replied disarmingly and flashed him one of her bewitching smiles.

So far, so good.

Bianca returned to the apartment, mindful of the need to look for any signs that Philippe might be emerging from the fog that had befallen him since Dr Wiseman had changed his medicine. Careful and painstaking, leaving nothing to chance, she never left the apartment for the next few days, although her every impulse rebelled against the constraints of living in this mausoleum. During this time, she studied Philippe the way a biologist studies an insect; the one thing she could not afford was for him to have enhanced powers of concentration at the wrong time. By the Tuesday evening, she was satisfied that his mental powers were still sufficiently intact for him to follow simple explanations, but anything else, she determined, was beyond his abilities.

The following day, Wednesday, May 19 1999, was an eventful one in the Mahfud apartment. Eli's replacement, Frank Alderman, was due to arrive at ten o'clock, two hours before Maître Aras, whose appointment Bianca had made to coincide with the time that Philippe awoke from his morning rest. However, Frank Alderman's flight was late, with the result that he arrived at the same time as Maître Aras.

Both men were greeted, as they stepped out of the elevator into the entrance hall of the apartment, by Erhud Blum. 'I'll escort you into Monsieur and Madame in a moment,' he said to Maître Aras, then, turning to Frank Alderman, he extended his hand. 'Welcome to Andorra,' he said 'Alvaro will be down in a minute and will give you a quick rundown then I'll put you through your paces. It's a lot easier than you might think.'

Maître Aras observed with interest how Frank just stood there, his mouth open and his eyes taking in as much as they could of this new environment.

'We don't want to keep Monsieur and Madame waiting,' Erhud said, turning to Maître Aras and, leaving Frank standing beside his plastic travel case on wheels, headed upstairs with the lawyer following him.

By the time they reached the master bedroom, Maître Aras was dazed by the splendid furnishings he passed on the way there. Never, in the whole of his life, had he seen anything so impressive.

Erhud knocked then, without waiting for an answer, walked straight in. In a scene that conveyed wifely devotion, Bianca was sitting demurely on the bed holding the hand of her husband, who was propped up in bed surrounded by large, Continental-style pillows. Even though Maître Aras did not know that the linen was Porthault, he could tell at a glance that each pillowcase must have cost a fortune.

'Ah, Maître Aras,' Bianca said, jumping up to greet him. 'How kind of you to come. I trust everything's in order?'

'Yes, Madame, it's all been so easy and straightforward...' he started to say.

Worried lest he should say too much, and thereby give the game away, she cut him off. 'You are too gracious,' she said, 'which is always what one wants in a lawyer, isn't it, Philippe? Graciousness makes life so much more pleasant than the hurly-burly prevalent in certain quarters nowadays.'

Then, in one of her changes of mood that always wrong-footed her opponents, she said: 'May I see the will? Now that my poor husband can't read, I have to be his eyes.'

Maître Aras opened his briefcase and removed the document, handing it to Bianca. She took it and, spinning around to face Philippe, said:

'Darling, let me present Maître Aras to you. He's the nice lawyer from down the street who you wanted to redo your will to include your bequest for Jewish Studies.'

'Ah, Maître, a pleasure,' Philippe slurred, extending a shaking hand in greeting to the lawyer.

'Monsieur Mahfud, it's an honour to serve you.'

'Good, good. Have a seat,' he said, indicating the sofa beside the bed where Agatha usually sat, 'while my wife reads the will to see that everything's in order.'

Monsieur Aras perched on the edge of the sofa, his posture betraying his anxiety to please.

Meanwhile, Bianca was standing on the other side of the bed, reading the will. 'Everything's as you wanted, darling,' she said when she had finished, addressing Philippe in French so that Maître Aras could understand. 'You can sign it.'

Bianca then handed Philippe the will. Maître Aras stood up, while Philippe laboriously scribbled something approximating a signature. That done, Maître Aras had Erhud Blum and Alvaro sign it as witnesses.

Philippe's time had just run out for him.

Chapter Twenty-Two

How do you kill someone who lives in an environment that is monitored by security guards and surveillance devices that pick up your every move? Bianca had turned the problem over and over in her mind before coming up with the solution. It was, in its own way, a brilliant plan, based as it was upon the principle that Philippe must be guided inadvertently into killing himself. All she needed was an unwitting stooge – someone who could help her to pull the trigger, so to speak, without even realizing that he was wielding was the gun – and Mary van Gayrib seemed to have provided her with one in the form of Frank Alderman.

During his first full day at work, Frank showed his potential by falling victim, like so many before him, to her legendary charm.

He was gently helping Philippe into a more comfortable position on the bed when she swung into action. 'Darling,' she said to her husband, making up a total lie so that she could use Frank's adopted children to establish common ground with him, 'when you're more comfortable, I want to have a word with you about Manolito. He telephoned last night,

383

and things don't seem too happy on the home front. That's my youngest son,' she said, looking directly at Frank. 'He's a real sweetheart. He's the only one of my four children who's adopted, but I love him as much as all of them and, to be frank, even more than my youngest natural son.'

'My children are also adopted,' said Frank, struck, as Bianca intended him to be by the coincidence.

Only the parents of an adopted child could know the strength such a bond creates with other adoptive parents, and Bianca played it for all it was worth. 'I can tell, Frank, that we're going to get along just fine, 'she said.

'I hope so, Madame.'

'I hope so too.'

'Maybe at the end of my contract, you'll get to meet my family, Madame.'

'I'd love to. I hope you're not going to miss them too much.'

'I will, but I don't have a choice. We've got a mountain of debts, and the only way we're ever going to clear them is for me to work here.'

'So you're here without your family so that you can keep them together. I admire that. Will you please fetch my handbag from my bedroom?' she asked Agatha sweetly before turning back to Frank again. 'I respect initiative,' she said. 'It should always be rewarded. And anyone who's doing what you're doing has initiative'

While Bianca beamed approvingly, Frank finished making the patient comfortable and gave him a sip of water. Philippe, by now so helpless and vulnerable that he was reminiscent of an overgrown and wizened little boy, was murmuring his appreciation when Agatha came back into the bedroom with the handbag. She handed it to Bianca, who opened it with a smile, removed her wallet and counted ten hundred-dollar bills, which she then handed to the new helper with the words: 'Here, Frank, send this back to your family by Fed Ex. They'll be sure to need something to tide them over until you're paid next week.'

'Madame,' Frank said, holding the bills in his hand with a nonplussed look on his face, 'I don't know what to say. You're like a guardian angel. If I could, I'd kiss you.'

Bianca laughed good-naturedly. 'Well, we don't want you going too far with your appreciation. A simple "thank-you" is more than enough.'

'Madame is famous for doing things like that,' Agatha said, by way of assurance. 'Only the other day, she gave me a handsome graduation present for my daughter.'

No one had ever been so generous to him in his life before; and Frank, clearly in shock, continued standing fixed to the spot with the bills in his hand.

'Now, now,' Bianca said in a mock-severe tone. 'You two don't want to make me too bigheaded with all this praise, do you? Go on, Frank. Tuck the money in your pocket. You can't stand there all day holding it in your hand. Not when you have to take such good care of Monsieur that you'll make a financial killing and return to your family with pockets rustling with hundred-dollar bills.'

Having seduced her unwitting accomplice with a show of generosity, Bianca moved in for the kill the following day. Philippe's erstwhile client Boris Budokovsky, together with his wife and child, had been gunned down in Moscow the day before, so she said to her husband, while Agatha was feeding him a lunch of strained vegetables, mashed potatoes and minced venison: 'I had a most perturbing dream last night. I dreamed that those Russians you used to do business with were chasing me down a blind alleyway. There were three of them. They had machine guns and, while I was running, they were spraying the ground with bullets. Do you suppose it's a premonition, or do you think my unconscious is just worried because of all the press reports about the Russian Mafia liquidating Boris Budokovsky and his wife and child?'

Having deliberately raised Philippe's greatest fear, Bianca shuddered visibly, as if this really were now her greatest fear too, and waited calmly to see if it would have the desired effect. Philippe's fear was already so pronounced that he refused to get out of bed to go to the bathroom until the guards, nurses and helpers had looked behind each curtain and door to see that no gunman was lurking there.

As Bianca had hoped he would, Philippe immediately panicked. What added to the effect was that, in his drugged state, he had not taken in the news from the day before. 'How did they kill Boris Budokovsky?' he asked, his eyes pools of horror.

'They smashed through the front door of his house. It was backed with reinforced steel, but they still got through. Don't ask me how. For the first time in years, I'm thinking that maybe you were right about those people. Maybe we are in greater danger than I thought. I'm now beginning to wonder whether I was wrong to dismiss your mania for security. Maybe you had a better estimation of the danger than I did, darling.'

Bianca rose from the sofa where she had been sitting and moved to sit on the bed beside Philippe. 'You know, darling, I can now see why you've taken the precautions you have. I always thought it was faintly ridiculous that you can't even go ten paces without everyone checking behind doors and curtains and sofas,' she said, gradually lowering her voice so that the surveillance equipment could not pick up what she was saying, 'but now I understand and want us to have our own secret code in case assassins ever break into this apartment. I only hope to God you'll remember it, though. Look, if you're barricaded in a room, and I say that you can leave, don't take my word for it unless the titanium shutters are up. If the titanium shutters are down, it's a signal that the hitmen have got me and are using me to entice you out of safety into danger. Will you remember?'

'Of course I'll remember,' Philippe said irritably. 'I may be a wreck, but my mind is still clear as a bell. At least, it is when I'm not doped up on those tablets.'

'OK, darling, just as long as you remember. The shutters are the key. If they're down, stay inside. The Russians have got me. OK?'

Philippe took her hand in his and haltingly but lovingly brought it up to his lips. 'You really are unique. Always thinking of everything.'

Bianca felt the blood rush to her head, as she turned puce. She did not trust herself to reply. Never before had she been so conflicted about a course of action upon which she was determined, but she couldn't see an alternative to remaining a prisoner of her marriage. Mercifully, Philippe brought the encounter to an end. 'Now I must sleep. I'm tired,' he said, and Bianca let out an actual sigh of relief.

Having heightened Philippe's fear, and got across the message concerning the code of the shutters, Bianca then waited until early the next week to implement the next stage of her plan.

An opportunity presented itself to her when she noticed Frank standing outside on the balcony having a cigarette. It was a Wednesday afternoon. The sun was shining brightly, and he was staring at the majestic and dramatic beauty of the mountains in the distance. Bianca, seizing the opportunity to arrange a meeting outside the range of the auditory monitors, joined him outside.

'So, Frank. Are you happy you came?'

'Yes, Madame.'

'But you miss your family.'

He looked at her, smiled bravely but hollowly, and nodded.

'You've fitted in so well that, if you keep going at the rate you are, maybe we can fly your family over at the beginning of the kids' summer holidays. Are those still in June? They were in the days when my kids went to school.'

'Oh, Madame, would you?' Frank said, more convinced than ever that she was the living embodiment of an angel.

'Well, my New York assistant is bringing the Lear over with some stuff from our Fifth Avenue apartment around then, so I don't see why we can't dovetail arrangements and have your family along as well.'

'It would mean the world to us,' Frank said.

'Let's see how it goes, Frank,' she said lightly. 'Tomorrow is your day off, isn't it?'

'Yes.'

'If you'd like, I'll meet you in Enrico's - it's a shop that sells toys and souvenirs near the Casino - and we can get a few trinkets for you to send to your children by way of a "hello" present from me. They'll feel much better about coming here if they think of Monsieur and myself as kindly grandparents instead of dreadful employers who've stolen their father from them. I suggest we meet at, say, eleven-thirty tomorrow morning?'

'You really don't need to, Madame,' Frank said gratefully.

'But I do, Frank, I do. Unless I invent little projects to get me out of this apartment for short spells, I'd go crazy. Believe me, you'll be doing me as much of a favour as it appears I'm doing for you.'

'Put like that, Madame, how can I refuse?'

'Eleven-thirty, then. You can't miss it. Enrico's. If you get lost, just ask anyone local and they'll direct you...oh, silly me, of course you can't do that. You don't speak French or Spanish. Well, not to worry. You won't get lost, but if you do, ring Erhud and ask him to direct you.'

Having successfully set the stage for the next act of the drama that only she knew was coming, Bianca slipped back inside.

The following morning, as she was being driven to Enrico's, Bianca had a stern talk with herself about pulling herself together. She was actually growing nervous.

By the time she walked into Enrico's, however, she was feeling more composed and gave no indication of being anything but upbeat and normal, as she greeted Frank, who was already standing inside. 'Choose anything you want for the kids,' she said graciously. 'Shall we say, at least three different presents for each child? Come on. Choose. Choose.'

'I'll get a wire basket.'

'You know, Frank,' Bianca said, as Frank looked around silently, 'it occurs to me when I look at those toy firemen over there: maybe you can help me with a problem I've been having with Erhud. He refuses to accept that the security in the apartment is a fire hazard and that it's endangering all our lives. I've tried to speak to him, but you know what some men are like. If an opinion or a warning comes from a woman, they dismiss it out of hand. Not, I hasten to add, that I'm asking you to have a word with him on my behalf. That course of action would be wholly inappropriate. No, what I was wondering is...could you help me highlight the problem with a demonstration?'

'I'll help in any way I can, Madame.'

'That's good of you, Frank. Tomorrow at six in the evening, in case you don't know, is the start of our Sabbath. I'm giving all the guards the day off from then. They deserve it, and frankly, we can't have the demonstration, if they're there monitoring all our activities.'

'What do you want me to do?'

'At six-thirty tomorrow evening...make sure none of the guards is around...go into the control room and turn off the monitors in the living room and all the other rooms downstairs in the apartment. Do not turn off the monitors upstairs in the bedrooms or in the passages and, under no circumstances, turn off the monitors recording the sound in the bathrooms. The only place we're concerned about is downstairs. Do you understand?'

'Yes, Madame.'

'Good. When you've switched off the surveillance and recording equipment downstairs, go into Monsieur's study and set the transparent burgundy part of the curtain alight. Unlike the heavy green damask sides, it's not fireproofed to EU standards. I bought it in India last year and it will go up in flames pretty swiftly. There are matches on the desk if you need them, but since you're a smoker, I shouldn't think you'll have a problem finding a light. Wait until the curtain is really blazing...by which time the smoke alarms will presumably be ringing...then rush upstairs and tell me that the apartment is on fire. That's all you need to do. Do you think you can do it?'

'Sure thing. It doesn't sound difficult.'

'It will be extremely easy, as long as you do exactly as you're told. No more. No less. It's supremely important that you leave the surveillance equipment and cameras on everywhere except downstairs. But you must knock out the whole of the downstairs floor, otherwise a recording will be made of you setting the curtain on fire, and that will get us both into trouble.'

'I've got it, Madame. I was a Mountie, you know. I'm used to taking orders and carrying them through to the letter. It's an honour to do anything that will assist Monsieur and yourself.'

'You're a good boy, Frank. You will have our undying gratitude.'

Having clicked the main piece of the puzzle into place, Bianca felt that she had just done a disagreeable job well. 'Well, we'd better be getting back,' she said.

Returning to the apartment in time for lunch, Bianca played the dutiful wife as only she could. She took the meal with Philippe in his bedroom, eating off a mahogany trolley which she had specially commissioned from the Belgravia-based London furniture-maker David Linley, nephew of Queen Elizabeth II and son of Princess Margaret and the Earl of Snowdon, who had taken those photographs of her all those years ago and which were still displayed in every Calorblanco building. As she ate, she recalled with wry satisfaction the Duchess of Oldenburg telling her that the Queen of England often ate her dinner alone in the palace off a plastic standing-tray while looking at television. 'Well,' she thought, 'Her Majesty might not care about quality, but I do, and I see no point in having the means to live elegantly, then turning around and living inelegantly.'

As soon as the meal was finished, and Agatha had left the bedroom to take the dirty dishes back to the kitchen, Bianca got up from the sofa where she had been sitting and headed for the bathroom. The time had come to click the next piece of the puzzle into place.

Making sure she was leaving a photographic and auditory trail that would establish her movements and actions as having been ordinary and innocent, she used the lavatory noisily enough for the monitors to pick it up. Having finished, she turned on the taps to wash her hands. 'You know, Philippe,' she said over the sound of running water, 'I've been thinking. I really overreacted the other day about Boris Budokovsky's death. Maybe you're right when you say we shouldn't have the guards working on the Sabbath anymore. It makes sense not only on practical grounds but on religious ones as well.'

She then turned off the taps and headed back into the bedroom.

Knowing that Philippe would ask her what it was she had been saying, she positioned herself so that her head would block out the monitor's view of him by leaning in to kiss him.

'What were you saying?' he rasped, the disease increasingly affecting his powers of speech.

By way of response, Bianca kissed him on the ear and whispered: 'It wasn't important, darling.'

'You know,' she continued, cleverly playing to both Philippe and the monitor, 'as you get older, I can see your Orthodox upbringing reasserting itself. That's lovely. It must be such a comfort to know that our religion gives one something to cling to in times of need.'

Philippe, used to his wife's sudden changes of subject, nodded in agreement just as Agatha came back into the room.

'Ah, Agatha,' Bianca said, 'could you please get me a... Actually, don't bother. I'll go myself. I may as well. I have to have a word with Erhud.'

Without further ado, she headed downstairs to the head of security's station. When she reached it, the door was already open, which was hardly surprising, for he knew from monitoring the conversation that Bianca was coming down to see him. 'What would you say if I told you that Monsieur has just decreed that all of you are to have the Sabbath off from now on? Amazing, no?'

'People become more religious as they near the end,' Erhud said. 'I've seen it with my own father and his father before him.'

'There really isn't any danger, is there?'

'Truth be told, Madame, I don't think there ever was. In all the time I've been here, there has never been an incident. Not, of course, that you can use the past to predict the future when you're talking about security matters. The unexpected is the one thing you must always calculate for.'

'I think we're as one on this issue, Erhud. Since there's no real danger, we may as well humour Monsieur. Tell your men not to worry. Your salaries remain the same whether you work on the Sabbath or not. But from now on, though, you're all off from six o'clock every Friday evening till six o'clock every Saturday evening.'

'I'm grateful,' said Erhud, who was the child of an Orthodox family and who knew the strict interdict against working on the Sabbath.

Indeed, Erhud's parents had never driven a car on the Sabbath, nor had they turned on or off electric lights. They had cooked no food. Washed no dishes. Heated no water.

That crucial part of the puzzle locked into place, Bianca departed from the security station with her stomach in knots. She was as nervous as she had been just before Ferdie's death. Despite this, she still enjoyed a surge of satisfaction at having successfully accomplished such a complex and crucial task.

Unsurprisingly, that night Bianca could not get to sleep at all. 'I've got to get some sleep,' she kept on telling herself, as she lay in the bed waiting for the one thing that eluded her. 'I cannot be tired tomorrow. I've got to be well rested. And to look it too.' So, at one o'clock, in desperation she got up and took two Temazepam tablets, knowing that their effect would last only four hours, after which the drug would wear off without leaving her with a hangover, the way many other sleeping tablets did.

For the first time, however, the Temazepam, which had previously guaranteed her a sound sleep, did not work. At two o'clock, she was still wide-awake, her mind racing. In desperation, she reached in the dark for the phial, which had once belonged to the eighteenth-century Regent Anna of Russia, and downed a third tablet with a glass of Evian water from the beside table, making sure not to turn on the light and thereby leave too distinct a record of the fact that, on a night that was meant to be just another ordinary one, she had been so perturbed that she had been unable to sleep.

The third Temazepam did the trick. Bianca drifted off into a deep and dreamless sleep, and - as ever - the effect had worn off four hours later, so she was wide-awake by seven o'clock.

Mindful of the necessity to appear as if nothing out of the ordinary was happening, she lay in bed as though she were still asleep, resolute about not getting up before her usual time. Now that it was morning, she found it easier to sleep naturally than she had during the night, and she drifted in and out of a fitful sleep punctuated by extreme anxiety until, just as she was due to be awakened, she had the most golden dream about walking through the rooms of Sintra, showing them to her houseguests:

the Queen of England and the Duchess of Oldenburg.

This magical dream was interrupted by the maid bringing in her breakfast at the appointed hour. Having been fast asleep, she now felt more tired than she had two hours before. This time she did not need to fake tiredness when she said: 'God, is it morning already? I could've slept for another two hours.'

'Would Madame like me to bring another tray later?'

'No,' she said, yawning mightily, 'it's all right. Now that I'm awake, I may as well get up.'

The countdown to eternity had begun.

At six sharp that evening, the nurses changed shift. Erhud and the guards, thrilled to be let off duty to enjoy the unexpected delights of the principality, left *en masse* in two minutes flat. Ten minutes later Alvaro and the night nurse, who had been on duty that day while Agatha went to the doctor, ambled out into the street on their way home.

Upstairs, Frank, who was meant to be on duty, and Agatha, who but for her doctor's appointment would have been off, were sitting with Philippe, while Bianca sat watching television in the living room. For the first time since Philippe had moved into it, the apartment was not crawling with security guards; and to Bianca, this created the oddest sensation. It was as if she could literally feel the atmosphere lighten. There was now space where previously the guards' presence had been an oppressive weight.

'Livings things, even when invisible, take up space,' Bianca reflected at this most telling of times. 'They make themselves felt, which has frankly been one of the burdens of having to exist in a cramped environment like this.'

At twenty past six, she rose with her customary elegance from the chair where she had been sitting and left the living room, walking unhurriedly upstairs to Philippe's bedroom, as if this were just another evening and she were a dutiful and loving wife about to minister to her infirm billionaire husband. When she reached his bedroom, Agatha was sitting with him, while they looked at television.

Frank was nowhere to be seen.

'Hello, darling,' Bianca said sweetly. 'I was feeling lonely downstairs all on my own and thought I'd come up here and watch TV with you. What are you looking at?'

'A video of *The Third Man*,' Agatha said.

'Not that old movie,' Bianca said good-naturedly. 'It's so creepy.'

Philippe patted the bed beside him. 'Come and sit here with me,' he said softly, his cow eyes suffused with love.

'Only if we look at something more contemporary,' she said playfully.

Philippe waved his hand to indicate to Agatha that she should take the video out.

'What would you like to see, Madame?' she asked.

'What is there?'

'We have a *Kiss Before Dying*...'

'Nothing deadly, thank you.'

'There's *Amistad*...it's about slavery...'

'That's even worse than death, Agatha.'

'And *Armageddon*. It's an adventure movie with Ben Affleck and Liv Tyler.'

'Let's have *Armageddon*, Agatha, and I really hope it is an adventure story.'

Agatha pushed the videocassette into the machine.

'Fast forward through the trailers please,' Bianca said in her most patrician manner. 'We can do without the Coming Attractions. Sitting through those was bad enough in the days when you had to go to a theatre to see a film.'

The nurse pushed the button, and the movie trailers were already flashing past when a smoke alarm started to beep downstairs.

'Don't tell me Frank is burning toast in the kitchen,' Bianca said disparagingly.

Before those words were properly out of her mouth, Frank had burst into the bedroom. 'Fire! Fire!' he shouted. 'There's a fire!'

'Where?' Bianca said calmly.

'In the study.'

'In the study?' Bianca repeated, ostensibly perplexed.

'Have you tried to put it out?'

'I came straight up to warn you as soon as I saw it.'

'I'll come down with you and have a look,' she said, jumping off the bed. 'Agatha, ring for the fire brigade.'

By the time they reached the study, the whole room was ablaze. Bianca was genuinely shocked by the speed with which the fire had taken hold and slammed the door shut to retard the flames.

'Christ,' she said. 'This is quicker than I thought it would be. We must turn off the air-conditioning, otherwise it will spread even faster. Do you know where the controls are?'

'By the security station,' said Frank.

'Turn them off then wait down here for me. I'll just run upstairs to reassure Monsieur.'

She then ran back upstairs to Philippe's room. Bursting through the door, she said urgently, 'Quick. You've got to get into the bathroom. We're being attacked. Agatha, help Monsieur while I seal us off.' With that, she ran to the panel of switches beside the bed and jammed her finger down onto the buttons controlling the shutters throughout the apartment. They all descended as one, sealing every room. She then dashed to help the nurse, who was walking the patient to the bathroom.

Philippe, having lived for so long in terror of meeting the end that he had contrived for Ferdie, was blubbering uncontrollably as he came face to face with the fact that he would most likely die in a similar way.

'Lock the door from the inside and don't open it until I let you know it's safe,' Bianca said, as she ushered him into the bathroom with Agatha.

'What about you?' Philippe said.

'Someone has to stay outside to liaise with the police and fire brigade when they come, and I've already sealed upstairs off from downstairs. We're in a steel-and-titanium drum, and there's no way they'll reach us now until it's safe for us to leave.'

'You be careful,' Philippe said, concerned.

'You too,' she replied, pecking him on the cheek and whispering: 'You remember our special code about the shutters?'

'Yes,' Philippe said equally quietly, so that anyone listening to the monitors downstairs wouldn't be able to overhear him. 'Down, stay in: up, get out.'

'That's my man,' Bianca said then turned to Agatha. 'Please see that you do exactly as Monsieur says,' she admonished. 'Now lock the door after me.'

As soon as the door was locked, Bianca crossed the bedroom, heading straight for the telephone. She dialled the police. 'Operator, operator,' she said urgently. 'This is Madame Mahfud from the Banco Imperiale

Building. My husband's male helper has informed me that we're being attacked by the Russian Mafia. They're downstairs and have set the apartment on fire. Get here as quickly as possible and please inform Monsieur Etienne Reynaud, your chief of police. He's a personal friend, as is the president.'

'Madame,' the Police operator said, 'I'll phone you right back to confirm these details.'

'There isn't time. The building's on fire.'

'I have to call you back. It's our procedure.'

'Then do it quickly, before we all get killed,' Bianca snapped. 'Trust the Catalans to be so bureaucratic,' she thought while waiting for the return call. 'If this were Mexico, they'd be on their way by now, and to hell with procedure.'

The telephone rang. It was the operator, as she had expected.

'Madame Mahfud?'

'Yes, it's me.'

'Just confirming the validity of your call.'

'Will you please get the chief of police over here before we're all massacred?' Bianca hissed, pressing the release button that had sealed off upstairs from downstairs.

'Yes, Madame, we'll send in the helicopters as well.'

'You do that,' Bianca said, thinking how much better than planned this was turning out. Philippe would be sure to think they were under attack from the air when he heard the helicopters. Nothing, but nothing, would then induce him to leave until he was absolutely and completely confident that it was safe to do so. 'Now, if you'll excuse me,' she continued, 'I have things to do to save our lives.' Then she slammed the telephone receiver back into its cradle.

Bianca ran back downstairs. Frank was standing at the bottom of the stairs, looking like a little boy lost in the forest.

'Frank, this whole thing has got out of hand. We're going to have to say that you interrupted some Mafia hitmen and prevented them from setting us all on fire. That's the only explanation Monsieur will buy.'

'OK, Madame.'

'We'd better do something to make it look good. Do you have a knife on you?'

'No.'

'Go into the kitchen and get one. Nick yourself slightly and say that you fought one of the assailants off.'

Frank looked dubious.

'Frank, you'll lose your job, and I'll be in hot water with Monsieur if he discovers we concocted this plan between us. You've got to do it, and you've got to do it quickly, before the fire brigade and police arrive. Come on. I'll help you get the knife.'

They dashed into the kitchen, Bianca leading the way. Once there, Frank took out a small knife from the knife drawer.

'No. Make it bigger but not too big. It's got to be convincing. The size of a hunting knife,' she said.

As receptive to orders as he had claimed to be, the former Royal Canadian Mounted Policeman replaced the knife with another. He put the tip towards his gut and grimaced. 'I don't think I can do this, Madame,' he said, clearly terrified.

'Yes, you can, Frank. Now, come on, be brave. You were a Mountie, after all.'

'But I wasn't a field officer. I was a lowly constable.'

In the distance, they could hear the screams of the sirens.

'Don't be such a sissy,' Bianca said as if she were speaking to a recalcitrant child of six and, without touching the knife herself, drove it into his gut by slapping his fist with stunning force.

'Fuck,' Frank said, the shock making him grimace.

'Sorry, Frank, I didn't mean to...but we've got to get our act together. Help is on the way.' Outside, the sirens were now blaring, and there was the sound of helicopters in the distance. 'Play the hero, Frank. Monsieur will reward you handsomely, and so will I. Don't let me down and I'll have a million dollars paid into any bank anywhere in the world you want. You've been loyal and helpful, so I want to reward you. Remember, Frank,' she said so intently that he knew she was giving him a very important message, 'I'll support you financially as long as you support me. Understand?'

'Yes, Madame,' Frank said, the pain starting to hit him.

'Good. Now I must rush back upstairs to see how Monsieur is doing.'

Left alone, Frank washed off the knife, dried it and replaced it in its rightful place in the kitchen drawer. He grabbed a bundle of clean kitchen towels to staunch the flow of blood then dragged himself to the front door to let in the firemen, who were immediately followed by police and ambulance crews.

In seconds, bedlam reigned as the professionals swung into action. The fire fighters ran to the study, trailing hoses, while, in the living room, the ambulance crew tended Frank's wound and set up a drip for him.

Before the paramedic had even set up the drip properly, however, a policeman started to interview Frank. 'Je ne parle pas française,' Frank said in a heavy North American accent, using one of the few stock expressions he had learned since arriving in Andorra.

This had the farcical effect of inducing the officer to question him further in French. 'Je ne parle pas française,' Frank then said over and over again until the officer finally realized that the injured Canadian really meant it.

This being Andorra, where most officials spoke Spanish and English as well as French, the policeman then switched to Frank's native tongue and once more asked for an explanation as to what had happened.

'I went downstairs to get something for Monsieur,' Frank said. 'I heard sounds coming from the study. I knew no one except the four of us...that is, Monsieur, Madame, Agatha the nurse and myself...was supposed to be in the apartment. So I opened the door to investigate. There were two hooded men there, and I tried to fight them off, but one of them stabbed me in the gut. I fell to the ground in agony, and the other assailant set the wastepaper basket on fire. Then they ran out of the study. I don't know if they're still in the apartment, or if they left.'

As several officers fanned out to find out whether the assailants were still on the premises, the policeman interviewing the injured man probed deeper, asking him question after question. Meanwhile, the paramedics were tending to his injuries.

Upstairs Bianca was also surrounded by a throng of policemen, ambulance men and fire fighters, none of whom could gain access to the bathroom where Philippe and Agatha had sought refuge.

'Isn't there a code to neutralize the system?' one of the officers asked her.

'There is, but I can't remember it,' she replied. 'I'll have to call our head of security. He knows it. I'll get him to come and give it to us.'

In an apparent gesture of cooperation, Bianca picked up the telephone and rang Erhud Blum at his apartment in Andorra de Vella. 'We've been attacked by the Mafia. You've got to return immediately. They've got into the apartment and set it on fire. Hurry. We need you to release Monsieur,' she said in Arabic, a language the former Mossad operative spoke fluently, but none of the emergency workers surrounding her understood.

She had pointedly failed to ask for the code.

She then hung up the telephone before Erhud had a chance to ask her any questions, turned to the policeman standing beside her and said: 'He'll be right over.'

'How long will he take? Your husband and his nurse don't have much time before the air gives out in there,' the policeman asked, surmising that she had asked for the code and the head of security had not had it on his person.

'He's coming right over. He'll be here as soon as he can.'

While Bianca was speaking to the officer, a fireman ran into the room. 'The injured man says someone up here knows how to raise the shutters,' he said. 'They must be raised. We can't fight a fire with metal shutters sealing off the place. It's a firetrap, and we'll all burn to death.'

'I know how to raise them,' Bianca volunteered helpfully and immediately crossed to the control panel, pressed the appropriate buttons, and all the shutters retracted as one, save those in Philippe's bathroom.

'Are they all up?' the fireman asked.

'All except the ones in my husband's bathroom. He's very old and very ill and he'll have a heart attack from fright if we raise them before you have this situation under control. I will not do anything to hasten his death, and I'm sure you wouldn't want me to either,' she said sweetly.

Then, looking at the policeman beside her, and remembering what a good alibi the wife of the Mexican interior minister had been at the time of Ferdie's death, she said imperiously: 'Come with me, young man. I need to reassure my husband, and I might need your help.'

Knowing the importance of this moment, Bianca allowed the policeman to lead the way to the door. Once they had reached it, she shouted to Philippe, making sure to do so in Spanish so that the policeman could bear witness to what she had said. 'Darling,' she yelled. 'It's me, Bianca. The police and the fire brigade and the ambulance are all here. You can come out. It's OK. The attack's over.'

'Monsieur says he's not coming out until he's absolutely positive that it's safe to do so,' Agatha said from behind the door.

'Are you both OK?' Bianca asked, her voice a testament to concern.

Agatha once more spoke on behalf of her weak-voiced patient. 'Madame, we're fine. Monsieur says to tell you he'll stay here till the danger's past.'

'Darling, there's no danger. You don't need to worry. I know you want to be cautious, and we understand. But there really is no danger. You can come out now. Here's a policeman. He'll tell you.'

'What your wife says is true, Monsieur. There is no danger. You can come out without fear for your safety. If you're worried, I'll give you my name and number and you can telephone the chief of police, and he'll confirm my identity.'

The occupants of the bathroom, however, had not taken a mobile telephone in with them, and there was no landline in there. But even if they had, Philippe would never have fallen back on such an obvious option as checking the identity of a policeman with the chief of police of any state. Not when he knew, from personal experience, how easily authorities were bought and sold when the price was right. And, he had no doubt, the Russians – or anyone else for that matter – who were capable of mounting such a sophisticated and concerted assassination attempt as to include armed gunmen breaking into his attack-proof apartment and helicopters flying overhead, could easily buy a chief of police. Looking at the titanium shutters sealing him off safely from harm and remembering the code he and Bianca had devised regarding the raising and lowering of them as a warning of whether it was safe to come out of his bunker, Philippe concluded that the assassins must be forcing Bianca to pretend that they were his rescuers, so that he could be induced to walk into a death trap. As images of stepping out into a hail of machine gunfire played vividly before his eyes, and he remembered the fate of Boris Budokovsky and his wife and child, Philippe decided that he would wait until the Andorran authorities forced open the door. In this situation, he reasoned, there was safety in numbers. Time was on his side.

Downstairs, meanwhile, Frank was still recounting his story when the chief of police, Etienne Reynaud, arrived. Amidst protests from the ambulance men, who wanted the injured man moved to the Hôpital Occitan without further delay, Monsieur Reynaud insisted on hearing a brief account from Frank himself. As soon as he had heard it, he rushed upstairs to see Bianca.

After a personable but perfunctory greeting, Etienne Raynaud recounted Frank's story to her. 'I'd be careful what you believe,' Bianca replied smoothly. 'This could be an inside job that has backfired. The security guards are away for the first time ever. Philippe insisted they take the Sabbath off from now on. Have you checked the surveillance tapes to see who's been recorded coming and going from the apartment? Check. You might well see something helpful. Everyone who enters this building is photographed entering and exiting. Every room, except our bathrooms, has video cameras making tapes of what happens there. Before you take anyone's word for anything, I'd suggest you go into the security control room and have a look at those tapes. A picture, after all, is worth a thousand words.'

Seeing the sense of Bianca's remarks, and still unsure whether Russian hitmen were lurking in the vast apartment, Reynaud headed downstairs just as the fire fighters were gaining control of the blaze in the study. It was at a cost, however. Black acrid smoke, caused by a combination of fire and water, had started to fill the apartment, and the ambulance men were now handing out portable oxygen masks to assist everyone with their breathing. Everyone, that is, except Philippe and Agatha, who were beyond reach.

Erhud Blum arrived at this crucial time. 'I'm the chief of security,' he announced to the policeman on the front door. 'What's going on here?'

The policeman radioed to his inspector, who in turn informed Reynaud of this latest development. 'Hold him for questioning,' Reynaud said, aware that if this were an inside job, even the head of security - especially the head of security, perhaps - should be treated as a suspect.

'Don't let him go upstairs. And make sure he doesn't escape,' he concluded, before returning to the task of checking the tapes. To his astonishment, they clearly showed that no one had entered or exited the Banco Imperiale Building between the departure of Alvaro and Olympia at 18.20 and their own arrival some time later. Moreover, monitors which Bianca had claimed should have been on had been turned off. This was ominous.

'Where's Frank Alderman?' Reynaud said.

'He's been taken to the Hôpital Occitan. He has a deep abdominal knife-wound and is scheduled to be operated upon imminently.'

'Go to the Hôpital Occitan,' Reynaud ordered. 'Find out what room Frank Alderman has been assigned. Post guards. And when he wakes up from surgery, question him again. I want to know how it is possible that he could've seen two hitmen in the study, when no one came in or left this apartment...unless, of course, they came in before the security guards left at six o'clock and left through another exit than the street door.'

By this time, the whole of the apartment had started to fill with fumes.

In the bathroom, Agatha and Philippe were having trouble breathing, and their coughing could be clearly heard through the door. Bianca, in a show of wifely concern, was standing with her cheek pushed up against it, two policemen and three paramedics beside her. Between gulps of oxygen, she implored Philippe to allow Agatha to open the door.

'Darling, I promise you: you'll be perfectly safe. The police are here standing right beside me and their chief is downstairs speaking to Erhud. Just let Agatha open the door. Do you hear me, Philippe? Open the door.'

'Madame, Monsieur says he's not opening the door until he's sure that the hitmen haven't captured you and forced you to lure him out,' Agatha replied, her voice a study in worry.

'They'll asphyxiate in there if they don't some out soon,' the policeman said, removing his mask.

'Surely your people can cut a hole through the steel from the outside to get them out,' she said, sounding ostensibly helpful.

'There are things we can do, but they'll take time. They've got to get out now.'

'Darling, it's me, Bianca, your wife. The police are telling me that you've got to come out now, otherwise you stand a chance of asphyxiating in there. Please, I beg of you, come out for my sake if not your own.'

Silence.

'Philippe,' Bianca repeated, dramatically banging her fist against the door, 'you've got to come out. You've got to. Please. Please. I'm imploring you. Come out before it's too late.'

'Come, Madame,' the policeman said, pulling his mask away from his face once again to enable him to speak. 'There's nothing else we can do. You'd better leave now.'

'If you say so,' Bianca replied sadly.

'I'll escort you off the premises.'

'No, absolutely not. I will not leave this apartment until I know my husband is safe,' she said bravely.

'As you please, Madame,' he replied, full of admiration for this devout wife.

'I'll wait in my bedroom,' she said and headed towards the room she had been using, the tears streaming down her face.

Bianca, knowing that the monitors upstairs were recording her every action, lay down on the bed, removed her oxygen mask and audibly prayed to God to make Philippe come out of danger safely. Then she put it back on, closed her eyes and waited.

When the police finally managed to cut through the reinforced bathroom door, they found Philippe and Agatha sitting on the floor, holding hands. Philippe was dead, asphyxiated; Agatha close to death. The medics oxygenated her before bundling her into an ambulance for the short drive to the hospital. The plan had worked to perfection.

Chapter Twenty-Three

Bedlam reigned, as Bianca stepped out of the apartment's private exit and onto the street that Friday evening. The whole place was crawling with soldiers in riot gear and gas masks. Policemen were barking orders as fire fighters pulled hoses through the lobby of the Assurance Meridien, adjoining the Banco Imperiale Building; and there to record it all was the press, in the form of television cameras, reporters, photographers and sound recorders. While local television crews were beaming news of the fire to European and American audiences, CNN was broadcasting it worldwide.

Before the fire had even been put out, the story had become an international *cause célèbre* far in excess of anything Bianca had anticipated; but, being highly instinctive, she was quickly able to assess the danger of the situation once confronted with it. As soon as she saw the throng of journalists, therefore, she recognized that they posed a danger unless she could contain - and hopefully, direct - their interest.

Before the police had even succeeded in clearing a path through the throng of humanity milling around, so that they could usher the grieving widow into the back of her waiting Rolls Royce for the short trip to the helipad for her to catch her helicopter back to L'Alexandrine, Bianca made up her mind to retain John Lowenstein's services as her press spokesman. 'I need an animal tamer to stay on the back of this tiger,' she told herself, 'otherwise it will devour me.'

With that in mind, she telephoned Mary van Gayrib on the car phone and ordered her to get in touch with the king of PR and put him on the job immediately. This being a weekend, Mary had to track him down to his Southampton retreat, but he immediately returned Bianca's call, catching her while she was in the air en route to L'Alexandrine.

'John,' Bianca said in her most matter-of-fact tone, 'we can't speak for long. It's dangerous for me to be talking at all on a cellular while I'm in the air. But we don't have a moment to spare. I need you onboard as my spokesman to deal with the press. I could hardly believe the interest this assassination has generated. If you saw the number of media people outside the Banco Imperiale Building, you'd think Philippe was Princess Diana. I have a feeling we're going to need your expertise in dealing with them. Would you be insulted if I asked you to come onboard for a retainer of...what shall we say...$100,000 a month, for a period of a year, at the end of which we can review the situation and see if we continue with the retainer or terminate it?'

In all his years in public relations, John Lowenstein had never been offered such generous terms so willingly. The speed with which he accepted owed more to his anxiety to agree before Bianca changed her mind than to any concern over a cellular telephone interfering with the flight mechanism of the helicopter. 'I'm mindful of what you said about the dangers of using a cell phone while flying,' he said nevertheless, 'so I'll simply say "yes" to your terms. Do you want me to get in touch with my contacts right now and start to field questions, or do you want me to wait until you're back at L'Alexandrine?'

'Start right now,' Bianca said. 'Line up a few journalists who are well disposed towards us, and I'll phone you when I get home. I should be there in half an hour, but, as Philippe would have said, we mustn't give the press a chance to find us uncooperative, otherwise they might make mischief in the absence of positive input from our side.'

'Right you are. Call me when you get home.'

'I will.'

No sooner had John Lowenstein disconnected from Bianca than he made the first of a multitude of telephone calls, offering his contacts in the media access to Bianca together with the 'inside story' on 'the Death in Andorra', as the affair was quickly becoming known in the media, before he even knew what Bianca's version was.

Once Bianca arrived back at L'Alexandrine she headed for the safety of her bedroom, where there were no monitors or electronic equipment to detect any of her movements, and telephoned John with the story of Frank Alderman and a botched assassination attempt, enabling him to put out a line heavily weighted in favour of his client: the grieving and unfortunate widow who had unsuccessfully and poignantly tried to get her husband to release himself from the bunker that became his death trap. John emphasized the role the police had played and even went to the lengths of speaking to, and getting quotes from, the officer who had stood beside his client while she implored her husband to open the door. Although John did not know it, Bianca was mightily relieved when he informed her that he wanted to stress the part played by the Andorran police: not, in fact, that he wished to protect Bianca against any gossip that might ensue but because it made for a more dramatic and newsworthy piece.

Relieved that John Lowenstein was preserving her interests by disseminating a story casting her in a favourable light, Bianca next turned her attention to maintaining her liberty against any encroachments she might not have foreseen. The lessons she had learned from Ferdie's death had come back to mind; and she realized that she had to take steps to silence the staff, especially as the press might induce them to indiscretions, with God knew what consequences. As soon as she hung up she dialled Juan Gilberto Macias on his cell phone in Mexico. 'Juan, it's me,' she said, knowing she needed no further form of identification.

'I just turned on CNN and saw you leaving Banco Imperiale...'

'I need you here with me. Right now. We don't have a moment to spare. Charter a jet and get to Nice by tomorrow at the latest. I'll have the helicopter pick you up from there.'

'It's done,' he said.

'I need you to come up with a formula for muzzling the staff,' she continued. 'As you can see, the media sharks have entered my pond, and frankly, I don't trust my minnows not to turn into piranhas. You know what servants are like. I needn't remind you of all the trouble the Mexican servants were the last time a husband of mine died tragically. I really can't go through another trauma like that, just because of a servant's idle chatter.'

'I'll have something ready for you within the hour.'

'Good. And phone me back as soon as you know when you're arriving.'

'Done,' he said.

While Juan's secretary organized the charter of a jet to fly him from Mexico City to Nice, he worked on a draft confidentiality agreement which was comprehensive in its simplicity, preventing each person who signed it from ever 'speaking or otherwise conveying information about or in any manner whatsoever communicating information about and/or pertaining to the late Philippe Mahfud and/or his widow, Bianca Mahfud...for a consideration of $100,000'. This document, which ran to only two double-spaced A4 sheets, was short, sweet and to the point. By the time he handed it over to his secretary for typing and faxing to L'Alexandrine, Bianca had also been exerting herself at her end. She needed someone capable and trustworthy to deal with the myriad enquiries and arrangements that had to be attended to; and there was, she knew, no better assistant on earth than Philippe's secretary, Gisele.

It was hard for this efficient and decent woman to believe that Monsieur, of whom she had grown so fond, was dead and that he had died in so terrible a manner. As she applied herself to typing up the draft confidentiality agreement that Juan had sent through on one of the three computers still housed in Philippe's office overlooking the helipad at L'Alexandrine, Gisele consoled herself with the thought that she still had a link to him through his family: for who had Madame turned to in her hour of need? This, Gisele knew, was small consolation in the circumstances, but at least she was still a part of Monsieur's way of life; and at least she could continue to serve him in death with the same loyalty and ability as she had done in life.

This loyalty would ultimately work to Bianca's detriment.

Having transferred the confidentiality agreement onto the computer, Gisele, believing that its purpose was to protect Monsieur's professional and personal secrets, consulted her list of the employees who would be required to sign it. There were the three nurses, their three male helpers, eleven security guards, and the eighteen household staff at both the Andorra apartment and L'Alexandrine.

Noting that each employee would receive the sum of $100,000, to be paid into a bank account of their choice anywhere in the world, she decided to offer to sign the agreement herself. After all, why shouldn't she and the other secretarial staff also benefit, especially as their jobs would most likely now be coming to an end?

'There's no need for you to sign it,' Bianca said sweetly, seeing exactly what Gisele's motive was, 'but if you want to, you can.'

'If the secretaries don't sign it as well, Madame, it will cause friction between the employees,' Gisele explained, widening the net on behalf of her assistants.

'Very well,' said Bianca, recognizing that the willingness of the secretaries to sign something they had not been asked to would encourage those members of staff who might otherwise have had objections. 'Let them sign it as well.'

In truth, Gisele's actions were prudent, for, as she suspected, all the secretaries were due for the chop: Bianca having already decided to terminate the employment of Philippe's office staff at the first opportunity. Those who signed the confidentiality agreement would therefore receive a bonus additional to the redundancy payments they could expect at the termination of their contracts. As far as the widow was concerned, the only minions she would be paying thereafter would be those who owed allegiance only to her.

By the time Juan Gilberto Macias arrived at L'Alexandrine at 15.47 on Saturday, May 27 1999, every single employee had signed the confidentiality agreement. Bianca was now safe from leaks to the press – or so she imagined.

Having provided the mechanism for containing the flow of information from the Mahfud camp, Juan then turned his attention to the rather more important matter of dealing with Frank and the authorities in Andorra. These had to be made to realize that the richest widow in their country deserved the deference that was her due. 'I want justice,' Bianca had said to Juan, employing the kind of doublespeak that had concealed her motives over the years. Although it was a necessary part of the game to pretend that Juan accepted at face value the meaning of the words, as they walked around the garden at L'Alexandrine, Bianca gave her lawyer his instructions in typically obscure but, to him, fathomable style. 'My husband was the fairest man alive, as you know only too well. I want you to get confirmation from the police of the reason why Frank set the fire. If it emerges that he really was trying to help Philippe, as Etienne Reynaud, the chief of police, says he's been saying since coming out of surgery... Whether it was the drugs or not, I don't know, but it turns out he's admitting setting the fire himself and that there never were any Russian Mafia hitmen... He simply used Philippe's fears to warn him about the dangers his security system was creating for him... If Etienne's comments are accurate, see that the way is paved for Frank to be treated with the leniency he deserves. After all, the poor man is as much a victim in this as Philippe or myself: he never intended to cause my darling husband's death. You know how to handle this sort of thing...and remember, Juan, money is no object,' she said, dropping the hint that she was ready to pay a sizeable bribe, 'I'd rather pay someone $2,000,000 to see that an innocent man is spared than save the money and see someone punished for a crime he did not intend to commit.'

'Leave it all to me,' Juan replied, understanding the subtext only too well, 'and we'll see that justice is done.'

'If you find out that Frank is as innocent as Etienne says he is,' Bianca continued, 'and if you manage to get the authorities to arrive at a deal which ensures justice for him, I'll see that you receive a suitable bonus.'

Juan, who over the years had become a rich man from the work he had done for Philippe and Bianca, remained silent, a small smile playing on the corner of his lips.

'I was thinking of something along the lines of $5,000,000,' Bianca said.

Juan, wrongly suspecting that the reason why Bianca was so anxious to protect herself was that she was afraid that Philippe's death might reopen an investigation into that of Ferdie Piedraplata, surmised that this might well be the last major deal she would ever call upon him to strike on her behalf. He was consequently aware not only of how much Bianca needed his negotiating skills to preserve her position but also how necessary it was to obtain maximum recompense for himself. Nor was he the Mahfud lawyer for nothing. There were few tricks he hadn't learned from that past master of negotiating wizardry, Philippe Mahfud. So, instead of driving up his demands, he skilfully deflected Bianca's attention away from his intentions by saying amiably: 'Bianca, I'm happy to do it for nothing, in honour of Philippe's memory.'

'I know how fond of Philippe you were,' Bianca replied, rightly interpreting the statement as a negotiating device but wrongly concluding that he suspected her of being involved in another husband's death. 'But I also know you have expensive tastes and, since I've dragged you all this way from home, I thought it would only be considerate to offer you a bonus. But, if you don't want one, I won't force it upon you. Shall we scrap the idea?'

'We don't have to scrap it entirely,' he responded smoothly. 'Why don't we say a bonus of $4,500,000 and fees of $7,500,000 to cover the negotiations with the suspect and the authorities?'

'Your charges are becoming rather excessive, Juan,' Bianca said, convinced by this demand that he definitely suspected her of involvement in Philippe's death, 'but one of the things I've always liked about you is your utter ruthlessness where your interests and those of your clients are concerned. That's what makes you such a good lawyer. Philippe thought so too.'

'Philippe and I always shared a refreshingly honest approach to deals.'

'Yes, Philippe valued your lack of pretence. That, and the fact that you always obtained the desired result.'

The time had come, Juan could see, to move the subject on. 'Unlike many other rich people,' he said, 'Philippe didn't mind paying...as long as he was getting his money's worth.'

Bianca took the hint. 'I think $7,500,000 is an excessive fee for only a few days work,' she said nonetheless. 'Don't you agree that $6,000,000 would be far fairer?'

Juan laughed amiably. 'How do you know it's going to be only a few days work? These things have a way of dragging on for years. By agreeing a flat fee with you, I run the risk of financing your lawyers' costs unless I can have it wrapped up quickly. That is surely in your interest as much as in mine?'

'True,' Bianca responded reasonably.

'Bianca, we've been friends for many years. You know me, and I know you. Why don't we stop this haggling and shake hands on a bonus of $5,000,000 and a fee of $6,500,000? That way you give something and I give something, and we'll both be happy.'

Bianca shook Juan's hand to seal the agreement, knowing she had struck a deal that would ultimately be to the advantage of both parties.

Juan would be receiving a big fat payment while she would be hiring the services of the one person she could trust to arrange for Frank to take the rap on her behalf. Not, of course, that either Bianca or Juan would ever put it in such crude terms. No, Juan would act upon his instructions to 'reward Frank for his loyalty' by making him know that she 'supported the admissions he had made so far', and that she would not 'lose respect for him if it emerged that he had come up with the idea to set fire to the study out of a sense of misguided concern for Philippe's welfare'. Indeed, if it emerged that his motives had been as noble as they appeared to be, she would reward him by depositing the sum of $1,000,000 in a numbered bank account in Liechtenstein, which Juan could open for him as soon as he signed a confession. A further $1,000,000 awaited him for each year he was kept behind bars; and another $1,000,000 would also be ready and waiting for him upon his release from prison, to 'assist his recovery from the effects of institutionalism as he readjusted to society'.

After all, Bianca reasoned, she was already worth some two billion dollars in her own right and had just come into several billion more dollars from Philippe. So the few million dollars she would have to pay out now wasn't that high a price.

It would not, however, have done to give voice to any of those sentiments. So, as she shook Juan's hand, Bianca also shook her head in mock resignation. 'You always were a tough nut to crack,' she said, smiling, 'but then, that's why I have you acting for me. Yes. OK. Fine. It's a deal. Now I'd suggest you get on the phone to the chief of police and ensure that justice is done.' And Juan,' she said, almost as an afterthought, although it was anything but, 'I want to be kept out of things as much as possible. Aside from anything else, I'm frantically busy making arrangements for the funeral, so please say to everyone you deal with that you're acting for Philippe's Estate and keep my name out of it.'

For the next two days, while Bianca, Gisele, Mary van Gayrib, John Lowenstein and the secretaries worked to organize Philippe's funeral, scheduled to take place at the St John's Wood Synagogue in London, and to contain the coverage of Philippe's death, which was dominating the French and Swiss papers and was being covered as far afield as Australia and Annapolis, Juan worked behind the scenes with the Andorran authorities to seek 'justice'. This took the form of renewing Bianca's promise to Frank that his financial future would be assured but only if he signed a confession in which he 'admitted setting the fire on his own, an idea he had conceived, again on his own, to help Monsieur, whose security arrangements had caused him, an ex-Mountie, concern for Monsieur's safety and well-being'. Juan also told Frank that he would 'use Bianca's influence in Andorra to see that this noble - yet flawed – plan would be treated with the consideration it deserved, so that any punishment he faced for having inadvertently caused Philippe's death, would be minimized as a result of his motives.'

Frank, unfortunately, was proving difficult to 'help'. He was too naïve, too afraid and frankly, too *dumb* to understand that Juan was tipping him a wink. All he needed to do was accept the conditions that were being offered in the subtle way these things were customarily done, and he and everyone else could breathe easier.

Frank, however, refused to sign the confession. Even when he was given two court-appointed lawyers, and they assured him that he would be given lenient treatment as long as he signed the confession, Frank stubbornly refused to do so.

Bianca and the Andorran authorities, however, needed him to sign that confession if 'justice' was to be done. When he therefore persisted in his refusal to sign, Juan came up with an apparent solution to the problem. He got Mary van Gayrib to telephone the recalcitrant helper's wife, Susan, and to offer her a return ticket, all expenses paid, including spending money in Andorra for a week, if she wanted to come to see her hospital-ized husband. Susan, however, did not have any available time-off from work, so sent their eldest child, the nineteen year old Louise, who flew out of New York on the evening flight to Paris. The following morning, she caught a connection to Toulouse, where she was met by a Mercedes-Benz from the Mahfud fleet, together with a driver and two bodyguards.

'How's my father?' she asked the man who identified himself as Benyamin.

'He's doing well. He's not in danger. Would you like to see him before or after you check into the hotel?'

'Before. Miss van Gayrib said you'd take me straight to him.'

'We will,' said Benyamin. 'Hop in.'

He opened the car door, Louise slipped into the back seat, and before she knew it, she found herself sandwiched between Benyamin and another bodyguard.

'How long a stay did Immigration give you?' asked Natan, the other bodyguard.

'I don't know,' Louise said, suspecting nothing.

'It's in your passport,' Natan said. 'Have a look.'

Louise opened her handbag, an obvious Louis Vuitton copy, and withdrew the document. She started to look through it.

'Here,' said Natan said. 'Don't trouble yourself. Let me.'

Deftly removing the passport from her grasp, he flicked through the pages. Then he said something to Benyamin in Hebrew that Louise did not understand before turning to her and saying: 'They didn't stamp your passport properly at the airport in Paris. It's not a problem. I'll take it into the Immigration authorities tomorrow and get it dealt with then, otherwise you might have trouble leaving the country.'

'The French are very bureaucratic,' Benyamin said, 'especially where access to their country is concerned. They're even worse than you Americans, always thinking everyone wants to come and live in your country. That's not a problem we Israelis have.' He and Natan laughed, while Louise let it go and surrendered herself instead to the joy of peering out of the car window as the magnificent scenery between Toulouse and Andorra flashed by. 'It's so beautiful,' she said.

'Yes. It is, though I personally prefer the view between the Airport and L'Alexandrine, where Madame Mahfud lives,' Benyamin said while Natan stuffed the passport into his trouser pocket.

'I've always wanted to see France,' replied Louise. 'Ever since I was a little girl. Is Madame Mahfud's house close to here?'

'Only by helicopter,' Natan said, the passport safely secured.

Just then, the telephone in the car rang. The driver answered it, said something in Hebrew, which was the trigger for Natan to stretch across Louise and take the receiver from him. Natan's response was to grunt something perfunctory into it in what sounded to Louise like Hebrew again and then hand the receiver back to the driver for him to replace.

'There's been a change of plan,' he announced. 'The police have withdrawn their consent for you to see your father. But don't worry, we'll take you to your hotel and keep you company until permission comes through. Madame's lawyer is working on it, and so are your father's lawyers, who are two of the best men to have on your side in Andorra.'

Louise, in a strange country and unable to speak the language, with no friends and no one to turn to except her father's employers, felt her spirits sink. Tears sprang to her eyes. 'Don't worry,' Benyamin said. 'One of us will stay with you all the time. You won't be alone.'

Louise remained silent and morose for the remaining hour of the drive to Andorra. Where minutes before she had been taking in the magnificence of the French countryside, now she stared unseeingly through the window at the scenery, blind to everything but her own anxiety about what was happening to her father, herself, her mother and her two siblings.

Finally, after what seemed a lifetime, they pulled into the Marmot Hotel. Natan and Benyamin jumped out and escorted her into the lobby, one on either side. They headed straight for the reception desk, where Benyamin said something in French, that she did not understand, to the receptionist. Louise was impressed to see that they didn't even need to wait for her to be checked in. The receptionist handed over a key, and they were on their way upstairs, while the formalities were attended to by the driver, whose name she never learned.

Within minutes of being shown into a pleasant but functional room, the bellboy arrived with her luggage, and Miss Louise Alderman was busy unzipping the vinyl case. 'You stay and keep our guest company,' Natan said to Benyamin, 'while I go to the hospital to see if the police will let her see her father today.'

Then Natan took her passport straight to Juan.

By this time, Bianca's lawyer had already seen to it that two of the police officers on the investigating team, as well as one of the public prosecutors, had lightened the Mahfud fortune to the tune of $240,000.

Juan now handed Louise's passport to one of the two policemen who were in his pocket. The man promptly took it to the prisoner in hospital.

'Go get yourself a coffee,' he said to the guard upon entering Frank's room. As soon as the guard had left the room, the policeman whipped out Louise's passport. 'The entry stamp in your daughter's passport is irregular,' he said. 'Here, let me show you.'

Frank looked and saw what appeared to be a perfectly regular entry stamp. 'It looks fine to me,' he said.

'Well, it's not. Now, I'm not accusing your daughter of anything; but the fact is, she has no valid right to be in France or Andorra, and Immigration in either country could detain her for an indefinite period. They could possibly even try her for breaking the Immigration laws – an offence, incidentally, which is punishable by a term of imprisonment in either country – but I don't think it needs to come to that. Not if we can establish a mutually advantageous and cooperative relationship.'

'How?' Frank asked cautiously.

'It's easy. You sign the confession you made when you were coming round from the anaesthetic, and we'll see that your daughter leaves Andorra and France without a problem.'

'And if I refuse?'

'We hold your daughter until you see sense.'

'Not a chance,' Frank said, terrified that he was about to fall into a trap.

'I'll give you until tomorrow to think things over.'

For thirty-six hours, Frank held out. During that time, his lawyers, who were as eager as the other members of the Andorran establishment to resolve this embarrassment before it spiralled further out of control, tried to convince him that it was in his interest to sign, pointing out that the confession was nothing more than an admission of having tried to help his employer. Each time they told him that, Frank came back with the same argument: suppose the authorities were trying to dupe him? Suppose he signed and ended up getting a long prison sentence? Over and over, his lawyers had to repeat that the authorities were not trying to dupe him. The harshest penalty the crime to which he had already admitted would attract was a maximum of four years in prison. If he cooperated in the investigative part of the proceedings, the judges would factor that into any judgement they handed down, so he might well get a lighter sentence. The quickest and cleanest way to solve the quandary was therefore to sign the confession.

'And if I don't?'

'Your daughter will be detained here until you do.'

'But she's done nothing wrong,' he objected.

'We're trying to do you a favour here. The authorities don't have to promise to release your daughter. We've got this concession out of them, because they know us and we know them, and because Madame Mahfud is an eminent citizen of Andorra. Passport irregularities might not matter to you Americans, but in France and Andorra, the authorities take them very seriously. If you keep on refusing to sign that confession, they might just lose patience with you and withdraw their offer to release Louise. Then you'll both be in jail, and who's going to defend her?'

Confronted by the possibility that both he and his daughter might end up incarcerated in the principality and assured by the lawyers that he would be able to see Louise within minutes of signing the confession, Frank signed.

Within the hour, his daughter was shown into his room at the Hôpital Occitan, where an armed guard still stood outside the door and another, English-speaking one sat dourly on a chair in the prisoner's room. With his right foot cuffed to the bed and with the guard in such close proximity, it was impossible for Frank to say anything that would not be overheard, so he and Louise deliberately limited their conversation to fairly innocuous family matters.

Only at the end of the visit, when Louise bent to kiss him goodbye, did Frank address what was happening to them. 'Leave Andorra tomorrow,' he said suddenly. 'Choose a late flight so you can come and see me again before you leave but make sure you get out of here tomorrow.'

'I can't just leave you like this, Daddy, ' Louise replied.

'You can, and you have to. Only when you're out of here and safe with your mother and the other kids will I be confident that they can't use you to reach me. Promise me that you'll do as I say.'

'Daddy, this is all so mysterious and puzzling.'

'It's a matter of influence, Louise. More, I can't say.'

'But I'd have travelled halfway across the world to see you for only a few minutes.'

'I know, honey, but you'll be of more use back home than here. You have to do this for me and the rest of the family, if not for yourself.'

'OK, Daddy.'

At the very moment that he was convincing his daughter to get out of Andorra, Philippe's body was being released by the authorities for burial.

Agatha was also released from hospital at the same time, badly shaken and still suffering the effects of smoke inhalation. Gisele had arranged, at Bianca's request, to have her flown out to Jamaica and to be given the princely sum, to her at least, of twenty-five thosand dollars US to cover the expenses of her recuperation.

Always a thoughtful and generous employer, Bianca wisely promised the woman a pension for life in the form of her salary being index linked and paid in advance on a monthly basis, together with a lump sum of $250,000 at the end of the second year 'to assist our beloved Agatha in adjusting to life after such a traumatic end to her employment,' as Bianca had put it, in return for which she was obliged to sign a waiver of all future claims against the Mahfud Estate.

When the time came, Agatha signed. She was simply too poor to cause a problem.

Philippe's funeral was scheduled for four o'clock on the afternoon of Monday, May 31 1999, and the St John's Wood Synagogue now became the venue for what would be a sensation. Bianca had wanted it to be as spectacular as Ferdie's had been, and it was - in ways that she had not intended it to be. Her first miscalculation was to leave instructions with Erhud Blum and the ten other security guards not to allow in anyone whose name did not figure on the guest list. Not only are all places of worship in England public places and you therefore could not prevent anyone who wished to gain admittance from entering but also a funeral is not a party or a charity première. Treating it as if it were seemed both frivolous and undignified. Some might even say pretentious and silly. As Bianca's aim was to contain the chatter and not inflame it, this was asking for trouble.

The real drama began when Raymond Mahfud arrived with his wife Begonia and his sisters Hepsibah and Rebecca at ten minutes to four.

'Name please, sir,' said the guard.

'I am Raymond Mahfud and this is my wife and sisters,' he replied in a voice that brooked no opposition.

The guard checked his list.

'I'm sorry, sir, there seems to be some mistake,' he replied, not realizing that Madame Mahfud had deliberately excluded all of Monsieur Mahfud's own siblings from his funeral. 'It must be an omission.' He was just about to let them in when the guard standing on the other side of the door shook his head. They had strict instructions not to let in anyone whose name did not feature on the guest list. 'Let me contact my superior, and we'll sort this out.'

The guard buzzed Erhud Blum on his walkie-talkie and asked him what he should do.

'How much do you want to bet that Bianca has deliberately left our names off the list?' Raymond said in Spanish to Begonia, while the guard was talking to Erhud.

'No. There must be a mistake. Not even Bianca would stoop so low,' said Begonia of her old school friend.

The guard, having taken his instructions from his superior, turned to Raymond and said: 'Monsieur Mahfud, the Head of Security will be along to see you in a moment. Once more, I'm sorry for this, especially at such a time.'

'You're only doing your job, young man,' Raymond said magnanimously.

Moments later, Erhud Blum stepped out of the synagogue and came up to them, clearing up any doubt of Bianca's responsibility. He was only too aware that he was not to let in any of the Mahfud family, but his Orthodox heritage was offended by his employer's wish to exclude her late husband's family from his leave-taking of this world. He was also prepared to put his job on the line for his principles - in the unlikely event that Bianca did not get rid of a security staff she had been complaining about for years. 'I'm sorry, sir,' he therefore said in a tone of voice which made his position clear. 'Our instructions are not to let in anyone who isn't on the list. Madame was most particular about that. But, seeing as you're Monsieur's family and synagogues are public places, we don't have any authority, beyond Madame's, to prevent you for entering. So if you want to step past us, there's nothing we can do to stop you.'

'Thank you,' said Raymond.

'Think nothing of it, sir' Erhud Blum said with respect.

Raymond, Begonia, Hepsibah and Rebecca walked around him and stepped inside. Stopping for a moment to get their bearings, they headed towards the casket, only to see that it was already closed.

'Why is my brother's casket closed?' asked Raymond, who had wanted to see his beloved brother's face one last time, of a guard standing nearby.

'Madame gave the undertaker instructions to close the casket at three o'clock, sir,' the guard said.

'Open it,' Raymond ordered. Around him, the invited guests continued to stream in and heads turned to see what the commotion around the coffin was all about.

'I'll have to get the undertaker to do that.'

'You do that,' Raymond ordered, as his sisters stood by quietly in tears at the sight of the coffin housing their brother's body.

The guard quickly returned to say that the undertaker could not open the casket once it had been sealed. 'The bitch,' Raymond spat out in Arabic to his wife and sisters. 'She did this deliberately so that we wouldn't have a chance to say goodbye to Philippe.' Then he turned to the guard.

'Please escort us to our seats,' he said.

'If you're not on the list, you won't have seats,' said the guard, embarrassed. 'They've all been allocated.'

'In that case, get chairs for us,' Raymond ordered. 'We'll wait here until you find some. Then you can place them where I tell you.'

So far, Bianca was nowhere to be seen. 'You'd have thought the Praying Mantis would be here to receive all her chic Fifth Avenue friends,' Hepsibah said.

'She must be planning a dramatic, last-minute entry,' said Begonia, accurately divining her intention.

'She thinks she's Norma Desmond in *Sunset Boulevard*,' Hepsibah said.

'She is Norma Desmond in *Sunset Boulevard*,' Rebecca said. 'Mad, attention-seeking and ruthless. Till my dying day, I will never be able to erase the vision of that woman marrying one man and sleeping on her honeymoon with another.'

Two guards then returned with four folding chairs. 'Follow me,' Raymond said to his wife and sisters, and they set off for the front row, where the Secretary General of the United Nations, the Commissioner for Refugees, various European politicians and three European princes, one of royal blood and two of the commercial world, were seated along with Dolphie Minckus, Walter Huron, and the Duke of Oldenburg. The men were on one side of the aisle, the women on the other. 'Here,' said Raymond to the guard, indicating the central spot, 'put mine here. And put the others beside it: in a row, like this,' he continued, pointing to the centre aisle which would then be almost blocked by the four chairs, for the gap between Raymond's chair and the ladies' was so narrow that only a thin person could get through with ease.

The guard did as he was told. He opened Raymond's chair, placed it where ordered then followed Raymond, who by this time had crossed to the other side of the aisle, where the women were segregated from the men.

'Put those two here,' he ordered, pointing to the end of the front row where Bianca's name and the names of her good friends Ruth Fargo Huron, Stella Minckus and the Duchess of Oldenburg were displayed on gilt chairs. The congregation by this time was transfixed by the drama that was taking place at the front of the synagogue, and there was a buzz of speculation as to what was going on in the front row. No one who saw Raymond Mahfud's face could doubt that he was furious beyond words, but no one in the congregation had any idea what the fuss was all about. All they could see was Raymond thanking the guards graciously then taking his seat, along with his wife and sisters, with great dignity.

No sooner had the Mahfud family sat down than Bianca arrived, on the arm of the European chairman of USNB, Sir Jonathan Richards, flanked by Stella Minckus, Ruth Fargo Huron and the Duchess of Oldenburg, as if this were a wedding and they were bridal attendants.

The progress upon which Bianca then embarked towards the front of the synagogue was more like royalty greeting an assemblage of acolytes than a widow heading towards her husband's coffin. She was so busy being gracious, constantly smiling to the right and left that she did not even notice how her arrangements had been altered until it was too late. Only when she could no longer turn back and walk down a side aisle, did she notice Raymond, Begonia, Hepsibah and Rebecca ensconced in the front row, preventing her easy access to Philippe's coffin. She was so surprised by their temerity in having crashed Philippe's funeral and frustrated her plans that she let out an involuntary and very audible gasp. Their presence forced first Sir Jonathan, then Bianca and her three female attendants in turn, to squeeze through the narrow passage single-file. While they were doing so, Hepsibah and Rebecca pointedly nodded to each other, knowing that by so doing, they would be sending a message to the watching congregation that would publicly embarrass Bianca.

Victory in the next round of this public squabble also went to Raymond. The funeral rites having just concluded, eight eminent pallbearers, none of whom had known Philippe well enough to call him a friend but all of whom were household names which bedazzled readers of glossy magazines such as *Vanity Fair* or *The Tatler*, stepped forward to lift the dead man's coffin out of the synagogue. Intent on not being excluded from an honour that was rightfully his, Raymond stepped forward, determinedly taking his place at the front of the company, and shoved his shoulder under the casket. In so doing, Raymond forced one of them to step aside as the deceased's brother assumed his rightful place as chief pallbearer. This position he maintained until the eight pallbearers had conveyed the coffin to the hearse, and, when it reached the North London burial ground, he once again resumed his place of honour to convey Philippe to the waiting grave. Only when he reached it did Raymond pause, casting his eyes over the open hole that would be his brother's final resting place. He took in the canvas canopy erected beside it, beneath which reposed little gilt chairs such as one customarily saw at couture shows. Further angered by what he perceived to be the undignified manner in which Philippe's widow had turned his funeral into a society show, Raymond relinquished his place of honour to the undertakers.

By the time Philippe had been buried, Raymond could no longer contain himself. Although a great adherent to the principles of dignity, he was so outraged by a funeral that he saw as both a farce and an insult to not only his late brother but also to himself and his sisters, that he was no longer prepared to contain his fury. On his way to rejoin Begonia, Hepsibah and Rebecca, who were standing at the end of a row of gilt chairs occupied by Bianca and her socialite friends, he deliberately chose to walk in front of his sister-in-law. Getting as close to her as it was possible to do, he brushed past her knees and forced her to pull in her feet under the chair to avoid having them trodden upon. As she glowered at him with the set smile that he knew meant hatred, Raymond glowered back at her. 'You think you're so clever,' he said. 'Just you wait.'

Pedro and Manolito, no longer surprised by any of Bianca's antics, moved in to restore a semblance of decency to their stepfather's leavetaking.

They approached Raymond in full view of everyone before he could reach his wife and sisters.

'Please accept our condolences, Uncle Raymond,' said Pedro, intent upon righting, insofar as he could, Bianca's wrong, 'and my apologies for my mother's deplorable conduct.'

'And mine too, Uncle Raymond,' added Manolito. 'Uncle Philippe must be dancing a jig at what's gone on here today.'

'Thank you, boys,' Raymond said. 'It's awfully decent of you to do this. I know how fond you kids all were of your Uncle Philippe, and I want you to know he would be proud of you right now.'

'Will we see you at the reception?' asked Manolito. 'It's in the ballroom at Claridge's.'

'I don't think so,' Raymond said. 'We haven't been invited.'

'That doesn't matter,' Pedro said. 'The Praying Mantis can't very well throw you out. If she tries anything, I'll say that I asked you to come.'

'It's good of you, boys, but no. We'll go back to our hotel and remember your Uncle Philippe the way he would really want to be remembered.'

'When will you be returning home?' Pedro asked.

'Maybe next week.'

'Me too. I'll look you up when I get back.'

'You do that. You too, Manolito, when you're next in Mexico.'

'Right, Uncle Raymond,' Manolito said and kissed Raymond three times Middle-Eastern style. The people surrounding them craned their necks to get a better view of Bianca's child and stepchild showing solidarity to the very person whom she had tried to exclude from the proceedings.

The time had come for Raymond to leave. So, having said goodbye to the boys, he crossed over to Begonia, Hepsibah and Rebecca and, linking arms with his wife, said: 'It's time we went.'

In declaring war on the Mahfud family so publicly and so callously, Bianca had not only hardened those four relations into real enemies, but she had also ignited the fuse of public speculation. Before the day was over, half the people in the congregation who witnessed the spectacle of the Mahfuds having to crash their own blood relation's funeral had spread the word far and wide about the war between Bianca and Philippe's family.

As so often happens when people have something important and painful to discuss, once the Mahfud family were in their suite, they delayed having their conversation about what to do next. First they changed out of their funereal clothes into something more comfortable and ordered a light supper of soup, white wine and fresh fruit. Then they decided to wait until it had arrived, for they did not want to be interrupted by waiters walking in with food while they were in full flow.

When the food arrived they thought it advisable to eat first, lest the subject they were about to discuss ruin what was left of their appetites.

Raymond, Begonia, Hepsibah and Rebecca were therefore on their coffee, with the afternoon's happenings still not touched upon, when the phone rang.

Being the nearest, Begonia answered it. She was monosyllabic throughout the call, which did not last long. 'That was Conchita Perez de Guellar,' Begonia announced after she had hung up. 'She's at Claridge's, and she says the party is in full swing. The only alcoholic beverage being served is vintage champagne. There's an array of fruit juices and a lavish buffet, with several two-kilo silver bowls full of Iranian gold caviar doing the rounds in the hands of liveried footmen. She says there's a real air of celebration and that Bianca hasn't stopped laughing since she arrived to hold court.'

'It's an outrage the way she's behaved,' Hepsibah commented to Raymond.

'I always said she was no good,' said Rebecca.

'There is nothing that woman does that surprises me,' Rebecca said bitterly. 'She is a monster. A pretty, sugar-coated monster. But a monster nevertheless.'

'It hurts me to think that we never got to see Philippe before his coffin was sealed,' Raymond remarked.

'She did that deliberately,' Rebecca said, 'to prevent us from seeing him.'

'I had a right, as his brother, to see him before he was buried. I had a right to say goodbye to him. To see him in death, as I had seen him in life.'

'We all did,' said Hepsibah.

'And how dare she bury him in North London, when he has an Israeli burial plot on Mount Herzl and always said he wanted to be returned to the land of our forefathers? What sort of person doesn't ask her own husband's family to his funeral but invites 830 guests to that same celebration...I mean funeral...'

'How do you know how many people she asked?'

'Gisele told me. There were only twenty-seven refusals.'

'You're right to confuse it with a celebration. The arrangements were more appropriate to a wedding than a funeral. Guards standing outside the synagogue with guest lists, checking off names. Ushers in morning coats walking everyone to their seats, all of which had been allotted as if it were a theatre or some other sort of public function instead of a funeral,' said Begonia.

'That woman is such a rampant social climber,' observed Rebecca.

'The whole event was more about her showing off to her smart social friends than saying goodbye to our brother in a seemly and dignified manner...an appropriate Jewish manner. By God, she's behaving like a shiksa, and one without any religion either.'

'Do you realize, if it hadn't been for the television and press coverage of his death, we might never have known about it until after his funeral? I mean, finding out from the television that your own brother has died as a result of a fire: is that any way to learn of your brother's death?' said Raymond. 'I don't know why she hates us so much.'

'It's because she's afraid that we can see through her,' observed Hepsibah shrewdly.

'She never used to hate us when she lived in Mexico,' Begonia said. 'On the contrary, she was all over me like a rash in those days.'

'Those days, dear wife, are long gone. Nowadays, we're small fry to her.'

'Is it true, what Juan told you?' asked Hepsibah. 'About the will?'

'Yes,' Raymond said. 'Philippe changed his will less than two weeks ago in favour of Bianca. She inherits everything except for small bequests to the two of you and to a university in Israel for a Chair for Jewish Studies.'

'Doesn't it seem suspicious to you, that Philippe would sell the bank and change his will then die in a tragic accident, all in such a short space of time? I detect the hand of Bianca behind all of this. I bet she engineered his death,' Hepsibah said.

'Never say that,' Raymond said sternly. 'Never. Not even to yourself.'

'I don't see why I shouldn't,' Hepsibah retorted, 'when everyone in Mexico has been saying for years that she killed Ferdie Piedraplata.'

'That is precisely why none of us must ever say that we suspect her of killing Philippe.'

'Raymond, what you're saying doesn't make sense,' Rebecca said. 'If Bianca has killed our brother...and killed another husband before him... what possible reason would we have for not going public with our suspicions? Don't you want to see your brother's murderess brought to justice? If Bianca really is behind Philippe's death, then she is his murderess whether she actually did the deed herself or not.'

'I don't want her being exposed...not when it will mean destroying Philippe's reputation and our family name.'

'I don't see how accusing Bianca of causing Philippe's death will destroy his reputation and our family name, if that's what she's done,' Hepsibah said. 'And, knowing her the way I do, I wouldn't put it past her.'

Raymond shook his head. 'Trust me on this one,' he said sadly. 'Let's just leave it alone.'

'No,' Rebecca said fiercely. 'Why should we? He was our brother too. She damaged our relationship with him during his lifetime. Now that he's dead, and she may have had a hand in his death, you want us to let her get away with it? No, I say. A thousand times no.'

'Then you leave me no alternative,' said Raymond quietly. From the expression on his face, they knew something momentous was coming.

'The reason why we have to let her get away with it is that Philippe is rumoured to have been the one who arranged Ferdie's death for her. Now that you're forced this out of me, do you see why we have to let this rest?'

'That's not possible,' Hepsibah said.

'It's not true,' Rebecca echoed.

'I'm afraid it is possible and, if the original investigation in Mexico is accurate, it's also true. I made it my business to get hold of the findings years ago.'

'Philippe would never have done something like that,' both sisters said in unison.

'Maybe he wouldn't have...maybe he would...I don't know. All I know is, Ferdie Piedraplata did not commit suicide and Bianca did not act alone.'

'Sweet Jahwe,' Hepsibah said as she absorbed the enormity of it all.

'That isn't to say that we have to let her get away scot-free,' Rebecca said. 'Let's wait awhile and see how much more press interest there is in Philippe's death. When things quieten down a bit, we'll sue her.'

'That's a good idea,' Hepsibah said. 'Remember how frantic she was when Clara sued her after Ferdie's death? I thought she was going to have a nervous breakdown.'

'Well, she'll be even more nervous this time. The last time there was no press interest. This time, what with the international attention Philippe's death has been getting, she'll be terrified that a skeleton will fall out of her closet. We might rethink things before the day, but for the moment I'd recommend that we get ready to dispute the will when the right time comes,' Rebecca said, looking directly at her brother. 'That will give her sleepless nights…and we can drag the process out for years. Yes,' she went on gleefully, 'years of sleepless nights, wondering which skeleton will topple out of her crowded closet next.'

While the Mahfud family were having that conversation at the Carlton Towers Hotel in Chelsea, a block away in Cadogan Place, Clara d'Offolo was sitting in Amanda's drawing room, talking about Philippe's death with Amanda and Magdalena.

'I've got the inside track on what's been happening in Andorra,' she announced. 'The story is that the manservant has confessed to having set the curtains alight to bring fire hazards caused by the security system to Philippe's attention.'

'Who told you that?' asked Amanda.

'Etienne Reynaud, the local chief of police and his wife Elise are good friends of my niece Delia's husband Charles Candower's brother and his wife, who are tax exiles in Andorra and live right next door to him,' she said. 'Either Etienne Reynaud's reckless – which I doubt – or he's spreading stories deliberately…which I wouldn't put past him, knowing how the Andorran authorities function. Whatever the reason, he hasn't been able to resist the temptation to show his friends that he's a central figure in the biggest news story to come out of the principality since its inception. They've passed on everything to Charles, and either he or Delia have been keeping Magdalena and me abreast of developments.'

'Philippe's death certainly smells fishy,' Amanda remarked.

'You can say that again. Knowing the way Bianca functions, I wouldn't be surprised if she didn't deliberately entice that male helper into setting the curtains on fire. I wonder if he knew that his actions would result in Philippe's death? Not, it has to be said, that I care much one way or the other how Philippe died. Over the years, I've come to recognize the part he played in Ferdie's death, so his end has a certain symmetry to it,' Clara said.

'I gather that crook Juan Gilberto Macias is here,' Amanda said sarcastically, 'holding that most fortunate widow's hand.'

'And acting on her behalf very openly, I might tell you. I spoke to him yesterday, just before lunch,' Clara said. 'He telephoned me, doubtless to pick my brain at Bianca's behest to see what I had to say for myself. He went on and on about what a terrible trauma this has been for Bianca:

how she had to be ushered out of the apartment by the police while pleading to be allowed to stay until she could see for herself that Philippe was safe. He said she broke down in front of the officers when they refused her request to stay in his bedroom. He said that they gave smoke and fumes as the reason for her to leave. Then he said...with a certain amount of disapproval, it has to be said to his credit...that Bianca had arranged for Maximilien to open up their shop especially for her yesterday, so that she could choose a new coat to wear to the funeral in case the weather turned. He said she bought a sable and – if you can believe it in this day and age – a new leopard-skin coat, muff and hat.'

'I didn't know you could still buy leopard,' Amanda said.

'It's now an endangered species. Furriers are not allowed by law to sell new coats. You and I can't buy a new leopard-skin coat, but Bianca can,' said Clara. 'I suppose the coat must have been made before the ban was imposed.'

'She did the same thing when Uncle Ferdie died, didn't she, Mummy?' said Magdalena.

'So Juan said at the time,' Clara said. 'I've always been able to see right through Bianca. My view is that she got Frank Alderman to set those curtains on fire by promising him a reward if he did so. She'll have also sent a message through the legal team that he'll be handsomely rewarded if he takes a dive. Delia says Etienne Reynaud told her that the Court's appointed two members of the Andorran legal establishment to act as his defence team, so we can safely assume there will be no surprises emanating from that quarter.'

'We all know the way those independent principalities function,' Amanda said. 'I can just imagine an edict being issued to the effect that this case must be cleared up with the minimum of damage being done to the principality's reputation as a haven for the rich and shady.'

'I think the Andorran government is also concerned about its reputation for probity, now that the French have accused them of being complicit in the money-laundering that takes place there,' Magdalena said.

'Uncle Piers says that they're among the biggest money-launderers on earth,' Amanda said. 'He says they even pushed through Philippe and Bianca's citizenship in record time as an inducement for him to move his headquarters from Geneva, along with all the drug-money Philippe laundered for the Colombians and for Manuel Noriega when he was still

president of Panama – that's aside from all the tainted Russian money he
brought with him. Piers says the authorities were up to their necks in it
with him.'

'Which is all the more reason why we're going to see a similar farce
akin to the one we witnessed when Ferdie died,' Clara said. 'Just you wait
and see. Now that Philippe's dead, Bianca will steer as wide a berth of
Andorra as she has of Mexico. Frank Alderman will be let off with a light
sentence. The authorities are already setting up the justification by letting
out the story that he set the fire for the noblest of motives and didn't
intend to harm Philippe in any way. He will be released from prison in
the near future to be greeted by the dollars that Bianca has assuredly got
Juan to pay into some bank account somewhere to keep him quiet. And
Bianca will trip off merrily to make herself known in every gossip column
and social magazine as the richest widow in the world. In a year or two,
Philippe's death will be marked down as a tragic accident and
remembered by no one except his family, his friends and many enemies,
and us. The whole thing is too sickening for words but, when you have as
much money as Bianca has managed to get her hands on, the authorities
bend over backwards to absolve you of suspicion, especially if they have
things to hide themselves.'

'I don't see why we should let her get away with it,' Magdalena said.

'There must be something we can do.'

'There is,' Amanda said. 'We can give her the Ann Woodward brand of
punishment.'

'What on earth's that?' asked Magdalena.

'Ann Woodward shot her husband like a dog when he threatened
divorce, leaving their two children without a father' Amanda said. 'Their
grandmother Elsie, who in her day was known as the Dowager Empress
of New York Society, decided that it would be too traumatic for the
children if their mother were charged with murder and possibly executed.
She joined forces instead with her murderous daughter-in-law, taking her
side when the Grand Jury investigated and passing the murder off as an
accident, then unmasked Ann as a murderess before the only court that
really mattered to either of them, the Social World: the court of smart
restaurants and couture houses, the major jewellers, the houses in the
country and houses in town, the social columns and the fashion pages,
Vogue magazine and Cholly Knickerbocker. Thereafter, every time Ann

Woodward entered a drawing room or a restaurant or merely walked down the street, there was a buzz of whispers. In the end, she couldn't take the ignominy any more than Bianca could when all Mexico was whispering about her. It was the most exquisite form of justice: punishment by social torture. Ann Woodward finally committed suicide. You could almost say she had been administered the death sentence when she realized she'd been given a life sentence from which there was no escape.'

'Bianca's too tough to kill herself,' Clara said. 'But I do like the idea of giving her a life sentence of public revilement through exposure. I say "yes". It's a good idea. Let's do it.'

'I say we get in touch with the Mahfud family and knock heads together,' Amanda said.

'I'm not so sure they'll go for it,' Clara replied wisely. 'Raymond knows that I'm aware of the part Philippe played in Ferdie's death. He's sure to think our interests are mutually exclusive.'

'Don't all businessmen abide by the maxim: my enemy's enemy is my friend?' Magdalena said.

'Raymond's too canny for that,' Clara said.

'Then let's leave Raymond out of it, ' Amanda said. 'But I will approach Hepsibah and Rebecca. I'd be very surprised if they don't provide me with as much information as they become privy to. They've always loathed Bianca, and they'll be hankering after justice, no matter what Raymond says. I'll let them know that anything they tell me won't be traceable back to them. With their information and ours, we'll be able to build up a comprehensive picture. We can drip-feed the information into the social world and the pages of the glossy magazines on both sides of the Atlantic. God knows, there are enough hangers-on who act as stringers for the gossip columns, earning their pin money repeating the gossip they overhear at every gallery opening, dance, dinner party.'

'I know several sieves in London,' said Magdalena. 'I can use them to leak stuff.'

'And I know several in New York as well,' Amanda said, 'It will be relatively easy to unmask Bianca. In fact, I'll go further and predict that the journalists will positively leap upon the story. All we need to do is whisper in the right ears, and I guarantee that within months, if not weeks, all the smart publications on both sides of the Atlantic will be doing stories on her. I should think we can quite easily make sure Bianca gets the sort of notoriety she deserves.'

'Punishment through opinion. Social death by informed gossip. It all has a wonderfully ironic ring to it,' Clara said, appreciating the symmetry with which natural justice would punish when formal justice could not.

'It's the least she deserves,' Amanda said.

'Shall I tell you something?' Clara said brightly, a large smile breaking through her features. 'In some ways this is the most effective punishment for someone like Bianca. Maybe there really is such a thing as justice, after all. Though, it has to be said, I've been waiting for it for an uncomfortably long time.'

Epilogue: September 21, 2000

It's late afternoon, and Bianca is already dressed and on her way to Brunswick House when the telephone in the Rolls Royce rings. The driver answers it.

'It's Mr Lowenstein, Madame.'

Bianca reaches for the telephone.

'John, what's up?' she asks irritably 'I'm on my way to the unveiling as we speak.'

'Bianca, I have the most dreadful news. It's such a disappointment, I don't know where to start.'

'Try just telling me what it is,' she retorts, impatient to dismiss whatever paltry nuisance is getting in the way of her moment of glory.

Contrary to the golden days of widowhood she had envisaged for herself while Philippe was still alive, the first year since his death had been a living nightmare for Bianca.

Hardly a day passed without her receiving a reminder of the notoriety that had increasingly become her Mark of Cain. She had achieved renown beyond her wildest dreams, but it was for being written about in veiled terms as a gold-digger who might also be a murderess. One day it was *People Magazine* running a four-page spread on its investigations into her husband's death, with ample photographic coverage of the glamorous widow, L'Alexandrine and the exterior of the Banco Imperiale Building.

The next day it was the *Wall Street Journal* dedicating three full columns to the latest developments in the case. Frank Alderman's daughter, Louise, also seemed to have a permanently open telephone line to the *New York Daily News*; and at least once a week there was some story stating that the authorities in Andorra were railroading Frank or were somehow disregarding due process of law and his human rights. The international press was up in arms about the length of time it was taking for Frank to be brought to trial. Through Louise, Frank had even publicly recanted the confession he had signed in return for the $1,000,000 to be paid into the numbered Liechtenstein bank account opened for him by Juan.

As far as Bianca was concerned, Frank more than anyone else was responsible for this public mess. He seemed incapable of comprehending that it was his own obduracy in doing things like recanting the confession that was prolonging his - and Bianca's - torment. However, he was not the only person to blame for the flood of information that was muddying the waters. Bianca could tell, from the detail of certain stories, that the secretaries, bodyguards, nurses and domestic staff who had taken the $100,000 apiece as a reward for their silence had violated their confidentiality agreements; and that some of them were now enjoying a roaring trade selling stories about her to the steadily growing number of publications which sent out reporters with an open chequebook and open ears in search of yet another nugget of information to lay before the public. As for the public, their appetite for a solution to the mystery of the Death in Andorra seemed only to be increasing, but at least, Bianca told herself, she had John Lowenstein and close friends like Ruth Fargo Huron, Stella Minckus and the Duchess of Oldenburg to lean on in these times of travail.

In truth, Ruth, Stella and the Duchess could not have been more stalwart. They were only marginally less incensed on Bianca's behalf than she was herself. Everywhere they went, whether it was to the Met in New York, Covent Garden in London, the Pompidou in Paris, the Palace in Gstaad or just to lunch, they spoke up on their beleaguered friend's behalf.

Nevertheless, the support of her friends, although uplifting, was not solving the problem, and Bianca hoped that John Lowenstein would continue laying the ground for doing so.

As Bianca saw it, her problem was basically a public relations one. She had acquired a bad reputation, and she needed to replace it with a good one. She could see no point in having all of what she had striven to acquire, all of what she had worked to achieve, if she could not enjoy it along with the reverence due, in her opinion, to the wealthy. She also needed the respect that went along with her stature. According to her reasoning, status was meant to bring fame. It was meant to be something that gave you clout, that obtained influence for you and allowed you to call the shots. Status was good, and it should bring good things in its wake. It was not meant to bring ignominy, pain and distress.

It was therefore inevitable that John Lowenstein would now become the architect of her rehabilitation. At first, he tried to accomplish this miracle by working his connections in the press so that the items he placed about her would counterbalance those that were cropping up on a daily basis from other sources. There was a vibrant and seemingly neverending supply of stories to counteract. His every instinct told him that someone out there was waging a deliberate and effective campaign of vilification against his client. His media rehabilitation was doomed to failure unless it could be backed up by something else from a new and better quarter.

'Bianca, we're going to have to up the ante if we're to win this struggle,' he said to her over lunch, eight months after Philippe's death.

'It's a war: not a struggle,' Bianca retorted. 'Of course, they're all jealous of me. That's why they're doing this. It's jealousy. Nothing but jealousy. Well, I've got the money, and I'm not going to allow myself to be hounded by them.'

'Who is "them"? John enquired.

'I'm not sure,' she said.

'It's always better to know who your enemy is. It's difficult to fight and win when you don't know who you're up against.'

'I wonder if the Mahfud family isn't behind this because Philippe snubbed those sisters of his in his will. Old crones. They look like buzzards, with those ghastly Orthodox wigs and that pasty skin Orthodox women get from that weird diet they follow... Or maybe I'm giving them too much power and it's just the journalists covering the story who are jealous because I have so much and they have so little.'

'You should be careful of "the little people",' John Lowenstein warned.

'However, it appears we now have two identifiable enemies: the Mahfud family and the journalists covering the story. If we're to win, Bianca, we must have a comprehensive strategy that targets both of them.'

'One thing I've decided is that I'm going to officially take up residence in London. The English have the harshest libel laws in the free world and, if I move there, I'll be able to use them to buy myself a measure of protection against the intrusiveness of the press.'

'That's a shrewd move, Bianca,' John concurred.

'I've looked at a house in Chelsea Square...that's the smartest square in London. I've put in an offer for it and am waiting to find out if it's been accepted.'

'You realize, don't you, that moving to London won't make the stories go away? It may quieten things down a little, but believe me, this is one that isn't going to disappear unless you position yourself very carefully. Even then, there's no guarantee that it will ever die down completely. I believe the best you can realistically aim for is to achieve such eminence in your own right that the brilliance of your reputation will outshine all the notoriety.'

'And how do you think we can achieve that, John?' Bianca asked, a trace of wounded bitterness betraying itself in her voice.

'I'm friends with Peter Rivers. He's the American agent for The Prince's Charity, the American branch of The Prince's Trust, the heir to the throne's own charity. He can deliver the prince in return for a large enough donation to the charity.'

'Deliver, as in, being seen in public with him?' Bianca asked.

'Absolutely. That's the whole point. The message couldn't be simpler. You're good enough for the heir to the throne of England, so you're good enough for anyone else. One photograph of you with His Royal Highness will be worth a million words of copy.'

'Aha,' Bianca said, a smile dancing across her face as she saw her place in the international pantheon as one of the world's leading socialites secured with the very people whose opinion really mattered to her.

'I'll talk to Peter and find out the quid pro quo: what sort of donation gets what sort of reception. The Prince's Charity is run on strictly tailored lines. You give X amount, he invites you to a party for five hundred supporters. You give Y, and he invites you to a party for two hundred supporters. Give Z, he invites you to a party for twenty supporters. Give

Z + P, and you get to go to the party for twenty supporters and have your photograph taken with him. It's later presented to you in a leather photograph frame embossed with his personal emblem in gold, personally signed by him. It will then be up to us how we use the press to let the world know the circles you're now accepted in.'

'And if I give Z + P +X +Y, multiplied by two?'

John laughed. 'Presumably a unique donation will elicit a unique response.'

'Why don't you work on it?'

'I will.'

In the coming weeks, John negotiated with Peter Rivers, and Peter Rivers negotiated with the Prince's private secretary. Meanwhile, Bianca bought the house on Chelsea Square.

During the months of its inevitable refurbishment, Bianca lived in some approximation of what her future lifestyle would be in a house owned by Lord and Lady Malteviot, of Belmont's, on the other side of Carlisle Square. What she had in physical comfort, however, she still lacked in social connections, despite the best efforts of John Lowenstein and Stella Minckus, who arranged introductions for her through friends of theirs. These few introductions, while they would prove invaluable in the future, did not provide a comprehensive solution to her problem of isolation. There was only so much you could see of people with full and busy lives, for they had neither the time nor the inclination to entertain and be entertained by - on a daily, weekly or even a fortnightly basis - someone they barely knew. Not when there were so many other equally well-placed people whom they knew better and whom they did not have the time to see as frequently as they would have liked.

As for Ruth Fargo Huron's introductions, they were, in Bianca's view, pathetic. She and her husband knew practically no one in London, and of the couple introductions they were able to provide, the only thing she got out of them was an education as to the limits of the social cachet foreigners possessed in English social circles. The Duchess of Oldenburg's introduction fared no better with this student of Society.

'Ha,' Bianca commented sourly. 'If possible she was even more of a disaster than Ruth's friends. At least they had money. She's nothing but a broken-down aristocrat: a penniless German countess whose father had been a reigning prince of a small German principality until it's abolition in 1918. She makes costume jewellery for a living. And she lives in Battersea. I ask you...'

A more immediate problem was the time that hung heavily on her hands when she was in London. One evening, on an impulse Bianca tried Mary Landsworth's old home number. Maybe she might know enough connections to make renewing the acquaintanceship worthwhile. To Bianca's surprise, Mary herself answered the telephone.

'Mary, this is a voice from your past. It's Bianca. Bianca Antonescu as was. Do you remember me? I used to be your client.'

'Bianca! How could I forget? You're one of the most memorable people I've ever known...if not *the* most memorable. How are you?'

'I'm well, thank you, and you?'

'Never been better. To what do I owe the honour of this call?'

'I'm living in London now and thought how nice it would be to get together with you.'

'I'd love that.'

'Would you prefer lunch at Harry's Bar or dinner at Mark's Club?'

'If it's dinner His Lordship has to come with me,' Mary said in a jocular tone that managed to convey the information that her husband had been made a Lord Justice without seeming to boast about it.

'Shall we then say dinner next Tuesday or Wednesday at eight o'clock?'

'Wednesday would be better for us.'

'Eight it is then.'

'What a treat this is! It will be so good to hear your news first-hand, instead of having to read all about you in the newspapers.'

'Yes,' Bianca said, the dejection breaking through her voice. 'I seem to have gone full cycle, haven't I? I'm right back where I was when I first had to come to you.'

'I wouldn't have put it quite like that, dear girl. Back then you had to fight off an intransigent sister-in-law. Now you're a huge media star and the queen of the columns.'

A huge media star: Bianca liked the sound of that, even though she knew there was a slight element of exaggeration about it. Certainly, she was being talked and written about. Did that make her a huge media star? No. But did it at least make her a star? The answer to that was 'yes'. For all her hyperbole, Mary was on the right track. Maybe people in the Establishment really cared less about her 'baggage' that she did. If that was the case, her rise to the peak might be easier than she had thought. All the same Bianca was beginning to regret her status as a widow. Life had not turned out the way she had expected it to. In her estimation, she had moved one step forward and five steps back. She now looked back on the years between Philippe's decline and his death as the real 'golden days'.

His very existence, she now saw, had offered protection in a way that only women who have been protected by a rich and powerful man would ever understand or appreciate. Invincibility had then been the cornerstone of her existence, and now it had died along with him. Bianca had to admit that she missed it.

It was at this juncture that John Lowenstein came up with a long-term plan that would serve both his and Bianca's interests in equal and inextricable measure. Philippe had now been dead nearly a year, and John was aware that his retainer would be coming up for its annual review within the next two months. Calculating that there was little chance of her keeping him on as PR advisor at a cost of $100,000 a month once Bianca had achieved her ambitions, he had devised a comprehensive strategy that delayed using Peter Rivers' connection with Prince Charles while at the same time feeding Bianca's growing hunger for social recognition.

He told her his idea over lunch at The Four Seasons in New York. 'Association with English royalty is the solution to your problem,' he declared. 'But you must save the prince for when your foundations are solid. Diversify in the meantime and then use him to crown you as the Queen of the International Set.'

'Only the Queen?' Bianca replied archly, an ironic smile playing on her lips.

John laughed, getting her point. 'OK,' he said. 'Empress then.'

'Just as long as we're clear about what my rightful position should be,' she said, still jokingly, but John also could tell there was an element of truth to her jest.

'I say we save the Prince of Wales until we're more established than we are at present,' he said. 'Get the house on Chelsea Square finished first. Have a few soirées and fly in all your friends. I'll get wonderful social columnists like Suzy or Richard Johnson to cover the events for you in the American press. That way, we spread the word in New York about how successfully you've made the transition from New York to London. Then, when we've primed the public to be receptive to your respectability, we pull the Prince out of the hat and have him crown you as the Empress by his presence.'

'But what's your suggestion for putting me in there?'

'Donate a major art work to the English nation in memory of Philippe,' John said.

'Yes,' Bianca said eagerly, knowing how successfully Ruth Fargo Huron and Brooke Astor had used such donations to cement their positions.

'But not just any painting,' John continued. 'In fact, not a painting at all. Something major and huge and imposing. Like a massive sculpture. Something that will jump out at people whether they want it to or not.'

'I'll get Ion onto it as soon as I get home.'

'No need. I've found the perfect thing. It's a huge Henry Moore sculpture. It was the centrepiece of the Wasserman Collection, but they're having to sell because stock in Wasserman Technology has plummeted in the last few months.'

'How much is it?'

'One point six million dollars. It sounds a lot, but it will put you on the map. It's as big as a house in Queens. Peter Rivers says he can have it placed for you in the middle of the piazza of Brunswick House. That's one of the former royal palaces on the Thames. It's being refurbished as a gallery of modern art. So you'll have a prime site, with royal connections. Peter says he can whisper in the right ear and get you one of the senior royals along for the dedication ceremony. In fact, he's already talked with the Queen Mother's private secretary, and she's amenable to the idea. The only risk we run there is of her dying before the big day. She is, after all, nearly a hundred.'

'If she dies, will one of the other royals take her place?'

'I don't know. I'll have to ask Peter.'

'You do that. And if the answer's yes, then my answer's yes.'

Peter Rivers' informed John that another royal would indeed fill in for Her Majesty Queen Elizabeth The Queen Mother should she pass away before the engagement. Having received the answer she wanted, Bianca gave John the go-ahead to acquire the sculpture and plan the unveiling in the presence of the last Queen-Empress of the British Empire.

Events of this nature always take a long time to execute, and Bianca now had to exercise patience while plans were made. Brunswick House wasn't due to be opened until the middle of September 2000, at which time the British Prime Minister, Tony Blair, would officiate at the opening ceremony. That meant that the unveiling of the sculpture by Her Majesty could not take place until afterwards. Telephone calls and letters now flew back and forth between 10 Downing Street, Clarence House and John Lowenstein's office on Madison Avenue in New York. Finally, after nearly two months of negotiating, an agreement was reached. Tony Blair would open the renovated centre for modern art on September 16, 2000, and Queen Elizabeth The Queen Mother would unveil the Henry Moore statue in memory of Philippe Mahfud on September 21.

Once the dates were set, there was no changing them, royal and prime ministerial engagements being set in stone. 'That's because all the royals have their diaries planned six months in advance,' John Lowenstein explained, 'and, as they try to do three and four different engagements in a day and the people organizing the events depend on the royal family not to let them down on such occasions, usually only death or serious illness prevent them from attending. Can you imagine the chaos if the Queen Mother didn't attend? Not to mention the disappointment and humiliation? It may be a palaver getting a royal to agree to an official engagement, but at least we know, once they've committed themselves to it, they never back out.'

To Bianca, this was both a relief and a torment.

'All this waiting will kill me,' she said, 'but I suppose the interval will at least give you the chance to drip-feed stories to the American public through Suzy and Richard Johnson.'

John Lowenstein chuckled. 'How well you know me.'

These now became days of hope and excitement, as well as of anxiety and distress for Bianca as she and her army of cohorts waged their respective campaigns to fend off her adversaries and prepare her life for ultimate victory. While her public image continued to receive a battering in the tabloids and glossy magazines, renovation work on the house in Chelsea Square house continued at its own pace.

As June became July and July became August, and August became September, Bianca became more and more panic-stricken. 'I was so hoping to have moved in by the 21st so that the dinner following the unveiling of the Henry Moore could be *chez moi*,' she confided in Mary Landsworth. 'Now I'm going to have to come up with another venue, and I can't think of anything suitable.'

'We can get you the Lord Chancellor's Apartment in the House of Lords, if that helps,' Mary suggested, keen to make herself useful. Since Bianca had returned into her life, she'd received only one donation for her Distressed Legal Gentlefolk Society, and that was for a paltry £20,000, but she was hoping that this offer would induce her former client to open her purse with more of that welcome generosity for which she was known.

'I like the sound of that,' Bianca said, thinking that she must run this suggested location by John Lowenstein. 'Are the rooms big?'

'Not particularly, but they are very impressive, and you'll be able to get in a select hundred or so without too much trouble.'

'Well, I wouldn't have been having more than that at home in any case,' said Bianca.

'So, shall we ask Derry...Lord Irvine of Lairg, the Lord Chancellor?'

'If you don't mind, Mary, I'll think about it tonight and let you know tomorrow. I don't mean to sound ungrateful, but...'

'It's quite all right, my dear. Makes no difference to me if you decide you don't want one of the most exclusive and hard to obtain venues in the land.'

John Lowenstein concurred with Bianca that the Lord Chamberlain's Apartment was unbeatable in terms of prestige, so she rang up Mary the following morning and accepted her offer, feeling optimistic for the first time in months.

Within an hour of hanging up the telephone in her office, Mary's secretary buzzed her on the intercom. 'Mrs Mahfud's driver is in reception. He says he has a note from her that he's been instructed to deliver to you in person. What shall I do?'

'Do you mind if we have a thirty-second interruption?' said to the client sitting opposite her.

'Not at all,' the client replied.

'Ask reception to show him up and bring him in,' said Mary. But only for thirty seconds. No more.'

Mary wondered what the note would say. She would not be surprised if it contained a cheque, although she could not be sure.

Her secretary soon showed the driver into her office. In less than thirty seconds he had handed over the envelope, she had thanked him, and he was out the door.

'Do you mind?' she asked her client once more, this time reaching for a silver Asprey letter-opener, ostentatiously engraved with her husband's coat of arms, even though Mary knew only too well that wives were forbidden by the College of Arms to use them. 'It might be something urgent,' she explained, knowing very well that it would not. She deftly cut open the envelope and peered inside. Before she even removed its contents, she could see a cheque neatly folded between the pages of a handwritten letter on Smythson notepaper. Sliding it out, she saw that it was made out to the Distressed Legal Gentlefolk Society and was for the considerable sum of £50,000. She felt her heart leap with delight. Bianca was back on track. 'Say what her detractors will about her,' Mary thought, 'the fact remains she has a thorough understanding of how the world works. There's nothing cheap or shoddy about her. She pays her way. No wonder she has such good friends.'

But Mary's surprises for the day were not yet complete: a massive arrangement of flowers arrived from Pulbrook & Gould, the smart florists near Sloane Square in the heartland of Chelsea.

It was after arranging for Pulbrook & Gould to deliver the flowers that Bianca, a study in chic, sailed out of the Malteviot house she was renting on Carlisle Square to walk to Sloane Street. Turning heads, she headed straight for Smythson's, the elegant stationers whom she had been using since the days when she was Señora Calman, living in middleclass Mexico City and needing to further herself socially with 'aristocratic' British traditions her family had never possessed.

For once, it was a beautiful day in London so, having completed the task of ordering invitations for the New Year's Eve party she intended to have in the Chelsea Square house she would have moved into by that time, she walked up Sloane Street to Tomasz Starzewski's showroom at the Knightsbridge end of the street. 'It's so seldom one has the chance to walk in London, but today is different,' Bianca reflected. 'It's as if God is celebrating my triumph in finding an even better venue for the reception than my house.'

With an irrepressible smile on her face, Bianca felt a surge of the high spirits which had always been such a characteristic of her personality, but which had deserted her since Philippe's death. The only other time in the whole of her life she had been so low was after Ferdie's death, but at least then she had had Philippe. Now she had no one. 'And yet,' she decided as she walked past Gucci after looking in its window, 'maybe I've turned the corner. The last fifteen months have been torment itself, but maybe now I'm back on track once more. After all, who but a lunatic would believe that there's any real mystery to Philippe's death when I'm so respectable that the Queen Mother and Lord Chancellor of Great Britain are prepared to have their names linked with mine?'

In the ensuing four weeks, Bianca felt more light-hearted than she had done since Philippe's death. Things really were going to be all right.

'How simple life is,' she told herself as this new mood of buoyancy took hold. 'You have money. You buy yourself influence. Queens and Lords, even the head of a kingdom's legal system, pay court to you. And all for a price that, in relative terms, costs you less than a maid buying a hairpin out of her wages.'

By the morning of September 21, 2000, the optimist in Bianca was now so confident that nothing could go wrong that she even took Pedro's call without fear that this most tiresome of sons would blight her mood on her big day. Nothing, but nothing, she believed, could touch her now. This was the crowning moment of her life. John Lowenstein had been right. After tonight, her place as Empress of English and International Society would be so firmly established that she could forget about everyone who had made her life a misery since Philippe's death. She would rise above their niggardly comments and mean-spirited slurs, treating them with the contempt they deserved. Soon they wouldn't be able to touch her anymore.

Meanwhile in a townhouse in Kensington, Delia Bertram Candower was sitting down to breakfast with her husband Charles. Theirs was a great love-match and still, after all these years of marriage, he pulled out her chair for her in one of the acts of consideration which had kept their marriage fresh. She slipped into it, and he eased it forward. While he was doing so, she reached for *The Times* and turned, as she did every morning, to the Court Circular. She quickly glanced to see the report on Princess Anne's activities of the day before then cast her eyes over the day's List of Royal Engagements underneath.

'I don't believe it!' Delia exclaimed. 'Charles, look here! Look at this!' She stabbed at the page with her index finger.

Charles read that at a public ceremony at Brunswick House later that day Her Majesty Queen Elizabeth The Queen Mother was due to dedicate a Henry Moore statue donated by Mrs Philippe Mahfud in honour of her late husband.

'She's done it this time,' he said.

'We can't let her get away with this. Queen Elizabeth can have no idea that the woman's a murderess who's killed not one but two husbands. We must tell "You Know Who",' she said, referring to her royal friend Anne, in case the staff should overhear what she was saying. 'If we say nothing, and Queen Elizabeth discovers somewhere down the line that Bianca is connected to us through marriage, she'll never forgive us for having remained silent. You know what a high moral tone she takes about everything.'

'Let's ring our friend right now.'

'Don't use your cell phone. Bring the landline over. The last thing we need is for someone to hack into our conversation and make it public, the way the Sun newspaper did with Diana and Camilla.'

Charles walked to the sideboard, brought back the telephone and placed it in front of his wife. Delia dialled. The butler answered.

'Good morning,' she said. 'This is Delia Candower here. May I speak with Her Royal Highness?'

'I'll fetch her for you right now, Mrs Candower,' he said, hearing the urgency in her voice.

The princess came on the line. Without preamble, Delia plunged right in. 'I've just been reading the List of Today's Royal Engagements. I see that Queen Elizabeth is unveiling a statue donated by Mrs Philippe Mahfud in honour of her late husband. Mrs Philippe Mahfud was the wife of my first cousin Magdalena's uncle, Ferdie Piedraplata. We have proof that she helped Philippe Mahfud murder him, and I've heard the Andorran authorities know that she's also responsible for organizing Philippe Mahfud's death. You've got to get in touch with Her Majesty's private secretary and warn him.'

Grateful to her friend for the tip-off, the princess agreed to do so immediately. And she did.

'Queen Elizabeth The Queen Mother's Private Secretary just called,' John Lowenstein explains over the phone to Bianca, as her Rolls Royce continues on its way to Brunswick House and the unveiling ceremony.

'He said Her Majesty has come down with a chill, and the doctor has ordered her to bed. He says she's been fighting it all day and had hoped to honour the commitment, but she's got steadily worse, and he's had to call in the doctor. He rang as soon as the doctor left.'

'This is a disaster,' Bianca said.

'It is. Had the old biddy given us more time, we could've got one of the other royals to fill in for her. As things stand, we'll just have to go ahead without any royalty at all.'

'So who's going to unveil the plaque dedicating the statue to Philippe?'

'You'll have to do it.'

'I've wasted over £1,000,000, and all I have to show for it is a brass plaque engraved with some nonsense about how Her Majesty Queen Elizabeth the Queen Mother unveiled it? It's outrageous, and I'm not having it! Tell them to honour their pledge to replace her if she's dropped out,' Bianca ordered.

'The pledge actually says that they'd replace her if she died. But she's not died. She's gone and caught a cold on us,' John patiently explains, seriously worried that his retainer is now in jeopardy.

'I don't care. I want another royal. What about one of her daughters or grandchildren?'

'I asked. He said everyone's otherwise committed and at such short notice it wouldn't have been possible to get them to cover for her even if they had been available.'

'I've never been so humiliated in my life,' says Bianca, distraught.

'We can turn this around. I'll get Clarence House to put out a story that she's taken ill, then I'll run with it and get us even more column inches than we would otherwise have got. What's better news? A Queen Mother who's unveiling a statue or a Queen Mother who can't because she's at death's door, but is so taken with Madame Mahfud that she was intent on honouring her commitment until her doctor ordered her to cancel an hour before the ceremony? The latter story is far more newsworthy...and you're still linked to the British Royal Family in the public mind. Who knows, Bianca? This might even be a blessing in disguise.'

'In very heavy disguise,' she says disconsolately.

Suddenly Bianca sees that, no matter how many column inches she gets, and no matter who ladles praise over her in the press, her detractors will use this no-show as evidence that she really is the social pariah they have been making her out to be.

'I'm turning into a freak in a freak show,' she wails. 'I must find a way to turn this around, otherwise this will destroy me.'

And, although Bianca has only a glimmering of it, the actual fact is that she is at the beginning of a life sentence. The world has become a prison, and she its most celebrated occupant. Justice in a very real sense has been done. Wherever she goes and whatever she does, she will know that a healthy proportion of the people around her will either despise her or laugh at her. All her money, all the influence she has so avidly courted, the people she has just as avidly cultivated and all the manipulations to which she will resort in the future are powerless to bring this punishment to an end. As long as she exists, Bianca now clearly understands, so will it. And the thought of it starts tearing slowly away at her insides.